THE PRISONER OF DEATH

"Whether you like it or not, whether you believe it or not, you know who killed your parents. It's been locked up inside your head all these years, and for whatever reason, it's just now starting to come back. If the Prisoner should get wind of this, he'll pull himself up out of whatever hole he calls home...

"And he will kill you."

PRAISE FOR GENE LAZUTA'S PREVIOUS THRILLERS:

"The most heinous serial killer... Even Clive Barker would flinch!"

—*Rave Reviews*

Diamond Books by Gene Lazuta

BLOOD FLIES
BLEEDER
VYRMIN
FORGET ME NOT

FORGET ME NOT

GENE LAZUTA

DIAMOND BOOKS, NEW YORK

If you purchased this book without a cover you should be aware that this book is stolen property. It was reported as "unsold and destroyed" to the publisher and neither the author nor the publisher has received any payment for this "stripped book."

This book is a Diamond original edition, and has never been previously published.

FORGET ME NOT

A Diamond Book / published by arrangement with the author

PRINTING HISTORY
Diamond edition / November 1992

All rights reserved.
Copyright © 1992 by Gene Lazuta.
This book may not be reproduced in whole or in part, by mimeograph or any other means, without permission. For information address:
The Berkley Publishing Group,
200 Madison Avenue, New York, New York 10016.

ISBN: 1-55773-812-2

Diamond Books are published by The Berkley Publishing Group,
200 Madison Avenue, New York, New York 10016.
The name "DIAMOND" and its logo are trademarks belonging to Charter Communications, Inc.

PRINTED IN THE UNITED STATES OF AMERICA

10 9 8 7 6 5 4 3 2 1

*This story is dedicated,
with love, to my wife, Sue.*

FORGET ME NOT

PART I

Jessie

ONE

1

The woman made the sign of the cross, touching her forehead, her heart, her right and then her left shoulder, and then her heart again. She didn't do it for God's sake, but for the benefit of the men who were watching her. She wanted them to believe her, and she figured that a little obvious piety probably couldn't hurt. Then she took a drink from the aluminum water fountain, tasting salt.

When she stood up, she used both hands to straighten her dress—a somber, blue and grey flower print cut in a sexy, 1940s style that was perfect for a gloomy winter's day, or a police interview—before turning to face the suspicious eyes of her questioners. The three fat men were waiting at the end of the noisy police station hallway, indicating the door to the room where the interview regarding her deposition would happen, and wearing guns.

Christ! she thought, starting toward them. I hope my face is on straight.

Using the linoleum ricochet of her high heels as a rhythm, she concentrated on keeping the roll of her hips sultry. In her mind she could see her reflection in the dressing room mirror backstage at school where she had created her costume: a beautiful twenty-year-old girl with long black hair pinned up off her shoulders in a "schoolmarm" style that emphasized her big, dark eyes—her most expressive feature, she thought—while providing an interesting, conservative contrast to the vampish dress she had chosen after hours of shopping. Her lipstick was very red: perfect for pouting. And her nylons had seams running up their backs. Overall, everything about her appearance had been carefully calculated to convey a particular impression.

Whether or not it would prove to be the impression she intended was the point of this exercise because sometimes it was necessary to do a little field work . . . to go out and experience life, free of the confines of the theater and the limitations of a script.

"Ready, Miss Reynolds?" a cop asked, in a tone that was queerly out of sync with his glowering expression.

The woman nodded.

"Good. Then let's get it over with."

He sounded bored, or irritated.

Entering the interrogation room, Jessica Reynolds saw the fourth man for the first time. He was sitting at a chipped Formica table, holding a foam cup and resting one big hand on a stack of folders. He was probably seventy years old, balding, and dressed in a shabby brown suit. His moustache was that dirty shade of nicotine-blond that grey hair turns to after it's been grey too long; and what hair he had left around the crown of his skull matched it, especially at the edges. His silvery eyes locked on her face the instant she appeared, and his upper lip twitched as he rose . . . not to speak, but because a lady had entered the room.

"Corroboration," one cop explained as he moved her through the door by the arm and followed her in. "He believes you."

"Really?" she asked the older man.

He nodded.

And somehow that made her feel better . . .

Though she didn't know why it should.

Getting the police to even talk to her had been a trial, and she had been forced to hard-sell herself over the phone. Once she got an interview, she became suddenly unsure as to whether she really wanted one or not. And on the ride downtown, she nearly abandoned the whole thing when she realized that she wasn't certain as to exactly what she intended to say . . .

"I remember people's faces and a lot of broken glass," she rehearsed in the car, waiting for a light at the corner of Euclid and East Ninth. "It was dark outside. And it was snowing. And there were colors."

Snowing and colors.

Great.

Only the chance to actually be the subject of a police interrogation—like she had seen in so many movies over the years—had prevented her from turning around and taking her "woman of mystery" character back home. But her acting career was serious to her; so serious, in fact, that she was willing to make the trip downtown just to get a taste of this experience . . .

Which described a lot of what she was all about as a person, because Jessica Reynolds saw herself as being on the outside . . . a woman apart . . . divorced from the rest of the world. Maybe it was her family background, which was a little on the unstable side, that had left her an observer instead of a participant. Her relationship with the people who had raised her was strange, and it may even have been one explanation for the ease with which she stepped in and out of the roles she played. Her parents had died when she was so young that she didn't remember either of them. And over the years, she had been forced to deal with an evolving series of feelings regarding their loss . . . from confusion at not having a mommy and daddy like the other kids, to resentment at their absence, to indifference, and finally, to what she suspected might be a deficiency in herself. The stage became her natural habitat. And "real life" was just another performance.

"Miss Reynolds, my name is Sergeant Wills," the largest of the three policemen said as he settled himself between his two companions on one side of the Formica table. The man in the brown suit sat alone opposite the cops, leaving Jessie the hot seat at the table's head. "Regarding your deposition, Sergeant Novak"—the man pointed left—"will assist me in this interview pursuant to statements you made in connection to acts allegedly perpetrated by persons as of yet unidentified. And Officer Temple"—he pointed right—"will serve as observer. This interview is being recorded on audiotape"—no indication as to where the microphone was hidden, or who was operating the machine—"and please be advised that holding forth false or misleading information as true is a punishable offense in the context of a homicide investigation."

That said, the man opened the file containing Jessie's deposition and coughed into his hand.

Jessie thought about leaning back and crossing her legs, but given the moment, she didn't think it would be quite right, so she stayed still. As an actress, she was constantly aware of the precarious balance between mood and event, and she expelled a great deal of mental energy noting the body language of the people around her. So far this morning she had been witness to a startling range of contradictions and cross-purposes, from the painful insincerity of a woman officer who was obviously unimpressed by her experiences, to the barely concealed skepticism of a Lieutenant Breznitski, her coffee-drinking "case officer" who didn't "have time to talk to you right now," but who assured her that anything significant revealed by her efforts would receive his "undivided personal attention."

She had just pulled her cigarettes out of her purse, figuring that she may as well be the one who started the old "smoke-filled room" toward its inevitable smokiness, when, without even lifting his eyes from the file, Sergeant Wills said, "I'm afraid there's no smoking in here, Miss Reynolds."

Making Jessie blink.

She had a whole routine planned around lighting, smoking, and handling her cigarettes—even though she really didn't smoke. And now she wasn't sure what she was going to do with her hands.

Sergeant Wills took a preliminary breath.

Jessie tensed, wondering which one would be the good cop and which one the bad.

And then both cops smiled.

The third, Officer Temple, was covering his mouth with his fingers.

FORGET ME NOT

"Okay, Miss Reynolds," Sergeant Wills said, leaning forward and tapping the file with a pencil Jessie had not seen him produce. "You're reporting the murder of four people, in a house, at night, in the dead of winter, by a man you don't know. You can tell us the position of the bodies, the color of the carpets, and what kind of curtains were hanging over the windows. But you can't tell us the address of the crime scene, who the victims were, or when this multiple homicide occurred. That the gist?"

Jessie nodded.

"It's *audio*tape, Miss Reynolds," the man with his fingers over his mouth offered, indicating the surrounding air with his free hand.

"Oh," Jessie said. "Uh, yes. That's the gist."

Bad start. Sounded nervous.

"On page four of your deposition," Sergeant Wills continued, "you state that, and I quote, 'I don't really know how I know about this. It seems like one morning I just woke up, and it was there. It started bothering me, and I thought at first that maybe it was something I'd read, or seen in a movie, working its way through my mind and getting mixed up with real life. But I'm sure that's not it. I just have this memory . . . like I forgot something a long time ago, or made myself forget it, and now it's back. I can see parts of it clearly . . . but for all those clear parts, there are others that I can't see at all. But it's eating me up . . . knowing how those poor people died. The whole family. Everybody in the house. They died.' End quote."

Wills closed the folder and looked Jessie right in the eye.

"Miss Reynolds," he said with infinite patience. "Do you believe yourself to be some kind of psychic?"

"No," Jessie responded, maybe a bit too strongly.

"Are you a murderer?"

"No!" she emphasized—better control, but still weak on the range.

"Then you must be a ghost."

Now both unspeaking cops had their hands over their mouths.

Jessie squirmed in her seat, searching for an emotion.

And Wills continued.

"You said clearly in the passage I just read," he said, "that everyone in the house, the 'whole family,' in fact, died at the hands of this unidentified assailant. If everyone in the house was murdered, and you know all about how it happened, then you must either be the killer, or you must be dead. Right?"

"No," Jessie insisted.

And the sergeant put down his pencil.

"From what vantage point did you witness the crime?" he asked, an edge creeping into his voice.

"I don't know."

"Did you speak to anyone?"

"I don't think so."

"Do you have any physical evidence in your possession?"

"No."

"Names?"

"No."

"Dates?"

"You know I don't."

"Motive?"

"How could I know that?"

"Have you ever heard of this crime as being reported in the media?"

"I don't think so."

"What does that mean?"

"It means that I didn't know anything about this until a couple of weeks ago, so even if I'd have seen something, it wouldn't have meant anything to me."

"And before that?"

"I didn't know anything about it at all."

"But now you do?"

"Yes."

"So you just suddenly remembered that you witnessed a murder, but you can't remember when it happened?"

"Yes . . . I mean, no."

"It just came to you?"

"That's right."

"How?"

"I don't know."

"Would you call it a vision?"

"No."
"A dream?"
"I . . ."
"Can't you find the right word for it?"
"That's right."
"But still you thought you'd come and share it with us?"
"Yeah."
"And what would you like us to do with it?"

Jessie glanced from one cop to the other, feeling suddenly inarticulate.

"Miss Reynolds," Sergeant Novak, who was there to "assist," cut in helpfully, "we're obligated by law to respond to any offer of information regarding a capital offense, no matter what. You maintain that you possess such information."

"That's right."

"So where'd you get it?"

And Jessie clammed up.

This was the absolute crux of her problem, and the very thing that had almost turned her around on the way down to the station that morning: she didn't know where the knowledge she seemed to be carrying had come from. Just a short time ago she had been a drama student at a local college, blissfully emoting on cue and untroubled by anything except her fear of graduation. And now she was a witness to murder. Maybe not in any way that these cops could appreciate. But she was a witness . . .

Goddamn it!

She was!

And she was about to tell them so when the man in the brown suit spoke for the first time.

"I'd like to go over a couple of the things you saw again, if that would be all right," he said in a rich, breathy voice roughened by a little of the gravel that fills the throat of a smoker after years on the weed.

Wills leaned back in his chair.

Novak sighed.

And Jessie perked up in her seat.

There seemed to be some kind of communication going on between the three cops on the one side of the table and the single man opposing them. Jessie wished she knew what they had been talking about before she entered the room, who they were, where they stood as individuals regarding her story, and what the man in the suit had to do with anything. She realized, with something of a start, that she didn't even know his name.

And something more:

"What do you mean *again*?" she asked, speaking to the older man. "I only told *them* about it an hour ago."

In response, he glanced at her slyly and said, "They let me listen."

"Just do it, Henry," Sergeant Wills complained. "It's almost lunchtime."

But the old man's attention never wavered from Jessie's face.

"My name is Henry Parks," he said.

And his eyes were very pale.

They might have once been grey, or even an icy blue. But now they had been washed by time to a thin shade of silver so indistinguishable from the whites that it made them look a little eerie behind the lenses of his glasses. It was almost as if the things he had seen in his life had scrubbed off all the color, leaving his eyes scorched clean.

"I'm a retired police officer," he continued. "And, as a professional courtesy, these gentlemen are indulging my curiosity."

"Retired?" Jessie asked, conscious of the slip in her voice. She was weaving in and out of character now, one part of herself trying to hold onto the "interview personality" she'd decided to wear, and the other becoming caught up in what was going on around her.

"Retired," Parks confirmed. "For nearly twenty years. I was originally forced out because of an accident."

That had something to do with your throat, Jessie thought, listening to the way his voice seemed to vibrate. It was almost as if he were squeezing the words from his body by passing air over waxed paper.

"I expect my retirement date coincides very closely with your first birthday."

"Why?"

"How old are you?"

"I'll be twenty-one the day after tomorrow."

"Near enough," Parks said, and smiled cryptically. "Now, to your testimony. The killer you say you saw . . ."

"Was tall," Jessie said, deciding to cut right to the heart of it. "Huge, in fact. He seemed to stretch all the way up to the ceiling."

"Stretch?"

"You know. Stretch. Like a building or something: narrowed by perspective."

"So to remember the narrowing effect of perspective, you must have viewed him from below."

Jessie blinked.

Then she glanced at Parks, saying, "Yeah. That's right." And, leaning toward him a little dependently, she added, "I hadn't thought of that."

"I wouldn't expect you to," Parks said, opening one of the folders upon which his hand had been resting. Picking up the pencil Wills had placed on the table, he freed a clean sheet of lined paper from a spiral notebook. "Now," he said gently. "Piece by piece, everything you can remember about the man 'narrowed by perspective.' "

And Jessie gave it to him, speaking slowly and pausing often to get the words just right. The three cops at the table kept quiet, and Parks spoke only in sentence fragments that amounted to rephrased bits of what she had already said. He scribbled a few words, here and there, but as he listened, at least half of his concentration seemed to be devoted to the sketch he was constructing of what looked to be the layout of a house, blueprint style, including segmented, arched lines indicating the different directions doors would open—in or out of a room.

When he seemed satisfied with her description—tall, pressing, dark, indistinct but menacing—he slid the paper in front of her and said, "Now, please mark X's where you remember the bodies to have been placed."

His use of the word "placed" rang a bell in Jessie's mind, and she took the pencil from him while studying his expression. She glanced down at the paper . . .

Sterile white with rectangles of smudged lead pencil lines.

And back up at Parks.

Pale eyes urging her on.

Then she moistened her lips and marked one X.

The effort required was greater than she would have anticipated because there seemed to be a dynamic involved in the space between her eyes and the page. In that hovering void she was mentally constructing the slices of, what?

Memory?

Illusion?

That had been creeping in on her from the hazy recesses at the edges of her consciousness, and teasing at ever more distinct images that hinted at solidity, but that were in fact as tenuous as the air.

She was dissatisfied with the placement of her second X, so she erased it.

Parks opened his mouth, but she hissed, "Shh!" without looking up.

"The window was here," she said, tracing an invisible line with her finger. "And the happy man was in front of it, sitting on the floor, his back to the couch, and his arms out, like this." She vaguely struck a crucified pose. "On the cushions . . ."

"The 'happy man'?" Parks asked.

"Happy," Jessie said, re-marking her second X. "Big smile."

She pointed. "The puppet lady was here, next to the happy man. She was real funny. All floppy, and bent and . . ."

She looked up, asking, "How did you know the shape of the room?"

Parks didn't answer.

So she let it go.

"The puppet lady was to the happy man's left," she continued, returning her attention to the page. "All folded up on a chair so that her arms hung down, and her head rolled back. On the other side of the happy man was Bert."

"Bert?" Wills cut in.

"Like in Bert and Ernie, from *Sesame Street*. Bert's the one with the long face and the tuft of hair on the top of his head. The person in the chair on the other side of the happy man had hair like that, so I call him Bert.

"And the flat man was here." Jessie marked the last X, completing a perfect circle.

"Where was the murderer?" Parks asked.

And Jessie put an asterisk in the circle's center.

"So," Parks said, taking back the drawing. "If you remember the window as ahead of you, with the flat man, as you call him, close by, the killer next, and then the happy man leaning on the couch, with the puppet lady and Bert on either side of him, you must have been seeing this scene from approximately here. Wouldn't you say?"

Parks marked an O near the wall facing the window so that the four dead X's and the killer were between the O and the couch, which he indicated with a line.

Jessie didn't respond.

"And what was the killer doing?" Parks asked.

And Jessie said, "Stepping up."

"Up?"

"Over the flat man."

"The flat man . . ."

"Was lying, flat on the floor."

"And the window . . ."

"Was broken!" Jessie said, her voice rising and her eyes going wide. She was seeing the scene more clearly now. For days it had been bits and pieces. But now, with Parks to lead her through it, she was putting those pieces together, like a picture puzzle, seeing it whole for the first time.

"I was looking right at him, and he was between me and the window. I was looking up at him, and he was tall. The window was broken, and the drapes were moving, with snow coming in. And there was a light . . . a lot of light . . . two colors of it. Red and blue. It was coming in the window, with the snow, turning everything red and blue . . ."

She was on her feet.

"What's going on?" she blurted, addressing Parks. "How did you know?"

Parks got up and gently sat her back down. The other cops didn't so much as stir in their seats. After fetching her a paper cup of water, the older man assured her that she wasn't in any immediate danger. Apparently, she was describing the scene of a killing that he was personally interested in solving, and his familiarity with the case came from that personal involvement.

Then he produced the photographs, laying them on the table...

One, two, three, and four.

"The victims," he said as explanation.

Making Jessie lean forward, only to find the faces unfamiliar.

The photographs were black-and-white vacation-type shots that were yellowed with age and ratty around the edges. Each showed the face of a single person—three men and a woman—blown up and grainy. Jessie decided that maybe she recognized one as possibly being Bert because of his fuzzy hair. But she wasn't really sure even of him.

"Happy man," Parks said, placing his finger on the first photograph in the line. "His name was Michael Sterns, and he was apparently the first victim. He was killed in the kitchen, and later moved to the living room, where he was propped against the couch. He was struck across the face with a knife, which cut through his cheeks and scored the jawbone. He bled a lot. The killing stroke came in a forward thrust to the heart. When he was found, the cuts on his face exposed his teeth in a grin."

Jessie felt suddenly cold, and watching Parks' finger move to the next picture, she flinched when he said, "Puppet lady. She was strangled to death, and in the process her neck was broken. She was Sterns' wife. Her name was Natalie.

"Bert's name was Phillip Jenner, and he was also stabbed.

"And the flat man was Dennis Wright; his skull was smashed with an iron bar."

Parks looked up, and in a tone that sounded very much like he regretted what he was saying, he added, "I was the flashing light. Blue and red. The bubbles on my squad car. I was forty-six years old."

Jessie noticed at that moment, for absolutely no good reason, that the room in which she was sitting was made of concrete blocks, and painted the same institutional green as every hallway in every high school in the country. There was an odor of

Lysol in the air. And somewhere, someone was pecking at a typewriter.

Her "mystery lady" character was gone.

This time, Sergeant Novak brought her water.

"I shouldn't even have been on a squad," Parks said as Jessie drank. "But we had a lot of guys out with the flu, and I was filling in.

"We got a domestic disturbance call at a little after midnight, and I took point, with my partner behind. I saw the busted front window, so I went straight through the door and into a living room that looked just the way you described it: bodies in a circle, big guy dressed in black in the center, you against the wall at the far end."

"Me?" Jessie whispered, her voice sounding dead.

"He was stepping over the flat man and reaching for you when I told him to hit the floor."

"Me?" Jessie repeated.

"And that's the last thing I remember," Parks went on. "I never saw anybody move so fast."

Sergeant Novak had apparently had enough. Rising from his seat, he said, "Henry got nailed pretty good. The guy tried to choke him, but Henry's partner got there before he could finish. When it was over, Henry was unconscious, his partner was dead, and the nut was gone, leaving the baby crying in the corner."

"Baby?" Jessie repeated.

"Henry was a hero," Sergeant Wills put in. "He got a citation, a pension, and a place in the history books around here. He saved the kid's life. But we never caught the guy who did the killing, so Henry ended up kind of making it his business to keep up with the case."

Parks was nodding his head in agreement.

"And you think that the baby you saved was me?" Jessie asked.

"I'm sure of it," Parks returned.

And Jessie was on her feet.

"This is crazy!" she said, stepping away from the table. "Where'd you guys come up with this?"

"Miss Reynolds . . ." Wills said, standing.

"Don't you 'Miss Reynolds' me . . ."

"*You* called *us*, remember?" Novak said, also rising from his seat.

And Parks placed one more picture on the table. It was the puppet lady, dressed in a summer sundress and straw bonnet, standing in front of a roller coaster and holding a child next to a man Jessie vaguely recognized. He was much younger than she had ever seen him, and thinner. His hair was longer, and thicker than it was now, and his smile was so broad that he looked almost absurdly toothy. But his eyes were the same, and his shoulders still rolled forward in that distinctive stoop that identified him as . . .

"Uncle Kevin?"

She picked up the picture, her hand trembling.

"Kevin Reynolds is the puppet lady's older brother," Parks said gently, without coming any closer. "After his sister and her husband were murdered, you ended up living with him in Columbus as Jessica Reynolds."

"But . . ." Jessie whispered, still studying the photograph. "Why didn't he tell me?"

"What good would it have done?"

"He said they died in a car accident."

"That was very kind."

"My real father probably took this picture. No wonder Uncle Kevin didn't want me to go to school here."

She glanced up. "You knew my name," she said. "So when I said that I was coming to the police, your friends just called you down. After twenty years, why so much interest?"

"Because we never found the killer," Parks said, taking the photograph from Jessie's hand. "And, after twenty years, he never stopped."

Jessie looked at him, and realized that he was trying to do something that he thought was important. She couldn't help but notice his effort, and at that moment, she respected it.

But that didn't change anything.

For her part, she wasn't interested in making Parks' job any easier. His story was so incredible that it shook her to her shoes and started a mental process humming in her head that essentially organized the significant events of her life—the first birthday she could remember, her first bicycle, etc.—into a chronology, like a time line, twenty years long. Quickly, she visited each stop on that line and tried to imagine what the moment must have been like for her Uncle Kevin. His sister's horrible death was surely branded onto his mind, and yet he had raised a little girl in an environment of love and security without ever once mentioning her loss . . . even as Jessica's maturing features naturally took on more and more of her mother's remembered beauty.

If what Parks said was true, Uncle Kevin's sacrifices and devotion were more than touching—they were heartrending. He had dedicated himself to avenging his sister's murder by making sure that the tragedy of it ended there, without ruining her only child's life as well. She suddenly wanted to cry, and to hug him . . . to throw her arms around his wide, stooping shoulders and make him blink and pull away shyly as he always did whenever she displayed affection.

And she wanted to slap Parks.

She got up, and he followed her out to the parking lot, where, against the grey, omnipresent backdrop of Lake Erie, he watched her pull off her black wig and shake out her strawberry-blond hair. It was cut as short as a boy's, razored over the right ear, and very trendy. He didn't seem surprised by her disguise, and it was only after she'd calmed down later that she realized he probably knew she was wearing a wig all along. In the cold, her breath turned to steam, and her cheeks flushed pink. To stop her from getting into her car—a gold convertible Mercedes two-seater with a winter hard top that Uncle Kevin had given her because "My Jessie's not hacking around town in any rust-bucket beater like college kids do"—he put a hand on her arm and . . .

"Just lay off!" she snapped, pulling her arm away and feeling real rage for the first time that morning . . . and possibly, for the first time in her life. "Enough!"

"Miss Reynolds! Jessica!" Parks pleaded, snatching back his hand and wrapping his suit coat around his brittle ribs against the chill of a stiff breeze whipping in off the water. "If you'd just hear me out . . ."

"I've heard enough!" she fumed, trying to pull her car door

shut against his resistance and starting the engine. "I'm not talking to you anymore."

He was very strong for someone who looked so frail, and he was able to prevent her from getting away long enough to say, "Other than me, and the man who killed your parents, you're the only person who was in that room who's still alive."

"My parents died in a car accident," Jessie hissed, pronouncing her uncle's history as fact in defiance of everything Parks had said to hurt her. "And if you don't leave me alone, I'll . . ." She stumbled for just one breath, and finished, "I'll call the police!"

And then she drove away, leaving Parks behind her in a swirl of snow that was as fine as dust. She didn't find the scrap of paper upon which he had written his name, address, and phone number, along with the words "If this means anything to you, call me right away," until later that night. He must have sneaked it into her purse sometime without her seeing. And stapled to that paper was a photograph she would soon come to wish she had never seen.

2

A coldness came over Henry Parks as he watched Jessica Reynolds—or Jessica Sterns, depending on how you looked at it—drive away. Red taillights flashed as she pulled out onto Lake Avenue. And then she was gone.

The coldness spread, starting in the center of his chest and ending at his fingertips. This chilling calm was his most potent weapon, translating into a machinelike state of mental control that he saw as his only defense against his adversary's explosive irrationality. In the face of the Prisoner's remarkable physical strength and agility, Parks' only protection was intellect and raw nerve. And they'd worked reasonably well so far.

When he turned, Novak asked, "Well?" from the police station doorway.

"Something jarred her memory of what happened to her when she was a baby," Parks said, approaching his friend and closing the door behind them. On the stairs, he added, "And I jarred it a little more. She's got my number. All we can do now is wait."

3

The library downtown had the Cleveland *Press* and *Plain Dealer*—the "Pain Feeler," or so went the old joke—recorded on microfilm going all the way back to the dawn of time.

The newspaper stories about the killing of her "parents" weren't hard to find. Parks had told her that he had been retired for twenty years, and her own recollections centered around snow. So she poked through the twenty-year-old back issues of winter months until she found the headline:

FAMILY KILLED IN HEIGHTS!

Now she knew the exact date that the events in her "murder memory" had occurred: January 17, 1972: her first birthday.

And she read: "unidentified assailant . . . husband, wife, and two male friends . . . child present . . . identity withheld by police . . ."

She had the articles photocopied and then got out of the library's dusty stillness because it reminded her of a morgue.

Back in her car, she read more carefully.

Officer Henry Parks, a twenty-three-year veteran of the Cleveland Police Department, was injured while intervening in the apparent assault on an infant girl. The child's name and whereabouts are being withheld by authorities as a protective measure.

"Protective measure?" Jessie said aloud to herself as she raced her car up the freeway ramp and blew into traffic, much too fast for the icy road, but as clean and sharp as if the pavement were dry.

"Protective against what? What did they think the guy would try to do, find me again?"

She didn't allow herself any mental comment on the fact that the word "me" was a part of her question . . . as if she might actually believe Parks' story, though she had continued to insist that he was lying.

But the doubt was there.

Where else could it be?

Her apartment was too warm, and after dropping her stack of photocopies on the kitchen table, she pulled a wine cooler out of the fridge and drank half of it down. Then she called her Uncle Kevin in Columbus, but he wasn't home. Instead of hanging up when she heard his answering machine kick on, she leaned against the sink counter, listening as his voice said, "You've reached the Reynolds Genealogical Survey and Research Group. I'm sorry, but we presently aren't available to personally attend to your call. But if you'll leave your name, number, and a brief message, we'll get back to you at our absolute first opportunity.

"And if this is Jessie, I love you, kid."

Jessie smiled. Uncle Kevin always put a personal message to her on his machine, just in case "I'm not home, and you need a little loving."

"But what about the people who call on business?" Jessie had asked.

"They'll all know how neat I think you are."

Jessie hung up. She hated answering machines, and thought talking to them was a little like having a chat with a CD player. Besides, if the machine was on at two in the afternoon, then Uncle Kevin was either down at the library or digging through records at a Vital Statistics Office in a city hall somewhere . . . which translated into anywhere. He'd jump on a plane and fly to New Orleans if it meant tracing a branch of someone's family tree. If he was home that night, she'd talk to him later. And if he was going to be staying out of town, he'd call.

In the hallway, something scraped a wall and then bounced on the floor. The people in 404 were moving out. There were boxes and suitcases scattered around a station wagon in the parking lot near the building's back door, and a mattress leaned forlornly against the wall by the elevator in the lobby. The elevator was a recent addition. Years ago, the building had been a fraternity house. But it had since been purchased by a private owner who had converted it into apartments. Located right across the street from the college Art and Drama Center—the sign on which had been recently defaced with spray paint to read, "Fart and Trama Center"—the place was a haven for music and theater majors, as well as some of the other well-to-do members of Lawrynce-Wynn University's undergraduate population too sensitive to live in a dorm.

From where Jessie was standing, she could see the theater through her front window. It looked like a big brick toaster. To her right was the door to her bedroom, and to her left, a wall on which the Joker grinned from a huge poster for the *Batman* movie that an usher friend had gotten her as an early birthday present. The poster had hung in the Village Cinema's lobby, and it featured Jack Nicholson, green hair and all, made up like a clown.

She hated it.

But someday it would be worth some money.

The Joker had been on her wall for about two weeks.

FAMILY KILLED IN HEIGHTS!

She finished her wine cooler, opened another, and realized that her hands were trembling. So she kicked off her shoes and lay across her couch.

The Joker grinned.

She turned around and lay the other way.

So where do I stand? she thought, trying her best to get her mind around the parameters of the question. That morning she had gone off on a lark to do a research project in a real police station. The "memories of murder" story had been her excuse for being interviewed. But to have a stranger actually verify it!

And now . . .

She didn't know who she was anymore.

Well, maybe it wasn't quite that bad.

But then again, maybe it was.

That was the problem: she wasn't sure how she felt about things. Not about her Uncle Kevin, of course. She knew how she felt about him: she loved him. If the story was false, she loved him. And if it was true, hell, she might even love him more.

But the idea of a woman carrying around the memory of an event that had occurred when she was a year old, with that memory hidden away like a time bomb, lurking in the back of her mind until, for some inexplicable reason, it decided to reappear and prove that just about everything she had believed about her life was untrue . . .

Christ!

There was a play in this.

She swore to God there was.

Maybe even a movie!

She sat up.

"But what if it's true?" she said, dangling the wine cooler bottle between her knees and hunching up her shoulders in unconscious imitation of her uncle when he was worried. "So what if it is?"

If her parents were really murdered by some nut twenty years ago, well, that was obviously a tragedy. But it didn't really make her feel anything. Not really. Not really *feel* anything. She had never known them. Even if the Sternses actually were her biological parents, they truthfully couldn't be any more to her than a couple of names in an old newspaper, no matter how cold an attitude that might appear to be. She couldn't be expected to put personalities to the faces in a photograph, and then to learn to love them for their own sake. She needed flesh and blood in her life. Not abstractions.

She'd like to know, of course. And she intended to ask her uncle about it just as soon as she could. But she wouldn't confront him. She'd ask nicely. Confrontation simply made him fall apart. Growing up, she'd learned that all she had to do to get her way was to raise a fuss and he'd buy her the moon. There frankly seemed to be no end to his money, or to his capacity for gentleness. It had taken a lot of work to convince her grandmother to let her move in with him when she was twelve. But it had been worth it. At times she considered him more of a friend than an uncle; at other times she saw him as her father; and yet at other times she wished that he weren't her uncle at all. Older men had always been attractive to her.

She frowned.
Some older men.
But certainly not Henry Parks.
He reminded her of a crow with a suit on.
She finished her wine cooler, opened a third, and got in the tub, watching steam curl and water bead on white tile. Sinking her head down so that the water filled her ears, she closed her eyes and listened to her heart beat, thinking . . .

FAMILY KILLED IN HEIGHTS!

Later, wrapped in a terry-cloth robe and toweling dry her hair, she found the paper Henry Parks had hidden in her purse. And the photograph.
It made her cry.
And then it made her call him.

4

The crow drank coffee as if he were pouring it down a hole. Cup after cup. Gulps of it, no matter how hot.
Jessie drank some too, to sober up. They were in a Denny's restaurant by the freeway. She didn't want him in her apartment. The photograph was on the table between them. It was nearly ten o'clock. And, save for a guy reading a newspaper at the counter in the smoking section, they seemed to have the place to themselves.
"Why?" Jessie asked, because it was the only question that she could manage without flying off the handle. "Why are you doing this to me?"
As she spoke, her right hand nervously massaged the base of her throat, unconsciously touching her scar through the heavy weave of her wool turtleneck sweater. It was that scar that had clinched things for her. That scar, and the picture on the table.
It was of a baby; a year-old little girl; her, if she could believe it . . .

Okay, goddamn it.

It was her.

She knew it was.

It had been taken in a police station, apparently, because the little girl—crying, naked, and terrified—was being helped to stand against a drab grey wall with black lines indicating inches from the floor. She was just a little over twenty inches tall. The arms that were holding her up belonged to a man, and while his right hand was cupped around her hips to keep her steady, his other was displaying a length of leather dog leash, doubled-up and close to the wall to show that, stretched out, it would have been a good five feet long. The leash had been tied around the little girl's neck . . .

Around *my* neck! Jessie thought.

And its end had been nailed to the living room floor in the house where the Sternses were murdered so that she wouldn't wander off during the proceedings. A terrible gash encircled the child's throat because, as described by the writing on the back of the picture, the assailant responsible for the killings had dangled her on the cord to carry her around.

Beneath her purple turtleneck, Jessie had a very faint scar—barely perceptible, unless you knew where to look—that ran all the way around her neck. It was worse in the front, presumably because that was where the leather had bitten most deeply into her flesh. Uncle Kevin had once told her that it was the result of a childhood accident involving a clothesline. It had nearly disappeared over the years, but it was there, and she could see it, especially after a really hot bath or if she let herself get a sunburn.

The picture was dated January 18, 1972, 3:15 A.M.

Parks finished his coffee, signaled for more, and said, "Everybody who's come close to this guy's got some kinda scar," as he distractedly lifted the photograph and examined it. "At least the ones who lived through it do. And there ain't a whole lotta them around."

The waitress filled his cup and left, but not before furrowing her brows when she caught a glimpse of the picture he was holding.

He turned it facedown on the table.

"Now listen," he said, and his voice sounded even rougher than it had been earlier in the day. "I never set out to screw up your life. I never even approached you over the years. I figured that you were too young to remember what happened to you, and that it would be better if you never knew. I spoke with your grandparents, and your uncle . . ."

"You talked to Uncle Kevin?" Jessie cut in, her tone indignant, as if Parks had violated some private property.

The old man was nodding.

"A number of times," he said. "And he's been very helpful. There wasn't a lot he could tell me, but he was anxious for me to find this guy and . . . Are you all right?"

Jessie was leaning back in her seat, with her hands flat on the table. She was breathing hard, with her eyes closed and her lips pressed tightly together in a bloodless line.

"I'm okay," she whispered. "Just go on."

The idea that her uncle had helped Parks in his investigation . . . and that Parks had spoken to her grandparents . . . and that her grandparents knew . . . and that everybody but her knew . . . and that all this had been going on her whole life . . . and that nobody had ever told her . . . and what the hell else had been happening that she didn't know about? . . . and . . .

"Just go on," she repeated thinly, an underpinning of anger barely concealed beneath a tone of overt passivity that neither she nor Parks believed was genuine.

Parks glanced around the room as if someone might be watching before leaning forward and saying, "You've got to help me find him."

"Who?"

"The Prisoner."

"Who the hell's the Prisoner?" Jessie asked, opening her eyes.

But instead of answering, Parks ordered breakfast food for them both. The man at the counter in the smoking section got up and walked over to the men's room, transforming himself from a stranger to Sergeant Novak right before Jessie's eyes. A pay phone rang once near the restaurant's front door, and a man that she hadn't even seen before, but who was just sitting there, as if waiting for the call, picked it up. And a cigarette lighter flared outside the black window as a figure—she couldn't tell if it was a man or a woman—loitered back and forth.

When the food came, Parks made her eat. When they were done they left without paying the bill. And in the parking lot the man with the cigarette materialized out of the gloom. Parks told him to "Take my car back. I won't need it anymore tonight." And then, with Jessie at the driver's door of the Mercedes, he added, "You drive. Your car's too nice to leave in a restaurant parking lot all night."

"Where are we going?" Jessie asked.

And Parks said, "To the airport."

"Why?" she asked more firmly, without making a move for her keys.

And for the first time since she'd met him, she caught what she believed to be a glimpse of the man lurking inside the husk that Henry Parks used for a body.

In the bitterly cold oxide light of one of the parking lot's halogen lamps, she saw a gleam come to his eyes that was at once clever and dangerous. If that gleam had been there earlier, she'd missed it—probably because she had been so concerned with playing her own part that she'd been taken in as he played his. But she saw it now. And it made her think that she had finally found some human motivation to which she could react: an angle . . . an opening . . . an opportunity.

She zipped up her leather coat and thrust her hands into her pockets with a defiant cock of her hips. Her hair was brushed straight back, and she wasn't wearing any makeup, so she knew that, with her sallow complexion, she must have looked ivory-pale in the stark white light. Her boots had a high, spiked heel. Her jeans were very tight, with a thin silver chain threaded through the belt loops. And she'd painted her fingernails black, for effect.

Her whole posture said, "I'm not budging without a very good reason."

And Parks gave her one.

"We're going to the airport," he said very slowly, "because, whether you like it or not, whether you believe it or not, you know who killed your parents. It's been locked up inside your head all these years, and for whatever reason, it's just now starting to come back. If the Prisoner should get wind of this, he'll pull himself up out of whatever hole he calls home . . .

"And he'll kill you."

Jessie got in the car.

5

"Are you rich?" she asked when she saw the plane.

"No," Parks responded. "It's a loaner."

The airport was only ten minutes from the freeway, and Parks had her park in the terminal's fire lane and give her keys to a large black man in a cream-colored sport coat who was waiting for them in the lobby. There were no tickets, gates, or counter clerks to deal with at all. They just stepped out onto the tarmac—the first time Jessie had ever been on a runway—and boarded a private Learjet, piloted by a faceless woman who did not so much as glance at them through the cockpit window. They buckled up, took off, and settled back. If it were not for the constant whoosh of rushing air outside, Jessie might have sworn that they were standing still, so smooth was the ride.

The interior of the cabin was done in leather and suede, which reminded her of her Mercedes . . . and money.

She was nervous.

She had never been to a murder scene before.

"Now," Parks said, sinking into his seat and rubbing his pale eyes. "What I'm about to say is between me, you, and Buddha. You can't repeat it, one, because some very important people would be irritated if you did, and two, because no one would believe you anyway."

Good start, Jessie thought.

She was glad that she'd left a message on her uncle's answering machine before leaving to meet Parks at the restaurant.

"Hi, Uncle Kevin. This is Jess," she'd said. "This is gonna sound really weird, and damn, I wish you were home, but there's this retired cop who's been telling me all kinds of strange stuff about the family. And . . . well. I'm meeting him at the Denny's near the ramp on 71. His name is Henry Parks, and there's a Sergeant William Novak I talked to this morning and . . . I'm not in any trouble or anything, so don't worry. But it's just that, well . . . I've really gotta talk to you when you get home. It's about my first birthday, and it's kinda important. So call me right away, okay? I love you. Bye."

Insurance.

Murder scene.

". . . been having this memory?"

"What?" Jessie blinked. She'd drifted off there a bit.

"I asked you exactly how long you've been having the memory that brought you to the police station," Parks said, studying her face.

"Two weeks, maybe," she responded. "I'm not really sure. It started off kinda hazy. And it just got stronger."

"And when I showed you those pictures of your parents, didn't they mean anything to you?"

"No. I've never seen them before."

"You've never seen your own parents?"

"They said that all the pictures were lost."

"Every one?"

"Every one."

"Didn't you think that was odd?"

"I guess I never thought about it."

"And the name Sterns?"

"Never heard it."

"That's interesting," Parks mused, before returning to the original subject with a wave of his hand.

"This airplane," he said, "as well as the phone call in the restaurant signaling us that it was time to go, and the one that called me down to the police station this morning, are all pieces of a privately funded effort devoted to identifying and apprehending the man who killed your parents."

"Why should someone give things to *you*?" Jessie asked.

The expression on Parks' face hinted that he appreciated the question.

"Because, like you, my patron lost a loved one," he said. "But unlike you, he remembers his."

Jessie frowned.

And Parks began talking about the Prisoner.

The term left his lips so easily that Jessie realized he had christened the killer with the name not only because of some insight he seemed to believe he had into the workings of the man's mind, but also because it gave him a handle on this nebulous, apparently faceless specter of death. "The killer," and even "the man who killed your parents," were descriptive phrases that did little but point a finger in a general direction without offering any hope of unveiling the unknown. But "the Prisoner" almost seemed magically accurate, like the naming of a hurricane: suddenly an incomprehensible force of nature became not a random event without motivation, but a being with an identity. It was now a particular thing, a living object, a finite quantity. By virtue of naming it, Jessie realized, Parks was implying that he could conceivably understand it. And once it was understood, it would be, at that exact moment, effectively contained.

It was a complicated dynamic, and more than a little primitive at heart. It gave Jessie a sense that Henry Parks believed he was facing something of such awesome power that it reached into the deepest memories of his soul and found that place where magic and superstition still live in us all. It also gave her a hint of his fear:

What he was doing was dangerous.

And what he was chasing was bizarre.

"I've had a sense of contact with him since that first night," he said. "And later, while I was recovering, I couldn't get him out of my head. I had a feeling that there was some purpose to what he was doing that went beyond simple murder. And that by killing those adults, and you, he was, in fact, pursuing a goal."

"How could you possibly know something like that?" Jessie asked.

But she may as well not have opened her mouth for all the impact her question had on Parks.

"He didn't kill again for almost sixteen months," he said. "But since then, it's been about three a year, for twenty years. That's sixty people.

"Sixty.

"And those are the ones I know about.

"Which is why I need private help. The authorities don't believe me when I say that just one man's responsible for all this. They think I've got psychopaths on the brain, and that I've been taking a bunch of unrelated crimes and lumping them together.

"But I know what I see.

"And so does the man who's sponsoring me.

"It's an honor to have someone place such confidence in me and say, 'Yes, Henry Parks, I believe that you can catch this lunatic. And I'll do all I can to help.' That's a heavy responsibility. It's been a long time, and others have thrown their hats into the ring. But in the end, the chase always comes back to me."

He sighed.

"But, Jesus! It would just be so much better if I could see the bodies when they're fresh. I used to be able to get in right away, but I can't anymore. The FBI put the word out: no Henry Parks. So when a killing happens that looks like it might be the Prisoner's work, I have to depend on somebody in the area to get me in late at night or the next day. Once the feds are gone, the city cops usually feel like they owe me: former brother in arms, maimed in the line of duty, dedicated to the philosophy of order and the rule of law . . . Blah blah blah. Happy horseshit all the way.

"I milk it for whatever it's worth. I'll even gravel up my voice, grimace like it hurts to talk—which it doesn't, but they don't know that—and hobble like a geriatric. I'm not proud. If it gets me in, I do it, period.

"But still I don't get to see every site. I don't have enough informants. And sometimes, even when there is somebody local who would call, they just plain miss the signs and overlook a job. So sixty deaths might be a little heavy, or it might be shy. Let's just say that it's a lot. Okay?"

Jessie nodded, feeling cold.

"And it's not like they're connected," Parks emphasized. "If I didn't know better, I'd swear they were picked out of a hat. Almost totally random, all over the goddamn country. Insane.

"But I do know certain things . . . Like the fact that the Prisoner is about five feet ten inches tall, right-handed, and quick on his feet. He's athletic, clever, has an almost unbelievable ability to vary the locations of his activities, and is a sadist and a pervert.

"But I've never gotten close to him with fingerprints, semen, saliva, or blood. He hasn't left so much as a friggin' hair for me to analyze. It's like he's got himself wrapped in plastic.

"Which is part of why I'm sure he's one man: killers always leave something. Only this one's perfect."

Jessie found "perfect" to be an odd choice of words, but Parks qualified it by saying that the Prisoner operated as if he were in battle. She'd see what he meant for herself soon enough if the site in Pittsburgh was a true Prisoner job.

"He comes in like a terrorist: in, out, bang, bang. Couple a minutes tops, and everybody's dead. No sound to alert neighbors, no chance to fight back. I've seen his technique evolve since that first night in your parents' house, and he's become a master.

"But that's not his genius.

"What's made him so hard to find is that sometimes he does things, and sometimes he doesn't. He's not dependable. It's almost as if he varies his operational technique specifically to mask his handiwork."

Jessie cut in, "But wouldn't that only make sense?" feeling a little embarrassed at herself for getting involved.

Parks looked at her curiously.

And she had to summon up her courage to say, "I mean, if you meant to keep doing something someone else didn't want you to do, wouldn't you try your best to be unpredictable? It would be like a part in a play.

"On the inside, an actor's always the same person, but on the outside, every role's different. That's the beauty of playing a character. And it's why people are usually disappointed when they find out what their favorite actors are really like when they're not playing the roles that made them famous."

Parks agreed. "But it's not quite so simple with a nut like this. He might be able to change the *way* he does something. But he's not going to be able to change the *why*. His underlying psychosis is going to drive him to repeat certain things, over and over again. There's a demon inside that compels his search for a kind of relief he can only get in a particular way. He can't change that. And he can't hide it. At least a 'normal' psychopath can't."

"But the Prisoner can?" Jessie asked.

Making Parks nod and say, "He's got tremendous self-control when it comes to concealing the clues to his real motivation. Sometimes they're there, and sometimes they're not. Sometimes they're so obvious that even the feds can see them, and other times they're all but invisible."

"But you can pick them out?"

"Yes, I can."

"How?"

No answer.

Jessie expected a big airport, but the one at which they landed was small—little more than a runway and a control shack; a group of sullen men blowing steam in the cold, but the car waiting in the lot was empty; a long, mysterious drive through snowy, midnight streets, but they were there in no time at all.

A little pink house . . .

But the place was a factory with broken windows.

Two of the anticipated, steaming men were standing at the factory door next to an unmarked Ford. They shook Parks' hand, glanced at Jessie without comment, and then explained how to find the murder scene. Apparently, not only were they not going to accompany them inside, they weren't even going to wait around until Parks was finished.

Is this legal? Jessie wondered.

And then Parks was moving.

"They paid for an hour," he said, nodding at the car carrying the two men away. "Since it's listed as 'murder with motive,' the feds aren't in on this one. The scene's been sealed, the guard went out for a hundred-dollar doughnut, and we've got a lot to do."

The victim called himself Mark O'Polo—real name Mark Opal—and he was a local eccentric. The factory had once printed a newspaper, but that was gone. In its place, O'Polo published a science fiction magazine called *A Time for Space*, which he wrote for, edited, laid out, and printed. His real job was simply guarding the building from vandals, but on the side he had about twenty-five hundred subscribers, and once every other month he carted three big cardboard boxes down to the local post office, bleary-eyed and unshaven after spending the night running off pages and stapling them together on a contraption that looked like an old sewing machine. The rest of the time he spent squirreled away in his room, pounding on an IBM P.C. and reading his mail.

"The locals think he was robbed, but they don't know what kind of stuff he kept around the office, so they can't tell if anything's missing," Parks said, shaking his head and producing a flashlight from his briefcase. "We'll start over there," he added, indicating a dark corner on the factory's southwest side. "And follow the Prisoner's approach. They've already removed the body. But everything's marked, so we should be able to get a pretty good idea of what happened without it. Here . . ."

He handed Jessie a flashlight from his briefcase, and then slid a small black gun into his belt.

" 'Cause you never know."

Terrific, Jessie thought.

Later, she would think of accompanying Parks through that old factory as having her first period and losing her virginity, rolled into one.

As he moved, Parks explained that the Prisoner always studied a target before the kill.

"He really knows what he's doing when he goes in. Like that second-floor window with the broken lock in Boston or the poisoned Doberman in Tampa."

(Jessie had no idea what he was talking about.)

"And tonight's no exception."

The building was only three stories high, but at least eighty yards long. O'Polo lived in a room on the second floor, overlooking a parking lot surrounded by a chain-link fence. On the opposite side there was another unoccupied building. And in the alley was a truck ramp to the basement, where supplies had once been unloaded.

Both streetlamps nearby were dark.

"Kids throwing stones," Parks mumbled sarcastically, heading for the ramp.

There was glass on the sidewalk, and it reflected the moonlight. The alley went totally dark in one abrupt lurch, making Jessie feel a little disoriented. Following the beam of Parks' flashlight, she descended the ramp behind him, listening as he said, "I'll bet he shot the lamps out days ago and then checked the doors."

Which were corrugated steel, twenty feet high, ran up and down on a track, and were locked to a ring in the ground with a three-foot chain.

Parks bent over and slid the door up far enough for them to crawl under. When they were inside, he dropped the door and it produced a deep, echoing thud that seemed to vibrate through the walls.

"With his target on the other side of the building, he could have blown the door open with a grenade and nobody would have been the wiser," Parks said, running his flashlight beam around the cluttered room. It finally settled on the black rectangle of an open door at the top of a series of steel stairs. "There," he said. "Now, be careful."

The main floor was one large room, three stories high, and cut into about a million slices of moonlight and shadow by the jagged teeth of its countless broken windows. Running down the center of the room was a tangle of sheet-draped machines, jutting, squatting, angled, and grimy.

"The presses," Parks explained in a whisper.

Looking around, he settled his light on an outside door and then ran it up a set of steel-tube stairs that entered a hole in the ceiling.

"According to my source," he said, "O'Polo got back from his shopping at approximately eight P.M. It was already dark outside, and after placing four bags of groceries on the floor, he locked the door behind himself and took two of the bags upstairs." The flashlight followed the stairs again. "And then he came back down and got the rest."

The living quarters were weird. Approached first through the floor—the metal stairway to which reminded Jessie of one that might be found in a submarine or a lighthouse—they started as an outer chamber that was separated from the main room by a three-foot-high partition wall of plaster, mounted by windows that ran to the ceiling. There was a door set into the middle of this wall of dusty glass, and from where Jessie was standing, the arrangement gave her the impression that she was looking at an observation tank or a museum display.

"Director's office," Parks said, his flashlight glinting around nervously. "Secretary's office out here, plant manager's in there."

The door to the main office was hanging open, but a yellow *Do Not Cross—Police Order* ribbon was tacked across its frame.

Parks pulled it down and stepped through.

The office was large, and set at the corner of the building so that two of its walls were made entirely of windows that amazingly had been left unbroken. Moonlight stained everything silver, and on the horizon the midnight lights of Pittsburgh twinkled gold. But the city disappeared when Parks hit the ceiling lights, which flickered a couple of times before fluorescent glare blazed along a dozen tubes, drowning the room in neon-white and turning the windows into black mirrors. The first thing Jessie noticed was herself, reflected as darkly as if she were swimming in ink.

And the next thing she saw was the blood.

Hard, splattered, and black.

Her legs went rubbery, and she gasped. Parks shot out one hand, catching her arm, but she pulled away to stand on her own.

They may have taken the body, but they hadn't touched the room. The scene was just as it had been found . . .

"Yesterday," Parks said. "He'd been dead for at least a week before they noticed he hadn't come to the post office for his bimonthly mailing."

But Jessie was only listening with one part of her mind. Another part was busy seeing, while still another was trying to back the rest of her body out the way she had come. The sensation of dislocation almost made her dizzy. An oppressive feeling of unreality overwhelmed her while her mind simultaneously insisted, It's true. It might look like a bunch of stage props, but it's not. Somebody died here. Now pull yourself together! She felt woozy and scared; frightened and alive. There was a theatricality to the whole thing to which she responded, while, at the same time, there was a depressing banality to the scene that was embarrassing.

If Parks saw her confusion, he chose to ignore it because, almost as soon as she pulled away from his touch, he started talking.

"Without knowing what you're looking at, you won't see what he was doing," he said, stepping deeper into the room.

Around him a remarkable arrangement of desks and tables were covered with mounds of papers—thousands, maybe even millions of sheets scribbled over or typewritten: letters, magazine pages, drawings, envelopes, manuscripts, and doodles—overflowing the furniture and spreading across the floor in heaps through which paths had been etched like canals in the sand. A cot lay in one far corner, away from the windows next to a battered refrigerator, a series of doors ran along the room's back wall, and O'Polo's computer sat, bleary and ignored, on a desk near his cot.

But the room's feature piece, and the object that commanded the most attention, because of its position and its size, was something that looked like a wooden workbench. Constructed of two-by-fours nailed together in a roughly rectangular frame and topped with a sheet of badly stained—and, was it, burned?—plywood, the table was centered in the room beneath a hanging cord at the end of which dangled a naked light bulb. There were leather straps screwed into the table's sides at the head, center, and foot. An empty steel pail sat on the floor nearby, and an extension cord wound its way from the wall to a place where it was secured to a table leg, as if to keep it from being kicked away.

But it was the table surface that was most disturbing, and it was here that Parks began his dissertation.

"They told me about this," he said, gingerly touching the side of the table with one finger and looking down at the stained, plywood surface. "It looks like somebody was tortured here . . . the straps, and the stains, here, at the spot that would be between a person's legs. And here, at the head. The local lab's analyzing samples. Then we have the electric cord . . . and the light overhead to work by. But, interestingly enough, there isn't any blood. Or at least none that I can pick out with my eye. Maybe I'm wrong, but I don't think so.

"When they told me that this thing was in here, I thought, 'Christ! He had that much time to prepare?' thinking that it was the Prisoner who had set it up. But after looking at the rest of the evidence, now I'm not so sure. I think this thing was here before the Prisoner ever came. And if that's true, then it would appear that O'Polo must have used it for something . . . God only knows what. This thing muddies the pool, so to speak. But as interesting as it is, we've got more important evidence to consider."

Parks stepped away from the torture table and entered a sea of clutter.

"Now," he said, with more feeling than Jessie had previously heard him express. "Watch the man's mind take shape . . . 'cause that's what this is: his mind. What he does to other people is how he gives his thoughts life. He's packed full of things he's imagined. And killing people is how he proves they're real. So . . .

"From his hiding place outside, he watched O'Polo leave to do some shopping, taking his car, which"—his right index finger shot up for emphasis— "has yet to be found.

"The sun set at between six-forty and seven o'clock, so he waited 'til dark and entered the building the same way we did, working his way up to here, where he hid . . . in there." The door standing ajar next to the cot. "Clear, unobstructed line of sight over the whole room."

Parks was standing in front of the door without opening it, indicating the area before him with a sweep of his arm.

"O'Polo came home, turned on the lights, and put his groceries in the icebox. The Prisoner, watching him around the door, waited until he was standing just about where I am now, ten feet away, and then he revealed his presence.

"O'Polo turned, and his assailant shot him: once in the stomach and twice in the head. The weapon is a Walther PPK, 9mm automatic with a homemade silencer. I know about the silencer from the bits of asbestos embedded in the body. And because of the paint chips left here, and at one or two other scenes over the years, I know that he's painted his gun gold."

Jessie blinked.

"By the time O'Polo hit the floor, he was dead. And that's when the Prisoner went to work."

With an almost comical spring to his step, Parks moved to the overturned table and demonstrated how the Prisoner would drag the dead body of Mark O'Polo, "after shooting him one last time, *blam!* in the heart"—a jerking finger gun fires a final invisible bullet—along the cluttered floor, leaving a trail of blood to the room from which the killer had launched his ambush.

"And now," Parks said, dropping the imaginary body and indicating the door, "an opening like this is the key. And it's why I call him the Prisoner. He seems like he wants to get out . . . to pass from somewhere, to somewhere else. I don't know where he thinks he's going, but sometimes he uses the bodies of his victims to get to openings like doors or windows because he wants to *get back to where he belongs* . . . wherever that is. I heard him say it the night he killed your folks. 'No one's going to stop me from getting back to where I belong!' I'll never forget those words.

"Now, he placed the body facedown on the floor, and . . ."

Parks arranged the invisible corpse.

"Walked over it."

Balanced with exaggerated movements of his arms like a tightrope walker traversing unsure terrain, he carefully stepped forward.

"Leaving footprints up the back, he crossed his bridge of death, and on the other side he . . ."

Still balanced, Parks leaned forward and pulled the door toward him as . . .

Jessie screamed when she saw the man standing on the other side.

6

Parks fumbled for the gun in his belt and dropped it. It hit the floor with a stupid *thump* that was as anticlimactic as it was final. Jessie's heart raced, and her throat hurt from the exertion of her scream, but she didn't move from her spot. And the man in the doorway stepped from darkness into light.

Her eyes followed the motion of his hand as it lifted the gun from the center of a yellow chalk line describing the awkward arrangement of a body on the floor. He was younger than Parks by at least twenty years, and his smile was the mirthless, mocking grin of someone who believed himself superior to all he surveyed.

Handing the gun back to Parks, butt end first, he picked up the older man's sentence where it hung in the air and said, "The Prisoner crossed his bridge of death and disappeared on the other side."

"Ellis!" Parks breathed, slack-jawed.

Even from where she was standing, Jessie could see that he was trembling.

The younger man's shit-eating grin faded as he said, "Hello, Harry, you old bastard."

And Parks put his gun away.

If sound-track music had swelled up from the floor at that moment, Jessie probably wouldn't have been surprised. A terrible sensation of unreality was choking her thoughts, and even when the man in the doorway said, "And hello, Miss Reynolds," she didn't respond. She was watching, studying almost, wishing that she had a camera as the younger man handed Parks some photographs and said, "Peace offering."

They were Polaroids.

And they were dark.

Parks shuffled through them, his expression hardening to stone.

"I was told about the shooting," he said, handing back the pictures. "But not about this. Nobody told me a word about this!"

"Does that surprise you?"

"What surprises me is that someone would take my money and then lie to my face."

"It wasn't *your* money, and he didn't lie. He omitted certain details."

"Don't quibble semantics," Parks snapped, his cheeks coloring. "He told me you wouldn't be here. He told me it was listed . . ."

" 'Murder with motive'?" Ellis cut in.

"He said no feds!"

"And there aren't any. I'm private. You're private; and now I'm private too."

At that moment, Jessie didn't understand that Wilson "Sonny Boy" Ellis was an investigator for the FBI who had, on more than one occasion, and by instruction of his superiors, told Henry Parks that his Prisoner theory was ludicrous. She didn't know that they were talking about an informant in the Pittsburgh Police Department dispatch office who was on Parks' payroll. And she wasn't aware of the fact that Parks secretly considered Ellis the best of the feds on the market.

Parks would have to explain all these things to her later. But for now, she was feeling very much as if she had just stepped into a theater and begun watching a movie somewhere in the middle.

"How private?" Parks asked, cocking his head to one side.

"I believe you," Ellis said casually. "That not private enough? Then how about this? I think that it's about time we stopped pretending that this guy doesn't exist and nail his ass."

"That's pretty private," Parks responded softly.

"They'd have me digging for Hoffa in Anchorage."

"Then why buck the party line?"

Ellis was about six feet tall, which set him almost a full head over Parks. He wore a dark grey, pin-striped suit, a white shirt, and a red necktie. His build was slight but solid, constructed predominantly of angles. He had a small, straight nose, thin, tight lips, and a pair of the most steady, glassy-blue eyes Jessie had ever seen. When he spoke, despite his earlier superior grin, Jessie believed what he said. And within moments she found herself more prone to trust him than Parks, who she still considered odd, cranky, and crowish.

"Because I'm tired of it," Ellis said with a shrug. "And because I'm not willing to go on protecting the nonexistent ass on a bureaucratic machine anymore. Ignoring a mistake isn't going to make it go away."

Jessie would stay lost on this point until Parks explained that the people at the Bureau had been insisting for so long that the Prisoner didn't exist that changing their minds had become virtually impossible.

"But can't they just admit when they're wrong?" Jessie would ask.

And Parks would respond, "The time you spend doing something often becomes more important than the thing itself."

"They're going to 'reevaluate' their position," Ellis said. "Go back over the evidence, look for new connections. And that'll take time. A lot of the evidence they'll be going back over came from you in the first place."

"So you figured that if you rubbed my belly I'd be so grateful that I'd just lead you to him," Parks said through his teeth.

"If you knew where he was, you'd have gone after him by now," Ellis returned, starting that awful smile again. "I know you, Henry. I know how the 'Dead Man' works."

Parks' posture stiffened, as if the younger man had hit a nerve.

"No joke, Henry," Ellis cut in quickly. "I want to partner up. You've been holding out on us, and we've been . . ."

"Holding me out."

Ellis shrugged helplessly. "It was policy. It wasn't personal."

"*This* is personal!" Parks nearly shouted, pointing at the blood on the floor.

"Then let's put our heads together and end it."

Parks' expression was one of absolute suspicion. "Everything?" he asked.

Ellis nodded.

"Why now?"

"He came unstuck."

"How?"

"You tell me."

Parks stepped toward the door as if he'd been challenged, concentrating on what he was seeing ahead of himself and mumbling, "I wanna see a printout of the latest personality profile, and the suspect list too. The latest one."

Moving aside to allow Parks to pass, Ellis said, "You will."

"The *latest* one," Parks emphasized.

And Ellis agreed.

Jessie caught up to him just as he stepped through the door. And when Ellis put his arm out to hold her, saying, "I don't think that's a good idea, young lady," she squirmed past him and made Parks hold her hand, shooting back a glance that was so indignant that Ellis just let her go.

Parks' hand was fleshy, and remarkably warm. She'd have thought it would have been cold. His skin radiated a pulse that reminded her of her neighbor's stereo. The man who lived in the apartment below her liked hard rock, and when he played it, usually late at night, she couldn't so much hear it as feel the bass throbbing up through the soles of her feet. There was an energy in Parks that felt like those hard rock rhythms: steady, harsh, and ridiculously macho.

At one time in his life, she realized, Henry Parks must have been a very hard man.

Now he said, "Holy Christ!" and squeezed her hand, making her squeak and pull away.

"Holy Christ Almighty!"

It wasn't anything that the Prisoner had done that was impressing Parks, it was their location. He and Jessie were standing on the facility manager's observation platform, a walkway with a railing overlooking the factory's main work area below. The ceiling stretched high overhead, practically invisible in the gloom save for a darkly tangled, impressionistic suspicion of girders and supports. The moon filtered in through the broken windows, emphasizing the depth of the place. And the shimmering sheets over the machines seemed to run for miles, like a pale train moving silently under a black bridge upon which they were perched. Their predominant impression was one of size and expanse. They seemed to be standing at the entrance to a cavern, having passed through a hole in space.

"It would be like a dream," Parks whispered, and Jessie turned, trying to catch his expression, but seeing only the glint of his eyes in the dark. "He'd want to touch it."

And then Ellis turned on the lights.

"The clinical explanations for his behavior are all bullshit," Parks was saying, his hands on the railing as he stared out over the now bright expanse of the abandoned factory below. "In their own way, the details are logical, and it's that logic that we have to accept. What he's doing is real to him, and it's got to be real to us too, or we'll never catch up."

Jessie was backing away, aware at once that she was suspended very high in the air on a walkway no more than eight feet deep from the wall, but uncaring in her refusal to take her eyes from Parks as she edged her way further from him. His image was the most awful thing she had ever seen, and through the rush of adrenaline and blood in her head she heard her own breathing, pounding heart, and shoes on cement . . . as if those things mattered. As if those things could ever matter any less . . .

Or any more than they did right now.

There were things painted on the wall around the opening of the doorway. Embellishments, patterns, talismans . . . God knew what. But they were done in blood. There were black, dried lines on the ground, exploding out from the door. And there was blood on the railing. Parks, hunched and rigid, was surrounded by it, his long coat hanging around his legs, his frizzled hair static-charged along the crown of his skull in the cold, dry air, his pale eyes shining as he spoke . . . to the building, to himself . . .

To the Prisoner.

"But he wants to go back to where he belongs," he said. "He must make things as they were before, and go back to where he belongs.

"Make things as they were . . . no witnesses.

"Back to where he belongs."

As he turned, Parks lifted his eyes to the gory effusions painted over the door, and added, "We'll get him because of this. I swear, with God as my witness, that this is going to lead us right to the bloodthirsty son of a bitch."

TWO

7

The morning after Jessie flew to her first murder scene, Ron Manning, one of her friends from the theater, went over to her apartment to see if she wanted to go and watch the fire. It was eight o'clock, and the January morning was very cold. There were cops and emergency vehicles all over town, and the rumor was that some kind of a fugitive was running around loose. Ron didn't believe the part about the fugitive, but since Jessie was always so hot to "experience life," he thought that she might like to roam around a little before lunch.

Her building was a beautiful old place known as the "Palace" because, by dorm standards, its rent was outrageous, its decor luxurious, and its imposing exterior reminiscent of some looming edifice in a Boris Karloff movie. Four stories high, and constructed of sandstone blocks stained nearly black with age, it had started life as a hospital during the Civil War, was purchased as an office building in 1902 by a wealthy businessman, and left to the Phi Tau Omega fraternity in 1937 as a part of the man's will, "in grateful recognition of the youthful years I spent as a member of this brotherhood. Honor, fidelity, and knowledge, I pledge myself to thee. Phi Tau Omega, a bond of fraternity." From 1939 to 1980 it was known as the Phi Tau House, but with the decline of the frat's membership, and the eventual dissolution of its Lawrynce-Wynn chapter, it was sold back into private hands in 1982, this time to an unnamed investor who converted it into apartments.

At first, Ron thought that the place was being evacuated. There were cars lined up along the side street, and the parking lot was loaded with furniture, boxes, and scuttling students and parents all grumbling indignantly as they packed their station wagons and patted their hands in the cold. Ron recognized a couple of people from the theater, stopped to ask, "What the hell's going on?" and was told that it was lease-renewal time.

"So?" he asked.

And a dour man whose daughter Ron recognized as an oboe major in the con, said, "The owner won't renew," as he stuffed a box of records into the trunk of a silver Oldsmobile. "We got the notice last week: out on the sixteenth. No arguments."

"Everybody?"

"Sure looks like it."

And Ron ran up to Jessie's apartment, number 401, corner room, overlooking the theater. He pounded for five minutes while people excused themselves around him, jostling lamps, bending mattresses, and making him feel a little like a refugee. Then he headed back downstairs, asking the people he passed if anyone had seen "Jessie Reynolds from the fourth floor," and wondering if she had already moved out, or if she just wasn't home.

It was in the Palace's lobby, amid a virtual turmoil of activity, that someone said, "Miss Reynolds? Yeah, I saw her," making Ron turn to find a man in overalls and a baseball cap holding a broom.

"Where?" Ron asked, dodging the ungraceful arch of a passing sofa.

"I'm John, the super," the man said, answering an entirely different question and starting down a set of stairs to the basement. "I look out for the kids in this building, 'specially the girls. You know, kinda make sure nothing bad happens. Now, who are you?"

Ron had to follow him down the steps to hear the end of his statement. And before he knew it he was at the bottom of the stairs, saying, "I'm a friend of Jessie Reynolds."

"Oh, yeah?" the older man asked, snapping on a light and grinning suggestively. "Been in her pants?"

"No," Ron said truthfully. "But I've been in her car. She's got a really nice car."

The janitor smiled. "Lyin' sack a shit."

And Ron got the sudden feeling that the guy was all right.

"So where'd you see her?" he asked.

And John the janitor said, "Hey. You got a minute to give me a hand with something? I ain't as young as I used to be, and I gotta pull a carpet scrubber up the stairs. Won't take long."

You foxy old prick, Ron thought.

"Saw her late last night, after eleven," the janitor said, leading Ron across the cellar floor to another door that opened on yet another set of stairs. "Subbasement," he explained. "Keep my shit down there. Place was built 'bout a hundred and fifty years ago. Made to last."

"But have you seen her today?" Ron asked, stepping down on the creaking wooden stairs and running his hand over damp sandstone for balance as he descended into darkness. At the bottom he found himself submerged in blackness, with only the faintest hint of light bleeding down from above, and an uncomfortable question forming in his mind about why an obviously aged man would want to keep his heavy equipment in a place where he would need to drag it up at least two flights of steep stairs every time he wanted to use it.

"Ain't been back since," the janitor answered, clumping his way into the gloom. "Now, stay where you're at till I find the switch. Damn, it do get dark down here, don't it?"

"Who 'ain't been back,' you or her?"

"Why, her, of course," the janitor answered from the dark very close to Ron's face a microsecond before the light came on. "'Cause I never left."

The hammer hit Ron squarely between the eyes, right on the bridge of his nose, breaking bones, dancing stars, and knocking him off his feet. The last thing he heard was a peculiar *dunk!* that seemed to come from somewhere very close by . . .

Then he realized that the sound was his head striking the stair behind him.

And then he was out.

The Prisoner checked his pulse.

Still ticking.

He hadn't wanted to kill the greasy little shit, but head shots were tricky, and it was easy to make a mistake. Especially with a hammer. You didn't have a lot of control with a hammer, and the metal could make for a lot of blood. But it couldn't be helped.

The kid folded like a paper kite, his knees going goofy and his skull bouncing on the stairs when he landed. There was some blood, but not nearly as much as there might have been, and the Prisoner probably could have dragged the body away without even getting his hands dirty. But he put his gloves on out of sheer habit . . . a lifelong habit . . . a habit that ran to the bone.

The kid wasn't heavy, but the Prisoner had a hard time moving him. That was all a part of the Punishment: that his body would weaken as the critical time approached. But he'd show them what he was made of. He hadn't come this far only to fail now.

The subbasement was damp, cold, and poorly lit, which were all reasons why he liked it. But there were other reasons that it reminded him of home: its walls moved, its solids were hollow, and its angles were hinged in a way that bent even the most predictable corner if you knew where to press.

At the touch of a secret brick a section of stone swung away and he pulled the unconscious body behind him into the opening of a tunnel. Water dripped, echoing through the dark. His boots scraped on the floor, and he imagined himself as a white blood cell moving through the arterial system of some gigantic living thing, dragging a parasitic intruder to its doom while his immense host dreamed important dreams that would have been impossible without his diligent struggles against disease.

FORGET ME NOT

He had to stop and rest twice, but soon he had the parasite securely locked away. The intruder never so much as stirred as he wound his hands and feet with black electrician's tape. His eyes stayed shut, and his head lolled limply on his neck. After locking up the cell door, the Prisoner moved to another room and checked another parasite. This one was awake, and when he caught a glimpse of the Prisoner's flashlight, he struggled on the floor, rolling his eyes and pleading in mumbling, incomprehensible groans for mercy.

But when had the Prisoner been shown any mercy?

Never!

All his years of confinement had transpired without so much as a single reprieve. No visitors, no time off, no comfort of any kind. Even the periodic visions of home, which he had originally thought were designed to soothe him in his suffering, were really just veiled torments, offering him glimpses of a place that would remain beyond his reach until he was sufficiently punished for his crime.

His crime . . .

Which had happened in this very place, many floors above the ground, on the other side.

Because there were two sides.

Here.

And there.

There was where he belonged.

Here was where they sent you when they wanted you to pay . . . and pay . . . until the retribution exacted guaranteed exemplary behavior for the rest of your life.

The system was harsh.

But it worked.

The premise was simple:

The Prisoner was being punished for something he had done on the other side of reality . . . the real side . . . the place where he was born. He had violated a cardinal law . . . a linchpin, keystone kind of edict that was one of the pillars that supported much of his society's weight. Similar laws were in effect here in the "Punishment Zone," as well. But in the Zone, they were rarely observed, since the entire phantasmagoric miasma of this alternate reality was nothing but an amazing technological advance in the art of criminal rehabilitation.

The Prisoner didn't know exactly when the Zone had been introduced into society. He seemed to recall being taught something about it in grammar school, and as long as he had been alive, it had been a part of his cultural literacy. But the actual date that the machine went into practice . . . well, that was kind of hazy. He'd probably known more of the particulars when he was first sent over—there had been a lot of things in his mind when he was first sent over that had faded since—but details like that weren't important anymore, and without being pertinent, they were soon forgotten, or at least moved further back in his head. He remembered the important things, like the crime.

She'd been so beautiful.

He slammed the observation window shut on the heavy plank door, leaving the conscious parasite to squirm in darkness, and headed back up, out of the tunnel. His knees ached, and his head hurt. He was tired, after having been up all night, and in his mind burned the afterimages of his most recent glimpses of home: the soothing visions he saw from his dreamscape shore at the edge of the surging night sea.

The principle of the Zone was this:

Physical incarceration and confinement were pointless, since all criminal activity had as its motivation intellectual objects. That is to say, people did things that were wrong because they were trying to gain something they imagined they wanted. Even crimes like rape were considered to be intellectually motivated, since sexual fantasies were carried on in the mind until the body could resist action no longer. With the root of all antisocial behavior identified as the mind, it naturally followed that punishment and rehabilitation would most effectively be achieved by intellectual experiences.

Thus, the Punishment Zone . . . was all in your head.

They put it there with a machine no one had ever seen. Or at least no one had ever seen it and then been able to describe what it looked like, because, when you saw it, they used it on you, and by the time they were done, you were a changed person.

The Zone changed you . . .

FORGET ME NOT

Forever.

In the Zone you were set a task. It could be anything: swim an ocean, right a wrong, fight a battle, live an entirely different life from beginning to end, die a thousand times. They were presumably all different for different people, being chosen specifically after consideration of your own particular crime. But what they had in common was that, as long as the machine was on, they were as real as real could be to the people living inside them. They could send you to the Zone for what seemed like a thousand years of Punishment, from which you would emerge back on the other side after only a couple of minutes of real time having elapsed. So in that way, the Prisoner was lucky: his sentence was reasonably short.

Just twenty-one years.

But his task was difficult . . .

So difficult that it still hurt to consider it, even after so many years of struggling through.

Or maybe it was a drug that did it, and not a machine at all. The Prisoner couldn't remember. But confusion was all a part of the Punishment. The only time he wasn't confused was when he was plotting and moving, moving and plotting . . . it was all he had left of his mind.

It was the Punishment . . .

To kill that which he loved most of all: the evidence of his crime, the most beautiful thing he'd ever seen.

And the time was drawing near.

He'd have just one chance, one opportunity to accomplish what he had been sent here to do. If he made it, he could go home. But if he failed . . . well, he wasn't sure as to what the consequences might be, but he was certain that they would involve another stretch in the Zone, another task, and another delay in release. So everything had to be exactly right . . . just as it had been. The preparations were many, complicated, and dangerous. But they were almost complete. Just a few more adjustments and he'd be ready for the seventeenth.

He could see the doorway opening for him. He could imagine its shape, and folds, its breathing, mouthlike structure that would transport him back through to the real world. It was how he had gotten here in the first place, it was the only way back, and it made him so excited that he had to do it. He couldn't help himself. He just had to. And he did, before he went back upstairs, under his protective clothing. Always under his protective clothing because nothing of his essence could touch this place. That was one of the rules. And since the onset of the Punishment, he had become very conscious of rules. He understood them at their root, could see through them to what they were really trying to achieve, and could gaze deeply into their heart to see the wheels turning inside the wheels that drove this world down its meandering path.

He could move among the creatures of the Zone without causing so much as an eyebrow to be raised because, with this second sight, he had learned to become invisible. He knew all the tricks, exploited every advantage, and most important, constantly maintained his perspective. He kept his objective firmly focused in his mind, and while those monstrous, fleshy things—so obscenely similar to the human beings he remembered from his world, while so horribly different in ominous, bone-chilling ways—bumbled along around him, acting out their machine-generated roles in obvious intellectual oblivion, he was busy weaving his way toward that glorious moment when the tunnel to his future would open before him, sucking him back through to the other side, where he belonged.

And it was all going to happen on the seventeenth.

Just one more day.

What he really wanted to do was to return to his own dark cell, pull the door shut, and lie down. There he could listen to the nearly perfect silence and slide in the syringe, filling his veins with the magic and returning to his midnight shore. The Night Shore was all he really had; and it was the thing that kept him sane. But there was just too much to do upstairs, and he didn't have time. Maybe later in the afternoon, when he could physically remain awake no longer, he'd go. But for now . . .

He'd finished doing it, and the crotch inside his rubber pants was wet. Suddenly he felt guilty, and frozen in his place at the opening to the tunnel in the subbasement, he stood, breathing hard, red-faced with shame and wondering if Molaine was watching. Molaine, the Keeper, was the Prisoner's personal monitor, and there was no telling when, without warning, a wall might pucker or the air might fold in on itself to reveal his disapproving eyes.

Pulling his hand away, the Prisoner hesitated a little longer, and then a smile crept over his face.

No Molaine.

He slid the stone wall panel back into place, sealing up the tunnel and hiding the parasites away.

Then he went back upstairs to watch the cyborgs.

8

Earlier that same morning . . . like much earlier . . . while the sun was still somewhere below the horizon mulling over its options regarding a rise, Jessie's uncle, Kevin Reynolds, was coming face-to-face with the ugly prospect of his own capture and arrest . . .

Again.

It was inevitable, and he was resigned to it. That didn't make it any easier to face, of course, but at least it took some of the mystery out of his future prospects, leaving room for him to concentrate on the task at hand . . .

Which was making as much noise as he could without being caught until the big event occurred.

Behind the wheel of his Corvette ZR-1, flying down Interstate 71 at a cruising speed of ninety-two miles an hour, with sweat on his palms, and the flashing blue lights of a highway patrol car in his rearview mirror, he had the terrible feeling that, as close as he'd come to being nailed before, this time there was no way out. But then he always felt like that: trapped, hemmed in, used. His life was a mess, and he was too weak to fix it. There was a gun in the glove compartment, five more in a storage niche behind the passenger seat, and enough incriminating paraphernalia in the trunk—including a pair of rubber gloves and a black leather mask—to start an avalanche of shit that would bury him up to his eyeballs if he gave it half a chance.

But he was driving fast . . .

So he still had hope.

He loved driving fast.

Especially at night.

He had known that his day was coming for years, but had been deliberately repressing both his knowledge of it and the anxiety it incurred. Even now, with another set of blue lights joining the first in his rearview, and a grimly satisfied smile spreading over his lips, he wasn't sure as to exactly what he'd do next. He was a cog in a machine, moving his particular part of a vast and complicated mechanism without really knowing why. He had a job to do, and how he did it was up to him. But beyond the start, he hadn't considered any specific route, intending instead to improvise by using anything that came his way.

Like the exit ramp ahead, at which he aimed the Vette while simultaneously killing his headlights.

When Jessie left her message on his machine, mentioning Henry Parks . . .

That unmitigated son of a bitch!

. . . Reynolds wasn't in Columbus. He was in Cleveland, occupying a room in a motel not two miles from her apartment building. He'd moved in about a month before, and had been secretly keeping an eye on her, living like a hermit, and listening to her every word through clandestine microphones hidden in her apartment walls and ceiling. Her phone was tapped, her mail monitored, and for a while there had even been talk of positioning a surveillance camera—like the ones they use in banks—behind a piece of two-way mirror in her bedroom. The camera idea hadn't panned out, much to his disappointment, and despite all his efforts, it was Jessie herself who had announced the beginning of the end.

But she didn't really understand.

And Parks . . .

That fuck-head, creep-show asshole.

. . . was only guessing.

Ten minutes after Reynolds heard his niece say Parks' name into her phone, he loaded up the Vette with as much "evidence" as he had handy, and headed for the Denny's she had mentioned. Even in the dark he had no trouble spotting the babysitters positioned around the restaurant: two men in a nondescript, late-model, four-door, American-made sedan huddled under a burned-out streetlamp near the parking lot's extreme north corner; and two more in a newer, Japanese two-door, reading newspapers beneath the car's dome light right up close to the building's front entrance as if, by being conspicuous, they might be fooling someone.

Keeping his violently obvious, bright red car to the shadows as much as possible, he parked around the dark side of a Perkins across the street and watched Jessie at a table, talking to Parks under a light so bright that it made them both look as if they were sitting in an aquarium. After about an hour, Jessie drove them to the airport, with the four-door-sedan baby-sitter running ahead and the Japanese two-door bringing up the rear. Reynolds followed, giving them plenty of room.

Normally, four cars riding in a perfect row so late at night might have resembled an impromptu parade. But traffic near the airport was thicker than usual, and apparently neither the babysitters nor Parks himself noticed, or recognized, the Vette.

Jessie and Parks disappeared into the terminal, and a large black man drove her Mercedes away.

For one terrible moment, Reynolds didn't know if he should follow his niece on foot through the terminal or stick with the Mercedes. But when the baby-sitters swung in behind the black man, shadowing him out of the airport and back to the freeway, his decision was made. At Jessie's apartment he watched the Mercedes park in its usual spot before its driver got into the four-door sedan and drove away. The Japanese two-door hung around the Art and Drama Center's lot for a while before finally getting bored. And about an hour after that, at nearly one in the morning, Reynolds cruised up to the biggest intersection in town, U-turning as he whispered, "Okay. Let's party!" and popping the clutch toward the freeway.

The Vette virtually screamed as he punched her accelerator, rocketing past the apartment house at seventy miles an hour. He was doing ninety when he hit 71, and in less than five minutes there was one cop on his ass.

Then two.

And then he was improvising and heading downtown, thinking about Jessie all the while. She was still with Parks . . .

That son of a bitch!

The first time Kevin Reynolds ever saw Henry Parks was nearly eight months after the murder of Michael and Natalie Sterns. He just appeared one day, without warning, full of suspicions and accusations, bullying, angry, and twisted. His scars had pretty much faded since then, but at that time he was a pallid scarecrow of a man with bright red suture tracks, an unsteady walk, and a voice like bicycle chains revolving in a clothes dryer. He was just embarking on the private hunt that would eventually turn into his life's work, and even though the local police had cleared Kevin of any involvement in the murders, Parks still arrived full of venom that he spit across the kitchen for everyone to hear.

Everyone, meaning Kevin's mother and father.

Mom, who was kind.

And Dad, who never let him forget.

Jessie was in a crib in another room, crying, and Kevin wanted to go to her, pick her up, and hold her close. He loved little things . . . children . . . so soft and helpless. He loved them. He did . . .

Kevin's father, Eugene Reynolds, was a man of influence and bile who thought that his son was a spineless neophyte. But he wasn't about to stand idly by while a stranger dragged their family's good name through the muck. So in a classic display of indignant outrage, he went nose-to-nose with Henry Parks and routed him. Parks was forced to retreat, leaving his half-baked suspicions about Kevin—"You're the right size and shape, buddy-boy! I saw the guy up close, and you're him to a tee!"—hanging in the doorway like the accusatorial finger he pointed with such enthusiasm, and a promise of "I'll get to the bottom of this yet! Money or no money!" ringing through the house.

Eugene Reynolds closed and locked the doors, paused for

one pregnant moment, and then said to his son, "Now get the hell out of my sight."

Kevin was twenty-seven years old then, as tall as his father, and just as educated. But the look in his old man's eyes, that fatuous air of superiority and power that said, "I know you fucked up. I'm sick of having to cover your ass for you!" reduced him to the physical and intellectual position of a stumbling adolescent. He couldn't think, couldn't talk, could barely walk, in fact. He heel-toed his way out of the room, using the tops of chairs as support against the rolling floor beneath him as his mother went to his father—always to his father—and their hushed voices blended into a single insinuating murmur that, though it didn't necessarily agree with the specifics of Parks' accusations, concurred unreservedly with his implied demand of recognizing Kevin's guilt.

"You may not have killed your sister and her husband, but you've done other things, haven't you?" that wordless drone seemed to say in its all-knowing, voice-of-his-conscience kind of way. "And we'll never let you forget it either."

So in Kevin's mind, Henry Parks assumed the role of personal tormentor. For years he would appear, interviewing friends and acquaintances, questioning, insinuating, poking around for inconsistencies, and pointing out contradictions, until Kevin started collecting alibis and noting witnesses for everything he did. It was as if his life were being audited, and he was responsible for the receipts. Maybe he should have gone to the police to claim harassment. But his father forbade it.

"Nobody sounds more guilty than the man who protests his innocence. Just keep your nose clean and your mouth shut" was his decree, and Kevin heeded it . . .

Even after the killings started.

After the killings started, Parks' attention turned out to be a blessing in disguise.

Because, after the killings started, all those alibis came in handy.

The Vette bottomed out at a spot at the end of the ramp where the concrete's incline suddenly leveled off, bouncing her chassis twice and throwing sparks in the dark. Her tires squealed as she leaned hard-left through a blinking amber caution light, and with her headlights turned off she resembled nothing so much as a dark bullet ricocheting off the pavement.

The cops followed only seconds later, one turning left at the light, the other heading right.

Kevin knew that, when improvising, the first move is invariably the most important because it sets the tone for things to come. He also had a tremendous sensitivity about being followed, and seemed to know, instinctually, what a pursuer might be thinking. As soon as he was off the ramp and saw West 25th Street stretching out straight and wide before him, he knew the cops would expect him to use the Vette's guts to high-speed up the pike toward downtown. So he turned at the first side street he saw, slowed down, turned again, doubled back, and ended up on a smaller, parallel street, which he followed for a few blocks before skipping over again.

Buzzing the electric window down and sticking his head out, he crawled down another side street, listening, not for the whine of sirens, but for the sound of fast-moving cars. The cops wouldn't warn him with their horns, but they'd still be in a hurry. They were like that everywhere he went: once they got the scent, they took it personal if denied a taste.

Improvise! he thought, chewing on the end of an unlit cigarette that he didn't remember placing in his mouth. It's like jazz . . . you know what key the jam's in, now run with it!

Improvise . . .

"Yeah!"

He saw it, circled once, pulled down a narrow alley, and stopped the car. Grabbing a few things from behind the passenger seat and popping the trunk, he bailed out, selected what he needed from amid the junk he was carrying, and took to the shadows. The next time he became visible, in a ribbon of light thrown against a brick wall by the space between two buildings, he was wearing his mask, and moving in that springy, silent way that someone who didn't know him wouldn't have believed possible for a man of his age and ungainly, paunchy build.

Check it out.

Set it up.

Move slow, but keep moving because once you stop, you might not start again because . . .

Ohhhhhh!

You don't want to do it.

Because . . .

Ohhhhhh!

The truth is the hardest part.

It's so terrible that you do the things you do. So terrible . . . but you do them anyway because there's no other way, and the time is coming. Just a few more hours . . . after years and years. If you can go years and years, you can go a few more hours.

But still . . .

Just do it.

"I don't want to!"

He wasn't going to cry.

Check the tools.

He absolutely wasn't going to cry!

I don't wanna do it!

Now . . .

I won't!

Go!

The woman was stepping up onto her Chevy van's running board after herding her two kids—one boy, age twelve, one girl, age nine—into the side of the vehicle when the man came up behind her out of the shadows. She was holding a bag of groceries she'd just picked up from the convenience store in front of which she was parked, and they weighed her down a little . . . not a lot, but enough so that it took her maybe an extra second to turn and face the figure she had seen rise up as a reflection on the dark glass window of her open door. By then he was on top of her . . .

And past.

She gasped, turned again, and . . .

Ice bled in a cold white rage down from her eyes to fill her chest and freeze her heart.

"I don't really want to do this," the man was saying breathily from where he sat on the plush captain's chair behind the steering wheel. There was something about his voice that sounded as if his mouth didn't work right . . . as if he were speaking through clenched teeth. "But it's my job."

He had Mary, the nine-year-old, one hand around her mouth so that she wouldn't cry out, the other holding a flat, ugly automatic to her head. The girl stood perfectly still, eyes wide with terror, and the candy bar that was her reward for spending seven hours in the van without crying was dangling in her limp right hand. The man was wearing black canvas trousers. His leather coat was black, and covered with pockets and zippers. He had on army boots. A knapsack or something was slung over his left shoulder. And he was wearing a hood . . . or a mask. In the dim light it was hard to tell exactly what it was, but it made him look bald, and emphasized his mouth—the lips of which protruded slightly through an oval cut in the gleaming black rubber.

"Now get in," he said in his weird, restricted way. "And try not to be scared. None of this is really my idea."

The woman quaked and trembled, her mind numb. But a jerk of the pistol decided her, and after placing her grocery sack on the pavement, she did as she was told . . .

Noticing, with amazement, that behind his ugly black mask, the man who was holding a gun to her daughter's head seemed to be crying.

He instructed her to hand over her keys and take a seat next to him up front. A momentary blossom of hope welled in her chest as a police car cruised up and paused not twenty feet from where the van was parked. But that hope died when the car turned, and crawled away. In the corner of her eye she saw the man in the mask watching, and his voice was brittle when he said, "Okay. Now nice and slow. I think we'll head that way."

He pointed with the pistol.

And the woman, whose name was Jenny Alexander, was silent for fifteen blocks before she was able to clear the choking dryness of terror out of her throat enough to speak. Keeping her tone soft, reasonable, and perhaps even a bit too deferential to be entirely convincing, she did her best to bargain: money—all she had, plus whatever she could get out of a bank-in-the-box, if they could find one that would take her card since she was from out of town; sex—any way he wanted it, she was willing . . . really; the van—"Take it, I got it in the divorce settlement and it's too big anyway!" Anything at all just "Please don't hurt us."

Or, "Please don't hurt my kids. I don't care what you do to me."

Or simply, "Please . . . don't."

But the masked man just stared out the window with tears in his eyes and little Mary seated on his lap. He didn't want to do this, he occasionally insisted. But beyond such protests, he behaved as if the tiny family, whose trip from Jersey City, New Jersey, to Detroit, Michigan, he had so thoroughly interrupted, were suddenly his own, personal property. And it was that air of indifference, that lack of overt malice or enthusiasm, that kindled a glow of hope in Jenny Alexander that maybe, just maybe, they'd come to a corner and he'd say, "Okay! Now get out." Or better yet, "Okay! Now I'm getting out."

It was only after a half an hour of driving that he shattered her hopes. They'd moved straight south from the city to the suburbs, and were on a brightly lit street in front of a local movie theater that looked like something out of a Normal Rockwell painting, when, in full view of a passing police car, he said, "I'm sorry," and swung his door open, making Jenny scream, *"Nooooo!"* as she lunged toward him, tangling her arm in the steering wheel and sending the van careening over the center line.

"What the hell?" the cop on the shotgun side said as the cruiser passed the Chevy conversion van with the smoked plastic bubble windows and the out-of-state plates.

What made him say it was the object that appeared as the two vehicles passed broadside to one another. The van's driver's side door opened, and something dark—and was it moving?—was launched into an arch that sent it directly into . . .

"Jesus!" both cops exclaimed, automatically lifting their hands to protect their faces as the body of a little girl struck their windshield, seconds before the sounds of shattering glass, crunching metal, and gunshots ruined the very peace the two officers were sworn to protect.

9

When Jessie woke up, hungry, blearly, and confused, it took her a couple of minutes of mental gymnastics to remember where she was:

A Red Roof Inn off a nameless freeway near Pittsburgh, on a double bed near the spot where two men who she had just met a few hours before were talking in whispers about things she could hardly bring herself to believe. One of them—she suspected that it was Ellis—had taken off her boots and laid a blanket over her after she fell asleep. The room smelled as if someone had been smoking . . . not cigarettes, but cigars. A phone produced half a ring before someone snatched it off its cradle and started mumbling into it. And somewhere either a television or a radio was playing, so softly that the words all ran together into one, unintelligible murmur.

It had been the phone that had awakened her.

For some reason she had the impression that the phone had been ringing a lot, but she couldn't tell if she'd dreamed the bells or heard them in her sleep. Either way, she could feel a heaviness in the room, an ominous kind of urgency in the hushed voices that led her to suspect that important things had been happening during her couple of hours of fitful, uneasy rest.

Without opening her eyes she lay still, listening as Parks said, "Yeah. Keep me posted," hung up the phone, and sighed. "That was Novak in Cleveland. They confirmed the numbers. It was him, all right. I just can't figure it."

"There's no way we're going to be able to keep this out of the papers," Ellis returned.

"Whether he's our man or not, he's still a monster. And monsters are news," Parks agreed.

"Well, maybe a little publicity'll make spin control easier later on."

FORGET ME NOT

"If it's him, there's gonna be an awful lot of uncomfortable questions begging to be answered. Like, how'd we miss him when he was one of the first people we ever questioned?"

"It's him, Henry. There's no other answer."

"There's always another answer."

"It's him."

"Either way, we're gonna have to nail down his movements, especially over the past couple of weeks. I've got Novak running down the Corvette. I figure he must have been holed up somewhere close. All I hope is that they give me a shot at him when they bring him in. I've got so many gaps to fill. I mean, Christ! I've got him listed as out of the goddamn country at least a dozen times over the last few years."

"And don't forget the blood writing. I can't wait to see what he says about that."

"If he's our man, I think we'll find that he didn't *want* to leave the writing. I think he *had* to."

"He's our man, Henry."

"We'll see."

"And you're sure he didn't fly into town for O'Polo?" Ellis asked, changing the apparently sensitive subject.

"Absolutely," Parks agreed. "They found O'Polo's car at the airport because the Prisoner left it there to throw us off. That's how he works: every step carefully planned. He had a gun with him, so he wouldn't have taken a chance on getting caught trying to sneak it aboard an airliner."

"Maybe he's got his own plane. That would explain how he got around the country so easily."

"It's a thought. But I doubt it. We'd better check the charters in and out, starting a week or so before the killing, just to be sure. But he loathes people, and the crowd at an airport would make his skin crawl. I think it's more likely that we'll find that he drove into town, and used the airport parking lot because it was a place where no one would notice an unattended car, even if he decided to leave it for a week."

"So how'd he get to the murder site, taxicab?"

"We'll have to wait and see. In the meantime, it can't hurt to check."

"Hey!" Ellis said, suddenly enthusiastic. "That kinda makes sense: he takes a cab out, and then, with his clothes bloodied from the killing, he takes O'Polo's car back to the airport, picks up his own car, and he's gone. That way, no one sees him after the killing, and . . . shit! It'll give us a blood type to match off the Vette's upholstery!"

Parks yawned.

Ellis scribbled in a pad, saying, "What I still can't figure is all that mutilation in the factory. He was never that bad before. I know the location was particularly secluded so he probably could afford to take his time more. But everything was so . . . extreme, so out of control. I wonder what pushed him over the edge."

And that's when Jessie sat up, making Ellis stop speaking. Impervious to her, Parks said, "I think we'll find that throwing O'Polo's guts into the darkness over the factory railing meant something too."

Ellis put a hand on Parks' forearm to silence him. Without looking at either of them, Jessie stepped up to the card table at which they were seated, carried the telephone back toward the center of the room, and called her apartment. Keying in her answering machine's touch-tone code, she waited to see if her uncle had left anything on her tape.

He had.

Pressing the receiver to her ear, she listened as his strained, urgent voice said, "Jess, listen. I don't know what you've been doing, or what's been going on, but stay away from Henry Parks! He's crazy! I'm not going to explain it all now, but just . . . well, just stay the hell away from him until I get there. I'm on my way now. It's just a little after ten-thirty, so I'll be there before one. Till then, sit tight, and don't worry. But please, Jess, for me, don't get wrapped up with Henry Parks. He's bad news. I love you, baby. See you soon."

She hung up, her mouth feeling absolutely dry, the image of Parks, still hunched over the table, filling her eyes.

What the hell am I doing? she asked herself, suddenly quite frightened. She'd never been frightened like this before—a quick, savage fear that raced up her spine and tingled her entire body before settling into an ache in her stomach. *What the hell am I doing in Pittsburgh, in a motel with two strangers? Nobody even knows I'm here! If they did something to me, nobody would ever even find my body! Oh, Jesus! Oh, Christ! I've got to get out of here! I've got to* . . .

God!

She couldn't even call her uncle . . .

Wait.

Where was her uncle?

It was what? Just after seven in the morning by the electric clock on the wall over the night table by the bed. According to the message on her answering machine, he'd left Columbus for Cleveland at ten-thirty last night. It was about two hours travel time on the freeway, so he should have been in her apartment long ago. He had a key. Why hadn't he answered the phone? Where was he? What was going on?

"Do you want to tell her, or should I?" Parks mumbled to Ellis without looking Jessie's way.

Ellis didn't answer, which seemed to indicate that he was unwilling to make a decision one way or another.

"Tell me what?" Jessie said, as calmly as she could, though she had a creeping feeling that she wouldn't like whatever their answer might be.

The two men looked at each other.

"Tell me *what*!?" she suddenly shouted, the emotion welling up in her like a retch.

Parks turned his pale, dead man's eyes her way, and said, in a voice totally devoid of inflection or sympathy, "Your uncle's Corvette was found abandoned on a Cleveland street at about two o'clock this morning. The police had been chasing him, and when they located the car, they found a number of very incriminating things in it. They're still looking for him in connection with . . ."

And that's when Jessie threw the phone at him. It might have hit him if the cord hadn't arrested its flight. But before it banged to the floor, Ellis had his hands on her thrashing wrists, and she was screaming into his chest, and she was crying, and Ellis was trying his best to calm her, and . . .

Parks never even moved from his chair as he turned his head to face her and added, "Now tell her what he did to the little girl."

"Asshole!" Jessie hissed back, yanking her hands around against the restraint of Ellis' fists and looking far to her left to avoid the sincerity in his eyes as he wrestled her to the bed, saying, "Listen . . . please! Just listen to him!" over and over again.

"Get off me!" she demanded. "Goddamn it, *get off*!"

But even when she stopped fighting him, Ellis didn't stir. Instead, he kept her immobile beneath his weight until he was satisfied that she was going to be placid, and then he said, "It's not what you think. They're supposed to take him alive!"

He finally moved to release her when Jessie started laughing. He looked a little bewildered, and Parks rose to his feet. Glancing back and forth between the two of them, Jessie felt a sinking feeling that seemed a mix of nausea and vertigo lying like mud in her stomach as the positive absurdity of her situation finally registered on her consciousness. It finally hit. It hadn't been real—really real—even at the murder scene. But here, in a motel room, in the earnest eyes of two men who were as different from one another as two men could conceivably be, it blasted in on her like a sonic boom.

And she laughed . . .

Through the tears drying on her cheeks.

Struggling up to sit on the edge of the bed, she shook her head, rubbed her face with both hands, and said, "You think he did it," with her shoulders still quivering. "That's what you think, isn't it? That Uncle Kevin is your Prisoner."

"Now, Jessie," Ellis began.

And that's when she made a break for the door.

She was nearly there before Ellis got his hands on her again. But this time, instead of restraining her gently, he forcefully picked her up with both arms around her waist and dragged her back, kicking and screaming, only to throw her down on the bed, hard. She was up in a flash, but he just threw her down again.

"This is kidnapping!" she screamed. "You can't keep me here like this!"

And Parks said, "He was a suspect years ago," opening a briefcase and removing a stack of folders. "But at least a dozen murders happened when he was out of the country. So I moved him off the 'hot' list. Now it looks like I made a mistake doing that."

They couldn't make her believe them, she decided from where she knelt on the mattress. She didn't care what clever tricks they used to confuse her, they couldn't make her believe anything else they said. This knowledge fortified her against them, making her position as inviolate as if they didn't really exist.

"But until they track him down," Parks continued, spreading the folders out in a crescent moon on the table before him, "we've got work to do."

"Forget it!" Jessie wanted to say aloud, but didn't. Instead, she said it with her eyes.

"Let's talk about him," Parks added. "He hasn't exactly lived like a monk."

Jessie didn't flinch.

"You moved in with him when you were twelve. Before that time, you saw him only under direct supervision, because your grandparents forbade . . ."

"My grand*father*," Jessie couldn't help but correct. "It was my grand*father* who did the forbidding, not my grand*parents*."

"Because . . ."

"He didn't do it," she said, climbing to her feet and brushing off Ellis' outstretched hand. "I know what you're gonna say, and it's bullshit, so skip it. Now, tell me why the cops are after him."

"The test results were confusing at best, muddied by politics and money . . ."

"I said, skip it! Nobody ever proved a thing. And even if they had, it was years before I was even born."

"And yet you know all about it," Parks mused, lifting his pale eyes as Jessie stepped closer to him. "You were never shown a photograph of your own mother, or told your real last name, and yet you know all about your uncle's psychological difficulties, and at the age of twelve were allowed to make the decision to move in with him."

"It was Grandpa," Jessie said, in a tone that implied that just mentioning her grandfather should explain everything. "He wouldn't let it go. He used it to hurt him, beating him with it in front of everyone all his life. He was a monster, and we all hated him."

"Him?"

"Grandpa."

"We?"

"Everybody."

"Including your grandmother?"

"Yes."

Parks shook his head, pushing his glasses back up his nose and saying, "So you waited until your grandfather died before disobeying his standing order and moving in with your uncle. Didn't your grandmother protest?"

"No," Jessie lied.

"You know, having a long-standing criminal record is a standard part of a violent psychopath's profile," Parks said, patting the stacks of papers on the table before them as if they were a cat. "Which to me is our problem. Since the Prisoner's anything but a 'normal' madman, it seems strange that he'd have such a predictable personality profile as the one the FBI put together."

And Parks started reading that profile aloud.

Jessie tried not to listen, but a part of her couldn't help itself. Automatically, she defended her uncle, as she'd been doing all her life. But there were questions that she'd been half asking since she was old enough to understand certain things that were lifting their noses and sniffing at the shifting mental breeze of her thoughts.

The profile Parks was reading was based on all the information gathered about the Prisoner so far.

"Why would the FBI have a profile of a person it doesn't believe exists?" Jessie interrupted.

And Parks' expression took on a curious pride, as if she had just verified something about herself that he had known all along.

But it was Ellis who answered.

"I did it," he said, taking a seat at the card table. "Once I decided to help Henry find this guy, I figured we'd need something to go on, So I reintroduced evidence into the computer model. The old profile was based on killings termed 'circumstantially connected,' so it was vague, and selective in what it used. I connected 'em all, and the computer did the rest."

What the computer had done was to plug certain "key" factors regarding the Prisoner's behavior into a character model that had been painstakingly developed after years of experience with serial killers by the FBI's Division of Behavioral Studies in Quantico, Virginia. The result was not so much a prediction of the specifics regarding the man's personality as it was an overview of his character type. It built a collage of traits and tendencies, one layer at a time, upon telling aspects of the things he'd done, until the shadow of a man began emerging through the fog of anonymity. There wasn't a face in there anywhere, but there was certainly a silhouette that, to Jessie, was uncomfortably familiar.

According to the model, the Prisoner would see himself as isolated from other people to an agonizing degree. He wouldn't be able to relate to others, confining his deepest secrets to the vault of his own mind. He might function in society, moving through a daily routine—and this word, "routine," was emphasized—without drawing attention to himself. But his true motivations, the fuel that drove him, would be a treasure he'd hoard for himself.

Motivation, in this case, was the key. The Prisoner, seen as a methodical man, was pursuing some goal, and to discover what that goal was, it would be necessary for an outsider to insinuate himself into his viewpoint enough to understand his ego system. Since that was impossible for any sane, nondeluded mind to do, it was important to realize that the man was not randomly picking up girls and killing them, Ted Bundy style, but proceeding *toward something*, as indicated by the developing intricacy of the "ritual" he apparently enacted at the scene of certain, but not all, of his murders. This "refinement" represented the best hope to someone hunting him because it indicated that he was sensitive to outside influences—such as the law—and such sensitivity implied that he was connected to reality enough to make his activities essentially predictable.

"If we knew what he thought he was doing," Parks interjected, lifting his eyes Jessie's way, "there's a good chance we could anticipate his next move."

"Dandy," Jessie returned unenthusiastically.

To the people with whom the Prisoner interacted on a daily basis, he would most likely appear as a withdrawn, bookish, perhaps even mildly irritating details-freak. He would probably be the type of man who never threw anything away; who saved string, plastic margarine tubs, and pennies; a man who held some job that involved long hours alone, deep in concentration on some subject that others would most likely find tedious, and who, if successfully drawn out, might be induced to engage in boring explanations of the most trivial details of his work. And in order to keep himself from being the center of anyone's attention, he would dress in a nondescript manner, assuming the overt affectations of shyness.

But this was the central lie. Though he might cringe from attention, avoiding eye contact when speaking, and keeping his voice low and uninflected, in truth, at the level of his deepest beliefs, he was essentially a walking ego. In his own mind, he was outrageously important, so much so that no one else in the world could possibly matter. It was *him* around whom the stars revolved, and the callous, inhuman manner in which he used the bodies of his victims indicated in just how much contempt he held the rest of humanity when compared to the intrinsic importance of himself and his mission. There would be some telling hint at this ego in his personality. It might manifest itself in something as subtle as a perfectly acceptable ethnocentricity, such as belonging to some patriotic organization; or it might go deeper, expressing itself in an overprotection of possessions . . .

Including people.

"Stop," Jessie said, lifting her hand for emphasis. "What does that last part mean?"

"It means," Parks responded, "that one way he might express his own maniacal ego is by lavishing attention on the people closest to him—as if saying, 'Since you are worthy of something so good as this thing I give you, imagine what treasures I keep for myself!'"

Jessie swallowed, thinking of her Mercedes. She had never, for as far back as her knowledge went, wanted for anything. And it was always Uncle Kevin who was doing the buying.

The Prisoner would have a record of past offenses with the police, the file continued in Parks' voice. In his youth he'd have made mistakes. They wouldn't involve anything serious enough to keep him permanently confined, since he would have been acting on an undeveloped psychosis, and not the full-blown delusional structure waiting in his future. But his testing of the parameters of his environment would inevitably leave some mark. On this point, the profile was unequivocal.

"Kevin Reynolds has a record like that, doesn't he?" Parks asked.

Jessie frowned.

"And I guess that's what bothers me," Parks went on, closing the folder. "I can see him splashed all over this report. If we'd have had this profile earlier, we would have said, 'God! It's so obvious!' Too obvious, in fact. Something about it stinks, but I can't seem to place exactly what it is.

"If the Prisoner were really the boring little homicidal accountant described here, we'd have caught him years ago. There's got to be something about him that the computer missed. No one lives in a vacuum. Someone must have felt a twinge in the gut that said, 'Something ain't right with this guy.' Someone who knows him, who maybe even loves him, must have sensed his essential lack of sincerity.

"Women especially can feel things like that. They know when their men are lying. Or at least it's been my experience that they do. Especially when that woman is as sensitive as, say, an actress might be. Then she'd really understand what it takes to play a role . . . the emotional effort . . . the contrivances of deceit. If she were an actress herself, she couldn't help but see when someone she loved was putting on a show. She might not admit it aloud, but in her heart, she'd know."

Jessie studied Parks' face, realizing that, despite the intensity of his voice, and the sincerity with which he punctuated his words, he had remained essentially unmoved by anything he'd said. She saw it in his eyes—those flat, milky eyes that had sparkled as he led her through a murder scene, while remaining reptile-cold as he verbally dissected what he thought were the workings of her mind.

"That's right," she agreed. "An actress would know when she was being lied to."

Parks put his pencil down.

And Jessie got off the bed.

"She'd know when someone was just saying his lines," she said. "And she'd know when those lines were meant to move the plot along—drive the narrative, as we say. You've been driving a little narrative, Mr. Parks, and it couldn't be any more obvious if you were holding a script."

"I need you for your memory," Parks said, looking right at her.

"I don't believe you're right about my uncle."

"All the better," Parks cut in, intending to say more.

But Jessie wouldn't have it. "I don't believe he's the self-centered egomaniac posing as a mild-mannered geneaologist you've described," she said, her tone of voice building steam and her expression set. "I don't believe he's been as good to me as he's been all my life as a reflection of his own megalomania. And I don't believe he's crazy.

"What I think is that you've spent twenty years building a monster in your head. And now that you're ready to give it a face, you can't find any that fit. So you want me to find one for you. Well, forget it. I'm not joining your pathetic little crusade. Count me out.

"If you won't let me go home, then we'll consider this a kidnapping and run it from there. You can play Don Quixote, Mr. Parks, Mr. Ellis can be your Sancho, and you both better pray I don't get away. Because if I do, you'll be explaining to the cops all about how you were only trying to save innocent lives when you forced me to have sex with the both of you in this motel room.

"Because that's exactly what I'm gonna say happened. And I'll swear to it on so many Bibles that the Pope'll make a special trip over from Rome just to slap your ugly faces!

"And I'll make 'em believe me too . . . Just watch."

And Jessie launched into her scene.

"They . . . those two men," she said, wringing her hands and looking up with big doe eyes as if speaking to an invisible judge. "Henry Parks and Ellis—I don't know his first name—they said . . . your honor . . . they said that they were policemen, so I trusted them. I thought they were trying to help, to do good. But they made me—oh, my God, I'm sorry . . ."

She started crying. Right there, on the spot, the tears flowing and the sobs coming in what started as brave little gasps held back at great personal expense until the emotion built into irresistible spasms of pain that squeezed her breath into the full-fledged, gut-wrenching moans of a classic stage breakdown. Her face glistened with tears as she cringed, squeezing her eyes shut and trying her level best to physically banish the horror of remembered agonies. But her efforts were in vain, and with perfectly timed inevitability she succumbed to her suffering's overwhelming power.

"Together . . . at the same time!" she exclaimed, her hands on her face, her eyes hidden. "Oh . . . it *hurt*!"

The startled look on Ellis' face betrayed just how genuine Jessie's passion must have appeared to him. But Parks remained unmoved. As Jessie went on, developing her scene toward the fit of hysterics that would naturally culminate in her physical and emotional collapse, Parks settled his reptilian gaze and stepped forward as he said, "According to the official police report, Kevin Reynolds was twelve years old when the event that would lead to his first recorded run-in with the authorities happened. He was twelve, and the little girl who he chose as his victim was five."

"I tried to get away, your honor," Jessie returned, cowering from him with exaggerated timidity until her back touched the wall. "I struggled, but they said that they'd kill me if I didn't do it. They said that they'd show me how bad they could make it hurt if I kept on fighting them . . ."

"Twelve's just about the right age for a pedophile to begin displaying some of the aspects of his twisted sexual preferences," Parks countered, stepping forward again so that Jessie had to slide along the wall to keep her distance, disturbing a painting of a covered bridge, and ending up in a corner, where she put her hands up in self-defense.

"And choosing Natalie, his younger sister, as his object of attention is about right too. It's usually a family member first, because they're so available."

"They showed me their badges, or I'd never have gotten in the car!" Jessie cried, knotting her fingers in her short blond hair and letting herself slide to the floor, burying her head in her arms and sobbing. "All night . . . over and over . . . both of them . . ."

"Since he was a minor himself, there wasn't all that much the authorities could do. It's still a little unclear as to who exactly called the police. But if the report I read is accurate, if that neighbor next door hadn't heard the little girl screaming, it's a pretty sure bet that nobody outside the family would have ever heard a thing about what was going on in that basement."

"The young one was just a brute, but Parks . . . the old man . . . he was sick!"

"Your grandfather paid for some very good psychiatrists. And I've got the record of their findings. They were expensive to obtain, but I've got them right here!"

"Parks brought a rubber thing with him. He kept it in a briefcase . . ."

"The only really unusual thing about these reports is Reynolds' aggressiveness. The degree of physical sadism indicated by these reports isn't usually a part of a pedophile's initial experiments. Violence and pain usually come later. It's very rare for a boy to start off as a sadist. It indicates a level of disturbance that runs very deep."

"It was the blood!" Jessie suddenly shrieked, thrusting her face forward and defiantly embellishing her story in voluminous counterpoint to the old man's narrative.

Ellis, standing off to one side and saying not a word, seemed

FORGET ME NOT

bewildered by the performance, and his eyes roamed back and forth from Jessie to Parks as if he were examining the two sides of a single coin. His posture seemed to indicate that some physical urge was rising and falling inside him that made him vacillate from intervening to allowing things to take their course uninterrupted, while his eyes betrayed a bafflement that, in itself, was sufficient to keep him immobile.

When Jessie mentioned blood, Parks stopped talking. As if sensing his momentary vulnerability—without understanding its cause—she pushed her way back up to her feet and, using the volume of her voice, thrust herself right at the old man, driving him before her with her words.

"It was the blood, your honor!" she shouted. "It got him off—at the factory, where he took me first to meet his partner. There was blood everywhere, and I could see him loving it. That's what he likes, your honor. I didn't know it, but he showed me later. He said he wanted me to bleed . . . that he was going to hurt me. He likes it when he gets to hurt someone. That's why he's so interested in this Prisoner thing. He's got a whole Prisoner scrapbook. And it was the blood that he kept talking about!

"He said he wanted to make me bleed so that he could use my blood to paint a chart on the wall like the one we saw in the factory—"

"A *what*?" Parks suddenly exploded, firing out a hand and snatching Jessie's wrist from where she had been flailing her arms about. "What did you say you saw in the factory?"

Jessie mentally stumbled, her concentration on her testimony scene momentarily derailed by Parks' sudden, and uncharacteristic, animation. She paused, recaptured the flow of her performance, and tried to pick it up again.

Parks grabbed her other wrist and shook her hard, shouting, "What did you just say?"

"You're hurting me!" she protested.

"A chart? What kind of chart? What were you talking about?"

Jessie squirmed, but Parks held tight.

"Let me go!"

"What kind of chart?"

When Jessie didn't answer, Parks grabbed her by the back of the neck and hustled her across the room to the table, where he bent her over with one hand while rifling through the contents of his briefcase with the other. Jessie saw glimpses of O'Polo's mutilated body sliding beneath Parks' nervous fingers until Polaroid shots of the doorway appeared and he said, "There. You said you saw a chart. Now, what did you mean? You used the word 'chart.' What the hell did you mean by that?"

"A tree," Jessie said, stubbornly breaking Parks' grip and rubbing the back of her neck. Glancing at Ellis and wondering why he had done nothing while the old man had manhandled her, she returned her attention to the table and added, "It's a family tree chart."

Parks was suddenly fascinated, and his silver eyes darted from Jessie's face to the photos and back.

"Go on!" he said, licking his lips. "Don't make me dig for it."

Jessie took a deep breath, grimacing at the stinging on her skin and wondering what had just happened. She saw quick bits of the scene she had just played, and its absurdity disquieted her so much that it was momentarily hard to think.

"Tell me!" Parks insisted, trying to touch her again.

But she slapped his hand away, saying, "Here," as she pointed at one of the pictures. "This single line connecting these four dots indicates a blood relationship. This double line connecting these two is a relationship by marriage. The segmented lines are divorced couples. And the waving lines indicate remarriage."

Parks was breathing hard, puffing his cheeks and working the tiny muscles around the corners of his eyes so hard that Jessie thought he might have some sort of a nervous reaction—like a stroke or a heart attack—at any moment.

Drawn by the familiarity of what the pictures represented, she allowed her own voice to calm her as she leaned on the table and concentrated on what she was saying.

"I don't know what it's supposed to mean," she said as Ellis joined them at the table. "And without a list of names to correspond to the blanks it's almost completely useless. But whoever put it together organized it around the doorway, as if the original progenitors of the line were there."

"What do you mean, 'there'?" Ellis asked, probably because he suspected that, at the moment, Parks couldn't.

"Well," Jessie said. "Look here.

"Here's the doorway, right? It must represent the origin of the family 'cause we've got three separate straight lines coming off the top, ending in three dots. Those would be the first three children of the original man and wife. One dot's connected to another with a double line, which means that that child was married. But the other two aren't connected to anything at all, indicating lifelong bachelors . . . or spinsters. Then, there's this dot connected to the married couple, meaning that they produced one child. As we move out, we get double lines, segmented, wavy, and all the rest, indicating the growth of the family through marriages, divorces, the birth of children, and everything else that happens over the course of generations. Whoever drew this thing spread it out around the door, which is probably why I didn't recognize it right away. Usually, when you see something like this, it's flat on a page, starting at the bottom and moving up, like a tree: a trunk below and branches above.

"But what I don't understand are all these spiky lines. See here? Up and down like lightning bolts. They connect almost everybody on the chart back to the doorway, as if everybody, including nonblood relations by marriage, is directly connected to the central progenitors in some way . . . which is impossible."

"So you've seen this kind of thing before?" Parks asked softly, as if concentrating very hard on his voice. "You recognize it?"

Jessie nodded. "Sure. After Grandpa died, Uncle Kevin took over his business. Between the two of them, I've seen these charts all my life.

"Grandpa was doing geneaological research fifty years ago . . . way before it was popular. That's where our family's money comes from originally. Years ago, when it was Grandpa's business, he worked almost exclusively for real rich families out east. You know, old money that could trace its roots back to the *Mayflower* type of thing. Then he started in on celebrities.

"But since *Roots*, everyday people have gotten interested in their family histories. And that's what really made Uncle Kevin rich. After Grandpa died, Uncle Kevin's had more business than he's known what to do with, since he didn't discriminate against clients whose backgrounds or personal achievements were more ordinary. I used to help when I could. He and I were partners, kinda. In projects as complicated as some of these can be, you've gotta have a partner to add a second pair of eyes, if only for perspective. If you try to go it alone, things can get really jumbled up. It was only recently that he hired on a staff to do the legwork."

"So this key . . . this single line/double line code, is it common to the trade?" Parks asked.

"Common how?"

"I mean, does everyone who does family trees use the same code?"

Jessie was suddenly wary. "I don't know," she said, the distrust naked in her voice.

"If the key is common to all genealogical researchers," Parks mused, staring down at the table, "then anybody who's ever done a family tree could be considered capable of producing this chart. But if it's not—" He looked up, and Jessie suddenly hated those milky eyes of his more than anything else in the world. "If it's not," he repeated, "then it's as good as a fingerprint."

Slapping his hand down flat and standing up, he pointed Jessie's way and added, "I knew you had what we needed in your head."

He was smiling. For the first time since Jessie had met him, he was really smiling—a broad, satisfied grin that was at once triumphant and sad.

"Didn't I say so?" he asked rhetorically, and with an eagerness that was disturbing. "Back at the restaurant, didn't I say that you knew things that you didn't even know you knew? Well, this proves I was right! It would have taken me weeks to figure out that those marks were a genealogical chart. And you knew. Right off the bat. You knew."

"He didn't do it," Jessie interrupted. "He's not the Prisoner."

"I know he's not *the* Prisoner," Parks affirmed. "But he's *one* of them."

Jessie blinked.

And Parks nodded.

"I see that now," he said, gathering up his Polaroids and stuffing them back in his briefcase. "I didn't understand. I was blind. The killings in the street clued me in:

"Naturally he was out of the country during some of the murders. Naturally some of the killings display the mental delusions of a particular mind, and some of them don't. Naturally we've got knifings, bludgeonings, and strangulations on the one hand and pistol shots on the other. Because the Prisoner isn't one man. He's two. The Prisoner's a partnership ... or something. I don't know exactly what yet. But it's two. I know it is."

"How?" Jessie asked, momentarily caught up in Parks' insistent, interior world again. "How do you know?"

"Because you just told me," he responded cryptically. "Now," he added, turning to Ellis, "while I clean up, you tell her about the old lady."

"What old lady?" Jessie asked, looking deeply into Ellis' eyes for some sign of hope.

But Parks killed any hope she might have found there before it could even be born when he said, "Your Uncle Kevin had a very busy night."

10

Even though he knew that the two cops in the cruiser would probably come rushing toward the van at any instant, Kevin Reynolds didn't let himself hurry after he'd shot the woman and the boy.

He had important things to do.

And he did them ...

Methodically.

First he apologized, first to the boy, for his youth, and then to the woman, for her suffering. Then he pressed a hand flat against the windshield, leaving a perfect palm print on the glass. And finally, he jumped out of the van and headed for a row of hedges, leaping over the line of shrubs and pressing himself against the icy ground.

From where he lay, he heard one cop shouting into a radio in the cruiser as the other cursed when he saw what was in the van. They met halfway between the two vehicles, nearly stumbling into one another in the middle of the street, as the one described the bodies and the other explained that backup cars and an ambulance were on the way. They then agreed, reluctantly, that it was better if they both stuck close to the little girl, instead of leaving her unattended, or having just one of them go running into the dark looking for a nut with a gun.

Reynolds smiled through the tears freely flowing down his cheeks as he crawled along the hedges, his equipment bag slung over one shoulder, and his pistol, reloaded and fitted with a silencer, cocked in his hand. (He'd shot the woman and her son without the silencer because he wanted the shots to make the cops hesitate before rushing after him. But any more shooting he'd have to do within the next few minutes would have to be done quietly, since what he needed more than anything else right now was a little operating room.)

At the end of the hedges he slipped into the darkness between two houses, cut across the backyard, jumped a fence, crossed a side street, and hesitated, waiting for any dogs in the neighborhood to start barking so he'd know in which direction not to run. No barking came, so he headed down a driveway between two nearly identical homes, cut across yet another backyard, and approached the rear of a huge, two-story brick house with a porch enclosed with clear-plastic sheets.

He had to stop for a second and catch his breath. Years ago, when this had all first started, he had been better at being what he needed to be . . .

Which was a terrorist.

But he was older now, and heavier, and he smoked too much,

FORGET ME NOT

and drank even more—which was forbidden. But who knew? Certainly not Molaine. He'd heard a lot about Molaine, but he'd never actually seen his disapproving eyes or his evil, revolving head.

The Reality Terrorist operated alone, without direct supervision.

Operated alone . . .

Following orders.

The house was dark, like all the others on the street. It was nearly three in the morning—too late for anyone to be watching TV and a little too early for anyone to be getting up for work. It was the magic hour, the secret time, that slice of late-night/early-morning stillness when Reynolds had the world to himself. It was his favorite time to strike—and he was a man who knew his business . . .

Even if he did laugh and cry at the same time while he was going about it.

So far tonight he'd broken his own cardinal law of anonymity any number of times. But tonight was unlike any other in his life. It's hard for a man to change the way he thinks, to turn his instincts upside down and to do things he would normally never even consider, like leaving fingerprints and license numbers for the police to find. It wasn't easy. Especially since some of his earliest memories were of deceit.

Lying is a way of life . . .

And life is a way of lying.

"You never—ever—let yourself get caught without an alibi," a voice in his head reminded him.

"You never—ever—let yourself get caught without a plan."

Wisdom.

"They'll put you away if they can."

The lock on the back door of the house snapped like a rubber band. He'd picked it by reflex. Such things were second nature. Entering a tiny kitchen, he withdrew a flashlight, aimed it at the floor, and pulled the door shut behind himself. His senses were sharp. His psychic powers turned on, his internal radar emitting highly pitched, mental beams around him. Anything living that was touched by those invisible ripples of power would automatically set off alarm circuits in his brain, alerting him to the presence of potential prey, or predators. He adjusted his rubber gloves—habit—and breathed through his mouth in the controlled, noiseless way his karate instructor had taught him, letting the whole inside of his head and chest taste the oxygen as it entered his bloodstream.

There was one woman in this house. An old one. He tasted talcum power, Ben-Gay, lilac, and skin. There was a cat in the house too. He tasted its shit.

His flashlight beam was muted by a plastic cover over its lens to keep it from being visible to any neighboring insomniacs through the window. There was a clock ticking in the living room. He had never understood how people could live with clocks like that, but they seemed popular. He couldn't count the number of homes he'd sneaked into late at night where mantel clocks ticked away like unnaturally rhythmic cicada wings. How could a person think in such an atmosphere? It was amazing that people weren't throwing themselves out of high windows with their faces contorted by panic as their brains melted down their spinal cords after years of subliminal ticking.

The street outside was dark grey and snowy. He saw it through the living room window. The woman who lived here was named Elsa McGreavy. She was a ninety-year-old widow with a car. Reynolds had unconsciously selected her house without his conscious mind's involvement in the decision. He did a lot of things that way. In that ancient, alligator part of his brain, he was always on the lookout for some angle he could store away for future use. Sometimes he amazed himself with the things he didn't even know he knew.

Like Elsa McGreavy.

As soon as he had jumped out of the van he knew that he'd be visiting her tonight. Over the past few weeks of watching his niece, he'd become familiar with the town. And though he hadn't been aware of it, Elsa McGreavy's house had stuck in his mind.

It was the oldest in town, and he had read a newspaper article about it when he had first arrived. There was a glass case in the public library containing the article, as well as a photograph of the house, which was a certified, historic landmark.

She was sleeping under a beautiful quilt that she had probably made with her own, arthritic hands. Standing in the doorway to her bedroom and looking down at her thin, curled figure—blue in the light of the digital alarm clock on the night table next to her bed—Reynolds thought of how she must have appeared: old and sweet, harmlessly hunched over a sewing basket and pushing needles through fabric as her cat lay curled at her feet, sleeping in the cheery glow of a fire burning in the grate. This mental picture was so serene, peaceful, and heartbreaking that it brought a lump to his throat . . .

A lump that he almost choked on when the doorbell rang as loudly as a fire alarm, and Elsa McGreavy sat up in bed.

The Reality Terrorist idea was one that had been percolating in Reynolds' mind since high school, and probably before. The term stemmed from a feeling he had that reality was a completely subjective thing. No matter what the facts pertaining to a particular event might be, public perception defined the reality of the event to a wider and more practical degree than anything so mundane as physical evidence ever could. For example: Eugene Reynolds, Kevin's father, was always seen as a pillar of his community. Before the explosion and fire that took his life in 1982—a gas heater out in the barn that he had remodeled as his office malfunctioned and blew the building off its foundation while he was working on the Hoopleman family history—he enjoyed the friendship of wealthy and influential people from coast to coast. Any random issue of *People* magazine a person might choose to peruse was bound to contain photographs of at least six celebrities that Eugene Reynolds knew socially, or had done some work for in the past.

In public, he was a soft-spoken man who didn't drink, gossip, or ask favors of his wealthy acquaintances; he was handsome, polite, and invariably well dressed, always willing to step aside so that a photographer could snap a shot of his cocktail party companion—which was an indication of his intrinsic understanding of his unspoken place in the circles of power: namely that he was a business associate, and not a friend; and, perhaps most important of all, he produced results that his clients were pleased to pay for, having a kind of sixth sense about what sort of heritage someone engaging his services might secretly desire.

But at home, this smoothly intelligent man was a very different creature. He drank heavily, often starting his binges on a Saturday morning and not stopping until somebody got hurt—usually his wife—late Monday or Tuesday night. He was verbally abusive, short-tempered, arbitrary, and conceited. He was constantly reminding his family of how much they depended on him, and how, without his talents and protection, they would surely starve. He invited strange women over to the house at all hours, and during these visits, Kevin's mother locked herself in her bedroom. He espoused bizarre opinions regarding religion and politics, and he had a lot of special pictures of children hidden in a locked closet in the basement. Kevin knew about those pictures because he was in a few of them. After swearing him to eternal secrecy with some of the most fearsome-sounding oaths imaginable, his father had used him as a model . . . which was fun, but felt a little funny, being naked like that . . .

It was on the day that Officer Sampson came that his father changed so drastically. And it was on that same day, when his sister Natalie screamed in the basement as if someone were trying to kill her, that Kevin Reynolds' world was turned upside down for good.

The cop named Sampson spoke in a strained, choppy way that made everything he said sound like an order. There was apparently something about him that was very frightening, because Eugene Reynolds sat on the couch, darkly drunk and hanging onto his wife's hand the whole time he stalked up and down the living room, red-faced and angry, debating aloud with himself about something that apparently involved Kevin . . .

But Kevin didn't care.

He wasn't even listening.

His head hurt too much for that.

Natalie was Kevin's little sister. She was five years old, and

Kevin was twelve. Something bad had happened to Natalie. That much Kevin remembered. Whatever had happened to her had brought Officer Sampson to the house, and had terrified her so thoroughly that she stayed huddled up close to their older sister, Lisa, for days thereafter. Lisa was fourteen. She was beautiful, quiet, smart, and so much older than Natalie that, with her long, golden blond hair hanging over the frightened five-year-old, she looked more like her mother than her sister.

It wasn't until days later, when the first of a string of doctors came to ask Kevin questions, that the details of Natalie's travails were discussed.

"Apparently," the first doctor said over his notebook, studying Kevin where he sat, hands folded on the couch in the living room, "while your mother was out shopping, and your father was working in his office, you took your sister down to the basement, stripped off her clothes, and tied her up with an electric cord you cut off the television. Now, what did you do after that?"

Kevin said that he didn't know. He didn't say that he didn't remember taking Natalie down to the basement, or taking off her clothes, because, when he'd told his father that he didn't remember doing any of those things, his father had hit him across the face so hard that it had reopened the terrible swelling surrounding his right eye. Kevin got that first black eye the day the pissed-off policeman named Sampson came to the house. Kevin vaguely recalled thinking that he had to warn his father that a police car had just pulled into the driveway—which was his job, as official lookout—when his father came running drunkenly up the basement stairs, grabbed him, and slammed his enormous fist into his face.

But his father said that wasn't how things had happened at all. He said that he had discovered Kevin in the basement after coming to investigate the girl's cries for help, and that he had hit his son in a fit of rage engendered by what he'd found the boy doing. Then he'd taken a drink, to settle his nerves. Kevin didn't know what to make of things, and, consequently, he didn't know what to say in answer to the questions first the police officer, then the doctors—who were kind of like the

"Thought Police" anyway—started asking the first chance they got.

"What did you do after you tied her up?" the doctor asked again.

And Kevin shrugged, refusing to speak . . . which seemed safe.

"You're a dirty little liar!" Kevin's father had screamed into his face, shaking him awake in the basement after knocking him out in the kitchen. "You dirty little pervert!"

"Mr. Reynolds, please," Officer Sampson had said.

"I can't believe you're my son!"

"Mr. Reynolds, I understand how you feel. But please. You'll only make things worse."

"I wish you had never been born!"

"My daddy's mad at me," Kevin told more than one doctor over the course of the next few years. "He says that I tell lies. But I don't."

"Do you mean to say that you believe the incredible things you say are true?" the doctors would ask.

"Yeah."

"That you didn't do anything to your sister?"

"Yeah."

"That you've never done anything wrong?"

"Yeah. I've never done anything wrong."

"Not one thing?"

"Not one thing."

"So why is your father mad at you?"

"I don't know."

"Are you mad at your father?"

"No. I love my father."

And Kevin did, because it was his father who taught him that there are ways to do the things you want to do, that you *need* to do, without anyone knowing anything but what you want them to know . . . because making people believe what you say is more important than anything else in the world.

"You never—ever—let yourself get caught without an alibi."

It was his father's voice that said that, speaking years later. And . . .

"You never—ever—let yourself get caught without a plan."
You never—ever—let yourself get caught.
Never get caught.
Never.

Reynolds stepped quickly aside, disappearing into the hallway as Elsa McGreavy climbed from bed, put on her robe, and hobbled down the stairs to answer the door. She obviously knew where every object in her house of nearly half a century was located, for she didn't turn on so much as a single light. In the dark, she walked right past the bathroom door, behind which Reynolds was hiding. He was just creeping down the stairs as she snapped on a lamp in the living room, flipped a switch for the porch light, and unlocked the front door.

A voice that belonged unmistakably to a cop didn't even wait for her to ask what was wrong before it loudly apologized for waking her.

"I didn't mean to scare you, Mrs. McGreavy," the policeman practically shouted. And from where he was crouched in the shadows, Reynolds could see that he had taken his hat off and was holding it over his heart, like an old-fashioned, Victorian suitor might. "But we've got some trouble in town."

Mrs. McGreavy invited the cop to come in out of the cold for coffee, making Reynolds' heart skip. But the policeman declined, saying, "No thank you, Mrs. McGreavy. I've got to hit the rest of this side of the street. We're waking everybody up. We followed a set of footprints in the snow to a backyard a few doors down from you, and we're going over that house right now. There's a fugitive loose in the neighborhood. And we want everybody to make sure their doors are locked."

"Goodness," Mrs. McGreavy said in an absurdly aged voice that made her sound like Aunt Bee from the old *Andy Griffith Show*. "Is this man dangerous?"

"Yes, ma'am," the cop said. "Once we're done knocking on doors we'll be coming back through to make sure he ain't hiding in somebody's garage. So you be looking for us. And until we come back, don't open your door to anybody unless it's a police officer. Okay?"

Mrs. McGreavy accepted her instructions, thanking the young man and locking and chaining the door when he'd gone. As she moved around the house, checking windows and doors, Reynolds watched from the shadows, finally realizing that not only was her eyesight poor but she was also hard of hearing . . . which wasn't surprising for a woman her age.

But what was a little weird was that her cat was deaf too.

The big, white, long-haired, blue-eyed Persian was sleeping on the sofa. Reynolds happened to know that any male specimen of that overbred strain was born deaf, its breeders having sacrificed its hearing for its looks. Mrs. McGreavy picked the cat up, making it mutter as it groggily looked around before it started purring as she rubbed between its ears.

"There's a bad man loose, Leonard," she said as she stepped into the kitchen, where she turned on the teakettle and chained the back door. "Isn't that terrible?"

It hurt Reynolds' feelings to hear this sweet old lady's pronouncement about his being "bad."

It hurt his feelings, because he wasn't bad.

He was just doing his job.

And if he didn't hurry, he'd never have the house ready for those cops when they came back.

11

The policeman's name was Spall, and he thought he saw a figure dart behind the garage in the old lady's backyard. He drew his gun and signaled to his partner, thinking about what the guy they were after had done to that little girl, and then to her mother and brother.

All he wanted was a shot at the creep.

Fuck an arrest.

Officer Spall wanted one clean shot.

"You sure it was him?" his partner, a man named Benjamin Hackett, nicknamed "Buddy," asked as he came around the side of the house.

"No," Spall said. "But let's check anyway."

FORGET ME NOT

Every cop in town had been called into work, and twenty or so guys from the next town south had responded to their dispatcher's call for help. There were two teams of policemen working the street, one on each side, while others wandered randomly and cruisers crawled around with their lights on. Two police vans were being set up with huge halogen lamps, and when they got going they would bathe the neighborhood in a ghostly, skim-milk glow that would make the place look like a movie set. Starting on the south end of the street and proceeding north, the search teams were going over every house from top to bottom, checking basements and garages, and being surprised to find that there were people who, at four-thirty in the morning, already knew about the murders by the theater. The footprints that had initially led the cops across two snowy backyards had abruptly ended at the dry pavement of Beech Street. But backup cars had arrived within minutes of the shooting, so the murdering son of a bitch who had made those prints couldn't have gotten too far.

Four guys were ringing the doorbell on Mrs. McGreavy's front porch as Officers Spall and Hackett headed around back to check the yard. When Spall glimpsed the shadow disappearing behind the garage, the first thing he did was glance down, verifying that there were indeed footprints in the snow. Then he started jogging forward with his weapon drawn, silently waving his arm for his partner to head around the left side of the garage and hoping in his heart that he'd get that one clean shot that would bring the killer down.

He'd never shot a man before.

Behind him the men on the porch were pounding on Mrs. McGreavy's door, calling her name and banging the front window with their knuckles. On the next street over, a police cruiser slid silently by, the tiny searchlight near its driver's wing mirror dancing a conical slice of glowing silver between houses to briefly silhouette Hackett as he made the turn around the garage. Nearly every window on every house Spall could see was lit a deceptively friendly amber. And like the prints that had originally led the cops into the neighborhood from near the theater, the marks in the snow Spall followed around the side of the garage simply ended in the dark.

Spall's heart was pounding, and he was actually sweating under his vinyl uniform jacket. It was cold out tonight—no more than ten degrees—but his forehead was moist, and so was his palm around his gun's rubber grip.

"Buddy?" he called softly, moving through the slice of shadow thrown by the garage until he arrived at the back of the building where there was a stack of firewood piled next to a perfectly flat patch of snow-covered ground he assumed was a garden in the summer. "Buddy?"

Spall's heart locked into a steady trot when his partner did not answer. He stepped further back, seeing in his mind's eye the ladder leaning against the garage at the base of which the footprints in the snow had stopped, and hearing the faraway sound of splintering wood and shouting voices as the men on Mrs. McGreavy's front porch broke down her door.

"The fucker's up on the roof!" Spall thought, licking his lips and craning his head as he stepped back even closer to the fence.

It was at that moment that a figure materialized behind him, emerging from the gloom and making him spin as he emitted a sound that was supposed to be "Stop! Police!" but that was instead a kind of startled gasp.

"What the hell's wrong with you?" Officer Hackett asked, stepping through the gate in the fence separating the two yards and adding, "Did ya see him?"

Spall was just about to speak when a voice boomed out over the snowy yard, making both men snap their heads up as a figure lifted itself against the deep purple-blue of the predawn sky. The voice might have said, "Surprise!" Or it might have said, "Sunrise!" Spall wasn't sure which it was, and he didn't have time to find out, because, before he could so much as open his mouth, something flashed atop the garage and a sound that reminded him of someone snapping their fingers went *pop!* And then *pop!* again. And then Officer Hackett fell over backward, striking the gate behind him so hard that he ripped it off its hinges.

Spall was frozen where he stood as the figure on the garage roof leapt, emerging as a sharp black form against the sky and sailing down with his legs braced for impact and his left arm clutching something close to his body as he landed in the next yard.

Spall thought, "Pop?" and having expected the *bang!* of a gunshot, his mental dictionary never had time to produce the word "silencer" because . . .

Hackett groaned weakly at his feet, men started shouting inside the house, and the fugitive ran across the yard next door, crossing the street right behind a passing police car and throwing himself to the ground in a tumbler's roll like a commando preparing for a blast.

It all took thirty seconds . . . maybe less.

Spall hadn't so much as raised his gun . . .

One clean shot?

Right!

He glanced down at where Hackett lay tangled atop the broken gate and saw that the older man's face was gleaming in the moonlight, deflated in an awful, unnatural contortion that made him think that at least half of it was missing.

The shouting in the house had taken on a uniform texture of outrage. And there was a dark figure in the amber of the kitchen window, moving toward the back door.

Spall glanced to where he'd seen the fugitive drop to the ground.

Drop to the ground?

And then his eyes went wide, his gun slipped from his fingers, and he stepped forward . . . just as the back door opened on Mrs. McGreavy's house, and a voice shouted, "Spall?" into the night. It was at that instant that everything—the whole goddamn world—went a hellish shade of yellow before a sound that was so loud that it felt hot exploded out from the house and tore the shingles off the garage . . .

And the flesh off Spall's screaming face.

12

Reynolds felt the concussion beneath him as if it were an earthquake. Huddled against the brick foundation on the north side of a house across the street and a few doors down from Mrs.

McGreavy's, he let the change in atmosphere pull the breath out of him, knowing that a blast as big as the one his bomb would have produced could rupture his lungs if he tried to fight it . . . even so far away. Pieces of flaming junk ricocheted around the neighborhood, and windows shattered for blocks around. A sickly yellow glow flickered in the bits of broken glass littering the snow, and an oily stench tainted the air almost instantly. His ears were ringing. His legs wobbled beneath him. And his crotch ached with excitement.

God!

It had never been like this before!

Never!

Never like this before!

The neighborhood was suddenly and absolutely alive with the cries of bystanders and cops. People were running. Somewhere the moan of a fire engine's siren insinuated itself into the din. Horns were honking, tires were squealing, phones were ringing through broken windows.

And Reynolds had caused it *all*!

He *liked* improvising, he decided. He'd never really done it before, or at least he hadn't in years. He'd always planned, charted, plotted, and prepared, setting up every little detail and taking every conceivable contingency into consideration before making so much as an airplane reservation. Any improvising he'd ever done in the past was out of necessity . . .

Sure, it was fun.

. . . but improvisation was invariably the result of a mistake, or a turn of fate, which, in the end, was just another name for a mistake . . . especially if you looked at things as his father might.

"Just remember," his dad had said long ago, "the whole world is full of people who want to do you dirt. They'll stop at nothing. If you give them so much as half a chance"—that was a big phrase with his dad: half a chance—"they'll nail your ass to a tree."

Reynolds was nine when he first heard that one: "nail your ass to a tree." And the mental image was more than a little disquieting.

He stood up, unafraid of being seen any longer as doors up and down the street opened and people stepped into the night clad in robes and shoes without socks. He moved away from the house, pausing for just one moment to place the thing he was holding on the hood of a car parked in the drive. He took a moment to consider the arrangement of the object, found it to his liking, and smiled.

Mrs. McGreavy's terrified eyes glittered with reflected flames. Her severed head rested on the hood of what looked like a Buick—but it was so hard to tell nowadays, what with the way Detroit kept making all the models look alike. The hood ornament fit into the base of her empty esophagus, keeping her head from sliding off. And her mouth was open just enough to give her that "Oh, God!" expression that Reynolds did so dearly love.

She looked like one of those amazing "believe it or not" things that are supposed to happen during tornados: like that legendary church in Kentucky, or Georgia, or wherever—it's different every time—that is totally blown to bits, except for the altar, which is miraculously left unscathed. Or the single blade of straw embedded six inches into the trunk of a stout Louisiana oak tree. Mrs. McGreavy's head looked like that: like it had been blown across the street and had miraculously landed upright on the hood of this car, facing its former house, where the rest of its scorched body lay incinerated.

Wow!

Leaving her to watch the fun, he slipped off his jacket and mask and walked boldly into the street, joining the growing number of people amassing there to watch the fire. Three houses were burning now, not counting Mrs. McGreavy's, which you really couldn't even call a house anymore. It was just a pile of jutting lumber—like the remains of a Thanksgiving turkey: a carcass of bones, stripped of flesh.

"What the hell happened?" someone asked, and Reynolds turned to find a man, maybe ten years older than himself, standing in the chilly night air in a pair of striped pajama bottoms and no shirt.

Reynolds couldn't bear to see him exposed like that, so he ran back to the yard where he'd left his jacket and returned with it, offering it to the man, who said, "Thanks. Now, what the hell happened?"

Before he moved deeper into the crowd, Reynolds responded, "I think it was a terrorist."

And then he was gone . . .

Hiding in plain sight, like any good terrorist might.

THREE

13

Jessie was beginning to think that maybe there was something a little bit nefarious about Henry Parks and his wealthy, secret patron who was financing his search for the Prisoner. He was apparently able to produce anything he wanted simply by making a phone call or reaching into his seemingly bottomless briefcase. He'd done it at the police station with the photographs of her parents; he'd done it in the motel with her uncle's psychiatric profiles compiled by the private doctors her grandfather had hired almost thirty years ago, and also by the FBI, who supposedly didn't even believe a killer like the one Parks was chasing existed; and though she didn't know it yet, he was about to do it in her own apartment, where he would make a list of names appear as if by magic.

It was a little spooky the way he did things like that. It made her feel like he might have possessed powers a normal man shouldn't . . . powers that set him apart.

From the motel, Jessie, Parks, and Ellis drove back to the little airport where the same faceless woman Jessie had first seen in Cleveland was waiting to fly them back in the same private Learjet. During the forty-minute trip, Jessie stared out the window, Parks shuffled papers, and Ellis studied the floor. At the Cleveland terminal there were two unmarked cars waiting for them, and Parks took one, saying, "I've got some running around to do. I'll meet up with you in about an hour," while Ellis drove Jessie back to her apartment in the other. It was during that drive that he opened up to her, adding yet another twist to the already incomprehensible knot her life had become.

"I think you should know that I'm on your side," he said, merging their car into traffic on the freeway and lowering the visor against the glare of the sun on fresh snow. "Henry's a loose cannon, and the Bureau sent me to make sure he stays anchored."

"Infiltrating the enemy camp in deep cover, huh?" Jessie mumbled, without looking at him.

By now she was feeling disgusted by virtually everything.

"Something like that," Ellis said.

"Isn't broadcasting your mission kind of a funny way to play spy?"

"Who you gonna tell?" Ellis countered. "Certainly not Henry. You don't like him any more than I do."

And Jessie was forced to both concede the point and consider Ellis from a new perspective . . . which was something she found easy to do because, to her, perspective was the key to just about every aspect of life. She'd picked up that little attitude while studying acting, but, if pressed, she'd have to admit that it was also one that she had developed, more or less on her own, long before she ever started college.

For her, getting into character was simply a question of seeing a particular set of circumstances from a specific point of view. A director could rant all day about character traits, enunciation, and verbiage, but if you couldn't understand a character's *perspective*—no matter how skewed or narrow it might be—then you'd never understand that character's motivation . . . and motivation was at the heart of everything. Life was linear, moving from one point to the next. Being equipped with their own particular quantum of intelligence, compassion, and creativity, most people spent their lives proceeding from one goal to another . . . from the cradle to the grave . . . ambition without end . . . amen.

"I want breakfast," a mind would say to itself. "And these are the things I must do in order to get it."

That's how Jessie saw life.

"I want sex."

"I want love."

"I want . . ."

"I want . . ."

"I want . . ."

It all tended to sound a little mechanical when she tried to explain it in words. But the almost limitless horizon of objectives a human mind could conceive, and the equally boundless variation of ways to go about securing them, made for a situation of staggering potential. And when you added to the equation the unavoidable crossing of one person's objectives with another's, with the conflicts, cooperations, and complications that were bound to result from so many different people wanting so many different things in the limited space of the world—or the stage—the potential results were positively profound.

"But Miss Reynolds," a drama professor had once argued in front of a class when Jessie was only nineteen, and very prone to blushing, "don't you see that your position precludes the possibility of spontaneous action? That it negates the idea of a person's doing something just for the satisfaction of doing it?"

"Then in that case, 'just doing it' would be the motivation," Jessie had countered. "And there's always the unconscious to consider."

"What about the unconscious?" the professor had asked with a smile, as if he were anticipating some response he could use to rip apart her argument.

"The unconscious mind is full of things we don't even know we know . . ."

Where had she heard that phrase before?

". . . and I'm sure that actions we call spontaneous are usually just people acting out desires that they don't even know they have."

"But that's assuming that there is an unconscious mind," the professor announced triumphantly. "Remember, Freud coined the term 'unconscious' as a way of referring to something he could neither see nor understand. He made it up, offering his view of how the mind works as a way to explain the symptoms he saw in his daily psychiatric practice. In truth, the unconscious mind is just a theory, it's not a fact."

"It is a fact," Jessie countered stubbornly, feeling her face darken and wondering why this mattered to her so much. "Believing something is what makes it true."

"To whom?" the professor asked.

"To the only person who matters," Jessie returned. "To the person doing the believing. Maybe the greatest of all human motivations is the desire to make a substantial object out of something that starts off as an intangible belief. Maybe that's why people can create: because they can imagine, and then they can believe in what they imagine strongly enough to make it real."

"You'll be a fine method actress," the professor had concluded with a grin. "Assuming of course that you can believe in the parts you play strongly enough to make them real not only for yourself but for the people watching you as well."

"Isn't that what acting is all about?" Jessie had asked.

And the professor had given her an A+ for the class . . .

Which was what he believed she wanted.

But Jessie wanted something else, though she had never found it in a classroom.

"What do *you* want, Mr. Ellis?" she asked as they approached the railroad tracks that demarcated the edge of town. It was the root question, the most basic pronouncement of interest she knew how to make. And she sincerely wanted an answer. That's what *she* wanted: an answer.

And Ellis apparently wanted to give her one because, as soon as they were over the tracks, he pulled the car into a doughnut store's parking lot and turned to face her as he spoke.

"Look," he said. "This is probably gonna be a little rough for you to accept, especially after everything you've been through. But it's really important that you understand that it's true. Okay? You've got to believe me. That's important."

Jessie considered smiling to put him at ease, but decided against it. If she weren't at ease, why should he expect her to be?

"The fact of the matter is that, despite what I said earlier about wanting to partner up, I'm not really here to help Henry Parks," Ellis said over the hissing of the car's heater. "I'm here because the Bureau sent me. Henry's had things pretty much his own way for a long time. And I can't deny that over the years he's actually done some good. There have been a number of times that he's contributed important information to cases that would ultimately prove to be unrelated to what he says he's looking for . . ."

"Which is the Prisoner," Jessie interjected.

Making Ellis nod.

"Who's supposedly my uncle."

"Do you see that?" Ellis asked, pointing out the window at the sky.

Jessie glanced up and looked at the dark stain rising up from somewhere south of where they were sitting. When she'd first seen it from the freeway, a blackish-grey column of smoke, dissipating and faint, as if something were smoldering about a mile away, she hadn't thought much of it. But with Ellis pointing it out, it became suddenly ominous.

"Fire?" she asked.

And Ellis described the explosion on Beech Street, omitting the discovery of Mrs. McGreavy's head on the hood of the Buick, then returned to the central issue, the identity of the killer.

"There was an awful lot of circumstantial evidence pointing to Kevin Reynolds left at the crime scenes," he said, choosing his words. "The cops found his Vette in an alley after chasing it off the freeway. They ran the plates and had him made in two minutes. The car was loaded with weapons, and . . . um, other things. And the store owner said that he saw a man come from the direction of the alley and get in a van that matches the one they found wrecked here this morning. Kevin Reynolds' fingerprints were all over the Vette, and on the inside of the van's windshield he left about the most perfect palm print the local evidence warden's ever seen. And, though you didn't realize it, he was following you last night."

"He was what?" Jessie snapped, turning her head.

"Henry's crew picked up his car when you were leaving the restaurant."

"That's impossible. He was in Columbus until ten-thirty."

"That's what he told you, but apparently he followed you to the airport, came back to the apartment, trolled past the building a couple of times, and decided to make a break for it."

"Make a break for what?" Jessie cut in. "Why would he run away?"

But Ellis' answer didn't quite seem to fit the question.

"It was almost as if he'd been looking for a way to make the biggest impact he could with the materials he had on hand," he said thoughtfully. "Nobody even knew he was in town. So why attract attention by driving a hundred miles an hour? And that little girl . . . when he threw her from the van, he instantly made himself the number one priority of every cop in town. He left his car running, fulla more shit than a prosecutor could ask for in his wildest dreams. And instead of heading away from the heat, he came right back at it by killing that woman and her son not six blocks from your apartment.

"It's amazing. If I didn't know better, I'd swear that he did it all deliberately to get our attention. I mean, Christ!

"Anyway, the cops were going door-to-door when the house blew up. That was at about five this morning. It's almost noon now, and since then he's disappeared. All we can do is pray that they find him before he hurts somebody else . . . if he hasn't already."

Jessie clenched her teeth, blinking rapidly without saying a word.

Ellis excused himself to run into the store. He returned with a bag of doughnuts and two large cups of black coffee, one of which he offered to Jessie. Rooting around in the bag, he produced a doughnut and handed it over, saying, "Cops and doughnuts. See what you think."

Jessie bit, tasted jelly, sipped her coffee, and nodded, licking icing from her upper lip.

Ellis smiled, and Jessie inadvertently noticed how good-looking he was. He was probably forty-five years old, maybe a little more, and when he smiled, good-humored crow's-feet crinkled at the edges of his eyes. There was a rough kind of stability in those eyes . . . kind of like a fireman's gaze: that silent

FORGET ME NOT

assurance of someone who knows what he's doing, and who cares.

"Now," he said, the steam from his coffee dancing on his lips. "Whether your uncle turns out to be responsible for this or not, my job is to make sure that Henry Parks doesn't do anything stupid. In my opinion, he's almost as screwy as the guy he says he's chasing. But inside, he's a good man. He's devoted to stopping what he sees as a great evil. God knows he's had ample opportunity to profit financially from this over the years. But all he's ever accepted is help in his investigation. His bank account's the same today as it was the day he started, twenty years ago."

"He sounds like an obsessive to me," Jessie cut in around another bite of doughnut.

"I guess it's all in how you look at it," Ellis said, shooting her that smile again.

"And how do you look at it?" she asked.

(What do you want, Mr. Ellis?)

Ellis sighed. "All right," he said after a pause. "I suppose that he is an obsessive. But that doesn't automatically make him unsavory. He's not just looking for revenge, although that's a big part of it. He's also searching for balance. He's been trying to put the world back to rights since the day his throat was crushed."

"Why'd he retire?" Jessie interrupted, the question having just popped into her head. "His injuries don't seem to have been debilitating enough to knock him out of his job forever."

"You're right," Ellis agreed, stuffing his empty coffee cup into the doughnut bag and sliding the car out of the parking lot. "Henry could have gone back. But that business with Sallovy changed everything."

Jessie didn't know what the hell Ellis was talking about, and said so.

And as he drove them through the first of what turned out to be a set of perimeters established by the police around the site of that morning's bomb blast, Ellis explained.

"It was right after he broke up your birthday party," he said, pulling the car over and flashing some kind of ID at a cop who had flagged them down. The cop examined the wallet Ellis offered through the window and waved them on. "Henry was lying around, unable to talk, drinking a lot—despite his doctor's ordering him not to touch booze while he was taking all those pain pills—and driving his wife nuts with worry. He seemed directionless and depressed. But that was before Mr. Sallovy showed up. It was that visit that really got things rolling."

Jessie was listening with one part of her mind while another part was watching the little town in which she had spent the past four years of her life slide by outside the car window. Ellis' narrative delivered in its calm, reasonable tone, contrasted powerfully with the weird, almost unearthly condition of things outside the car. On the surface, the town appeared virtually unchanged, with its quaint century-old homes and cutely named souvenir shops all arranged in perfect rows beneath that air of moneyed, suburban elegance that only time and effort can achieve. But in the corners of her mind a gathering storm cloud of unreality was spreading its ominous grey veil over the sun of her perceived rationality, creating a twilight atmosphere in which nonsense was made less hard to accept, and the distinction between lies and fact became, at best, a blur.

"The man's name was Sallovy," Ellis said through the haze of Jessie's distraction. "Harland Sallovy. At the time he was the owner of a pair of pharmacies in town, and his brother had been murdered in one of them about a year before. The killer had never been caught, and after months of frustration with the cops, private investigators, and even a little amateur detective work of his own, Sallovy had heard about Henry's injuries, and decided to pay him a visit.

"I don't know exactly what transpired at that meeting, but Sallovy and Parks apparently reached some kind of instantaneous spiritual communion. Though Sallovy had accepted the fact that his brother's killer would probably never be brought to justice, he also wanted to help destroy an evil he could identify—just one evil that his money could pay to wipe out.

"But remember, Henry's jaw was still wired shut at this time, and he had had a lot of surgery on his throat. He couldn't talk. All he could do was sit there and listen to Sallovy's proposition, which was this:

"Since it was obvious that the conventional authorities were unable to do a competent job in dealing with criminals who didn't fit an ordinary pattern, Sallovy wanted to secure the services of Henry Parks, injured police officer, and known straight-shootin' guy. When Sallovy's brother was killed, it effectively punched a hole in his life, and he wanted the bastard who'd done it trussed up and disemboweled. Not arrested. He wanted the man killed.

"But since that was apparently impossible, there being no clues as to the killer's identity, and no motive anyone could discover, he settled for the next best thing: to help Parks destroy his own personal demon. He was offering to hire Henry as an assassin, plain and simple. That was the deal. He wasn't interested in anything approaching justice. What he was interested in was revenge. And he was willing to help bankroll whatever it took to buy it.

"At the time it might have sounded like a harebrained scheme. But Sallovy was a business genius. Those two drugstores his brother's death left him sole owner of eventually became Rex-Saver, the nationwide chain. It's gotten to the point where hunting the Prisoner is the only thing Henry Parks lives for. Maybe at first his intentions were good, and he never meant for things to go as far as they have. But after Sallovy's visit he started following his hunches, investigating murders, and racing all over the country. More and more people agreed to help him in his hunt, more money came his way, more information, and . . . I don't know. It just seems that he started seeing himself differently . . . as if he consciously took on his crusader's persona.

"To tell you the truth, his 'Dead Man' nickname wasn't even his idea. As I remember it, a coroner down in Atlanta hung that name on him. After Henry had looked at some bodies down there, the doc turned to a street cop standing nearby and said, 'Did you see that guy's eyes? There's nothing there at all. He's a dead man.' And from then on, when you say 'Dead Man' to just about any cop, just about anywhere, he knows that you mean Henry Parks."

After weaving through all kinds of disrupted traffic, meandering students, curious residents, and wary cops, Ellis had finally navigated the car to Jessie's apartment building and parked. But before they got out, he put his hand on her forearm and finished his story earnestly.

"The point is that I'm not really on Henry's team," he said. "I'm a federal investigator, a representative of the government. I really am. No shit. I'm here to see that Henry Parks stays in line. Now that things are happening, it's more important than ever that somebody be here to watch him. Before, when he was talking about the Prisoner as being this master serial killer who was stalking the whole country, he was almost safe. It was such a fantastic idea, and he had so little evidence that he couldn't really do any harm.

"But now, with you, and your uncle, and all, there's the potential for a very serious problem."

"Tell me," Jessie said, driving her gaze deeply into Ellis' eyes. "No bullshit anymore. Tell me. Do you believe in the Prisoner? Is he real?"

"Personally?"

"Yes."

"No. He's not real. I don't think Henry's right. There've been too many killings, too many chances for one man to have been caught. I think Henry's been connecting all sorts of unrelated occurrences into a big conspiracy theory that reflects his own paranoid frame of mind. Or at least that's what I thought before I came here."

"And what do you think now?" Jessie asked.

"Now? I don't know. Things look bad for your uncle, so that makes what Henry's been saying look better. And Henry showed me those psychiatric reports he bought, which I'd have never seen without a warrant, and there's some pretty disturbing stuff in there. From all indications, you were raised in a very fucked-up family, and I don't mean that to scare you. But I don't think you're even aware of half the shit that went on around you while you were growing up . . . or even worse, of the totally messed-up family life your uncle had before you were born."

"Messed up how?" Jessie whispered. "What exactly did you find out?"

"Now's not the time to go into it," Ellis said, withdrawing his hand and opening the car door. "What I wanted to make you understand is that I'm not interested in revenge, or retribution, like Henry is. I'm here to make sure that the laws are respected, no matter what the truth turns out to be. And that nobody, and that means Henry Parks, or anybody else, elevates himself to the position of judge or executioner. With that explosion this morning, it makes my presence even more natural. Any use of explosives in a criminal act is a federal offense."

"So you'd have been called in this morning anyway?" Jessie asked.

And Ellis nodded, putting his finger over his lips to indicate that she should not say any more . . .

Because Henry Parks had just pulled up.

14

The apartment building looked like a sinking ship, with everyone aboard abandoning the vessel with their possessions in their arms. People were everywhere, and Jessie suddenly found herself thinking of the explosion near the theater. The city was in turmoil, but surely everybody in her building couldn't be trying to escape at once. She wanted to ask someone what was going on, but the presence of Parks and Ellis served to constrain her, so she simply followed them inside.

Three men were tearing her apartment apart with crowbars and hammers, using weird electrical devices that they had dangling around their necks like stethoscopes to find spots on the walls at which to aim their efficient, experienced *whack*s and conferring in hushed, professional voices that ceased as Parks led Jessie through the door.

"Hey!" she cried when she saw the wreckage they had made of her home. "What the hell's going on in here?"

She was just about to try physically restraining a burly young man in a sickly green suit when Ellis took her by the arm and moved her aside so that Parks could slap a notebook down on the kitchen table, which was now resting in the hallway off the living room. Arranging an overturned chair next to the table, he pointed and said, "Take a look at this and tell me what you think."

Jessie wanted to tell him what she thought, all right, but not about the notebook. The notebook was a distraction that she was going to sweep away with her hand when she noticed that the handwriting on it was familiar.

"Where'd you get this?" she asked, just as someone tore her Joker poster off the wall and draped it over the couch.

A man appeared behind Parks and produced a handful of wires that Parks took and displayed for Jessie to see.

"See these?" he said. "They're microphones. You've been bugged."

Jessie stared at the wires, and then at Ellis, whose blank stare told her everything she needed to know.

"Who?" she asked.

And Parks threw the microphones on the table near the notebook.

"Your uncle had a system of voice-activated recording equipment set up in a motel room down the street from here," he said, wiping his hand on his trouser leg as if the wires had been greasy. "Sergeant Novak found the place by running down the Corvette—unusual car for somebody to be tooling around town in this time of winter. Most Vette owners up North have enough cash to afford a beater for the sloppy months, so he just went to each motel in town until he found one where a guy recognized the car as belonging to someone who'd been staying awhile.

"You got a VCR?"

Jessie pointed to a closed cabinet under the television, and Parks kicked away a stack of movie magazines and textbooks in front of it.

"Novak found this in the motel room too," he said, pushing a tape into the machine and turning his head Jessie's way. "Now get ready. It's nothing graphic, but it's not going to be pleasant for you to watch."

Jessie was about to say something when Parks raised his hand to silence her. He had not taken his eyes off the screen, and everyone in the room fell silent as the pre-image snow disintegrated into jerking, vertical lines.

FORGET ME NOT

The screen went dark, and music started. It was that hokey, drippy-drama bombast of the opening of the theme from *2001: A Space Odyssey*, recorded, it sounded, by playing the record in the same room as a camcorder. As the darkness faded, an image took shape. At first it was fuzzy, but then it came into focus as the drapes over a very large window.

"That's the inside of the motel room," Parks explained.

Red, green, and yellow lights suddenly flickered up from the floor, overpowering the automatic focus on the camcorder a couple of times and washing the screen blank before whoever was operating the camera got things right.

"He had one of those revolting Christmas tree stands set up in the middle of the room, and a camera on a tripod near a boom box that plays CDs," Parks offered flatly, while fingering the remote-control unit, which he'd found on the floor near the sofa. "He had a bunch of lights set up too. And all the furniture in the place was pushed to one side so that he'd have a stage."

As Jessie watched, a man stepped up onto what must have been the revolving Christmas tree stand Parks had described, placed his arms flat against his sides, and began slowly turning. Parks let the tape run long enough for him to turn completely around three times before he said, "There's six hours of this. Do you recognize what he's wearing?"

Jessie didn't answer.

And neither did anyone else.

There was a disturbed, altered-reality sense about this tape . . .

Six hour long, did Parks say?

Six hours of this?

. . . that silenced everyone in the room, and filled the air with the interminable sensation of voyeurism.

"It's a shock-therapy hood," Parks said, ignoring the silence. "It's made of a heavy grade of leather, padded on the back and sides, and reinforced with hard plastic bands that run from above and below the ears to the corners of the mouth, forming a V on either side of the face, one below each eye. The points of the V's are connected to one another by a hard rubber rod, about as thick as a man's middle finger. The mask is padded so that if a person receiving shock treatments jerks around, he won't hurt himself by banging his head on the table. The rubber rod across the mouth opening is for the patient to hold onto with his teeth to keep him from chewing his tongue off.

"But they don't use masks like that anymore, so this must be an old one. They stopped because there was something about the design that seemed to encourage patients to . . . well, to fixate on them. They're autoerotic in that way. Similar masks with zipper mouths are sold in S&M shops—and they ain't exactly used for therapy."

The image on the screen suddenly started spinning like the beater on an electric mixer as Parks hit the fast-forward button on the remote control.

"That outfit he's wearing looks like a modified wet suit: rubber, or something like it, covering him from head to toe. That's why we never found any physical traces: he's literally sealed in plastic."

Jessie's mouth was absolutely dry.

At the end of his tornado-like twirl, the man launched himself off his pedestal and then leapt back on as his little TV world resumed a more rational pace.

Now he was wearing combat boots.

Parks hit the fast forward without further comment, and continued keeping his remarks to himself as he stopped, let the man revolve a few times, sped him up again, and stopped him, on and on, to the end of the tape. Each time the figure returned to his revolving stage he wore some new item of clothing. After the combat boots came black canvas trousers, a baggy shirt of a similar material, a leather jacket covered with zippers and clasps, shiny black gloves, a stocking cap over the shock-therapy mask, various belts and buckles, a backpack and survival knife, and finally, a gun . . .

Or, more accurately, a lot of guns, which he produced one by one, did a few turns while holding, and then set aside in order to give some other weapon its share of time on-screen.

By the time it was over, the tape had taken him from just the wet suit and leather hood to a state of total military preparedness, intimately displaying each step in the transformation.

The title on the tape's box read, "Son Rise," written in careful, block-style, black ink letters.

When the fuzz at the end of the tape finally erased the image of the man, blackly clad in leather and canvas, displaying an assault rifle that he held across his chest with both gloved hands, everyone in the room breathed a sigh of relief, and was then quiet while the machine rewound. Even Henry Parks seemed to need a little time to collect his thoughts before he turned Jessie's way and said, "There were other things in the room, but the tape and the notebook were the most immediate. According to the desk manager, he'd been living there for about a month. And according to the records he kept, he'd been watching you."

Because she needed something to do with her hands, Jessie glanced down and opened the notebook. The first page was dated, the date underlined, and the rest of the page filled with a description of what she had done on that particular day. Her cotton-dry throat ached and her jaw muscles squirmed as she read the details of a day over three weeks ago, filled with the mundane routine of settling herself back into her apartment after having spent two weeks at home in Columbus for Christmas. Uncle Kevin had followed her back. He had been watching her, "washing her filthy windows," as the notebook described it, and "stocking up on junk food; beating rugs in the snow; and making many trips to the drugstore, probably for condoms, Lord knows she needs them."

Jessie turned the page, and then turned it again, skimming over line after line of scribbled notes detailing all the things she had said to friends in her apartment, as well as verbatim transcripts of her telephone conversations, and a particularly disquieting smattering of one-sided monologues during which she had wandered around, talking to no one but herself. Finally, when the descriptions stopped with, "went to meet that pig, like a common hustler seeing a john"—"The pig's me," Parks needlessly explained over her shoulder—she paused, and allowed the old cop to turn a few more pages so that she could see the list of names at the book's end.

The last name on the list was Mark O'Polo.

Parks knelt down next to her, gathered up her moist right hand in both his dry ones, and said, "Jessica. This is where we're at: he made that videotape for himself. For hours and hours over the last couple of weeks, he was sitting alone in that motel room, watching himself on TV and listening to everything you said and did, all day and all night. Do you understand that? Do you get a feeling for what it is?"

Crazy! Jessie wanted to respond. But she didn't. First, because she couldn't bring herself to speak. And second, because she felt that saying such a thing to Henry Parks would be tantamount to betraying Uncle Kevin's trust.

"Your first response to that tape has probably got something to do with sex," Parks offered gently, as if he understood that he was treading on unsure terrain. "That's the 'in' thing nowadays, the bugaboo for the nineties. Sexual psychopaths have captured the headlines and established themselves and their disorders as the most fearsome menace most people can imagine. That leather hood your uncle was wearing, the dismemberment at the factory, and those references in the notebook to condoms and prostitutes, they all season this thing with an abnormal sex-drive flavor. But they're misleading. Even the folks down at Quantico, where Mr. Ellis ran his profile for me, believe that sexual dysfunctions play only a small part in the general structure of this guy's disorder . . . if they play any part in it at all. We're dealing with very murky water here."

"Why would you show me such a thing?" Jessie interrupted, withdrawing her hand from Parks' grip as if she were extricating a spoon from a jar of peanut butter. "Even if it's important, why would you do this to me?"

Parks' milky eyes were immutable, and severe, locking onto hers with a gaze so steady that she almost welcomed it, almost wished that she could simply stay there, protected by his commitment, or obsession, because—and she couldn't seem to quite work this part out just right—but, in that gaze, she felt as if there were something strong, or intelligent, that was a little deeper than any one man could ever hope to completely control. Whatever that something was, whether it was the spark of purpose or the glow of a madman's fire, he seemed to be offering her its protection. It was as if Parks' eyes spoke more eloquently than his lips, describing his willingness to take her in, to offer her shelter, and to give her all he had to give, just to keep her safe.

Which was fine.

But what did he have?

And did she really want it?

"If it were up to me, you would never even have heard a word about this," he said. "I'd have settled things between myself and the Prisoner, and that would have been all. I would even have tried to do it in such a way as to keep it out of the papers. You would have never known . . . But the happy man changed all that." Parks pointed at the Joker poster lying wrinkled on the couch. Jessie looked at the Joker's insane, unnatural grin.

Parks returned his attention her way, swinging that sincere, pale-eyed gaze of his before him like the beam of a lantern.

"You lived with him for years," he said. "You know how he thinks, how he responds to other people, and how he sees himself in the world. You can't go on fighting me. You can't go on denying what's happening around you. That mask—" He was pointing at the television now, still kneeling before her but resting his free hand on her knee for support. "He was seen wearing that very mask as he climbed into the van in which a woman and her son were shot. That very mask. That very one! It's him, Jessie . . ."

He was looking at her again, and she hated him for it.

"It's him," he said more gently. "That jacket—the one he was wearing in the video. A man who was watching the fire early this morning was arrested for wearing it! The same store owner who saw the man in the mask getting into the van identified that jacket too. When the cops saw the guy in the street wearing it, they nabbed him, thinking they had grabbed their killer. They lost a lot of valuable time thinking that they already had their man because of it. But it turns out that your uncle just walked up to this guy and offered him the coat because the guy was standing in the cold without a shirt. He just walked to him and gave him the jacket!

"Does that tell you anything about how calculating he is? About how thoroughly detached he is from the emotional content of what he's doing?

"He's a deeply disturbed man, Jessie. And as you saw for

yourself on that tape he made, he sees himself as some kind of a soldier. His enemy's the rest of society, and every cop in the county's looking for him. His picture's been faxed from here to Kentucky, and they've got your grandmother bundled up and on her way up here from Columbus right now. She'll be in this afternoon. They're still trying to locate his older sister, Lisa, to bring her in too, and . . ."

"How do you know all that?" Jessie asked.

And Parks' eyes narrowed.

"If all this just happened within the last few hours," she pressed on, as if maybe asking questions would give her time to think, "then who the hell are you that you know the details so fast?"

Parks stood up and put his hands in his pockets. He was still wearing that same baggy brown suit he had on when Jessie first laid eyes on him in the police station interrogation room.

Sighing, he looked out the window and lowered his head as he said, "I'm the only person in the world who really knows that something alien is among us."

He looked up and studied Jessie from beneath his bushy grey brows.

"Does that sound too dramatic?" he asked. " 'Alien'? That's a hell of a word. It makes it sound as if I think we're being invaded; like I belong in one of those squirrelly little groups that meet once a month in the basement of a library somewhere to discuss UFO sightings."

He paused.

Everyone in the room was watching him.

"But alien's just what it is. The Prisoner's unlike anything anyone I've talked to has ever seen. And if you don't believe me, ask Mr. Ellis. Most serial killers pick a particular type of victim, but not the Prisoner. He kills everybody. It ain't women and children that necessarily interest him. Today was the first time kids have been involved. Up until now it's been all adults, predominantly male, and of an age that could conceivably have made them dangerous as targets. The Prisoner's victims could actually have fought back. They could have defended themselves. And some of them did.

"So unless I'm missing my guess by a psychological mile,

we're not just talking sexual psychopath here. Though the sexual aspect's obviously involved, I think we're dealing with a different kind of killer. One with a completely different aim in mind."

"And what aim is that?" Jessie asked, unable to hold her tongue any longer. "You've been saying that same thing over and over again: that this guy wants something; that he's got some overpowering goal in mind. Once and for all already, what is it that you think he wants?"

"He wants to 'go back to where he belongs,' " Parks answered, pointing at the notebook. "I heard him say it that first time I saw him, twenty years ago. Where the hell 'back to where he belongs' is, or how he expects to get there by doing the things he's been doing, with whoever's been helping him do them, those are the problems we've got to solve. We're closer now than we've ever been before, but, at the same time, we're further away, because, though he may not have displayed the same behaviors that are expected of a 'standard' sexual psychopath, he is exhibiting one classic symptom: he's loosing control. It's taken him twenty years to reach that point, but it's finally happening.

"He completely abandoned his usual style of operating, leaving us everything we needed to identify him but an autograph. He even left us that palm print. That alone could have done it. But we didn't really even need it because he very thoughtfully left us his car, with his address book in the visor!

"Now that he's hit this apparently irrational stage, things are going to start moving very fast. There's no telling what he'll do next, or even where the hell he is. Which is why we've got to figure out what he wants. And that's where you come in.

"Look at that notebook. The Polaroids of the thing he left over the doorway at the factory are in that envelope. You said that all you needed were the names that would fit into the empty slots on that family tree and you could make sense of it. Well, I'd be willing to bet that the names in that notebook are the ones we've been looking for. Fit 'em in . . . and tell me what they've got to do with one another."

"Me?" Jessie protested.

"Like it or not," Parks intoned grimly, "you're the closest

thing to him we've got. You're his 'daughter,' after all. If anyone can figure him out, it's you."

I'm *not* his daughter! Jessie considered shrieking. She also considered throwing a chair across the room, screaming for help, pulling her hair and pitching a fit. What they were doing to her wasn't right. It wasn't fair. It wasn't . . .

Legal?

Parks hadn't answered her question about the details regarding his knowledge of the local police department's activities. He had skirted it neatly, as if it were of no importance. And that convenient oversight told her more than all his preachy explanations:

Legal had nothing to do with Henry Parks. Legal had nothing to do with anything he was doing. He was his own ultimate authority, and somehow, with money, words, and loyalties, he had convinced at least a portion of the real upholders of the law to respect his position and aid his quest. The police in uniform didn't stand a chance of finding their man before Parks did because he had the advantage of their work without the constraint of their rules.

So what could Jessie hope to do in the face of such knowledge?

Who could she go to?

Who could she tell?

Her first impulse was to run to her uncle. Throughout her life she had always looked to him for support and comfort. But this time she was on her own, in a room full of strangers; a room that, up until a few hours ago, she had considered home. Now it was occupied by an invading force, wired for surveillance by someone who she had thought loved her, and pressing in with its broken walls and an ugly poster of a strange, grinning man with green hair who was able to reach into the deepest hollows of her mind and pull out horrible memories of events she didn't even know she'd witnessed.

Get them out! her mind screamed.

Get them the hell out of here!

"Okay," she said, to that end, glancing down at the page. "If it's the only way, I'll do what I can."

Her words seemed to physically diminish the pressure in the

room. It was as if she had opened an imaginary window and released a cloud of sweaty-smelling steam into the biting cold. Parks studied her thoughtfully, and Ellis fell in at his side. The silent men who had been ripping her apartment apart when she first arrived hesitated a moment, as if waiting to see if anything else might happen that would be interesting, and then, like a crowd dispersing after a good house fire, began drifting back to their work. A hammer fell, and then two, and then a muttered word was passed between two investigators, and soon everything was sound and movement again except for the eye contact that was still passing between Jessie and Parks.

"I'll have to stay here, won't I?" she asked, though it wasn't really a question.

"It's for your own protection," Parks agreed.

"And though you aren't a policeman, and none of these guys are either," Jessie continued in that same, flat tone of voice Parks had used, "I can't leave when I want. They're going to be keeping an eye on me, watching me, following me around and telling me what I can and can't do. Isn't that right?"

Parks was silent.

And so was Ellis, who, standing next to the old man, was looking at her with a pained, somewhat forlorn expression. He appeared to want to communicate something to her, something like, "Don't worry; I'm here." Or, "It'll just be for a little while. Make the best of it."

But Jessie wasn't interested in the FBI man anymore either. All she wanted was to have these men removed from her presence. The investigators ripping through her walls and examining wires were just your average techies. She'd dealt with people like them behind bank counters, and in electronics stores, before. Alone with them, she was sure that she could improvise something clever enough to secure her escape. She didn't know exactly where she'd go once she got out, perhaps just as far as the freeway for sure. And after that, maybe just a motel somewhere, like in Canada, or New York state, it didn't matter. But she'd take some time off, hit a bank-in-the-box and grab some cash, aim her Mercedes in any direction facing away from Cleveland, and blow. Then, when everything was over, she'd come back ... or she wouldn't. She'd see. Right now, there were no absolutes ...

Other than getting Henry Parks the hell away from her.

Because Henry Parks had X-ray eyes.

"How do I reach you when I figure out the notebook?" she asked.

And Parks handed over a card, saying, "That's my beeper number. The minute you think you've made any sense out of that thing, call me."

"And what will you be doing?"

"Killing your uncle," Jessie heard Parks respond in her mind, though in actual space he said no such thing. As a matter of fact, he didn't say anything. He just frowned, and headed for the door.

"Keep this locked," he told one of the men standing near a hole in the wall that was as big as a fist. "And be careful. I'm sure Reynolds won't come anywhere near here, but for all we know, he might have paid someone to work with him. He's got the money, God knows. And things have changed since yesterday."

Parks exited without so much as looking Jessie's way again. But Ellis flashed her one of his most winning smiles and said, "Good luck," before he followed Parks out the door, taking one of the three techies with him.

Then Jessie was alone with her uncle's notebook. True, there were two big men in the room with her, but they may as well have been cardboard cutouts, or posters, like the Joker ...

Happy Man.

Michael Sterns.

Father?

Jessie wanted very much to cry.

But after a moment's thought, she decided that no, she didn't want to cry. She wanted to be angry. Parks had done more than disrupt her life. He'd taken it apart. Like these strange men dismantling her apartment, Parks had come in with mental hammers and crowbars and destroyed everything she could call her own ...

Or had he?

Had any of it really been her own to start with? There was

that picture of her crying in the police station, after all. And the killings when she was a baby. There was the burning house, the vague memories, and the videotape . . .

The videotape.

She was about to put that tape back into the machine and look at it again, just to verify that she had actually seen it, when someone knocked on the door and everyone in the apartment froze. One of the guards drew a gun from a holster under his left arm, and the other went to the door, looked through the spy hole, and shrugged before pulling the door open.

Jessie was on her feet before she knew what she was doing.

The man in the hall . . .

The janitor with the rolling, canvas laundry cart.

The man . . .

"Oh, God!" she gasped, making both of her defenders look her way . . .

Just as the Prisoner stepped inside.

"It can't be!" Jessie shrieked in a voice of utter despair. "This just can't be happening!"

15

She stumbled back against the wall, trembling. She'd never experienced a feeling like this one before, a total shutdown of her mental capacities that left her jellied in mind and spirit so thoroughly that she actually had to concentrate on keeping her knees locked so that she would not fall into a heap on the floor. Suddenly, a very odd, disjointed part of her mind that seemed never to be active except at the most inopportune times, said, "So this is what it feels like to be paralyzed with fright, to be so scared that you want to faint. In all those old movies you've seen, when the heroines start swooning, this is what they're supposed to be feeling. Next time a script calls for fear, shock, or terror, this is what you'll remember. If you can re-create this emotion, you'll knock 'em dead!"

The two investigators were still looking at her—it had only been about three seconds since the one had opened the door to admit the old man dressed as a janitor, though they couldn't have known that the apartment building's real janitor was a Polish guy who lived in Cleveland and who Jessie hadn't seen in about a week—when the man in the hall produced a gold automatic pistol capped with a strange-looking silencer. The sounds that the gun made when it fired were inappropriate, and sharp. They were so quiet, in truth, that the second man only flinched when he heard them. The first man didn't react to the sound at all. He reacted to the impact of the bullet striking his head.

The young man in the sickly green suit was the first to die. He was the one holding his pistol, and the man in the janitor's outfit seemed to zero in on him reflexively, drawing his bead and firing in a motion that was so smooth and efficient as to appear magical. The *snit!* of the weapon was almost instantaneously erased by the queasy sound of breaking bone as the man's head exploded, spraying blood and brain in a halo over flailing arms and legs.

Just as the second man's face was registering the first hint of horrified understanding, and even before he could move his hand toward his own weapon, the janitor very calmly swung his gun around, aimed, and placed a bullet directly between the man's eyes. The back of his head burst, and the wall—which he had just been so engaged in investigating—received a new hole and about a quart of the contents of his skull.

Jessie wasn't even able to scream.

She was frozen in her spot as the janitor quickly entered the room, slammed the door, and moved directly at her. She was just lifting her hands—as if to protect her face—when the man drove his left hand into that spot just above her stomach where all the air in her lungs seemed to be collected, knocking the breath from her and leaving her gasping as he collected her up and dumped her into the laundry cart.

She was trying to fight, but the air was full of sparkling stars drifting past her nose. Her arms and legs were fumbling uselessly, and her hands felt swollen. She tried to push the clothes the janitor was piling atop her off, but her movements were vague and childish. She was curled like a child . . . like a child hiding in a basket. She was fighting . . . she was trying . . .

She was trying to breathe, trying to pull air into her screaming lungs. And she was beginning to do it through her open, straining mouth, shaped like an O . . .

Just as the janitor put a rag over her face.

And the smell of ether drowned the familiar face of the man who was kidnapping her. The familiar face, that she had not seen in years.

The familiar face . . .

The face . . .

Of a man who had tried to kidnap her once before, years ago . . .

As the happy man watched with a grin.

PART II

The Dead Man

FOUR

16

Parks led the way into the hall, closed Jessie's apartment door, and . . .

His personality completely changed.

"Okay," he said excitedly, putting his arm around Ellis' shoulder and pulling him in close with a grin. "Sonny, I'm tellin' ya, things are rollin' now!"

The throng of people in the hall was not nearly as thick as it had been when Parks had first arrived at noon, but the presence of so much activity when he had important, even amazing things to say still irritated him, so he led Ellis and the guard from the apartment toward the stairs. Just as they were passing the elevator, the doors slid open and people spilled out, leaving the car empty. Parks stepped inside, closed the door, and sighed contentedly at the silence blurring the babble of disrupted students and their parents. He closed his eyes, leaned his back against the wall for a second, and felt the elevator jerk as it headed for the lobby.

In his head a rush of information was spinning faster than the fast-forward image of Kevin Reynolds in his rubber suit had on Jessie's TV. He almost didn't know where to start. When he opened his eyes, Ellis was watching him expectantly, and the man from the apartment . . .

"What's your name?" Parks asked.

"Lemon. Sir."

. . . Lemon, Sir, was practically standing at attention, as if he thought there was a chance he might be subjected to some kind of an inspection at any instant.

Parks smiled. "At ease, soldier."

And Lemon's shoulders visibly sagged to a less exaggerated height beneath his ears.

The elevator door opened to reveal not the lobby, but a dingy room of concrete block in which one wall was lined with canvas laundry carts, and another with three pairs of washers and dryers. An old man in a khaki-colored uniform kept his head down as he pushed one of the laundry carts onto the elevator, forcing Parks and his two companions to exit. Ellis was about to protest, but Parks signaled for him to be still, allowing the doors to close.

Then he said, "Novak's still at the motel. I brought back the tape, and the notebook for Jessie to work on because I wanted to keep her on ice for a while. I've got guys watching for anybody fitting Reynolds' description going in or coming out of the building, so she'll be safer here than running around with us.

"But the big news is that I think I finally know why we were never able to get a handle on the fact that the Prisoner was two people. Jessie got my wheels turning on the idea when she said what she did about helping her uncle do his genealogical research. Remember?"

Ellis was nodding. "Yeah, I noticed that too. She said something about needing another pair of eyes to give you perspective on a complicated project or you ran the risk of getting things all jumbled up."

"Exactly." Parks grinned, and if any of the men who had called him the Dead Man over the years had seen him at that instant, they wouldn't have recognized him. His face was so full of life, and his eyes so bright with excitement and passion, that he looked as if he had lost twenty years off his age, and had recently had a booster shot of vitamins, and maybe even a little testosterone to boot . . . just for luck.

"And not only did she say that she believed the rule," he continued, "but also that she'd learned it from her uncle."

"So?" Lemon asked.

"So," Parks echoed, turning on him like a professor. "When Novak ran down the Vette, he found that it wasn't Reynolds who signed the register book at the motel."

"Christ!" Ellis said through his teeth. "He's got a partner?"

"He's got a *woman*!" Parks said, turning to Ellis triumphantly.

"Holy shit!" Ellis exclaimed, his jaw dropping slack. "Holy fucking Jesus! No wonder the profile's so fucked up! A woman! Fuck!"

"Right!" Parks grinned, slapping Ellis' back.

But Lemon was lost, and his facial expression broadcast it like a radio signal.

"We were looking for a man," Ellis explained without prompting.

"*One* man!" Parks chimed in.

"We were looking for one, single man, acting alone," Ellis returned. "And we were looking for him so hard, we weren't letting ourselves find anything else."

"Bingo!" Parks agreed. "Every goddamn personality profile we've ever run has come up the same: 'behavior indicates the presence of two distinct motivational patterns serving to negate the relationship of different acts.'"

"Translation," Ellis said. "We kept blowing the computer's mind because we were feeding information into it that it insisted came from two different sets of crimes. Its conclusion was that some of the killings were done by one individual who had certain ritualistic tendencies in relation to the disposition of his victims. And that the rest were the work of someone else, possibly a lot of someone elses, and that they had nothing to do with the first, positive ID."

"For years now, I've been arguing with a glorified adding machine," Parks complained. "I've been trying to convince it that I know what the hell I'm talking about. But since the machine didn't agree with me, the feds didn't either."

"And now it makes sense?" Lemon asked.

"You're goddamn right it makes sense," Parks said. "Now it makes so much sense that it doesn't make any sense at all anymore. Though we seem to have solved one mystery, our solution's created another one. Which is: how the hell would a nut like Kevin Reynolds end up picking a woman to partner up with?"

"And what kinda woman would get herself wrapped up with a he-man woman hater like him?" Ellis cut in.

"Hey," Lemon interrupted. "You guys are kinda leaving me in the dust here."

Lemon was a "hire-on," as Parks termed the temporary help. As such, the man's qualifications were in his specifics, which in this case Parks had set down as "young, physically fit, and willing and able to engage in deadly force when ordered to do so, without question."

They were getting near the end.

Parks could feel it.

And the end would entail some shooting . . .

He hoped.

But the hire-ons didn't need to know too terribly much about the details of the problem, and consequently, they didn't. All they were told was that Henry Parks was going to be their boss—spelled with a capital B the size of the Hoover Dam—that they were going to be chasing a very nasty killer with absolutely no redeeming social graces, and that their pay was going to be very, very good.

"Kevin Reynolds, Jessie's uncle"—Ellis pointed at the ceiling to indicate upstairs—"the guy in the videotape with the shock-therapy mask, has got a psych history as long as both your arms and the hood of your car. He's had so many doctors shrink his head it's amazing his eyeballs still fit."

"Profiles out the ass," Parks emphasized. "Since he was twelve years old. Enough documentation to drown a research grant. His old man had him studied inside and out until he was too old to be legally forced into therapy without a hostile commitment to an institution, although even then the kid agreed to sessions for a few years.

"And you should see the paper.

"It's like a road map, leading through every dip and valley in a classic aggressive, dysfunctional progression. When he was twelve he was busted for abusing his younger sister. Tied her up naked and shaved her head. Had an electric razor all buttered up with Vaseline, God knows why, and a clothes iron hot on the table next to her when his father broke it up.

"Imagine what finding his son doing something like that must have done to the old man. Christ! You just know that he figured it was his genes in the kid. He couldn't have helped but feel a little responsible, no matter what anybody said. It's no wonder he spent so much money trying to get the little shit bent back into shape.

"But it didn't work.

"The doctors put him through intensive tests, but his condition never really improved. His dysfunction centered on what seemed to be a deeply rooted, obsessional hatred of all things female. He confused arousal with disgust, attraction with repulsion, and desire with pain. His dreams were filled with vivid, all-consuming images of mouths filled with teeth, and black-hole tunnels to hell. He saw intentionally arranged, precognitive messages in the basic architectural structure of the buildings around him, and in the design of everyday things from toilet seats to shoes. He was screwed up good ... and tended to act on his terror by lashing out: verbally at first and then with his fists.

"During his years in therapy, he vacillated from complete denial, to confusion, to catatonic fits in which he'd just sit still for hours without acknowledging anyone or responding to stimulation. When he was talking, it was always to express paranoid delusions that his father and older sister were really not who they seemed to be, and that his mother was somehow hollow inside, and not really human. He felt that life was a series of tests designed to entrap a person who didn't see through the fabric of the trick to the pitfalls awaiting them. And he held fast to a disturbingly vivid scenario in which he would one day do something that would end, once and for all, this mental connection between himself and his father, because that's where he thought his bad dreams came from: his father. It was his father who had the problems, not him. And he resented his doctors for not being able to see that they were treating the wrong person.

"Of course, when questioned, the father had no idea what the kid was talking about. And the older sister, a nice girl who really didn't deserve all this shit, named Lisa, was appalled that her brother harbored such a maligned view of her as a person.

"The shock treatments went down when he was about seventeen. I've seen pictures of him during that time. He looked like he was a survivor of Auschwitz. Hollow eyes, gaunt, dried-up. An old man before he was even old enough to shave every day. It was during that same time that drugs were introduced into his therapy. And it's the drugs that seem to have brought him back around. He straightened up well enough to go to school, and he even struggled through college somehow. A real turnaround. A medical success . . .

"On the surface.

"But what I think happened is that all those doctors just taught him how to act sane, and didn't really do anything to cure him. They taught him the rules with the carrot and the stick until his psychosis went underground, so to speak."

"Jesus," Lemon said, shaking his head appreciatively. "You really know this shit. And after all that, all you want to do with the guy is kill him?"

"What else is there to do?" Ellis asked, his face darkening.

Lemon shrugged. "Well, Christ, I don't know. Maybe they could study him or something. You know, like maybe help somebody else after they see what went wrong with this guy."

"You don't study a mad dog," Ellis said, not even giving Parks an opportunity to open his mouth. "You shoot it. And that's what we're paying you for."

Lemon had made a tactical error, though he didn't seem to know exactly where it had started. But instead of trying to smooth it over by pursuing a subject he didn't really understand, he fell back on the old standby of any subordinate in such an awkward situation, which was to say, "Yes, sir!" and shut his mouth thereafter. That seemed to satisfy Ellis, the liaison who ran most of the interference between Henry Parks and the various police organizations he dealt with.

Ellis' reputation was well known around the country. He was an FBI man who had taken a two-year leave of absence in order to help Parks full-time. It was said that after his initial involvement with Parks he had been so impressed with the efficiency and dedication to purpose of the hunt that he was willing to stay on the trail for as long as it took, even if that meant never returning to his government position. But Parks wouldn't hear of him sacrificing his pension in that way. He was steadfast in his assurances that the Prisoner mystery was on the verge of being solved, and that Wilson "Sonny Boy" Ellis was going to be in at the kill.

Lemon's faux pas changed the tenor of the meeting, and Parks assumed a more commanding tone and bearing. He stopped trying to explain his thinking, at least in front of Lemon, who wasn't one who needed to know any of this anyway, and laid out what he had learned from a man in the local police station about the specifics of the terror Kevin Reynolds had caused earlier that morning.

"He blew up the old lady's house with a plastic explosive, probably rigged on some kind of motion trigger that the cops set off while moving from the front of the house to the back," he said. "He accomplished the decapitation of the woman by means of what appears to have been a very large, heavily weighted knife: like maybe a machete. According to a guy on the ambulance, it looked as if the killing stroke came in one clean motion."

"How much do the cops know about Reynolds?" Ellis asked, in a tone of professional detachment, as if Lemon had been sucked off the face of the planet.

"Practically nothing," Parks returned. "They're scrambling around looking for information, but they've got a lot of catching up to do. They haven't traced the Vette to the motel yet because it's registered in Columbus, and for all they know that's where it came from. Novak'll have the place cleaned out in an hour or so, and we're paying the desk clerk to keep quiet."

"Who's flying Reynolds' mother out?"

"We are."

"No word on Lisa Reynolds yet?"

"None. She hasn't lived at home in years. Her brother's problems drove her out."

"And what if the local cops connect Kevin to Jessie and decide to come around and talk to her?"

"She won't be home. Everybody's moved out of the building."

"Are we responsible for the move?"

"No. But it's convenient."

"Why is everybody moving now?"

Parks' eyes misted a little and he drifted off with the question. It was one that had been bothering him, and he decided it was time to clear it up.

"Lemon, head over to the records bureau and find out who owns this building, contact them, and see why the place is being emptied today."

Lemon accepted his orders gratefully, as if he felt relieved at the prospect of having something to do that would take him away from the ruminations of the higher-ups.

His good mood was gone, Parks realized with a start. He didn't know where it had fled to, but such was the makeup of his personality. His own psychiatrist, the one who had spent six months after his injuries trying to help him "accept the trauma of a major affront to the physical integrity of your body, and the emotional integrity of your masculinity"—what a dink—had noted his tendency toward a certain "manic-depressive frame of mind, depending on how engaged your attention is at the moment." That was about the only observation that the man could be credited with making that made any sense:

Parks felt good when he was working, and useless when he wasn't.

And it was time to get back to it.

He led the way back up in the elevator and entered the flood of people in the lobby, exiting just as a uniformed policeman came blowing off the staircase with a woman partner who wasn't in the least bit winded from the climb. Their frustrated faces told Parks their story. The local cops were sharper than he'd expected. They'd already connected Jessie to Kevin Reynolds and had come to see her . . .

But the guys upstairs had had enough sense to keep the doors locked.

He smiled.

It certainly paid to employ men who could use their heads.

17

Christ! the Prisoner exclaimed in his mind as the elevator door opened in the basement laundry room and he found himself almost face-to-face with Henry Parks.

He had to consciously restrain himself from launching his body over the canvas cart and putting his hands around Parks' throat to finish the job he'd started twenty years before—the job that only Molaine could have prevented him from completing.

But he didn't launch himself to the attack. Instead he jerked his head down, moved past without so much as a stutter in his step, and went upstairs to take Jessie as he knew he needed to do.

The guards in her apartment were child's play—your typical incomplete cybernetic junk that populated the fringes of the Zone. The further away from the major players in his punishment you went, the further from complete personalities did the sundry cyborgs have. They were like clay pigeons by the time you got to the guards. They fell like lead.

When the elevator doors opened on the basement again, with Jessie hidden under the laundry in the cart, the Prisoner's heart was pounding so hard he was a little afraid that it might pop.

What if Parks and his two cronies were still down there?

What would he do?

But the three men were gone, and he scurried across the laundry room and through the back door in privacy. The cart bumped when he dumped it over, but Jessie didn't stir as she tumbled out onto the floor. He gathered her up in his arms, thrilled that she was so petite that he could still carry her, even after all these years during which his body had gone so frail, carrying her down the second set of stairs to the subbasement, where he had hammered the boy who had come looking for her about five hours before. After sliding open the wall panel to the tunnel, he considered putting her in the same cell with the last parasite he'd taken—at about one o'clock that morning—but decided against it. She deserved her own cell. So he gave her one.

Laying her down, he could not hold himself back from taking a moment to examine her lovely face: that beatific, adorable visage that he thought so resembled his own . . . as it should have, because, after all . . .

She was his daughter.

And he was the most beautiful man he had ever seen.

Even in the Zone, he had retained his beauty . . . or at least he had until recently. They had allowed him that—his beauty— and his glimpses of home over the night sea. Those two things had kept him sane over here. Only those two things were strong enough to have done it. If either had been held back from him, he knew that he would not have been psychologically strong enough to carry on as well as he had. He'd have fallen apart, ending up a random entity in a world of random entities, completely incapable of performing his task so that he would become an unwillingly permanent resident in the Zone . . . a "lifer," as the term went, with his physical body frozen like a statue where it lay strapped to the punishment table, and his eyes staring blankly ahead until he died of old age without ever again knowing the simple peace of occupying one physical world, and one mental reality. How long would it seem like he suffered then? Ten thousand years? A million? Eons?

The prospect was horrendous and had spurred serious legal and ethical debate at home. Was it humane, it was argued, to continue relentlessly punishing someone long after he had lost any idea of why he was being punished, or even that he was being punished at all? What was the point? Did it make any sense to so thoroughly confuse a man as to his place in the world that he couldn't understand that his punishment was over once he was allowed out of the Zone?

It had happened that way, or so the Prisoner had heard. There were recorded cases of men who, having been brought back home after their tasks were finished, refused to believe that their ordeals were over. These men, it was said, thought that they had entered another stage of their sentence, and even professionally administered readjustment sessions had been unable to convince them otherwise. So instead of a rehabilitated citizen with a sense of creativity and interest in life, the state was duly presented with a ruined husk of a man who might perform any labor set for him in strict obedience, but who never actually believed that the world around him was real. Such a man was reduced to a plane of existence similar to the cybertrons populating the Punishment Zone, and were useful as factory workers, and soldiers, but as human beings . . .

They were referred to as being "Zoned."

And someone who was Zoned was forever after considered an "it," and never a "he."

But such was not the Prisoner's fate, because he had two crystal-clear kernels of remembered truth stored safely away in the treasure chest of his mind. Vaulted permanently side by side, these memories were of his own face as it had appeared before it began degenerating in the Zone, and of the picture-perfect landscape from which he had come, first emerging on the Zone's beachy shore, dripping wet, and confused, shortly after his crime . . .

His first set of recollections was centered on his life before the crime, when, at home in the "real world," he had been happy and free. The specifics of this time were often so clear as to make him ache, and little things like the way the moon glinted on an icy road, or the sound of an autumn wind rustling leaves, could raise a nostalgic tear so bitter that he sometimes wept aloud.

The second part of his personal history was a chronology of the events that had transpired since he had first awakened to find himself in the Punishment Zone. These memories were as substantial as the first set, and provided him with a detailed portrait of his life's direction during these past twenty-one years.

But the last set, the strip of confused information that lay between, was of that transitional period through which he had passed from one world to another, from reality to the Zone. It apparently was not a simple journey, nor was it one that was entirely smooth. He remembered some of the events quite well, but others, well, he just didn't have a handle on them at all.

What he remembered about the transition started just after the crime itself. As soon as he had done that terrible deed he'd known that he had made a profound mistake, and that he would end up regretting it for a very long time. But he hadn't been able to help himself. She was perfect, lovely, and available for the first time in exactly the right way. He'd been drinking, so had she, so had everyone around them, and the atmosphere had been one of relaxed limits and easy transgression—a stage set for tragedy.

But that didn't change the magnitude of his affront. And it didn't buffer his poor judgment. No sooner was he on his feet, standing over her body, than the wash of guilt assailed him with all its gut-wrenching force. It literally took his breath away just contemplating what he'd done, and in a fit of sheer animal panic, he ran from the building and into the night.

The moon blinked merrily overhead, drifting through a clear sky. Music played in the distance, and the streets were empty. Launching himself at his car, he tried, through the use of speed, to escape the sensation of rolling power that seemed to be gathering behind him, racing down roads he had never driven before and seeing, in his rearview mirror, the twinkling lights of the city on the horizon behind him, pursuing him with all their undeniable authority, as if the glass itself held the reality and was not a mirror at all, but a window through space to a place capable of being held in a state beyond the laws of man.

And in truth, that was very much what the city was. The Prisoner's society had evolved into one that respected individual responsibility over everything else, and that required its citizens to maintain a strict code of ethics in their lives. Human dignity was paramount to its very fabric, to its success and power, and its moral correctness was represented by the complexity and beauty of its architecture. Seeing the buildings silhouetted against the night sky terrified the fleeing man, who, though he knew intellectually that his flight was in vain, could not prevent his animal side from making him want to run and hide.

"God!" he cried aloud, tears streaming down his face and his knuckles white on the steering wheel. "Oh, God! Why?! Why did I do it? Why did you *let* me do it?!"

The sensation of something building, a collecting force of growing consciousness that was the indignation of the good and decent society behind him, rolled like thunder over the city, focusing its energy and prickling the nape of the man's sweating neck. If the sky itself should crack and air come rushing down to crush him, it would have been no more than was his due, no less than he deserved. If he should be found by a mob, pulled from his car, and strung up from the nearest tree, naked by the neck, for people to gawk at until dogs ate his legs off to the knees and his head was pulled from his spine by the weight of his bloated body, he could not have disagreed with his treatment. He was a worm, a filthy scum on the clear pool of society's silver water. He was a man lower than dirt . . .

And everyone knew it.

Already, even before any physical act indicated that he would be apprehended, his punishment had begun inside his mind. As tears streamed down his face, the images of the girl he had so cherished began changing in his head. He blinked, grimaced, and hissed, "No!" between his teeth, feeling simultaneously the ever-increasing pressure of the anger building in the air behind him, and a sinuous, slithering tentacle of cold flesh squirming through the back of his skull, worming around his brain, and coiling behind his eyes. He shook his head, his entire body reacting to the feeling as one hand went automatically to his face and pressed trembling fingertips to the flesh of his cheek.

There were pictures flashing in his mind now, quickly and then disappearing, only to be replaced by others. It was as if a stranger had found a photo album and was paging through it, pausing at different shots and then proceeding on in search of something interesting. Most of the pictures faded quickly. But the ones of her . . .

"No!" he cried, swerving the car on the wet pavement as the speedometer climbed toward seventy miles an hour. "Leave her alone! Don't you touch her."

The girl was magnificent. In every instance her face was perfect, her eyes a clear, icy blue so true as to resemble the finest gems. Her skin was pale, and rich, lacking so much as a blemish. And her hair was heartbreaking—so blond as to shine with what looked like its own light. She was an angel, growing up behind his eyes, developing from a toothless, grinning baby to a delightful toddler, to a sweet schoolgirl, to an adolescent ripe with the budding promise of womanhood. But it was as if a brute were fingering fine pieces of porcelain plucked from a curio shelf. These fragile curiosities, which were in truth the man's life as he'd known it to that time, were being handled gently for the present, but there was an implied expectation that at any instant the gentleness would vanish and one of these irreplaceable pieces would slip fatally to the floor.

"Oh, God!" the man begged aloud. "Please. For the love of Christ! Don't do that!"

And it was his own guilt that was leading his tormentors to him, opening the way for their rebuke. It was the beacon of his overpowering shame that was showing those who would see him suffer exactly which of the memory-pictures they chose to cull were the most precious to him. And he couldn't help it. He reacted physically to the memory of the girl on the morning of her fifth birthday . . . the birthday on which she'd received her first bicycle: sky-blue, with long white streamers hanging off the handlebars. She had been so pleased with the gift that her smile had outshone the sun on that bright August morning when the little family was gathered together in love.

But as he watched, the image changed.

Was twisted.

Behind his eyes.

"No! Please! Not that!"

The car swerved, squealing tires in the dark as another car appeared around a corner. The man had drifted off his side of the road, and adjusted only in time to avoid the oncoming machine, which bumped onto the shoulder, stopped, cocked its wheels, and started flashing red and blue lights in a dusty cloud.

But the Prisoner didn't care.

He saw only the little girl on her new blue bike . . .

Her new blue bike bought not for her birthday . . .

"No . . . please . . ."

But as a bribe to keep her quiet after what he'd done to her the previous day.

"Oh, Lord . . ."

It suddenly wasn't a fine morning that he remembered anymore, but a gloomy afternoon the day after the police had come. He wasn't a good father with a loving child, but a terrible man with a secret, trying to blame others for his failings, and to buy off a child's affections though she was truly afraid of him. The woman standing behind the little girl was no longer beaming at him with devotion and love, but grimacing through a forced smile as she held up the bike for the child to sit on, both of them knowing that if they didn't do what they were told the old man would get nasty and yell at them, or hit them, or something worse, because he wasn't the perfect husband and father that he had just been a couple of seconds ago, but that he was, in fact, a beast, a louse, a sick, twisted specimen of a lying pervert who . . .

"Don't do this to me!" the man shouted as the memories in his mind were modified by that reaching touch.

Lights flashed madly behind him but he did not slow down. He was driving faster . . . eighty, ninety miles an hour over twisting, two-laned streets through a tiny town, heading for the bridge over the river and away from the city where he lived. Streetlamps flashed overhead in a single blur of white, and a moaning siren pursued him as the sensation of impending power swelled to the bursting point and the collective, invisible wrath of a vengeful society came hurling at him.

It was at the bridge, a single-laned affair covered over with a barnlike roof, when everything came together and knocked him into the Zone.

The bridge was ahead, and he was concentrating on trying to keep his memories as they had been and not let them be changed. The river was glimmering beneath the moon, looking so welcoming that he thought he might actually make it across . . . because, for some reason that he could not explain to himself, he had the feeling that if he could just get across that bridge and over the river before the city sent his fate crashing down on him, then everything would be all right. So he was straining, pressing his aching foot into the floorboards with the accelerator pedal beneath it, and leaning so far forward that the steering wheel rubbed his chest. The opening of the bridge yawned as blackly as a mine shaft, and the police were just coming up over the hill behind him as . . .

An explosion of silver light blazed up in the bridge's arched mouth, and the Prisoner shrieked, pulling the steering wheel to the right as a truck materialized directly in his path. His car was launched, as if out of an immense cannon, over the curb with a crash and hail of sparks, through a yellow guardrail and into the air. The engine screamed as the machine entered free space, and the world tilted madly ahead. Then came a crash, and a sickening sensation of pressure, and then came darkness, and cold, and . . .

This is where that jumbled conundrum of misdirected memory that lay between the Prisoner's life in the real world and in the Punishment Zone begins.

Things get fuzzy.

And the pieces don't always fit.

The next thing he knew he was standing on the bank of the river. He was soaking wet and facing a very black place with few features save for the tangle of leaves and twisted branches that shimmered with reflected, pulsating light. He was knee-deep in icy water, and his clothes weighed about a thousand pounds. His entire body was numb, except for his head, which lurched with his every heartbeat and roared with a sound like that of wind being forced through pipes far too narrow for the purpose. It was almost a whistling sound that he heard. And then came a thunderous crash and he staggered and was on his knees on rocks. And then he was up. And then there were men in white, and a woman with rubber tubes . . .

But no.

Because first there was the water again.

And he was turning to see one car sitting on the opposite bank of the river behind a drifting grey cloud of exhaust that vibrated with twirling emergency lights as two men climbed down after him. And another car, or rather a truck, which was also sitting in a cloud of exhaust, parked at the side of the road where a man was standing by an open side door, silhouetted in the mist, his arms hanging down at his sides. And yet another car, one with a very familiar back end, jutting up out of a bubbling pool of water as black as ink with taillights blinking an amazing, redundant hazard signal of red, red, red.

But over it all was the city. And, from where the Prisoner was standing, dripping wet and dizzy, he could see the majesty of the place, its glimmering skyline and ominous, portentous size, jutting up over the feeble line of trees that was the horizon, undeniably justified in its action, which had been to pass its judgment on a fleeing felon.

"The punishment has begun!" the Prisoner's racing mind screamed down his spine for the rest of his body to hear. The sentence was unclear, the specifics even more vague. But the change had happened sometime while his car was in flight over the river, and now he was standing, facing the opposite direction from which he had been going in his haste, confronted by his invisible accusers as two dark figures splashed into the water, and the silent, beautiful city looked down on him in his shame.

The time between the river and the hospital was a single line of unclear motions and bouncing images. It was during that time, the Prisoner was sure, that his physical body had been taken from the scene of the "accident" in the real world and transported to wherever it was that a prisoner's body was kept while his sentence was served. He seemed to recall seeing the vehicle they moved him in as brightly lit in the Zone, all full of attendants and shiny steel, while in the back of his mind he saw the real-world ambulance as a kind of hearse, or morgue vehicle, lacking so much as a single guard and driven by one sober man who never even looked back over his shoulder to see how his charge was bearing up.

He heard voices during this period, of that much he was certain. They said things that didn't make sense about his physical injuries—apparently part of his sentence was to come into the Zone in pain—and they also described much of what his sentence would entail, and the purposes for each of the specifics . . . though these explanations were couched in mystic references designed to make him work for their true meaning. Some of the things he heard he did not understand for years . . . until Molaine appeared.

Molaine came because, even with all the information he had been given, the Prisoner never did understand everything without him.

Molaine was almost like an exclamation point at the end of the paragraph that was the prisoner's docket.

"Do you remember how you got out of the car?" a woman asked sometime after he came awake in the hospital.

Her voice was toneless but helpful. Her hair, a rat's nest of grey and blond wisps, was poked through with pins beneath her peaked white paper tiara. She had long red fingernails, and a little badge on her meager breast that said "Cynthia Porter" over a strip of radiation-sensitive material that she explained away as her "glow button." She said that she was required by the hospital's radiology department to turn the badge in at the end of each week so that they could keep a record of her exposure level, even though everyone knew that people who worked with X rays all died young. She didn't know what good the glow button was except maybe for giving her an excuse to live her life as if every day were her last.

"Know what I mean?"

The Prisoner listened to Cynthia Porter jabber brightly as she adjusted the portable X-ray machine over him. He was lying in traction, in the ICU ward, studying her with steely hard eyes from behind the bandages covering his face, and wondering how the hell he was supposed to relate to her. She was so alien that he stiffened with fright every time she reached down to touch him, and her references to current events, like Vietnam and civil rights, were like listening to a foreign language. Apparently, she was younger than she looked. But what was young for a creature like this? He had no point of reference. He had nothing. When the "doctors" came, he remained mute. And the same for when he was examined by the "nurses" or the "specialists" or visited by his "family."

His "family" was admittedly the hardest to face because they were not exactly his family anymore. They were the new family that his modified memories—and modified life—provided him with. Where he had always enjoyed the warm glow of true love from his wife and children, he was now the subject of their wary, caged-animal looks. They were mistreated innocents who were trying hard to hide their secret desire that the monster—him—who was responsible for all their suffering should die and set them free.

It broke his heart the way his "wife" dutifully sat at the side of his bed, holding his hand when the doctors allowed her to do so, and repeating softly to him that "everything's going to be all right, darling," without sincerity or feeling. And the kids, God ... he'd actually cried—real tears, which caused a bit of a stir among the staff and sent two pasty young women running for a doctor should he damage his dressings. Even though he knew that these cyborgs were only artificial re-creations of his own children, they looked so authentic that his heart nearly broke when he saw them standing back from his bed as if loath to approach it. His real children would have been all over him. It would have taken half the staff of the hospital's trauma wing to keep them from hugging him, crying, and pleading with him not to die.

"They said that your car sailed thirty feet into the river," Cynthia Porter said, tightening the belt on the lead vest she wore and triggering the X-ray machine, which went *zzzit, ping* and was done. "Another ten feet and you'd have been on the other side. It's amazing you weren't killed. But I'd still like to know how you got out of the car underwater like that."

So would I, the Prisoner thought.

When he was alone, he studied things, moving his hands over the sheets and himself as much as he dared because even the slightest alteration in his position sent glass beads and plastic tubes tinkling, which invariably brought a nurse on the run. But what touching he could covertly engage in, he did, marveling at the substance of this fantasy world, impressed beyond all measure at just how real everything felt. If he didn't know better, he would have sworn that nothing physical had actually changed, but that the entirety of his punishment had been accomplished by some clever surgery that simply altered his perception of the things around him.

But he knew that that was wrong because every so often he'd glimpse a seam ... like the time he was observing a member of the cleaning crew mopping the floor in his cubicle. The woman had finished the area directly in front of his bed when she reached over and opened a door to a tiny bathroom he had seen a doctor or two use in the past. With the door open, the woman stuck the mop inside and swished it around a few times before leaving, but instead of the bathroom the Prisoner had expected to see, there had been nothing inside the room . . . not a thing! The door opening was filled with absolute darkness, and it was like seeing a theater's chipped brick wall through a hole torn in a stage's florid backdrop. It glared at him until the woman blocked his view by closing the door again and moving off to mop something else. It had only been a glimpse. But it had been enough to convince him that the things he saw around him were nothing but a veil. They covered his consciousness with illusions of reality that looked, felt, and smelled authentic, but that were actually a clever charade through which he would need to pass before returning home.

And then there was the Night Shore, which he visited by means of a drug.

One day, he didn't know how many into his sentence but it couldn't have been more than five or six, a doctor came and stood at the side of his bed. After looking down at him for a long time, the young man took a deep breath and started talking.

"I assume you can hear me?" he asked.

And the Prisoner looked at him from within the depths of his swaddling bandages.

"You've been conscious long enough that I'm hoping you've reordered yourself."

Reordered . . . now, there was a word!

"You're very lucky to be alive."

Lucky?

"But I'm afraid there are complications in your new condition."

The Prisoner listened, trying to decide exactly what was happening with this man. He looked like a cyborg, but he spoke words that were closer to his understanding. Maybe they were finally going to tell him what he was doing here and what was expected of him before they'd let him out.

"I know you're listening," the doctor continued. "And this is between you and me."

He took another deep breath, and the Prisoner noticed that his hands were clenched into fists.

"Your wife and I have been talking," he went on uneasily. "And though she hasn't come right out and made any accusations, I've seen symptoms of abuse before, and I've seen lives ruined by sin.

"What I'm saying is that you've been given a second chance. You've had a lot of trouble in your life, and you nearly died. You should have died. But you were spared. Now, I don't know if you believe in God, but I do. I've taken Jesus into my life as my personal savior. I've been saved by his love, and from where I'm standing it looks to me as if God's love has sent you a pretty clear message to change your ways.

"I'm not making any accusations. I'm simply pointing out that not everybody gets a chance to prove themselves like you've gotten. Not everyone can start over and erase their mistakes. You've got a chance to make things over. To do things right. To make things as they were before your troubles started. Don't mess it up. Do you understand?"

It was just at this moment when the first real pain the Prisoner could remember since the "accident" hit, emphasizing the doctor's message with an underscoring so profound that only a corpse could have missed it. A bright white light started right behind the doctor's head, blossoming out and wiping the Prisoner's vision clean.

The next thing he knew, the doctor was standing there again, drawing back with a syringe in his hand and an unsettling look in his eyes. He watched for a moment and then seemed to notice something that caused him to say, "That's the complication I was talking about. We don't know why, but you seem to be having some kind of seizures. You display some very strange brain patterns while unconscious, and you just did it again. Other than your obvious injuries, the broken bones and abrasions, you seem to have some . . . dysfunction." He paused. "Are you there?"

The Prisoner blinked.

"It might be chemical in nature. Or it might be a hidden injury we haven't found yet. We just don't know exactly, so until we figure it out, all I can do is try to keep you stable."

He held out the syringe and the Prisoner's eyes settled on it as if it were something magical.

"This is a new tranquilizer. You've been responding to it better than anyone I've seen so far. Now you just lie back and think about what I was saying about making amends. This could be a whole new world for you, if you let it. If you really tried you could do penance for your transgressions and be shown the gates to paradise. Don't let your chance go by. It's not even important that the things you do be directly related to your previous mistakes. As a matter of fact, it would probably be better if you changed things close to them, instead of dredging up old pains. If you could make things different without stirring up a lot of resentments and troubles, you'd be surprised at just how different your life could be."

The Prisoner listened and then closed his eyes. His head was throbbing, and a dull ache muted the area around his elbow where the doctor must have administered the syringe. A weird, disjointed sensation of floating overcame him, and even though he popped his eyes open, he could not make them stay that way. They suddenly felt so heavy that he grew frightened enough to try and speak for the first time, but to his horror, his lips would not part. His entire body had become as thick as concrete, and in his mind, he drifted, spinning . . . seeing himself spinning, through a darkness that took him to a . . .

Shore.

A Night Shore.

And he stopped fighting in light of the view he was seeing.

It was of the city . . .

Home.

The world!

The specifics of the vision were similar to the last glimpse he had seen of the city immediately after his accident. There was the city, ominous and dark against a poorly lit night sky, twinkling in all its golden perfection. But instead of standing on a riverbank, the Prisoner found himself on a sandy beach. How far the ocean stretched before touching the shore of the city on the horizon was impossible to judge. But be it a mile, or a thousand miles, the Prisoner knew that it was too far for him to ever swim. He was barred from this place by an uncharitable gulf, and could do nothing but gaze up in awe at that place he had so foolishly thrown away when he had flaunted its laws.

This was the Night Shore.

And this was the vision he would use to stay sane for the next twenty years.

But if he had known at the time of his hospital confinement that he was going to be spending twenty years in the Zone, he wouldn't have been able to stand it. At the time he was too busy trying to sort through the tangle of new things happening to him each moment to think about the implications of his presence. All he knew was that he was not where he was supposed to be, and that he wanted to go home. That was the paramount thought in his mind: going home. But as the days passed, his wounds started healing, the visits of his family became more regular, and the little details of everyday life started repeating themselves and becoming familiar.

He'd been in the hospital for six weeks when a pair of policemen came to tell him that, in light of his nearly having been killed, and the intervention of some influential, unnamed parties, the charges of reckless operation of a motor vehicle he normally would have been facing had been dropped.

Flowers, cards, and candy from some very famous people he had done genealogical work for in the past cluttered the room around him as he silently lay, receiving his pain shots and drifting off to the Night Shore to spend time gazing at the unreachable city across the waves. His wife's hand in his almost always greeted him when he returned, until one day, pulling himself back up from the depths of a drug-induced visit to the Shore, he came round to find his wife and daughter looking down at him apprehensively. When his eyes flickered, his daughter's hand brushed her mother's shoulder and she whispered, "Darling, are you awake? We've something important to tell you."

The Prisoner nodded. Still, even after . . . what was it, six weeks? Eight? . . . he had not spoken. And he was very seriously considering never speaking while in the Zone at all. He didn't want his Punishers to have the satisfaction of hearing the fear in his voice as he begged for mercy, which he knew he'd do if he so much as opened his mouth.

So he nodded.

And his wife said, "We're going to be grandparents."

And that was all.

That did it.

The news was like a bolt of lightning.

The Prisoner's eyes moved to the girl standing at his bedside, the perfect, beautiful girl with the heartbreakingly golden hair and the blue eyes as clear as the finest gems, and he saw through her, literally, for an instant, into her body to where the child she was carrying was growing . . . her child . . . and his . . .

His crime.

His misdeed.

His shame.

Not only had he assaulted her, he'd impregnated her as well. They . . . the authorities . . . the Punishers in all their twisted wisdom, had deemed it appropriate that he should see the result of his transgression bear fruit . . . in the most literal way imaginable. The idea that a daughter should bear her father's child.

"His name is Michael, Daddy," the girl said, interrupting the Prisoner's thoughts. "And I love him very much. We're getting married just as soon as you can get out of bed and be at the wedding."

There were tears in the girl's eyes. My God! There were actual, honest-to-Christ tears glimmering in her eyes. She was crying. She was wringing a tissue into a tiny little ball, she was chewing her lower lip in fear, she was pregnant, and she thought it was her boyfriend who'd done it, she didn't know that it had been her father, and she and the boyfriend—Michael? Michael who?—were getting married, and she wanted him, her father, her loving, doting, raping, son-of-a-bitching father, *to be there* when she married her boyfriend who was not the father of her baby but who thought he was and who would do just fine as long as the kid wasn't born retarded or something because of the genes being mixed too tight.

And then, in a flash of insight and understanding that came from somewhere very close to the Prisoner's heart, he grasped it all, saw it all, and embraced his position and task as being comprehensible and, in a way, just. He saw the logic of it, and the cruelty. He saw the simple balance of it and marveled that it had taken him so long to figure it out and that he had not seen it coming.

Of course the girl was pregnant.

She'd have to be.

And of course she didn't know it was him who had made her that way. That would have been unacceptable.

So this was where he stood:

He was a prisoner in a hostile world in which everything he saw and felt was specifically designed with the purpose of tormenting him in mind. The whole world, everything, was centered around him, and causing him pain and discomfort was the world's ultimate purpose. He was a stranger here, but no one knew it. He was infiltrating an alien society that had a very different understanding of him than he did of himself. The cybertrons that were playing the parts of his family and friends all remembered him as being different than he remembered himself. In their view he was a beast with a history of abusing his wife and children. In the logic of this world it was that abuse that had ultimately culminated in his sexually molesting his own daughter, and now his daughter was pregnant with his child, although she thought it was someone else's.

It made sense.

And he would have to deal with it.

And he did.

With his wife holding his hand, and his daughter standing over him with tears in her eyes, he opened his mouth and spoke for the first time since he had entered the Zone. His words were carefully calculated, and sincere. And they were the first part of the façade he would need to build and maintain if he was ever going to achieve his ultimate goal.

"I . . ." he started, his voice weak and cracking. "I . . . have something important to say."

Both women at his bedside leaned in closer, their faces fitful knots of concern and their eyes brimming with tears.

"I know I haven't been right . . ." the Prisoner said, almost choking on the content of his statement but determined not to let his internal disgust at having to lie so thoughtlessly damage the sincerity of his tone. "I know that I've been a selfish, heartless man . . ."

His wife and daughter actually made to protest, but he lifted his hand feebly and silenced them.

"Please," he strained in contrite piety. "Don't. You're both so good, and so beautiful, and so wonderful to have put up with me all these years . . . after all I've done, the drinking, and the rest . . ."

They were all crying now, all three of them, and the Prisoner was amazed at just how easily he was able to make the tears roll from his eyes.

"I've been doing a lot of thinking, lying here these past . . ."

"Seven," his wife whispered.

"Seven," the Prisoner said, "weeks. I've had a lot of time to go over my life and think about all the things I've done."

He would have listed a few of the terrible things he was responsible for, but he couldn't think of any. But by their faces, he could tell that both his wife and daughter were able to supply plenty of their own examples, and he let them fill in the blanks for themselves as he went on, pleading for their forgiveness and swearing that he had undergone a complete change of heart while lying at death's doorstep, with his devoted family ever-present and ready, nurturing him with their love, which, though he had not earned it in the past, he intended very much to earn in the future.

"You've wasted a lot of pure and sincere affection on a man who thought of no one but himself," he said, his lips trembling with emotion and his wife's hand clutched tightly in both of his as he strained to lift himself into a sitting position on the bed. "You, my sweet daughter, have had your childhood tarnished by the cloud of a father with no self-control, with the embarrassment of never being able to bring friends home for fear of what they might have seen . . ."

"Daddy, don't," the girl cried.

"No, it's true," he insisted, taking her hand so that he held both his wife and his daughter simultaneously. "I'm not going to deny it anymore. Pretending that something isn't true is no way to live.

"All I'm asking is for a second chance. I know it's a lot to expect after all the suffering I've put you through. But if God can give me another shot, and He did, make no mistake about that, I figure that my wife and kids might be able to see their way clear to giving the old man another swing at being the kind of father and husband I know I can be.

"I've relived every mistake I've ever made these past few weeks. Lying here with my bones aching and my mind numb on dope, I've seen every bad thing I've ever done in my life as if it were happening right now. It's been awful, and ugly. Even more so because I know that every ugly thing I've seen was my own fault. I can't stand it, but it's over, and all I can do is try to fill the years I have left with as much love and good works as I can and hope that you all will forgive me a little, if you can . . . Because I didn't really mean to hurt you. I just didn't know any better. I just didn't think!"

And then he cried, and his wife threw her arms around him, and so did his daughter, and they practically destroyed the spider's web of monitor cords that the doctors had spent so much careful time weaving over him, and nurses came running, and even a priest showed up—God knows from where—and it was an honest-to-goodness dramatic moment for them all. The Prisoner included. It was a miracle, or so everyone said. It was an example of the mysterious ways in which God does His work, taking a sinner like him and straightening him out once and for all by showing him the error of his ways.

And, wow, wasn't it something!

And . . .

The whole time, the Prisoner studied faces. He watched them through his own tears, monitoring the effect his words had on different people and noting every reaction because if he could learn to play these cyborgs like musical instruments, then the task of erasing his mistake would be all the easier.

And Jessie's eyes flickered.

The cell was dark and cold. Jessie was lying on an old mattress on the floor, and a single shaft of light was cutting its way into the room from the open door. That door was behind where the Prisoner was standing, hovering over the girl and studying her face with the intensity of an artist. For years he had done this, covertly, it was true, but he had done it with a mix of pleasure and terror since the girl was born. His features were emblazoned on Jessie's face, and he could pick them out when he tried: the fine form of the jawline, running softly from the ear to the chin, not too harsh, but with a subtle curve that implied strength beneath a veneer of sensitivity and grace; the full lips, quick to smile; the polished forehead; and skin free of blemish—why, she hadn't even had pimples when she was a teenager. All the things he remembered about her were there . . . and more. Since he had last been able to see her from this close she had become a real woman. She looked so much like her mother. Her poor, deluded, dead mother . . .

Whose hair was so blond that it was heartbreaking.

The Prisoner had been watching Jessie from afar for years. But now . . .

Her eyelids flickered again, and the Prisoner stifled a squeak of excitement as he momentarily panicked.

What to do?

Should he let her see him again?

Should he lock the door?

Yes!

He should back away, get out of here, leave her alone before . . .

"No!" his mind protested.

But there was no denying it.

He should get away before that same desire that had led him to his crime on the other side, in the world, drew him down to her and forced him to repeat his atrocity with his own daughter again . . .

A different daughter.

But she looked so much like him.

The whole world was out to get him.

"No!"

The time wasn't right.

And Jessie's eyes flickered for a third time, and opened, bleary, unfocused, searching in the darkness until they settled on his face. He was panting, for God's sake. And he could just imagine what he must look like hovering over her this way. He was panting like an animal. But he couldn't help it. She opened her eyes, looked at him, settled, and then broke. Her face changed. Her brows knit. Her mouth opened and it looked very much as if she intended to scream for an instant during which the Prisoner almost screamed himself, from the portent of it, from the sheer emotion of coming together again after so many years apart.

Jessie looked as if she were about to scream.

But she didn't.

Instead, she mouthed one simple word, as a question, before rolling her eyes and laying her head back as the anesthetic the Prisoner had used on her reclaimed her protesting mind.

One word she whispered.

But it made the Prisoner nearly swoon with pleasure.

One word.

She whispered . . .

"Grandpa?"

18

Kevin Reynolds watched from the fringes of the world as the authorities mounted their best efforts to find him on the morning after his "coming out." For the first time in his life he was able to hang around and actually follow the process of the hunt. And it was a very educational experience. He'd never imagined it could be so interesting, which was lucky, because, if he'd have known that it would be so much fun he just might have done it earlier, at different crime sites over the years, and that would surely have led to his capture. It was self-restraint and inhuman cunning that had kept his identity a secret all these years. And it was his training that had kept his mind on course from the start, to now.

The start, he remembered, had been during the first week that his father, Eugene Reynolds, had come home from the hospital after wrecking his car on a road not far from the Phi Tau fraternity house, which had been converted into the apartment building where Jessie lived today. What he had been doing driving so fast so early in the morning on that particular road was a mystery. The police said that he was behaving as if someone were chasing him, although no other car was ever observed. Some college kids said later that they had seen him at a fraternity party earlier in the evening, and that he was drinking and carrying on as if he weren't forty years old, but twenty, like them. So maybe he'd been drunk. No one knew, and he wasn't talking. All he was doing was repenting for all the bad things he'd done in his life before the accident, and acting as if he had seen the error of his ways and come in from the cold of a mean man's solitude, to the warmth of human contact.

Which was bullshit, and Kevin knew it.

The old man had seen the error of his ways, all right, but it had nothing to do with the things he'd done . . . it had to do with the way he'd done them.

"Never get caught . . ."

It became a constant refrain in the back of Kevin's mind. It became like sound-track music playing in the edges of his life. And it was so much a part of his personality that the meaning of the words were physically etched into his flesh.

Never get caught!

Never . . .

. . . get caught!

Never!

He had them tattooed on his chest, over his heart, emblazoned on a curling ribbon that festooned the picture of a bloody dagger, four inches long. He'd had the tattoo done in San Francisco ten years before, on a lark, when he was drunk after a killing. He'd been killing all his life, it seemed. And he didn't quite know how he was going to stop once "the event" was over.

"Never get caught!"

Probably the most interesting thing he learned while watching the police during the hours between the explosion at Elsa McGreavy's house and morning was that the authorities were essentially unorganized. As the sky lightened from absolute, predawn blackness to the first hints of a midwinter's morning, the streets became crowded with uniformed men and women, milling around and shooting suspicious glances at everyone not wearing a badge, and even at some people who were. Equipment arrived and orders were issued, radios crackled and houses were searched. Reporters materialized as if by magic, producing microphones into which no one would speak, though everyone wanted to. And civilians looked on as, essentially, nothing happened. It was all a bit of a circus . . . or so it seemed. And Kevin Reynolds watched it from the warmth and safety of Pam's Family Restaurant, a greasy spoon located right next door to the Village Cinema. The window was dirty, but looked out onto the street. And Reynolds ate breakfast, drank coffee, and read the morning paper for nearly two hours while people drifted in and out, bringing the latest bits of news with them and keeping him up to date.

At six-thirty he slipped into the men's room, fished around in his knapsack, and changed clothes, abandoning the tweed coat he'd found in Mrs. McGreavy's closet—a leftover from a dead husband, no doubt—and altering his appearance so thoroughly that, when he reemerged, Pam didn't even ask him if he intended to pay for his breakfast. He squeezed his way through the crowd of eight-o'clock-classers glowing with the cold near the cash register and waiting for tables, smiling demurely as gentlemen stepped back to let him pass . . .

Or to let the lady pass.

Because he'd become a lady, dress and all.

Just what was Kevin Reynolds underneath the exterior he allowed the rest of the world to see? That was a question that even he might have had a hard time answering with any conviction . . . or accuracy. If he did answer it, whatever description he might offer would surely be different the second time around, should he be compelled to run through it twice, and then different again the third, because the truth about him was locked up so tightly beneath a secretive veneer created, modified, and polished by his father over years of careful psychological manipulation that even he was constantly re-creating himself to suit his immediate surroundings, and he did it automatically, without even thinking. The funny thing was that although he knew what his father had done to him, and was aware of almost all the insidious twists and turns in his brainwashed history, he really didn't care. He accepted his place as being inevitable, and fatalistically believed that his only way out was by doing what he was told.

Which he always did.

Without question.

Like a good son.

Son Rise!

He practically had to run to catch the bus, which was just about to pull away from the curb when he came scooting across the street, waving and smiling at the bus driver. At the door a policeman stood, eyeing passengers as they boarded. But he didn't give Reynolds a second glance. The cops were looking for a man.

He rode all the way to the rapid transit station on Brookpark Road, turned around, and caught another bus heading west, toward Lorain. There he got out, and glanced up and down the street until he selected a late-model Ford parked beneath a tree as his target. He crossed the street and punched a hole in the left front tire of the car with a switchblade he was carrying in one of Mrs. McGreavy's purses—which he'd found in the same closet as the dress and coat that he was wearing, though they both were way too small for him. And then he stood by the car, looking worried and confused until a blue Nissan pickup truck stopped and a young man with long red hair, jeans, and a denim jacket got out, saying, "Got some trouble, ma'am?"

Reynolds smiled wanly as the man bent over to look at the flat tire, the Nissan truck still running with its door open. Then he placed his pistol's silencer against the man's left temple and blew his brains all over the parked Ford's fender with a *pop* that was barely loud enough to frighten a kitten.

Then he got into the Nissan and drove away, leaving the body in the street. With the Ford on one side and the Nissan on the other, not so much as a single person had seen the gun. And it took ten minutes before a passing motorist stopped to see what was wrong with the young man dressed in denim who was lying next to his disabled Ford in a pool of oil that turned out to be blood. But by then Reynolds was on the freeway, heading south at exactly the speed limit, listening to the news about an explosion in a tiny, college-town suburb and thinking about his father and the two sides of the personality he thought of as himself.

His father was lying on a bed under a tangle of silver tubes.

He hated his father by then. After a lifetime of psychiatrists, accusations, dissections, and treatments, Reynolds associated his old man with nothing but deceit, problems, and pain. Through all the words of penance spewing from the man's mouth, he still heard the old father's cunning underneath. Through all the tears shed by his mother and younger sister, he still was able to see the foxy gleam in his father's eye, even when his father himself was crying. He didn't believe a word of what his father said, and he didn't believe that anything other than the same old lies and manipulations was happening on that hospital bed.

And he was right.

His father proved it when he said, "So, how have your treatments been going, you little sicko?"

His father found such references amusing, knowing, Kevin was sure, that they cut him to the bone. For the life of him, Reynolds couldn't remember doing a single thing the doctors accused him of doing when he was younger. He couldn't remember having so much as a single one of the thoughts they said were his most secret fantasies. Although, the truth be known, so much dwelling on acts of violence and what they meant in the larger picture had been putting things into his mind. Things that weren't there before. When those ideas got really bad was when the shock treatments started.

Those were the worst.

But they were also the best.

God . . .

Life was confusing sometimes.

And although he didn't know it at the time, it was about to get even more confusing still.

"I know things now, Kevin," his father said conspiratorially, after his mother and sister had gone away. The pair of them, father—looking like death, hooked with wires to every machine in the room and probably to some that were in other rooms—and son—thin, twenty-five years old but looking younger in the body and older in the face—were only a few inches apart, with Kevin sitting in the same chair that his mother usually occupied to hold the hand of the "new and improved Eugene Reynolds" hour after hour. Outside it was already dark, and the lights of the parking lot made greasy, prismatic halos in the window glass.

The room smelled of alcohol and metal. The door was closed. And a beaded line of sweat adorned his father's upper lip like a string of clear pearls.

"All these years you and I have been together in our secrets, and not once were you able to convince anyone that what you said was true," his father said, making Reynolds' spine stiffen. Never had his old man come out and spoken like this. Even between them the lies each of them told were valued as truth.

His father's eyes glared at him as his hand shot out and took Kevin's off his lap.

"Listen to me," the old man said, his voice as intense as if these words might be his last. "I know what you remember about me. And I know what you remember about yourself. But none of it really happened that way. Understand?

"What you remember as having happened to you is all an illusion. You've just become a victim of the same terrible punishment that I have. If you help me, I can help you get back your past! I can help you reclaim the past you deserve!"

Wow! Reynolds thought, feeling the heat of his father's flesh on his hand, as well as the intensity of the old man's gaze. This is a new one. And it's good!

Kevin Reynolds was taking about 130 milligrams of Thorazine a day at that time, as well as a little Valium, and a Lithium or two, his discretion, since he'd been on it so long that even his doctors figured he knew when he needed it better than they did. As a result, his contact with what other people might have called reality was considerably more "fluid" than it maybe should have been . . . than it definitely should have been if he was going to be expected to deal with his father's newest life scenario. So, as medicated as he was, his father's words, spoken in an intense, hypnotic cadence, were absorbed, and accepted, almost directly into his brain stem, where they were deposited, unchallenged, for future study and assimilation.

The gist of his father's speech was that they were actually on the same side in a great and important struggle. He understood that Kevin might be a little leery of believing anything his father said, because he had a "pretty good idea of what they put in your mind about me." Who "they" were he was a little vague about, and the idea that someone put something in his mind was

FORGET ME NOT

a stunner. He'd always had the feeling that someone was doing things to him, but he had always thought that it was his father who was doing them. And he suspected that his father was doing it again this time, but when the old man said that he knew a way they could beat the odds, and free them both, Kevin listened. Not because he necessarily believed what he was hearing, but because even a nebulous opportunity for a little mental autonomy—even though the idea was honestly scary by that time—was too good to pass up.

"I did something wrong, and now they've messed up my life as a punishment," Reynolds' father said sincerely. "But I know I can put things to rights, with your help."

Reynolds assured his father that he would do whatever was necessary. And his father said that what was necessary first was that he go out and steal some drugs.

"They were giving it to me a couple of times a day for a while," the old man whispered, as if the room were bugged. "But now they've stopped. I need it. And I think you need it too. This is what it's called."

Kevin took the paper his father handed him.

"Get all you can. I don't care how."

Kevin read the paper again and put it in his pocket.

"And remember, they're all out to get us. The only reason other people are here is to stop you from doing your job, and to make us miserable. Be careful. And hurry. But don't bring it here. They're letting me out tomorrow. Take it home and wait for me. And just remember, if you give those robot bastards half a chance, they'll nail your ass to a tree!"

Walking out of the hospital that night, Reynolds considered his father's words again and again. There were parts of his statement that broke through the confused veil of his chemically softened intellectual capacity, striking chords that ran deep through his heart.

A "they" were out there pulling the strings.

Okay, he could accept that. After a lifetime of having doctors and other authority figures tell him where to sleep, when to eat, and what to think, the idea that his destiny was not his own, and his will subject to the whim of others, was anything but hard to accept.

This "they" were powerful enough to catch even his father up in their insidious influence.

Okay again. If they could do it to Kevin, why couldn't they do it to his father too?

Together, father and son could beat the "they."

Bullshit. Kevin had been trying to beat his own personal "theys" for almost as long as he could remember, and, as anyone who's ever confronted a "they" already knows, "they" are not to be outwitted. "They" have resources and intelligence that make "they" omniscient. The best one can hope for is a stalemate lacking pain.

But the idea that his father was willing to even try was amazing to him. And that he wanted Kevin to participate in the effort . . . wonderful! So, okay.

He'd give it a shot.

"Razomethihanichloride," read the paper in his pocket.

Sounded pretty promising.

Maybe it would even work.

But Reynolds didn't have any idea of how to get some. If they had been giving it to his father up until recently, then they must have had it at the hospital pharmacy. Maybe he should go back and try to get it out of there.

No.

The hospital was too crowded, for one thing. And he'd seen at least five security guards during his brief visit just this evening. He wasn't an accomplished thief—as a matter of fact this would be his first job—so he wasn't expecting things to run smoothly. What he needed was a small place, somewhere out of the way, where he could make his mistakes and still get away with the goods. A mom-and-pop drugstore, preferably in a run-down neighborhood where the cops wouldn't respond to a call for help right away, if at all, and the local residents were accustomed to crime . . . that was the ticket.

But would they have something as esoteric as Razomethihanichloride?

Was Razo . . . methihani . . . whatever, esoteric, or was it a fancy name for something like aspirin or birth control pills?

He cruised for an hour before he settled on the right store. The Rex-Saver was a tiny shop nestled in next door to a dry cleaner—which had closed over three hours before, at six—and a 7-Eleven, which was open twenty-four hours a day. The place was nothing but a big front window, a high counter behind which the pharmacist stood, and some shelves, arranged into four aisles and filled with little bottles and tubes. The pharmacist, a small, bald man, was busy tallying his register, and the clock on the wall behind him indicated that he had locked the door five minutes before, at nine. The parking lot was dingy, with two of its five lights broken. And, judging by the purchases of the people he saw going into and coming out of the 7-Eleven, the main staple of the local diet was forty-ounce torpedoes of Olde English 800 beer.

Which was fine.

Rustling up his courage, Reynolds assumed the most harmless, confused, and worried look he could contrive to wear, tapped on the glass of the drugstore's front window, and waved the paper his father had given him. The pharmacist looked up from his work, shook his head, and pointed at the clock. But Reynolds was persistent, waving the paper vigorously as if he had come on an errand of life or death. Still, the pharmacist was unmoved—this was, after all, a fairly rough neighborhood—and Reynolds, in what he would later come to regard as his first real indication that he was actually cut out for this line of work, pulled out his wallet, opened it, and held it up as if offering everything in it in exchange for whatever was written on the scrap of paper his other hand still waved. The pharmacist cocked his head, and Reynolds smiled hopefully, feeling a juicy gush of excitement when the man stepped out from behind his counter and opened the door an inch to say, "What's the big emergency?"

Up close like this, Reynolds judged the man to be about fifty-five years old, maybe a little less, but he obviously didn't take care of himself and his paunch and baggy eyes made him look feeble and hung over. He had a gold pinky ring with a black stone in it on his right hand, a gold chain on his left wrist, and fingernails that looked just a little too shiny to be altogether natural. Beneath his white smock he wore a turtleneck sweater. And he needed a shave.

Without real consideration, Reynolds launched into his pitch.

"My father's very sick," he said, with real concern in his voice. "They gave him some pills, but now they're all gone. He's in terrible pain, and he's sweating, and shaking, and ... uhh ... he's throwing up blood. I don't know what to do. We need some more of those pills before he dies."

"Why didn't you call your doctor?" the pharmacist asked, and Reynolds noticed the chain holding the door strung taught just under his chin.

"We did, but all we get is his nurse who says that he'll call us back in the morning."

"Typical," the pharmacist sympathized, without making any move to undo the chain.

"So, could you please help me?" Reynolds begged. "I know that it's late, but I'll give you anything you want. I don't care what it is. But I've got to get my father's pills before he dies."

"Why didn't you call an ambulance if he's so sick?"

"When I said anything, I meant, *anything*," Reynolds said softly, leaning his face in closer to the door and holding the paper up so that the pharmacist could see what was written on it.

"That's some pretty heavy stuff," the man said, licking his lips nervously, glancing up and down the parking lot, and then at his watch. "I haven't seen you around here before, and it's really a weird time of day, you know what I'm sayin'?"

Removing his cap, Reynolds stepped back from the door, pushed a lock of his long hair away from the side of his face with the back of one hand, and slid his other hand into the pocket of his jeans, opening his jacket in the process and displaying one hip and half his crotch.

"Gimme the wallet," the pharmacist ordered, and Reynolds handed it over, nice and easy.

The man counted off the money inside, which totaled nearly five hundred dollars, and then checked the ID. He looked at Reynolds' driver's license and then at his face. Seemingly satisfied, he said, "Go around back and wait," closing the door and turning the lock without giving back the wallet or touching the money inside.

The alley behind the drugstore was almost totally dark, lined with trash Dumpsters and filled with the scurrying noises of living things humping around in the night. The door with "Rex-Saver" scrawled across it in yellow chalk was a big, sheet-metal thing, dented and rusty. There was a light fixture sticking out of the wall over it, and the bulb was out.

He waited almost five minutes before the door opened, again only a couple of inches. There were two chains holding it in place, and the pharmacist didn't step too close.

"I can't give you what you want," he said, pausing as if he expected a protest. "And this is some nasty-ass shit. You'll have better luck with Dollathine, or Tellichloride anyway. The shit you want'll kill ya if you give it half a chance."

Still, there were no pills. Just a voice.

"Where you from?"

"The west side," Reynolds responded truthfully. After all, his address was on his license.

"Why'd you come here?"

"I don't know. Took a shot, I guess."

"You hard up?"

"Yeah."

"You look pretty hard up. You done time?"

"Yeah."

"Prison or mental?"

"Both."

"You got a lot of money for a junkie. Nice clothes too. Either you just got out and you been hookin', or you're a fucked-up little rich kid who thought that a couple a hundred bucks could get you what you wanted without you having to see a real dealer. Now, which is it?"

"I just got out."

"You been hookin', then?"

"Yeah."

"You protect yourself? Condoms, and all that?"

"Yeah. Well enough."

"Good. Now, where you belong is the rehab clinic down the street, not here. But if you're gonna be stubborn and hang around, which you probably are, you better know the rules around the neighborhood.

"Rule one: don't ever come back here again. You need something, you find a guy named Rings 'n' Things. He's always around. Rings'll know how to get you stuff.

"Rule two: stay away from the cops. They ain't here for you, so keep clear.

"Rule three: never give nobody your wallet like that again. Never use your real name. That's stupid. I'd think that somebody that did time would know better. But I guess you can forget. Just don't forget no more.

"Understand?"

"Yeah," Reynolds said.

"Last rule, rule four: don't you ever fucking come back here again! Same as rule one. Understand?"

"Yeah."

"Understand?!"

"Yeah. I said yeah already."

"Okay."

Reynolds' wallet hit the pavement at his feet. There was no warning, and no sign of the hand that had thrown it. He picked it up and found his money untouched, and a tiny paper packet squeezed in under his driver's license. There were five pills in the packet, and the word "Dollathine" was written on the paper.

"But this isn't want I wanted!" he protested.

"It's the same thing you could get down at the rehab for free," the voice answered. "So I'm savin' you the trip."

"No!" Reynolds shouted, grabbing the edge of the door and holding it so that the man could not lock up. "I need the other stuff. I can't make it with this!"

"Okay," the man inside the building said, quite amiably. "Slide it back, and I'll see what I can do."

Reynolds took the packet and flipped it into the opening, trembling with rage and frustration. His heart was hammering, and his eyes were alight with an intensity unlike anything he'd ever felt. It was anger, and it was aggression . . . and both of those were familiar. But more important, it was a sensation of need . . . not anything so paltry as a desire, but a clear, undeniable *need* to do as his father had told him.

"Okay," the man said again after the packet of pills was inside. "Now you got nothing. That's another rule: you take what you get. Or you get nothing. I ain't gettin' screwed by no undercover cop. I don't care how cute you are."

The door slammed, and the sound of the dead bolt being drawn put a period on the encounter.

Reynolds looked at the closed door for almost an entire minute before he snapped. When he did, when that barrier in his head that had started as a tiny hole was blown fully open and he was possessed by another, more aggressive part of himself that he had only suspected even existed, he made the first conscious move he had ever made as the Reality Terrorist, even though the name for what he had become was still in the making.

When Reynolds emerged from the alley he moved with a purpose and grace that had been invisible in him before. Every hint of his former clumsy, ill-at-ease, unsure self had disappeared, and without hesitation he approached the glass front of the Rex-Saver, saw the pharmacist holding the telephone to his shiny pink head, and picked up a trash can which he pounded on the window until the glass cracked and then shattered. The pharmacist let out a yelp and dropped the phone, stumbling backward into a cart of pill bottles and turning it over so that plastic and medicine went shattering over the linoleum floor.

"You're crazy!" he shouted, his former, streetwise, in-control persona vanishing as stark terror lit his face.

Who had he been talking to? Reynolds thought, climbing through the hole in the window. The cops?

No.

In this neighborhood the pharmacist's first thought would be to call his protection and tell them that there was a weirdo hanging around the store looking for some strange kind of high and waving a lot of money around. He'd say that maybe it was part of some kind of a half-assed sting operation looking to nail crooked pharmacists, or maybe it was just a particularly flipped-out junkie. But either way, he wouldn't be moving until somebody came over and made the kid hit the road. So Reynolds had to hurry. He'd have just a couple of minutes to do his thing before some goon came rolling up in a Cadillac to make sure that a merchant who faithfully paid his shakedown money each month didn't get hurt.

But when the pharmacist reached under the cash register, Reynolds knew that he was going for a gun.

Where exactly the Terrorist came from was something that would remain a mystery in Reynolds' mind for pretty much the rest of his life. Feeling this new personality rise up from inside him to take over the actions of his heretofore nonathletic physique was like discovering that he actually had a third arm dangling from his body that he had never noticed before. He became suddenly strong, and skilled in things he didn't know he knew how to do.

The gun the pharmacist produced was a ridiculous thing, huge and chrome and unwieldy. It took Reynolds less than two seconds to realize that the man had probably never even fired it. And if he had, it had only been once or twice, just to see if it worked.

"You should have given me my pills," he said, assuming a stalking posture and moving to his right, away from the broken window, where already there were spectators gathering from the 7-Eleven next door.

"I thought you were a cop," the pharmacist returned, holding his gun with both hands and fading back a step. He was trembling from head to foot, and the black eye of the pistol quivered uneasily, exaggerating the liquidity of his arms. Then, without turning his head, he seemed to notice the people on the sidewalk, and shouted, "Help! Help me! Somebody call a cop!"

But no one moved.

No one, that is, but the Reality Terrorist, who lunged without warning or preamble, launching himself over the high counter as the pharmacist pulled the trigger, making his big gun explode with white fire.

The sound was deafening and sent the rubberneckers outside scattering like birds. The first shot slammed into the wall and punched a hole straight through to the dry cleaner's next door. The second shot was followed by the third into the ceiling. By the time the fourth was due, Reynolds had his arm around the little man's throat and was pulling him back into the aisles of pills and preparations. He'd moved down one aisle after his leap over the counter and had simply come up behind the panicking proprietor, who, as soon as he realized he'd been fooled, threw his gun down and began whimpering.

"Okay. Anything you want!" he gurgled, hardly even struggling. "Just take whatever you want and go!"

But Reynolds knew things weren't going to be that simple anymore. He figured that he had another couple of minutes before someone nasty pulled up . . .

But he didn't care.

As a matter of fact, he was kind of looking forward to their arrival.

"This!" he hissed, shoving the paper in front of the pharmacist's nose. "Now! And all you've got!"

"But . . ." the little man began.

And Reynolds cupped the back of the man's skull in his hand and slammed his face into the metal of a shelf, sending pill bottles jumping and watering the man's knees. But instead of letting him fall, Reynolds turned him around and savagely kneed him in the groin—a trick he'd learned while in "therapy," which was, if a patient is distracted by one pain, give him another to take his mind off it. The pharmacist immediately went rigid, and stayed that way until Reynolds pushed him, hard, sending him into the series of shelves behind him with sufficient force to tip the whole thing over and send it clattering into the aisle behind it.

The man was instantly entangled in his own coat, squirming amid a lake of pill bottles and broken glass, settling at a strange, cockeyed angle as the flimsy steel structure of shelving came to rest on its neighbor and sagged beneath his weight. Reynolds gave him a second to think things over and then reached down, taking two fistfuls of lapel and dragging him out of the mess and onto his knees. Then he kicked him in the face one last time, sending him sprawling. And that's when he spotted the gleam of a box of overturned syringes on the floor.

The next thing he knew, the pharmacist was telling him absolutely everything he wanted to know.

The little man's face was a mess: cut, bleeding, already swollen, and tear-stained. His body was like rubber, and he didn't even try to defend himself anymore. The gun had been a joke. And a mistake. It had pissed off the Terrorist, who, holding the largest syringe he'd been able to find like a knife, was kneeling next to the helpless man, pressing his head firmly into the floor with one hand on his chin, and aiming the needle at the man's left eye as if he intended to stab it.

"Blinding time," he hissed. "Now, where is it?"

And the man told him: aisle, shelf, color-coded section, "You can't get pills, only injectable solution," how much he had, when he was getting more. He told him everything he could possibly think of . . .

And when he was done, Reynolds punched the needle right through his closed eyelid and made him shriek like he'd never heard any living thing shriek before in his life. Then he left him there, rolling on the floor with both hands up over his bleeding face, and calmly went over to the aisle the man had indicated and scooped everything on the shelf into a bag he found under the counter by the cash register. Then he grabbed the man's gun and stepped over him as he proceeded to the back of the store and exited through the big steel door where he'd been begging for crumbs not twenty minutes earlier.

And no one saw him go. Everyone was busy crawling around trying to get a look at what was going on inside the drugstore that would make a man scream like the pharmacist was still screaming. And when the thug from the neighborhood gang showed up, a cop car was wailing its way in behind him, so he never even got out of his Cadillac, but glanced around as if he found the crowd distasteful, and left.

Reynolds walked the ten blocks back to where he had parked his car, head held high, back straight, and the Rex-Saver bag dangling from his hand as if he didn't have a care in the world. The next day he read about what he had done in the morning paper with all the detachment of a patron skimming over a movie review. He'd maimed the man horribly, and though the paper didn't go into the gory details for fear of "compromising the efforts of the authorities to apprehend this vicious criminal," he could tell by their description of the man's condition that the needle had penetrated his brain and caused some kind of damage . . . which he regretted. If he'd just have pushed a little harder he probably could have killed the little son of a bitch . . .

(It wasn't until weeks later that he learned that the brain damage he'd done to the pharmacist was sufficient to keep him from explaining how he had been assaulted. He was unable to describe his attacker, or say what his assailant had wanted. Since Reynolds took everything off the shelf where his father's drug was kept, it was impossible for the police to determine specifically what chemical he was after. And, since the cash register was untouched, the motive of robbery was finally excluded. The Rex-Saver job eventually entered the books as a crime of manslaughter after the pharmacist died of complications stemming from his injuries, having never uttered another intelligible syllable, and taking Reynolds' name, and the identity of the drug he had wanted, along with him to the grave.)

Christ, Reynolds thought, lowering the newspaper and glancing out of the kitchen window to the driveway, where in just a couple of hours a private ambulance would be bringing his father home. I actually did it.

He hadn't taken so much as a milligram of anything since the event. No Thorazine or Valium or anything else. Not even an aspirin. And he felt great. Strange. But great. The second personality was gone now—the one that had apparently known ahead of time that something terrible was going to happen and had unconsciously prepared him by making sure that he had worn gloves, a dark, featureless coat, and a stocking cap to hide his hair—but he knew that this new personality, though gone, had not disappeared. The Reality Terrorist, for "terrorist" was the term used by the *Plain Dealer* to describe anyone who could do what he had done, was still there, lurking in the dark corridors of his mind, waiting for the proper time, perhaps even waiting for the *opportunity*, to step forward and do it all again.

Such knowledge might have frightened another man, but to Reynolds, it was a comfort. No longer would he be at the mercy of the doctors, nurses, and therapists who treated him as if he were an animal, and whose therapies were just this side of tortures themselves. No longer would he be at the mercy of anyone, for inside himself he had a secret ally, a big brother, in a sense. And he knew that his big brother wouldn't take any shit from anyone. He knew that his big brother was the kind of ally who wouldn't let him down.

• • •

And now he was wearing a dress and blinking back the tears of memory. From that first taste of violence until today, his skills had been improved, and his contact with the Terrorist portion of his personality refined. The drug he had stolen, though enough to keep his father happy for weeks thereafter, turned out to be a big disappointment to him. From the way his father had talked it up, he'd been expecting something really special. And despite the fact that it had an apparently amazing effect on the old man, it only made Reynolds sleepy. A few weeks later, he sought out a drug dealer who secured for him a steady supply of what his father called the "Razor," paying a remarkably small amount for it, since it was nothing but a perfectly normal sedative. Its only qualifying feature seemed to be that it was a little stronger than most drugs people took for fun. But his father demanded it, and Reynolds was willing to oblige.

The radio report about the explosion at Elsa McGreavy's house was vague and disjointed, which was about what he expected. One of the first things he'd learned about public media was that the news never got the whole story right the first time, and rarely the second. There were a number of reasons for this, but the two most important ones were that the reporters didn't know what they were doing, and the cops didn't want the public to know how much they knew. But if a person knew what to listen for, he could get a pretty good idea of what was really happening by spotting the things that didn't make the air. And judging from the mess he heard crackling from the Nissan's dashboard speakers, the explosion near Lawrynce-Wynn University had pretty much shaken the shoes off everyone.

Okay, he thought, glancing at the traffic around him. One more little distraction, and then it's on to Henry Parks . . .

That son of a bitch!

His father would be so proud.

19

The cop saw it all, but there wasn't a thing in the world he could have done about it. As a matter of fact, he was lucky that he wasn't killed himself.

The blue Nissan pickup truck moved with traffic past the 150th Street ramp as smooth as ice cream, and he didn't do more than glance at the woman who was driving it. He was running radar, and when she cruised by he was a little surprised by how perfectly she was maintaining her speed at exactly fifty-five miles an hour. He was used to people slowing down when they saw his car parked on the left berm, but he knew she hadn't even noticed him. She seemed distracted, looking straight ahead and holding the wheel with both hands. Later, when they would ask him to describe her, and he would be able to recall a veritable wellspring of details, he wouldn't be able to explain why he remembered so much about the big woman, in a drab coat, piloting a little blue truck in unusually heavy traffic for the time of day, which was shortly after ten in the morning. He just would. And it would be weird how that happened.

A Camaro flew past doing seventy just after the Nissan, and the cop, whose name was Joe, was about to hit the siren when all hell broke loose. Cars swerved ahead and he gasped when he saw a plume of black smoke, smeared yellow and red, burst into the air over what looked like a tangle of tires and flying auto parts. The speeding Camaro was still flipping, end over end, careening hysterically into the depression dug between one side of the freeway and the other, while more cars slammed into a semi-trailer that lazily yawned into a terrible jackknife that all but blocked the road. The sound of screeching rubber and crunching metal went on forever, it seemed, and the cop, forgetting all about the traffic behind or to the side of him, tried to pull out onto the freeway, only to be banged right back onto the berm by the violent contact of his car's front fender and a taxicab's side door.

In the end, forty cars were involved.

It was the driver of the semi-truck that had jackknifed so efficiently who—miraculously unhurt—eventually described what had happened. Joe the cop took it all down in a notebook as the pair of them stood off to the side of the auto graveyard that Interstate 71 had become, smoking cigarettes and shaking with the terror of it as ambulances bounced and flashed their lights in every direction.

"She fucking blew his head off," the trucker said, shaking his finger out at the horizon where the little blue Nissan had disappeared. "This guy in a Camaro came flying up on my left. She was almost right in front of me, and when he pulled up to pass her too, she just stuck her arm out the window and shot his car. And I'm talkin' five, six times. Sharp. Every one at the driver. Not random like you'd figure a woman might do. But just straight out, *bang, bang, bang!* I saw the guy's head explode, just like that clip of when Kennedy got shot, you know? Pink spray all over the inside of the car. And then the Camaro went tumbling. And the next thing I know my rig's sideways and there's cars slamming into each other. And . . . Fuck. Something blew up. And . . . Gimme another cigarette."

And Joe the cop did, saying, "Christ!"

FIVE

20

"But I'm tellin' ya, and no shit, it was a woman gave me the jacket," the man protested as Parks looked on through the observation window. "I know the difference between a man and a woman, haircut or not. And this was a fucking female!"

It was just a little after three in the afternoon, and since his meeting in the basement of Jessie's apartment building, Parks' mood had darkened. The elation that had led him to slap Ellis on the back and proclaim things to be really "rollin' " had given way to a sinking sensation of impotence in which he imagined himself watching events spin inexorably out of control. Again. God knew it had happened before. He'd come close, really close. He'd followed the evidence, organized his case, locked onto a suspect who seemed to make sense, moved in, taken what he thought was control of the situation, and come up empty. And unless he could untangle the mess developing around him now, he was afraid that he just might come up empty again.

The man in the interrogation room was tired, unshaved, and angry to the point that he had begun threatening the police department with lawsuits about an hour before. He was the witness who had been found wearing the black leather jacket with the zippers on it, standing in the street, watching Mrs. McGreavy's house burn. They probably should have let him go. But he'd seen the man responsible for all their trouble, and they wanted his brain picked clean . . .

He'd seen the *man*!

Who he insisted was a woman.

"Woman, goddamn it!" he was shouting. "Like, no dick. Get it?"

Woman.

Like the driver of a certain little blue Nissan pickup truck who was supposedly responsible for the worst single auto accident in Cleveland history, which had taken place not three hours before and had thrown the police station into an uproar which still hadn't fully calmed down.

Woman . . .

Not man.

Parks was sitting alone at a table in a dingy observation room behind a piece of two-way mirror positioned so that he could watch the interrogation without influencing its dynamics. A tiny speaker on the wall translated what was being said on the other side of the glass into a harsh, crackling chirp that he could have done without. But there was no way to shut the thing off. So he turned down the volume as far as it would go and returned his attention to the objects on the table before him.

They'd been found in a restaurant's men's room, stuffed in a canvas knapsack behind the toilet. Pam's Family Restaurant was located right next door to the Village Cinema, almost directly across the street from where a woman and her son had been shot in a Chevy van. The little girl who had been thrown into the police car was still unconscious, but she was expected to live—though her spinal injuries meant that she might never walk again.

Another scar.

Another reminder.

In the knapsack was a machete—obviously the one used to decapitate Elsa McGreavy, although they wouldn't be positively sure about that until the lab got through with the blood tests, and the process of matching the weapon's blade to the wounds inflicted on what was left of the old woman's neck. The machete itself was down at the lab, but a photograph of it was on the table.

Among other items in the knapsack was a two-month-old copy of *A Time for Space* magazine. Parks had three photographs of the magazine on the table, as well as a copy of that same issue which he'd picked up at the factory where Mark O'Polo had been killed. It was about the size of a *Reader's Digest*, and was part of a stack of things Parks had removed from the murder scene for future examination. The one found in the knapsack had its spine broken, so that it fell open to a story called "The Gates of Paradise," and, on the table before him, his own copy lay open at that same page.

Parks had read the story while the man in the interrogation room reiterated his familiarity with the differences between the sexes . . .

And now his entire body felt ice-cold.

His heart was beating slowly, and, save for the nearly imperceptible motion of his breathing, he was holding himself perfectly still. He was almost in a trance of concentration, thinking, Wrong, with a frown. Just about everything I thought was right is wrong.

But if it's wrong . . .

Then what's right?

For nearly twenty years, Parks had made a career—no, that wasn't the right word—he'd made a life out of finding the man he called the Prisoner. It was an obsession, and like any obsession, its very one-dimensionality made it easy to describe but impossible to explain.

Kevin Reynolds did it, he thought, mentally verbalizing the driving belief that he'd been carrying in the deepest part of himself for years. Even though I had the evidence that proved that it couldn't possibly have been him, I've known in my heart that he was guilty, and I've been deliberately blinding myself to every other possibility.

Why?

Why have I been doing that?

Because Kevin Reynolds has a history of mental problems, he forced himself to admit, hoping that order might bloom from chaos if he put things clearly and honestly to himself without prejudice.

What he absolutely knew as fact was that Reynolds had spent his life between the ages of twelve and twenty in and out of institutions in an ongoing, apparently futile attempt to wean him from his violent sexual preoccupations. When he was twenty-five, and had proved that he had been at least marginally "cured" by completing college and staying out of trouble for four years, his father was in a nearly fatal automobile accident that put him in the hospital for almost two months.

One month after Eugene Reynolds was released from the hospital, his daughter Natalie married Michael Sterns, a boy she had been dating at college. Seven months later, Jessie was born, and on her first birthday, the Prisoner struck for the first time. Jessie then went to live with her grandparents and later her Uncle Kevin, who Parks, on no evidence but a gut feeling, considered the main suspect in the murders that had orphaned the child. But after dogging Reynolds for years, Parks was unable to positively connect him to so much as a single killing.

And then his father died in an explosion.

"Okay. All right. Have it your way. Maybe it was a guy who gave me the coat," the man in the interrogation room conceded through the wall speaker in exhausted frustration. "But if he was a guy he was sure one funny-looking son of a bitch!"

Parks turned his head, closed his eyes, and sank into himself so deeply that he literally shut off the outside world.

Now, *think*!

The death of Eugene Reynolds did nothing to alter the activities of the Prisoner, which meant that whoever the Prisoner was, he was not Eugene Reynolds. Initially, the names on Parks' list centered around the males in Jessie's immediate family, since murderers rarely kill strangers . . . or at least they're not supposed to. Since a number of killings had happened in faraway cities at times when Kevin Reynolds was under surveillance at home, and since serial killers are male loners—or, again, are supposed to be—his name too was grudgingly excluded from the roster of possible suspects.

New lists were developed, money was raised, and Parks chased leads fruitlessly for years.

And then, at the exact same time that Jessie came to the police with a story about seeing people killed by a madman dressed in black, Kevin Reynolds came roaring up out of the past, blatantly making it known that he was the vicious bastard Parks had always suspected him of being. He was so blatant about it, in fact, that . . .

What? Parks thought. What's that shadow on my mind?

Reynolds was so blatant about his guilt that Parks just couldn't believe it was really him.

There, it was out.

It wasn't Kevin Reynolds.

But again, Parks possessed no evidence to support his conclusion . . . and quite a bit, including Kevin Reynolds' almost perfect palm print, left on the windshield of the van in which two people had died, to the contrary. All the physical indicators he'd amassed in the past few hours pointed squarely in one direction, while his gut feelings pointed in another.

But . . .

He had the story, "The Gates of Paradise," and it was an eerie summation of an uncomfortably familiar scenario.

A piece of hack writing so awkwardly done as to be almost unintelligible in spots, "The Gates of Paradise" was the story of a man who, through the use of esoteric chemicals, finally escapes the reality surrounding him, which, though rendered in perfect, lifelike detail, is actually a complicated illusion designed to cause him pain. Moving from one plane of being to another, he frees himself of his bonds and returns to his own world, where he is greeted by the friends and loved ones he'd left behind. His life at the beginning of the story, it turns out, had actually been a punishment, inflicted on him by the authorities of an advanced society through the use of some incredible machine. And his crime, though never detailed, is ultimately erased from his record . . . his debt having been paid by his successful completion of his task.

Bells were ringing in Parks' mind.

Connections were being made.

The story fit . . .

Especially the part where the "Criminal," as the author referred to his hero, was described as stalking through the streets of the dream-world reality in which he was trapped, seeing everyone around him as being somehow less than human, and wondering who it was he had to eliminate in order for him to find his way home.

Had the Prisoner written this story as a kind of Jack the Ripper "Letter from Hell," meant to explain himself without revealing his identity?

Or had he—they . . . it . . . she—simply seen it and responded to something about it that struck home so hard that it forced him to seek out the man responsible for its publication?

Either way, it was a link—an honest-to-God, solidly substantial connection between Parks and the Prisoner. And he felt sure that both he and the madman whose activities he had used to define his own value as a human being for so long had shared this page. He also knew that the only way a person could get a copy of *A Time for Space* was by subscription. On the table was a copy of Mark O'Polo's subscription list, faxed in from Pittsburgh not twenty minutes before. There were two thousand names on that list, and two thousand addresses . . .

But Kevin Reynolds was not among them.

It was Novak who had supplied Parks with the evidence he needed to verify Reynolds' innocence. With one simple phone call he had again eliminated Reynolds from the hunt.

"He's been seen at his office every day for the past three weeks," Novak said on the phone. "I called and checked. The motel owner said that he's seen a woman and a man go in and come out of the motel, driving a red Corvette, for two solid weeks. Reynolds couldn't have been in two places at one time. It just can't be him. I don't know who the guy with the woman is, but I know who he's not. He's not Kevin Reynolds."

A knock at the observation room door opened Parks' eyes, and a young policeman stuck his head in and said, "I'm sorry to disturb you, Mr. Parks. But there's a lady here making a real fuss about seeing you right away."

"A lady?" Parks asked, rising slowly from his ruminations and steadying himself with a hand on the table. "What's her name?"

The policeman read "Lisa Reynolds" off a card, adding,

"She's pretty upset, but as far as we can make out, she says she's here to help you find her brother."

21

Parks had spoken to Lisa Reynolds maybe four times in the past twenty years. But when it came to faces, his memory was nearly flawless, and his first thought at catching sight of her in the police station lobby was that she hadn't changed a bit. She hadn't aged. She was constant.

His next thought was, What the hell is she doing here now?

Lisa Reynolds was a tall woman, and remarkably statuesque. That was one thing about the Reynolds family, Parks thought, every one of the women in it was beautiful, without exception. At fifty-two years old, she had clear, emerald-green eyes, full, silver-blond hair cut in a businesslike fashion, and the body of a dancer: solid and muscular. Facially, she bore a striking familial resemblance to her brother, but instead of the softness that made his expression so constantly indecisive, there was, in her features, the unmistakable tang of iron and will. She was obviously not a woman who avoided confrontation, and her confidence in her own abilities was most eloquently expressed in her steady gaze and the boldly forward thrust of her head, which gave her a resolute, no-nonsense posture that made a person approaching her on the street instinctively want to step out of her way.

She'd been educated at Ohio State University, where she'd received a bachelor's degree in business administration. She'd never married, or at least not that Parks knew about. And the last time he had seen her was in 1984, shortly after her father's death. Her mother had been hospitalized for observation after a nervous breakdown brought on by the loss of her husband, and Lisa and Parks had encountered one another in the hospital's coffee shop. Her reaction was sheer undisguised outrage that Parks would show his face at such a time. And with a blustery display of anger that was reminiscent of her father's famous temper, she had a pair of security guards escort him out, threatening legal action if he ever "harassed" her, or what was left of her family, again.

Then she dropped out of sight, returning home only periodically for brief, unexpected visits that, with her father gone, she seemed to neither enjoy nor prolong. Parks never bothered tracking her down, but bits and pieces of her life did drift back over the years:

Lisa showed up for Christmas driving a BMW and wearing a mink coat; Lisa's last letter was postmarked London; Lisa visited her father's grave and put flowers there on some holiday; Lisa attended her murdered sister's funeral wearing dark sunglasses and never so much as speaking to her brother.

What she did with her time, the logistics of how she received and disposed of her money, and where she lived, no one knew, because there were more important things to spend Mr. Sallovy's money on.

Why she'd left when she had, what was the source of the animosity between her and the rest of the family, and why she never spoke to her brother, ever, all remained unsolved, because no one could ever get close enough to her to ask.

What she really knew about Kevin, whether or not she had ever discussed him with anyone, and why she was listed on all his hospital admittance records as his next of kin, no one seemed to care, because, for all anyone knew, she was just a little rich girl, alone in the world, living off Daddy's fortune.

But now she was back . . .

And she was furious.

"Henry Parks!" she shouted the instant she caught sight of him across the crowded lobby. She was standing by the front desk with three uniformed cops forming what amounted to a human barrier between her and the rest of the building. She was pink in the face—either from the cold or, much more likely, knowing her, from rage—and she was holding her clenched fists straight down at her sides as if she were straining to maintain her self-control by keeping her entire body stiff. "It's about time!"

"It's okay, boys," Parks said, ignoring Lisa Reynolds and speaking to the cops blocking her way. Holding his hand out as if to lead her, he added, "The lady's a friend of mine."

But Reynolds would have none of it. And, pointing one perfectly manicured finger his way, she shouted, "Where's my niece?"

"What?" Parks asked, taken off guard.

"Jessie," Reynolds said. "What have you done with her?"

"Nothing," Parks said, still holding his hand out helpfully. "She's at her apartment with two of my men to look after her . . ."

"I just came from her apartment," Reynolds interrupted loudly. "And there's no one there, you stupid son of a bitch!"

22

After calling Jessie's apartment and listening to the phone ring thirty times without a response, Ellis, Parks, and Reynolds raced behind an escort of three police cars that all had their lights spinning and their sirens howling like hell. Ellis drove, Lisa Reynolds sat silently beside him, and Parks leaned his head up between the pair of them from the backseat like a dog.

They got to the apartment house in less than ten minutes and found that the place had quieted down considerably since morning—the crowd of students and parents having thinned to the point that the lot was now virtually empty. After squealing the car to a stop, Ellis led four cops up the stairs while the remaining three positioned themselves by the doors and Parks huffed his way into the lobby, grabbing one of his plainclothesmen along the way and asking if anyone had seen Jessie leave the building.

The man shook his head.

"How about the description I gave you?" Parks asked hurriedly. "Have you seen anyone around who could have been Kevin Reynolds?"

And again the guard responded, "No."

By the time Parks got to the fourth floor, Ellis had forced Jessie's locked door open, and even from down the hall, the older man could smell that something tragic had happened. Be it by gun, knife, or bludgeon, murder has a distinct, olfactory signature that reaches into some very private parts of the human mind to hit some very old buttons. In this case, the acrid stench of gunpowder would probably have been enough, but the odors of blood and shit were so bad that Lisa Reynolds, fast-walking in her high heels at Parks' side, reflexively hesitated ten feet from the door.

Even amid the wreckage of the living room, Parks still found himself guiltily exhaling a sigh of relief when he saw that Jessie's body was not among those on the floor. One guard, whose name he didn't even know, was lying flat on his back, arms at his sides, staring at the ceiling with a little round hole centered perfectly between his eyes, and most of what looked like his brain dried in running streaks on the wall behind him. The other man had taken out the coffee table and was sprawled across the couch atop the Joker's grinning poster face, so that his head hung down, dangling thick, meaty red lines into a brown puddle on the floor. The yawning exit wound that had blown most of the back of his head off was exposed in all its ragged detail.

Ellis emerged from the bedroom, saying, "She's definitely not anywhere in the apartment!"

"These men have been dead at least a couple of hours," Parks said, indicating the congealed blood on the floor and heading for the hallway, where he confronted Lisa Reynolds straight on by saying, "Why did you come here? How did you know?"

But Reynolds had regained her composure, and instead of responding to the strain in the old man's voice, she answered calmly, "My mother's not coming here . . . like it or not. I told her not to. When she called to tell me that your people were bothering her, I phoned Jessie to warn her about you. But her answering machine was on. The next time I spoke to my mother she was practically hysterical. On the request of the Cleveland police, the Columbus authorities had contacted her to see if she'd seen Kevin lately. So I called Jessie again, got her machine, and decided to come up here and see what was going on for myself. When I got here I found her door locked, and nobody could tell me what was going on so I came looking for you."

"But how'd you know where to find *me*?" Parks asked.

"I asked one of the men sitting in a parked car across the street."

"And he told you?"

"Obviously. But . . ."

Reynolds grew quiet when a policeman emerged from Jessie's apartment and started stringing yellow ribbon across the door. Moving down the hall and forcing Parks to follow, she leaned her face in so close to his that he could smell her perfume as she said, "But the reason I came to you is that I think I can help."

"Me?" Parks whispered back in surprise. "You want to help *me*?"

"You were right about him," Reynolds said, her hard, green eyes going cold. "Hearing me admit that should make you very happy."

"Nothing about this makes me happy," Parks said.

But Reynolds' expression was doubtful.

"I spoke to him," she said, prickling the hairs on the back of Parks' neck. "He called me."

Cops ran by, three at a time, and radios crackled up and down the hall.

"When?" Parks asked.

"About a week ago. He called late at night, like at two in the morning. Since we hadn't spoken to one another in years, things were a little awkward. He apologized for all the trouble he'd caused, but he insisted that the things he'd done had all been necessary. He said that he had a couple of more things to do, and then everything would be fine. 'My debt will be paid,' he said. Those were his exact words. Then he referred to a story in some science fiction magazine that I'd never heard of, much to his surprise. As if this magazine were so important that everyone reads it. He said the story was called 'The Gates of Paradise.' I remember because he ended up sending me a copy."

"I've seen it," Parks said.

And Reynolds raised her eyebrows.

"Well, then, I won't bother summarizing. What Kevin said about it was that it was the story of his life."

Parks said nothing.

"He didn't know who'd written it, but he was sure that it was part of a plot to expose him—a secret message directed at his greatest enemy, who is you. But it didn't matter if you knew the truth or not, he said, because it was already too late. He was too near the end of his sentence, and nothing you did could stop him."

"My God!" Parks murmured. "But why didn't you tell someone?"

Reynolds looked at Parks as if he'd lost his mind.

"Mr. Parks," she began, suppressing what might have been part of a laugh, or her anger, building up again. "My brother's been the way he is—and at times considerably worse—for almost as long as I can remember . . . since he was a little boy. I've heard him say all sorts of strange things over the years. And I've always taken them as his way of getting attention. Just like the doctors all said.

"But I was wrong, and so were they.

"And now he's going to hurt my niece! You can save her, Mr. Parks. But to do so, you're going to need my help. And to get my help, you're going to have to promise to do things my way."

A deal? Parks exclaimed in his mind. Jessie's been kidnapped out from under the noses of a dozen armed guards by some madman who she may or may not be related to, there are dead bodies lying practically at the feet of this woman who may or may not be that madman's sister, and now she's offering me a deal? What in the hell's going on around here?

"What's the deal?" Parks asked aloud, consciously keeping his voice from rising.

Lisa Reynolds didn't so much as blink when she said, "I want you to kill him."

Parks wasn't sure if he'd heard her right, so he asked her to repeat herself.

Which she did.

"Kill him," she said firmly. "In exchange for my helping you find him, I want your personal guarantee that he won't be taken alive. I don't care how you do it, and I don't care about the legality of whether it's murder or justice—and neither do you, I'm sure. All I care about is finishing this, finally, after a lifetime of suffering, once and for all.

"It's been better than forty years that I've been living in his shadow, and I won't put up with another day of it. If he's captured there'll be a trial, complete with the accompanying scrutiny of his life, and mine. With him alive psychiatrists and experts are going to be researching books and articles, splashing every piece of dirt they can find about our family anywhere someone will pay them to do it. It'll be a media circus, just like these things always are. I won't put my mother through that. And I won't have Jessie's life tainted as mine has been. I want this stopped before she has to move to some anonymous town and change her name like I did. One exile in the family's more than enough."

"But why didn't you just say this to start with?" Parks nearly shouted, infuriated at Reynolds' suddenly calm expression and calculating tone of voice. "If you know where he is, then every minute counts."

"We've got nearly seven hours," Reynolds responded. "And I still haven't heard you promise."

"Seven hours?"

"He won't harm her until midnight."

"Midnight?"

"She'll be twenty-one."

"Her birthday?"

Reynolds nodded.

"His sentence?!" Parks exclaimed. "Where's he taken her?"

"Your promise, Mr. Parks?"

"I promise!" Parks shouted in his excitement. "I fucking promise! Now, where is he?"

Reynolds eyed him for a moment before saying, "He's in Pittsburgh at the Gates of Paradise."

Parks felt Ellis standing behind him, and when he turned to face him they both said, "The factory!" together, as if their brains had become suddenly connected.

There were arrangements to be made, and explanations to be given, and Parks wanted as many things as possible to be done simultaneously. After instructing his men to disappear when the local cops took over the building, he led Ellis and Reynolds back down to the parking lot, flipping orders at Ellis and holding onto Reynolds' arms as if he were afraid that she might simply vanish into thin air. They needed to mobilize, he was saying, his face flushed and his armpits damp. They needed to get things humming. First they'd line up the airplane again. They'd be in Pittsburgh in less than an hour, and that meant that, even if Kevin Reynolds had started driving there at noon, they should still beat him to the factory.

Secondly, while they were on their way they'd need to have some guys move in and secure the factory in preparation for...

"No!" Lisa Reynolds insisted, taking her arm back and refusing to get in the car. "If you leave him alone, he'll wait until midnight to do whatever he's planning. But if he sees your men trooping around, there's no telling what might happen. He's had a lifetime of practice at being clever. If we want him, we'll have to be more clever than he is. We'll have to go after him ourselves."

"We?" Parks asked, and over the roof of the car he caught sight of Ellis' expression.

Ellis was standing on the driver's side, holding open his door and looking at Parks. Lisa Reynolds had her back to him, so she didn't see his face as he shook his head and rolled his eyes.

He knows something, Parks thought. Something's going on here that I'm missing, and Sonny has an idea about what it is.

But despite Ellis' silent protest, Parks agreed to take Lisa Reynolds along, and, folding her into the car, he cut off any further protest from Ellis with a quick shake of his head. But at the police station, he took the younger man aside and led him into a men's room, leaving Reynolds at the receiving desk. Inside he said, "Okay now, Sonny. What the hell's wrong?"

And Ellis said, "Just before you sent us tearing over to the apartment, I was on the phone with Lemon. He found out who owns the apartment building, like you told him to. But when he called to find out why everyone had to move out today, the secretary told him that the owner wasn't available to give any explanations, not even to the police. She said that if it was important he could leave a message and the owner would return his call in a couple of days."

"So?" Parks asked impatiently. "Whose place is it?"

Ellis frowned and tilted his head toward the door as he cocked his thumb and said, "Hers. She wasn't available to talk on the phone because she was on her way here. The Reynolds Genealogical Survey and Research Group is listed as the owners of the property, and Lisa Reynolds is the company's president."

"Lisa Reynolds is the president?" Parks said, momentarily perplexed. "But Kevin's been running the company since his father died. Lisa hasn't even been in town more than six or seven times that we know of. Christ, we don't know where she's been!"

"That's right," Ellis agreed. "We don't know where she's been for years. But now we just might know where she's been for the past two weeks."

Parks went pale. "Not the woman at the motel?" he asked, his jaw going slack.

Ellis nodded. "While we were at the apartment, I had Novak run her picture under the desk manager's nose. I figured, why not? We're looking for a woman, and well . . ." He trailed off, glanced at the door, and continued. "It's an older picture, about the time of the explosion that killed her old man, but with it we got a positive maybe. The desk manager said that he can't be absolutely sure, but he said that it could be."

"Then . . ." Parks began, the implications arranging themselves into astonishing patterns of deceit in his mind. "If she's who she just might be, then her brother could easily have been seen at work every day, all things normal, running a diversion so she'd be free to stay here and do all this shit."

"Or he could know nothing about it," Ellis interrupted. "The guy at the motel didn't recognize Kevin Reynolds' picture. He said 'could be' again, but he wasn't nearly as sure. He said that he thought the guy at the motel was thinner in the face. He was a big guy, like Reynolds is, but he was maybe thinner in the face."

"So there might even be another accomplice," Parks said, his eyes going wide so suddenly that he felt a pain in his temples. "Or . . . " He snapped his fingers and grabbed Ellis' arm, whispering so loudly that spit flew. "Did the motel man ever see them both together?"

"What?" Ellis asked, apparently lost.

"Did he ever see the man and the woman come or go at the same time, together, arm in arm?"

The understanding crawled across Ellis' face like the ripples in a pond radiating out from a central point where a stone had landed. Starting with the bridge of his nose, his features seemed to blossom as his mouth and eyes opened and his brows climbed his forehead.

"I don't know!" he responded, the excitement in Parks' voice insinuating itself into his. "Jesus Christ, Henry. I never asked!"

"Find out," Parks ordered. But when Ellis moved to obey, he stopped him with a hand on his chest. Leaning his face in close and feeling Ellis' heart beating through his shirt, he added, "We could be wrong. She might not be involved. We could be back to square one, with Kevin Reynolds as our suspect and an unknown woman helping him.

"But . . ." he lifted one finger. "We've still got to keep an eye on her. Because is she is who we think she is, then, Sonny, she's one wicked bitch."

Ellis frowned, patting Parks' shoulder and straightening his brown tie like a son helping his father get ready for church. "Don't worry, Henry. If she's who we think she is, then she's one *dead* wicked bitch."

23

Jessie came awake to the sound of dripping water, in the dark and cold. She lay stock-still for a moment before her thoughts, completely of their own accord, fell into a kind of loose order centered around the face of a man . . .

Which lifted her body into a sitting position up off whatever it was that she was lying on and pulled a gasp from inside her so abruptly that it made her already tender head swim.

Leaning back on one hand and rubbing her forehead with the other, she watched stars dance before her closed eyes and felt a distant, rhythmic pounding in her temples that she instinctively understood was her heart. Every nerve and vein in her body seemed to be connected directly to her chest, and with each shuddering beat her eyes throbbed and her stomach twisted into a queasy knot.

She held herself still and waited.

No, she thought. I won't puke.

It was a solid conviction on her part, and she meant to live up to it. But her body had other ideas, and five minutes later, after a retching series of dry heaves, it finally let her down.

Which made her feel a little better.

But also made the room smell bad . . .

Or, more accurately, it made it smell worse than it already had.

What the hell did I have in my stomach to bring up? she wondered distractedly for a moment, wiping her eyes. When was the last time I had anything to eat?

Then that face that had roused her from the void returned to her mind and she stiffened and crawled to her feet.

The floor swayed beneath her, and she staggered around drunkenly until she found a wall for support. Hanging there, she forced herself to study the gloom until, just barely, she made out the faintest hint of an irregularity in the otherwise total darkness, focused on it, and remembered it as a . . .

Door?

And the face hovering over her was . . .

Grandpa?

She'd whispered the word herself, she thought, recalling the sound of her own voice as an echoing reverberation spinning back at her from the depths of some endless, twisting tunnel. She remembered the sensation of being disjointed, or dismembered, of having her personality separated into distinct sections that were each useless, one without the other. She recalled it as a weird, dangerous feeling, brought on by . . .

The bitter taste of a rag in her mouth, and some awful, chemical smell in her nose when an old man in a khaki-colored outfit came at her across her living room after . . .

Shooting someone!

She gagged again, forced herself to remain upright on her feet—one hand over her stomach, the other on the damp stone wall—and clenched her teeth, seeing . . .

That face.

Shooting.

Grandpa.

"But he's dead! Grandpa's dead!"

What the hell was going on? Had she been hallucinating

when she saw the face of her grandfather hovering over her, aged beyond all account, thin, with scrawny, pallid features and the red-rimmed eyes of a madman? Was her image of him a dream brought on by some kind of trauma or shock? Where was she? What was she doing here? Where were the men Henry Parks had left to guard her?

Smoke and fire.

Blood.

So much blood!

Had all that been real?

Pushing herself off the wall, she took three steps through the darkness before she stumbled over something soft. Without any light, she could not gauge her distance from the floor, and when she fell she landed hard, on solid ground, nearly knocking the wind out of herself and launching her stomach into another series of those awful, stabbing spasms. Feeling around with her hands, she sought out the thing that had tripped her, found it, and, after a moment, decided that it was a mattress. Then, instead of risking another fall, she lifted herself to her hands and knees and crawled toward the faint light, which went from a thin, dirty grey to a more distinct smear the closer she got to it.

The light was coming in from the outside, under a door made of . . .

Wood, she decided, running her hands up and discovering a steel ring.

She yanked on the ring, knowing ahead of time that she would be wasting her strength. But she did it anyway, producing a grinding of old metal and a baleful moan from the ancient frame. The door didn't so much as budge.

Back on her knees she aimed one eye under the door, trying to see out. But the light was so faint that she found nothing but a continuous greyness . . . a feeble and disappointing monochrome that didn't give her so much as a hint of what lay beyond the door. She was about to call out . . .

Why?

She wasn't sure.

But it seemed like the thing to do. Honestly, she couldn't remember how she'd gotten here, and she didn't have a clue as to why she was so confused. The idea that she was being held prisoner brought with it all sorts of terrible fantasies, most of them centering around rape and murder. She could feel herself trembling, and tears were boiling up in her eyes. She could feel herself wanting to pee, and she made herself tighten every muscle in her body because she was not, absolutely not, going to lose control. She could feel the steel-wool bristle of firing nerves prickling her skin as a building steam of panic began swirling . . . first as a series of images in her mind, then as a sensation of helplessness and fear, and finally as an irrational, animalistic instinct to run and preserve her own life. But that heavy wooden door, invisible in the blackness, stifled her hopes and left screaming, crying, tearing her hair, and throwing herself into the dark as her only options. And before she did any of those things—as she knew she would, as she knew she'd have to, sooner or later, no matter how hard she tried to avoid them—she wanted to try making contact . . . try making a reasonable, rational sound.

And she was going to . . .

Just as someone started screaming outside. And that sound, filled with terror, pain, and dread, all but pushed her over the edge.

That sound made her pull her knees up to her chin and cry . . .

Because she recognized the voice.

It was one she knew as well as her own, familiar despite its intense distortions. It was a voice wailing in the dark, hopelessly moaning and tearing her heart even as it wrenched tears from her eyes and ruined what was left of her self-control. She wanted to answer back, to call out and say, "I'm here. Don't cry. I'm here, Uncle Kevin. We're here together . . ."

But she couldn't.

It was Uncle Kevin, screaming from the darkness down the hall . . . sounding crazy with pain and terror . . . sounding crazy . . .

Crazy.

Uncle Kevin . . .

He was a prisoner too.

24

Hearing Jessie whisper, "Grandpa?" so softly, and with so much feeling, sent surging blasts of excitement through the Prisoner that were so intense that he almost lost control of himself and went for her right then and there.

But he didn't. It wasn't easy, but he was able to hold onto himself, and with his teeth clenched and his hands trembling so hard that he was almost unable to harness their nervous energy, he gently lowered her lovely head to the mattress, backed his way out of the cell, locked the door, and leaned on it, breathing hard and dripping sweat.

"No!" he demanded of himself, because he had to respect the limitations of his position, and fulfill his sentence. "I will not! I *can*not!"

He stopped, jerked his head up, and glanced down the hall. Molaine would be watching, he knew. Even if the Prisoner couldn't see the spinning, self-righteous, son-of-a-bitching Keeper who found it so easy to say things like, "A task is that which needs to be done, and other considerations are only emotional confusions of responsibility," he understood that he was always there, somewhere, waiting to emerge from the air, or come seeping through a wall with consternation in his eyes and rebukes on his bloody lips. He was always present, no matter what the Prisoner did. And now, with the end of his sentence within reach, he couldn't afford to give the Keeper even one excuse for anger.

But God!

Jessie!

God!

She was so beautiful.

On wobbling legs the Prisoner forced himself from her door and down the hall, glancing around for the Keeper and all but dragging himself away. When Jessie awoke, she'd be sick and confused from the ether. She'd be frightened, and desperate to escape. But they were so deeply buried beneath the apartment house that even when she regained her senses enough to understand her peril, no one would ever hear her screams . . .

No one would ever hear her.

No matter what he did.

"No!" the Prisoner demanded. "I will *not!*"

Yet.

Moving down the hall, he resisted the urge to glance into the various cells that lined the way back to his own living quarters. He'd been mentally preparing for tonight's physical passage back to the world for twenty years, and he'd been getting things ready at the apartment house for almost a month. A couple of the "guests" who'd been "invited" early on were getting a little weak, and they probably wouldn't have as good of a time as the others. But fun was where you found it, and the Prisoner couldn't worry about their pleasures now.

In his room he turned on a light, closed the door, and wiped a hand across his forehead, finding himself wet with perspiration, which was not a good sign. Even though his room was the warmest of the bunch—being filled with a tangle of heater pipes on the ceiling—it was never much better than being just this side of unbearably cold. And the dampness could go right through a seventy-year-old man's flesh and leave his bones tender in a matter of minutes. So he shouldn't have been sweating. He was sweating because he was late with his drug.

"How close?" he wondered aloud, stripping off his janitor's outfit and tossing it onto the cot that was his bed. "The guards I killed should count as two, but they were so far from the center of things . . . Christ! How can I be sure?"

Next came his rubber suit, peeling away from his skin and leaving his damp, hairless flesh to goose bumps in the chilled air. The suit followed his overalls onto the cot with a hollow rustle, as did the Prisoner's hair. His scalp itched when the toupee was removed, and gratefully he scratched, enjoying the sensation of tingling nerves right down to the soles of his feet. (He had started losing his hair in the hospital, immediately after the accident that knocked him into the Zone, a side effect of the drug they were giving him to keep his brain seizures under control. Since his release he had continued taking the Razor almost daily, and consequently, he didn't have a single hair left anywhere on his body.) He left his shoes on because the cold concrete floor was hard on his arthritic ankles. And before he did anything else, he removed his glasses from the drawer in his desk. He hated wearing glasses, but they were a concession to age that he had to make.

For a dead man, Eugene Reynolds moved with remarkable ease. After so many years of practice, filling the syringe from the tiny glass bottle and raising an artery in his arm with the rubber tourniquet were like second nature, and his hands did them automatically while his mind concentrated on thoughts of the night sea. He knew that once the drug was in, he'd wake up closer to the golden city than he ever had before. Each time, he got just that much closer, and this time, he knew, he'd be practically there.

His arms looked like the leg of a rat: all bone, gristle, and vein. Up and down from his elbow to his wrist was a linear pattern of needle scars and track marks that attested to twenty years spent on the Razor. His skin was actually callused in the spots that covered the arteries he had used most often. And it took him three stabs to score a hit. His two failures didn't even bleed, and that, too, wasn't a good sign. But once the plunger was depressed and the clear liquid preparation moved through the needle from the syringe to his bloodstream, that old familiar sensation of peace melted his concerns, moving through him from his arm to his heart in a single blossom of warmth that would make everything worthwhile by tearing down the veils that separated the Prisoner from his goal . . . the world from the Zone.

Quickly now! he thought, placing the syringe down gently so as not to damage it and pressing a tiny piece of cork onto its tip to protect its point. He had plenty more, but old habits were hard to break, and needles weren't. He could still remember times in strange cities, when, for want of a needle, he had been forced to take ridiculous risks. Moving to the cot, he stretched himself out, concentrating on his muscles as they seemed to disappear, visualizing himself as his body deflated, leaving only his skin and bones, and then only his bones, and then nothing at all as everything that was him was moved from one plane of being to another: from the Punishment Zone to the Night Shore.

And he found that he had been right.

He did wake up closer.

Normally, he savored these trips, even if his destination was really only a kind of limbo. Any reprieve that removed him from the Zone was something to be experienced slowly, and with deliberation. But today he was in too much of a hurry, and wrenching his eyes open as quickly as he did ruined his balance and sent him pitching forward onto the sand. He always came back to himself in an upright position. Having left the Zone lying down, he invariably awoke standing on the Shore, facing the city. And today was no exception.

Raising his head, he opened his eyes again more slowly, feeling water lapping over his buried hands and ignoring it. Overhead, glowering black clouds boiled in a purple, moonless sky. Before him the night sea swelled darkly, ribbed with glowing slivers of gold on the crest of every wave. Beneath his hands and knees, the beach's sand was as ivory white as ever. And before him . . .

The city was almost close enough to touch.

"God!" he choked, emotion surging through him uncontrolled. "Oh, please . . ."

Every killing brought it closer.

Every one.

Sitting down on the beach, Eugene Reynolds rinsed off his hands in the cold water of the sea before rubbing them over his face and feeling the wonderful tautness of his skin, the marvelous firmness of the muscle and bone beneath his strong fingers, and the incredible luxuriance of his beard. Then he scooped water over his hair, feeling twenty years' worth of it—practically down to his waist and as full as a horse's tail. Though his body had been ravaged by time and age in the Zone, his muscles turning to butter, his brain to mush, here on the Shore he had remained the same age as he had been when he had first committed his crime. His hair had continued to grow, as did his nails—in true dead-man fashion—but the rest of him stayed the same. He was even dressed in the same clothes, though they were worn almost to rags.

When he was clean and refreshed he stood, straining his eyes to sea and looking for the movement that would prove the effectiveness of his plan. The waves surged and swelled endlessly, the eternal motion of the void, offering so much space in which to hide that again, like virtually every other time he'd come, the Prisoner almost despaired of seeing his kill. But again, like virtually every other time, he did see it, at that exact instant that he was about to give up, waving from the distance, indistinct but familiar . . . first one and then the other . . . waving . . . the guards in Jessie's apartment . . . out there in the surf, maybe a quarter of a mile out under the glimmering reflection of the city. There were two of them poking up from the sea as if the water were only a few feet deep, barely covering them to the waist. The Prisoner could not make out their features, but their silhouettes were enough for him to recognize that familiar, one-handed wave of acknowledgment that said, "Yes, Eugene Reynolds. We're here with you. We were two who needed to die. Thanks for bringing us back."

Perhaps all the cybertrons in the Zone were actually other prisoners serving out their own punishments, and Eugene Reynolds was setting them free by killing them. He just didn't know. He'd often thought about the possibility, and a couple of times, when he was feeling particularly brave or frustrated or reckless, he'd even ask Molaine. But Molaine ignored the question, as he did all questions, answering instead to whatever he felt was important at the time without giving the Prisoner's inquiries any weight at all. But still, it was an interesting possibility, interesting enough to drive the Prisoner to read reports in the newspapers of other killings, other strings of deaths being enacted in distant parts of the country. Were those reports really the descriptions of other prisoners performing other tasks? Should he go and offer himself as another prisoner's victim? Would that shorten his own sentence? Would he, after dying at the hands of some other poor soul, awaken in the night sea, waving to a stranger whose sentence he had just shortened by playing his part? Who was innocent in the illusionary world of the Punishment Zone . . . and who was damned?

The questions were beyond his intellectual reach . . . for now and forever. And, as always, he waved back to the hailing forms in the sea and watched them sink with a final, satisfied flourish, down beneath the waters, out of sight. Then, as always, he turned his back on the image of the city looming on the horizon, and made his way to the tree line where a craggy rock outcropping held the cave in which he had constructed a shelter for himself almost twenty years before. It was in that cave that he had spent almost half his life since his crime . . . the better half of his life . . . the half in which his Punishers allowed him at least a shred of dignity.

Even if that dignity was solitary.

Because this was, after all, the Night Shore, that line between the real world and a dwelling of fantasy and madness. Here, reality and madness mixed, making anything possible, and the Prisoner had given up trying to make sense of things a long time ago. Instead of expressing wonder or loathing or anger, he was reduced to simply being grateful for pretty much anything he got . . .

But he wasn't grateful for Henry Parks.

Henry Parks was trouble both in the Zone and on the Shore. In the Zone, he looked human. On the Night Shore, well, he looked more like himself . . . more like what he really was, inside, beneath the veneer that camouflaged his true form. On the Night Shore, everyone looked more like themselves. And maybe that was the part that had given the Prisoner the most trouble, years ago, when . . .

The ambulance brought the Prisoner home from the hospital after his accident.

His whole family was there, waiting at the door. The attendants bumped him up the porch stairs on his stretcher and settled him into his own bed, which he hadn't seen in two months, while his wife took her place holding his hand, and the kids scurried around finding blankets and towels, and generally getting in the way. Despite knowing that none of what he was seeing was real, the Prisoner couldn't help but feel a certain warmth radiating from the scene. It resembled what he remembered about his own home so much that twinges of nostalgia moistened his eyes. And when his wife saw his tears, they started her own flowing, and two or three times before the morning was done, things had to come to a dead stop so that she could throw her arms around his neck, and he could hold her, and the pair of them could cry for no apparent reason while the kids stood and blubbered in the bedroom doorway.

All except for Kevin, that is.

Kevin never cried.

He just stood there, watching, like a reptile, with those cold eyes of his that never seemed to blink, but that drank everything in, as if reality were a liquid with which he was trying to fill his skull.

The first time the Prisoner visited the Night Shore after he got home was that same evening, late, when everyone else had gone to bed. He wasn't really supposed to walk around too much until he got his land legs back, but short trips down the hall to the bathroom were permitted, and since his wife had surprised him by announcing that she would be sleeping in the same bed as he—something she had stopped doing about a year before the accident because of the crappy way he treated her—he was forced to make this first, home-port foray out of the Zone while sitting on the toilet in the new "Snoopy and the Red Baron" pajamas his kids had bought for him special, because "We all know how much you love airplanes."

His youngest child was Natalie, who was eighteen years old at that time, and yet the three of them were buying him pajamas with cartoon characters on them. What the hell kind of a way was that for adults to behave? And . . .

He could feel a twinge of anger rise.

And he stopped it.

Because that wasn't him.

That was a part of the new personality the Punishers had devised for him, and he was not going to let it rule him, no matter how hard it was to control.

The drug and syringe were waiting under the bathroom sink, right where they were supposed to be, and rolling up his sleeve, he thought about the newspaper article he'd read over lunch in which the assault on the Rex-Saver druggist was described. That article had been bothering him all day. It seemed like such a high price to pay for a few bottles of clear liquid and a half a dozen needles . . . unreasonably risky and a bit foolish. But there was also something that ate at him about the man's name, given as Sallovy, Peter, of Garfield Heights, Ohio. Married, two

FORGET ME NOT

children. Police request any details on the assailant, no names necessary. Reward for information leading to a conviction of person or persons involved.

Peter Sallovy.

Sallovy.

Peter.

The name rang in the Prisoner's head all day, until that evening, after dinner, he asked his wife to bring up his daughter's college yearbook. And in it, he found what he wanted.

The Phi Tau Omega fraternity had their all-member picture printed beneath the letters of their organization in the "Greek Life" section of the book. There were about forty young men, sitting on the front steps of their fraternity house, across the street from the Art and Drama Center. Under the black-and-white picture, which was about the size of a postcard so that the faces were passable but hardly distinct, were the names of each and every member present, and then a short listing of those who hadn't made it to be photographed. All told, there were fifty-six Phi Taus, not including the fraternity's "sister organization," the Delta Lamba Delta sorority, page 107. In the sorority's all-member photograph, Natalie Reynolds stood in the third row, fifth from the right, wearing her cheerleader's sweater and smiling through shiny, freshly scrubbed cheeks.

Michael Sterns, his daughter's husband-to-be, was front and center in the Phi Tau picture, looking like Mr. Macho, dying for his graduation so he could get out there and do some business.

But there was no Sallovy anywhere. Not in the frat, and not in the sorority. But there was a Sales, and the boy's face fascinated the Prisoner for hours.

Sales.

Sallovy.

He studied the names, writing them on a pad and looking at them until he couldn't look anymore. There was a relationship there. He just knew it. It was just a matter of finding out what it was. And if there was anyone in the world capable of finding out about a person's background—because what better way was there to really get to know a man than to follow his family tree?—it was Eugene Reynolds, genealogist extraordinary and researcher to the stars.

As a matter of fact . . .

The vein bulged on his arm and he pushed in the needle far easier than he had anticipated. The dosage was the one he had seen the nurses give him at the hospital, less one little line on the syringe to be on the safe side, because he didn't know how strong his batch of drug would be compared to what the hospital used.

As a matter of fact . . .

The warmth in his arm felt right.

Just right.

As a matter of fact . . .

That was the answer!

Sitting there, in his Snoopy pajamas, at three in the morning, stoned on his ass and spinning, Eugene Reynolds saw the awesome, complicated, absolutely simple logic of what was happening to him, and sighed with contentment. If that was all there was to it, then he was going to be okay. He could do it. He'd make his mark, and serve his time, and be out of here before he knew it.

The doctor with the God complex had given him part of the answer, but it had been couched in the vagaries of the Zone, so it had taken the Prisoner some time to figure it out:

"Not things directly associated with your past crimes," the young man had said. "But things related to them."

So it wasn't Sales, a kid who had actually been present at the fraternity party where Eugene Reynolds had committed his crime, who was important. It was Sallovy, someone who was in some way *related* to Sales. Sales was a witness to the Prisoner's misdeed. He was one of the snot-nosed, drunken, rich-kid bastards who had cheered the Prisoner on, shouting, "Come on, Grandpa! You can do it!" as he drank, and staggered, and danced, and felt parts of himself that he never, absolutely *never*, allowed to come out in public, rising up from the depths of his personality and dragging his attention around the room, from young girl to young girl, until his eyes finally landed on the most beautiful girl there, who was Natalie, his own daughter, as drunk as the rest and doing what it was that he had found her doing!

But his task was not to take his revenge on the people directly responsible for his crime. His punishment was to see them go free, while he spent his life searching out people who were in some way associated with them.

People nearby.

Like the "innocent" druggist . . .

Peter Sallovy.

The Prisoner knew that, when he looked into Mr. Sallovy's family history, he'd find something that would connect him to the Sales family. It might be something as small and apparently inconsequential as a common city of origin, or a particular spelling of a name, but he knew that, whatever it was, there'd be something there for him to find. In fact, he was so certain that he would uncover the connection that he decided he wouldn't even waste his time looking. Instead, he'd start digging around in the rest of the fraternity's membership and see what was in their backgrounds, see who their families knew, and which of those acquaintances were the ones he had to deal with. Instead of looking back on things already done, he'd look ahead, to the future, and his release.

He came awake on the Shore just as what he thought were the final details of his punishment fell into place in his mind. By now, after having spent the time of his hospital confinement visiting the Shore almost whenever a nurse came into his room, he was familiar with the place, with its sights and sounds, its smells and personality.

But today, something was different.

Today, he wasn't alone.

The first creature he noticed was the figure of the dead pharmacist, waving at him from the sea.

And the second was a woman. He heard her before he saw her because, as he raised his hand to wave back at the white-coated figure in the waves, she said, "Hello, Father."

And he nearly swallowed his tongue.

Eugene Reynolds was fifty-three years old at that time. And though his physical body was weak and sore in the Zone, here on the Shore he was virtually perfect—strong and healthy. As startled as he was by the woman's voice—both by its proximity and by the fact that it was there at all—he leapt straight up and clenched his fists. When his feet came back down on the sand, he found himself facing the voice's source, and he crouched like a wrestler, ready to fight. He remained in that posture for exactly three seconds . . . and then his attitude softened because standing before him was a creature of such beauty that he could hardly bear the sight of her. She was undoubtedly the most magnificent, perfect, alluring, and attractive specimen of a woman he had ever laid eyes on. And just seeing her, just being close to her, just knowing that such a woman as this was possible at all, numbed him to the bone and made it impossible to do anything but stare, openmouthed and stupid.

The woman was glowing.

She was standing about ten feet away, dressed in white robes that made her look like an angel, and smiling. She was barefoot in the sand. And her hair was as golden as sunlight. All around her was a sheath of translucent brightness that sparkled like falling snow. And her eyes, as blue as the soul of a flame, bore through the golden light to hold the Prisoner in their gaze.

Cocking his head, Eugene Reynolds lowered his hands, his fists breaking open, his fingers going limp. In every feature of her face and every curve of her body, he could see some part of himself in this woman . . . some sliver of his own appearance and form, some indication that he was somehow responsible for her. And though they had never met, he knew that she was the daughter he was yet to have. Somehow he understood that this perfect, shimmering angel was the child his daughter Natalie was even now carrying.

Without a word, Eugene Reynolds stepped forward, extended his hand, and reached through the shimmering envelope of golden light surrounding his perfect child. He didn't know why he did it—he wasn't actually thinking in any way that made sense—but he felt that he had to touch her. He simply had to make some contact with her, if only for a moment, if only to verify that she was real.

And as if someone had read his thoughts, his hand passed through the girl's arm as if she were smoke.

Instantly, he snatched back his hand, feeling it tingle.

And the girl spoke.

"For now, I have no name," she said, staring at him through what looked like a haze of descending gold dust, shining around her. "For I am yet to come. As of now, I am almost without substance, for in time, I am to be. I have been sent to show you your goal . . . for it is me."

The Prisoner didn't understand. Actually, the first few words the girl spoke hadn't gotten through the awe in his mind, sounding to him a little like, "Azzohow, I the same." And it wasn't until somewhere around "yet to come" that he started picking up the meaning in her voice. Then he looked at her, sorted through what he had just heard, and asked, "How can you be my goal?"

"There will come one who will show you your way," she said, her eyes all but staring through him. "His name will be Molaine, and he will be your Keeper. Your crime is that of narcissism, for your love of yourself drove you to the woman who most resembled you in all the world . . . your own daughter, Natalie. I will be made even more in your image, and to look upon me will fill you with joy. But to pay your debt and accomplish your task of sentence, you will have to erase that image of yourself with your own two hands. If you destroy yourself in the Punishment Zone by destroying me when your Keeper so instructs you, I will then be allowed to serve as your passage back to the past you remember and the life you left behind."

The Prisoner was listening with every fiber in his brain. He was stamping these words on the flesh of his mind so that he could write them down, go over them, memorize and repeat them. For this was the single most important communication he had had so far with those responsible for his torment.

He was about to ask a question, but the girl had one final thing to say.

"Look to Molaine and complete the pattern," she said.

Then she was gone.

And the Prisoner's eyes flickered open. He was sitting on the toilet and the sun was just making the sky pink through his bathroom window. Groggily, he gathered up his syringe and bottle, hid them, and wobbled around, rubbing his forehead for an instant before hustling his way unsteadily down the hall to his office, where he found a pen and wrote, word for word, exactly what the vision of his future daughter had said.

"Complete the pattern!"

That rang true.

Then he went to bed with his head pounding in galloping rhythm, and he slept until three that afternoon, without so much as a sliver of a dream.

25

Natalie married Michael Sterns, and the baby grew inside her. The Prisoner didn't kill during the time of her pregnancy, but he did think about it. He spent a lot of time doing research on the boys in Michael's fraternity, which Michael thought was flattering. Here he had a nationally known genealogist looking up the family trees of his fraternity brothers as a wedding present. Good deal. The guys in the frat were thrilled, helping Reynolds all they could by answering the questions Michael asked them on his new father-in-law's behalf, and by asking their parents for information that they didn't know themselves.

Michael's college graduation day came quickly, and Eugene Reynolds attended—his first big day out since the wedding—standing next to his grinning daughter and her freshly graduated husband—Natalie was through with school now that she was married—so that his wife could take a picture, and afterward presenting the happy couple with a pair of tickets to a cruise along the Mexican coast as a kind of late honeymoon present. They were so excited. And so was his wife, who approached him that night in a way she hadn't in years. They made love tentatively, so as not to aggravate any of his tender spots, and when they were through, she cried.

The accident had changed him, she said.

She was so glad not to have to be afraid anymore.

He promised that she would never have to be afraid of him again.

On the Night Shore, the image of his soon-to-be daughter came and went, losing a portion of its supernatural glow and becoming more substantially lifelike each time he saw her. He and the girl spoke for hours while the surf pounded the Shore, and strange gulls that were oddly dark and silent appeared briefly, circled, and flew off. She instructed him in the rules of the place, showing him where he might find materials with which to construct a shelter, and identifying the very cave he would come to use as his haven from the ocean's spray. He followed her lead, approaching the tree line that started after about thirty yards of scrub bush along the beach's edge, and listening to the movements of animals in the dense woods that brooded as far up and down the Shore as he could see. She told him that he must never enter those woods because, as the one side of the Shore was the city on the horizon, which was beauty and civilization made tangible, the opposite side was the forest, and within its interior there were terrors beyond comprehension.

"But will I be safe on the beach?" he'd asked, holding a branch that he had just twisted off an evergreen tree.

"Nothing will harm you on the sand," his spirit daughter answered.

And that was fine.

He tried to touch her often, and she let him. As she became more solid, going from a tingling, insubstantial smoke, to a warm sensation of gelatinous promise, to very nearly flesh, broken only when the Prisoner pressed too hard, his touching lingered and became caresses. To these she didn't respond, saying only that their time would come and that the Shore was not to be their place.

But when his new daughter was finally physically born into the Zone as a baby named Jessica, her glowing form stopped appearing on the Shore. The Prisoner called for her for hours, walking the beach and shouting himself hoarse. But she didn't answer. She wasn't his anymore. She was a cyborg in the Zone now. Her spirit was gone.

And still he didn't kill.

But he thought about it.

And by the time of Jessie's first birthday he had a chart of names, all tied back to Natalie and Michael, and that even included two of the friends who had been at the party the night Jessie was conceived. Those two friends were also at Jessie's first birthday party . . .

Which was the night that Molaine appeared for the first time.

• • •

It was one year after Jessie had arrived on this side of the world, and the Prisoner was going to try ending his sentence by destroying her . . . as her glowing, golden figure had instructed him to do. It was hell waiting through the nine months it took for her to develop into a physical being inside the cyborg that resembled the Prisoner's daughter named Natalie. And it was even harder staying away from the baby during the year between her birth and her first birthday, which the Prisoner assumed would be the demarcation of her self-awareness. Lurking through the darkness outside his daughter's little house, he watched through windows as people gathered together and celebrated his misdeed, waiting until there were only four adults left . . .

Waiting.

Until he couldn't wait anymore.

Close to midnight he crept into the house, moving as quietly as the Angel of Death, which is exactly what he was, really: a killer, pure and simple . . . a machine, hardly any better than those he had been sent to slaughter, which was probably the greatest indignity of all: that he had been debased to such an extent that his actions against the mental perversions of those bent on his pain should bring him unease, and guilt, as if they were directed at real human beings. It was like feeling guilty for eating a hamburger, like agonizing over the harvesting of a pig. But he couldn't deny it, the feelings were there, and they made him careful . . . maybe even more careful than he needed to be . . .

But obviously not careful enough.

For after he had killed the larger ones—the parents and their last two remaining friends—he moved next to the girl—the guilt, the Jessica—and that's when the defenders burst in, waving their guns and shouting orders as if they had a right to dominate *him*!

In seconds he had his hands around the white policeman's throat—the policeman who he would one day come to know as Henry Parks, his most dreaded enemy—using a technique he knew in which pressure was applied to a spot just at the base of the neck that would rupture both the trachea and the esophagus, collapsing the breathing apparatus. Once that collapse was accomplished, even if he should remove his hands, his victim would be unable to draw air and would die in slow, gasping agony.

The first telltale *pop* that meant that he'd cracked the ribs on the cop's esophagus came, and the Prisoner bore down with his thumbs. But just as he felt his victim surge with pain, and saw his eyes widen—as if understanding that his mortality had just been exposed—the black policeman named Little stumbled in, and the Prisoner was forced to let go. After dispatching the younger man with a savage blow to the throat, he was just turning back to finish off the first cop when a strange and awful thing happened, seizing his attention and paralyzing him with fright.

The air opened, and the Keeper came through.

Henry Parks, gasping and clawing at his throat, overturned a torchère lamp near where he'd collapsed into a heap on the floor. In his legs, muscles twitched as nerves randomly fired, sparking their tiny electrical charges without sufficient oxygen to organize their messages into any coherent action, so that his shoe beat an erratic tattoo on the rug. He whistled when he breathed, a strange and plaintive pitch that vibrated though the wreckage of his throat and kept him—just barely—alive. There'd be some brain damage, though . . .

You couldn't diminish a man's oxygen supply by three-quarters and expect his system to keep on going as if nothing had changed.

Something had to give.

But to the Prisoner, the dying cop had ceased to exist because the thing he saw in the air had seized his attention, and the thrill of it tingled his entire body.

The air curved in on a spot just over the dying cop, and it wasn't the visual images of the things seen through the air that changed, but the air itself, as the Prisoner watched, was altered . . . twisting, moving, looking very much like the distorted picture one might see through a concave lens should that lens be turned, or how the world might look if viewed through somebody else's prescription glasses, like that little bubble window in Grandma's bifocals . . .

Yeah!

That was it!

It looked like there was suddenly a concentration of bifocal glass forming over the Prisoner's eyes and making everything he saw blur in his sight. It looked as if he had just that second developed a glass cataract, and that it was starting to impact his ability to focus. He rubbed his eyes through his stocking mask and gawked in disbelief as, from that smear in the air, a motion began to evolve, developing first into a smooth pulse and then into an undulating current that resembled . . .

What?

An invisible heartbeat, pumping smoke?

A thrashing fish, rippling water?

A transparent throat, gulping drink?

A head?

Yes!

A head!

The cop wasn't whistling anymore, but the Prisoner didn't care. The walls, the floor, the ceiling, and himself . . . none of them seemed solid anymore, but the Prisoner couldn't have cared less. The world wasn't predictable anymore . . .

But now everything was clear.

Blood came from the head in the air. Suspended as it was, six or eight feet over the floor, it produced crimson droplets that sprayed out, splattering a three-inch pattern up the wall behind it, over the ceiling, and then forward and over the floor . . . as the head spun, end over end over end . . .

Tumbling in place, spraying blood from its parted lips, wide-eyed and watching.

"No!" the thing said, without interrupting the bloody spray. "The time isn't right for this one yet. The Jessica must not die yet, and neither must the Parks! You must run away!"

And without even thinking, the Prisoner moved to obey, as much to escape the spinning head as to follow its instructions.

"No! Not that way," the head announced. "I am Molaine, the Keeper! And I say, look to the gate!"

And the Prisoner froze in the doorway.

Molaine! he thought, ice rushing through his veins. He'd heard the name before . . . from the lips of his own daughter's spirit, beneath golden layers of light on the Night Shore beach. He knew that name.

Turning, he found that the spinning head had moved to the broken window, where it hovered, splattering the ceiling and saying, "The gate!" over and over again.

"The gate!"

"The *gate!*"

The Prisoner took a step forward, and the head said, "To approach the gate, you must use the bridge!"

And the Prisoner stammered, "Wh-what bridge?"

But the head did not seem to hear. As the Prisoner would discover soon enough, it would never respond to any of his questions directly. Instead, it behaved as if he were too insignificant to bother with, imparting only its information and then disappearing back the way it had come, without a trace, or a mark of its passing.

"The bridge," it repeated, "is at your feet."

And the Prisoner glanced down to find the motionless body of the black policeman, Elson Little.

"Use the bridge to exit the gate.

"The bridge . . .

"The *bridge!*"

And the Prisoner arranged the body, thinking about the vision, the murder, the blood, and the gasping cop still struggling for life in the room's corner.

"What about Jessie?" he suddenly wondered, standing straight up after having pulled the corpse up on the couch.

"The bridge," the Keeper said. "There are years that must pass before the debt is paid. Now *go!*"

Jessie was screaming, so it was hard to leave her behind. But the Prisoner dared not to defy the Keeper, for, when he glanced back to where the child was tied to the floor, he found that Molaine was revolving directly over her, splattering her with its spraying blood and looking right at him.

Stepping up on the body, he found that it was so hard to keep his footing that he thought maybe the corpse was unwilling to support him. He had to struggle to walk up the man's back. The window was already broken—one of his victims had thrown a chair through it in a vain attempt at self-defense—and the flashing lights of the squad car parked in the driveway spun merrily, glittering in the cracked patterns before him.

Stepping over the dead flesh of the man whose life he had just extinguished, he felt a strange sensation of power tingling up through his feet. He had his palms pressed up flat on the ceiling, and was balancing himself before the broken window, listening to the crackling police radio outside and allowing the pulsating waves of something wonderful to leak up from the corpse and thrill him through to his spine as the Keeper said, "You are feeling the power that will keep you alive while you're here, in the Punishment Zone." Appearing outside the window, in the dark, blotting out the moon and revolving over the lawn with the clouds of nighttime moving behind its gleaming eyes, Molaine continued, "The death of a cyborg will be the only real food that will fuel your quest, giving you the strength to move on to the next killing, and the next again, and all those that are to come. For each cyborg you can kill, you will bring yourself that much closer to your final gate.

"Now . . . come!"

And the Prisoner stepped through the gate and landed on the snowy lawn.

"I'm going to need help," he said the day after the Keeper had prevented him from killing the baby Jessie. After spending a very bad night crying on the Shore, throwing stones into the sea and contemplating just walking into those terrible woods that lurked so darkly behind him so that some faceless horror could end his misery, the Prisoner had decided to fight. He knew his sentence would last right up to the moment that Jessie was twenty-one years old. And he knew that in the meantime he had a lot to do. His chart—the thing the vision of Jessie he had so enjoyed seeing on the beach had called "the pattern"—was filled with names. There were people all over the country who were in one way or another tied both to him and, more important, to his problem. He could never hope to deal with them all alone, without getting caught. So . . .

"I'm going to need *your* help," he said.

Recruiting his own child.

"Secrecy is the most important thing," he explained, withdrawing the Pattern and running his finger along the complicated series of interrelationships between apparent strangers that he had discovered. "We've got to be coordinated. It can't seem as if the same person is killing them all or we'll be caught. We've got to vary the way we do things. I'll do some, and you'll do the others."

"Okay," said his new partner. "I'll do anything you want. But why have you been ignoring me since I got you the drug? I thought you were mad about the druggist."

"I wasn't mad," the Prisoner said, pointing to a spot on the Pattern where the name Peter Sallovy was written. "But deception has got to be our first concern. We must protect our identities . . . use whatever means we can to remain anonymous. We must never get caught."

The partner's eyebrows rose.

"I'll teach you to rise above the confines of this world. I'll teach you to . . ."

"Rise?" the partner asked.

And the Prisoner nodded.

"Like the sun."

"Sunrise?"

"Son rise."

Their joke.

And also, the key to keeping his partner's identity a secret.

It was twelve years later that Eugene Reynolds decided to die.

The killings had been going reasonably well, and except for the occasional harassment by Henry Parks—that son of a bitch!—there had been no official interest expressed in either the Prisoner or the Reality Terrorist—the name his partner had assumed shortly after the pair of them had started erasing names off the Pattern Reynolds had drawn on the wall of the office he kept in his backyard barn. As time passed, the team's technique improved, and with the Terrorist free to move about unrestrained, and Reynolds almost as free to travel on business, they enjoyed twelve good years of hunting before the Prisoner decided that things were moving too slowly and that they needed to make a change. There was simply too much time being expended on providing him with alibis, too many hours spent on coordinating cover stories and backup plans. If he could disappear, he could move more freely and get more done.

No one is freer than a dead man.

So, on February 21, 1984, Eugene Reynolds was tragically killed when the gas heating system in his barn malfunctioned and blew him to the moon.

That accident took six months to plan.

The best part was the crowbar . . .

They never even knew the old guy's name. They found him sitting under a cardboard box on a heating grate down in front of the county courthouse at three A.M. on a cold, late-December morning, and coaxed him into the car with a fifth of Canadian Club. He was dressed in about seven shabby coats, was unshaven, smelled bad, and had a pair of bulging, milky eyes that seemed to independently revolve in a mess of pulpy pink tissue that was swollen and tender. He took two drinks from the bottle, threw up all over the backseat of the Cadillac Seville that the Terrorist was driving, and passed out. The whiskey had been generously laced with Razor, and the tranquilizer's effect on the bum, exacerbated by the alcohol, was profound. He didn't wake up for nearly twenty-four hours. And when he did, the Prisoner broke his arm.

The bum screamed in terror and pain and then passed out again. Standing over where the man was tied to a steel bed frame, the Prisoner studied his own X-ray charts for a moment or two, and then finished administering the proper damage with the crowbar. The medical materials were those recorded about him after his accident, and they'd been released to him after the hospital settled his malpractice suit—out of court because they admitted that they should have been more careful with a drug their patient obviously had an allergic reaction to—with a cash payment of nearly a million and a half dollars, and every document relating to his injuries they had in their possession. Reynolds used his X rays as his blueprint, breaking a collarbone here, smashing fingers there, knocking out these teeth, fracturing that rib. It took four hours . . . partly because he wanted to be very accurate, and partly because he waited for his victim to come back from his swoon a couple of times so that he could hit him while he was awake.

FORGET ME NOT 211

When he was finished, and the man on the bed frame had been reduced to a black-and-bloody mess, he set up an IV of tranquilizer solution and left the man alone. The next morning, he was dead. Too much dope. They had to do it again, and they had to get rid of the body, which they dumped off the Dennison Avenue bridge, where it landed on top of the Cleveland Zoo's hot dog stand, breaking every unbroken bone it had left, crashing through the roof, and landing on the deep-fat fryer used to make elephant ears. (The body stayed in the fryer for nearly a month before it was found. The zoo was closed for the season, and it was only after a snow that a security guard noticed a dark spot against the fresh blanket of white that was the hole in the concession stand's roof.) Later that same night, they recruited another bum, much in the same way as the last, and repeated the process, taking care to reduce the chemical doses, and successfully keeping their subject alive past morning.

The man remained in a state of semiconsciousness for nearly nine weeks, his injuries healed, and he was fitted with a brand-new set of false teeth that were identical to the ones Eugene Reynolds wore to replace the teeth he had lost in his accident.

On the morning of February 21, Mrs. Reynolds was sent shopping, and the bum, dressed in Eugene Reynolds' favorite work clothes—a terry-cloth robe, slippers, and a pair of silk pajamas—was propped up behind the research desk in the barn, and blown to pieces by a gas explosion so powerful that the upper plate he was wearing was eventually recovered in a neighbor's woodpile, two hundred yards away. After blowing out the pilot light on the furnace and rigging the timer on the fuse that would allow the building to fill with gas fumes before sparking the final explosion, the Prisoner and the Terrorist retired to the top of the hill, a mile away. When the barn went up—looking like a balsa wood model throwing paper planks like snow an instant before a rumble rolled up the hillside that sounded like thunder but that died more slowly—the pair threw their arms around one another and then opened a bottle of champagne.

"Here's to a successful finish," the Prisoner toasted.

And the Terrorist grinned, saying, "How's it feel to be dead?"

But the Prisoner didn't respond. In his mind, he'd been dead since that first moment he stepped from his sinking car, in a river of freezing-cold muck, almost fourteen years before.

The authorities didn't get much of a body to examine after the fire went out. A piece of a leg here. A chunk of arm there. But the pieces they did recover—most important, a collarbone, right side—as well as the testimony of Mrs. Reynolds, who had seen her husband, dressed in the robe they found tattered across the yard, and with his false teeth in, enter the barn only an hour before the blast, led the police to identify the victim as one Eugene Reynolds, local genealogist and part-time celebrity, personal worth in excess of ten million dollars, who would be mourned by many beautiful people, and who was a really nice guy . . . everybody said so.

Everybody.

Except his son, Kevin . . .

Who was glad he was dead.

But then again, Kevin wasn't right in the head, even if he had straightened up and gone to college. And everybody knew it.

From a motel bed not thirty miles away, Reynolds made his trip to the Shore the night after his own death. All the arrangements had been made ahead of time, and he had clothes, money, a new identity, and an organized family history, complete with pieces of his new self scattered through wallets, photo albums, and the trunk of his car: a late-model Ford he had chosen because of its anonymity. But despite his being a new man as far as the cyborgs in the Zone were concerned, his position and identity hadn't changed on the Shore. Nothing ever changed on the Shore . . .

Except that the golden city looked just that much closer. And that was enough.

The pain in his head nearly killed him outright when his eyes flickered open and the familiar view of his boiler room ceiling focused in at him from the blurred wash of liquid sight. There was a screaming in his head that, at first, he took to be his own agony crying like a siren in his skull. With his hands up over his face he added his own calls of pain and outrage to those in his head until the tears streamed down his face.

"God!" he gurgled, drawing up his scrawny knees nearly to

his chin and balling up his body as he rocked on his back and tried, through an act of will, to overcome the terrible fire burning in his head. "No, God, please! Please, not when I'm so close! Don't let me die in the Zone! Don't let me die."

When he finally lifted his head and withdrew his hands, he found blood on his fingers. Touching his upper lip, he discovered that his nose was bleeding. That was all . . . just a nosebleed.

His heart was racing, and his lungs hurt. His body disgusted him as he glanced down and saw his thin, hairless legs planted on the floor over the edge of the cot. And it was between those spindly, birdlike, old-man's legs that he saw Henry Parks' severed head lying on the floor. It was hairy and bloody, and its eyes were open. It looked insanely ugly, stark and awful on the concrete, so well defined in the light of the Prisoner's desk lamp as to resemble a dick on a plate.

The blood froze in Reynolds' veins, and he practically chirped when he tried to speak, producing, instead of a word, nothing but a movement in his lips and a shudder in his sunken chest.

And Henry Parks' head rolled, by itself, so that it faced up from the floor as it said, "You'll never get out. I'll fuck it up for you . . . so help me!"

It was just starting to laugh when Reynolds jumped up from where he was sitting and kicked at it, swinging his foot hard and screaming . . . really screaming, without a sense or purpose save for the natural, unthinking release of emotion that screaming could be . . . he was screaming, and stamping his feet, and shaking, and waving his clenched fists when he came back to himself about a minute later, stopped, and swallowed his rage . . .

He was alone in the boiler room. No Henry Parks.

"Molaine?" he whispered . . . he didn't know why. "Are you here?"

There was a terrible pressure surrounding him that he could not explain. And a ringing in his ears. There was a horrendous expectation of impending events that weighed in on him so heavily that it served to blot his senses into a single bulbous numbness, leaving him to thump around the room on feet that felt like clubs, looking under the cot for Henry Parks' head, or

Molaine's spinning face, or anything else that might have followed him into the Punishment Zone. He recoiled every time he put his face down close to an inconvenient corner, half expecting to find a bloody chunk of something or a lump of squirming worms. He worked himself into a state of almost total exhaustion by simply making a circuit of the room, and he was about to sit down and catch his breath when the rush of sound that filled his head seemed to give way and he was left with a single audible strain that he recognized, wailing in at him from the hallway outside.

Instantly, his exhaustion left him, and he threw open the door and rushed into the hall. The moaning rose and fell in pathetic waves, moving from out-and-out screams of horror to throaty gasps that filled the gaps between each louder shout.

"Shut up!" the Prisoner snarled, stumbling down the hall, naked, dripping sweat, trembling, and staring fixedly, his pupils still dilated from what would be his last dose of Razor and his hands working along the wall as he seemed to crawl like a spider past door after locked door, toward the cell where the source of the screams was housed. "Shut up!" he repeated, drool running from his lips unchecked. "Shut up! Shut up! Shut up!"

And from the last cell in the row, the screams and moans of pain finally formed one single statement of shock . . .

26

"They cut off my hand!" the voice screamed, and Jessie snapped her head up from where she had buried her face in her hands in the dark and shouted back, "Uncle Kevin! Uncle Kevin, are you all right?"

"Shut up!" another voice responded. An ugly voice. A voice of gravel and phlegm that seemed on the edge of breaking as it repeated its entreaty against the staccato slaps of bare skin on stone and the clanking of metal and wood.

"Shut up! Shut up! *Shut up!*" Jessie heard that voice bellow as she pressed her ear to her locked door and heard another door's hinges grind in echoing protest as her Uncle Kevin screamed, "Daddy, *nooo*!" in a high-pitched voice that sounded suddenly like a child's, and her grandfather . . .

Her grandfather was dead!

He was fucking *dead*!

. . . shouted, "Shut up, you baby!" just as the first in what would turn into a very long, very painful series of blows began to fall.

"Uncle Kevin!" Jessie screamed, climbing the invisible door and clawing at the wood as the blows fell from down the hall and her grandfather swore and her uncle shrieked like a little boy and . . .

"Uncle Kevin!"

And . . .

It went on for days . . . weeks . . . months, or years . . . and it didn't seem like it would ever end. Uncle Kevin cried and cried, screaming and pleading as blow after blow rang out with the sickening sound not of open-handed slaps but the heavy, drum-like quality of closed fists on a cowering back. He said things that didn't make sense. He promised to be good, to do what he was supposed to, to let his father do anything he wanted to him, "I won't tell!" Not like a man of fifty, but more like a tiny child who didn't understand the workings of an adult world and was desperate to find one foothold for a slice of mental balance.

Her grandfather . . .

Was dead!

. . . for his part, didn't speak after a few moments, but simply began a series of grunts that preceded and followed each blow as the beating entered into a kind of savage rhythm.

Jessie shrieked until her throat was raw, hysterical in her fear and tearing her nails on the wood barrier between her and Uncle Kevin. Even after Uncle Kevin stopped crying and fell silent—which was perhaps even more terrifying than his awful screams—and even after the blows stopped falling and the footsteps down the hall began approaching her door, she kept screaming, unable to stop. She knew she was drawing HIM to her. She'd seen HIM . . . he who just fucking could not be real, her dead grandfather, who she had always hated, who she had avoided at all costs, and at whose funeral she had cried tears of joy that pleased her grandmother, who thought they were tears of sadness . . . that fucking monster beast who had looked at her with those crazy eyes when he thought no one could see him, and who used to hole up in that fucking barn for days at a time with his fucking red chalk drawings on the wall . . .

Oh, Jesus!

The drawing on the barn wall!

She'd forgotten all about it!

How the hell could she have forgotten? How could she have failed to recognize that photograph of the pattern drawn over the factory doorway in blood as being almost identical to the family tree chart her grandfather had drawn on the wall of his office in the barn? She wasn't allowed in that office when she was growing up. It had always been strictly off limits. So, like any child confronted with a barrier, she had sneaked up one day when her grandfather was out of town on one of his frequent business trips and taken a look. Just the once. Maybe that was why she hadn't recognized it.

Maybe that was why!

Why?

"Grandpa, *no*!" she cried as a key was turned and her door swung open so that she saw . . .

"*Be still!*" he commanded, just as the lights came on with all the force of an explosion.

The light switch had been right there on the wall the whole time. Right there, just to the left of the doorway, at waist height, an old metal wiring box with a cheap switch strung at the end of a line that was wrapped in something that looked like canvas, and that ran to a ceramic knob near the ceiling. It had been right there, and . . .

The lights were like the sun.

They were set into the ceiling in a circle, aimed toward the center of the room, halogen spotlights that almost instantly started throwing heat, and that filled the tiny cell with so much white light that the walls seemed to expand as if the room had suddenly grown to twice its size. The mattress upon which Jessie had been lying—a filthy, urine-stained rag that she would not have touched with a gloved hand had she had the choice—was positioned so that the ceiling lights seemed targeted to ignite it with the sheer intensity of their power. And, stumbling back, she watched as the figure of her grandfather stepped from what was the absolute gloom created in the hall by the ceiling lights, to the merciless brightness in the room.

He was naked . . . scrawny, bowed, and ugly. His skin was pink and hairless, puckered and wrinkled as if he had spent years wrapped in rubber. His head shone bright under the lights, as bald as a skull, and his eyes, sunken deeply into a pair of violently dark circles beneath what had been his brows, burned with an attention and force that was inhumane in its single-mindedness. His hands were like flippers, so large did they look when compared to his meatless forearms. And up and down from his wrists to his shoulders, his flesh looked as if he had been tattooed with red and blue ribbons. There were needle marks dotting these tracks, which, even in her innocence of needle-born drugs, Jessie recognized as the etchings of blood poisoning.

Dirty needles! she thought, and the image of dirty needles, squalor, addiction, and insanity balled together to form one howling voice of panic in her mind that drove her back away from the door so quickly that she stumbled over the mattress, fell, backpedaled on the ground, and started screaming again, just shrieking, clawing backward, and staring up at the monster who had once insisted, with her on his knee, that she call him "Dad."

"Stay away from me!" she called, trembling and mad with terror. "Just . . . stay away!"

But her words had no effect. Grandpa moved as if drugged, like one of those zombies from the movies, or a wino on the street stumbling through the last stages of delirium. As her eyes adjusted to the ridiculous intensity of the light, she saw the blood speckling his pink flesh, dripping from his hands and sprinkled over the rest of him as if he'd been baptized with it. His hairless crotch seemed to move independently as he began rising into a feeble erection. And his tongue flicked over the bloody line of his lips as he stepped closer and lifted one finger to point, saying, "It's time, Jessie," in a voice like that of a sideshow hypnotist. "We can be together . . . like we were on the beach. We can finally fulfill the promises we made to each other on the beach."

"What beach?" Jessie stammered, thumping the wall of her cell with her back and ending her retreat. She nearly whimpered when she felt the barrier of stone behind her. But she bit her lip, clenched her fists, and settled herself to . . .

Run.

She lunged without warning, crying as she went, diving down so that she ran in a crouch that would take her under her grandfather's swinging arm and past him to the doorway. Once there she'd slam the door shut behind herself and turn the key her grandfather had so conveniently left in the keyhole, locking him safely away as she then took her time finding her way out of this underground hellhole to call the police.

But her grandfather, despite the ragged, washed-out appearance of his body and face, moved with the quickness of a snake, and as she tried to duck past him he snapped out his arm and hit her across the side of the head. Her knees were the first things to go. When his hard fist touched her, she staggered, saw the hallway, visualized herself turning the key, and saw the floor, an instant before she hit it, scrambling to stay upright, and ending up in the corner, huddled like a baby.

She heard the *click* before she saw the manacle. She felt the tugging before her balance was restored enough for her to stand. She saw her grandfather pulling her arm up, with one side of a pair of handcuffs snapped around her wrist, and the other looped through his fingers. He was talking again—something about the "special place" being gone, about some cave that she had shared with him that was no more, about an ocean that had disappeared, and about how he would almost be sad to see it all end—as he heaved her to her feet and placed himself behind her door.

Her senses were just coming back as he pulled her arm through a little window in the door she had not noticed before, and then, with her still in the cell, and him in the hall, he closed the door and heaved, slamming her face into the heavy oak planks and pulling her arm through the window right up to the shoulder. She screamed when he bent her arm down and held it, locking the other side of the handcuffs to the door handle so that she was left virtually hanging, her toes barely touching the ground, the bottom of the little window pressing on her breast and armpit.

"Now, don't go anywhere," her grandfather's voice said, his lips very close to the window so that she could feel them moving against the flesh of her upper arm. "The party's going to be starting soon. The party. You remember the party, don't you? The party where you were conceived? It's going to be starting, the guests are assembled, and I've taken care of everything. No one will interrupt. No one knows we're here. And when it's done, we'll be together like we were on the Shore. Won't that be wonderful?"

"Grandpa," Jessie sobbed, squirming where she hung in an attempt to ease some of the pressure on her protesting breast. "Please, Grandpa . . ."

"But first," her grandfather said, kissing her arm just over the elbow, "the Razor."

"Grandpa! No!"

"We'll have to introduce you to the Razor. The Razor's everything."

"Please, Grandpa, don't."

"And after the Razor," her grandfather said, impervious to her protests and moving away from the door, leaving her hanging, helpless, and afraid, "I'm going home.

"I'm finally going home.

"After the Razor.

"I'm going home!"

He was gone, and Jessie was fighting, flopping on her side of the door like a fish and crying tears that streaked across her face in glistening trails. The handcuff bit into her wrist, and her shoulder ground, bone on bone, in her ear, but she kicked and whimpered and struggled through the pain. She was trying to turn the doorknob. She was trying, at an impossible angle, to turn the handle and open the door. What she'd do once the door swung open she had no idea. But getting out of her cell and into the hallway filled her mind because . . .

Grandpa was crazy!

Crazy and . . .

Alive!

For so long she had forgotten about him, placing his memory

in that brain file where the deceased reside. Seeing him again nearly overwhelmed everything else, ripping the veil of sanity from what was left of her understanding and leaving her in a frame of mind that was very much like a dream. Nothing could surprise her anymore. She wasn't going to waste time and energy denying what her eyes showed her. She was going to get away, and worry about explaining things later. She was going to get away . . .

As the door handle turned.

The latch went *snap!*

And her grandfather's footsteps started in the hall again.

"No!" she whispered, pushing the door and feeling it swing. "No, not yet! Oh, God! Not yet!"

It was opening! The door was actually opening, and the sensation of moving on tiptoe over the stones and into the hallway was exhilarating. But the sensation of flying back the way she had come and hanging with all her weight on her screaming wrist and armpit jolted her as her grandfather heaved the door shut and the wood slammed with dreadful finality.

He should have said something like, "So, you thought you could escape!" But he didn't. He didn't say a word. He simply came up behind her where she was hanging helplessly and slammed the door shut. Jessie started immediately into a stream-of-consciousness kind of monologue not unlike the one she had just heard her Uncle Kevin babble while he was being beaten, but it made no impact at all. As she kicked and cried and pleaded, her grandfather, invisible behind the door, swabbed her arm with something cold, kissed her again, and ran something sharp up and down her flesh for a moment before sticking it into her.

Jessie squeezed her eyes shut, biting her lip so hard that she drew blood as the needle slid in.

"This is the Razor," a voice of absolute evil whispered as if from within the solid plank of the door itself. "The key to the escape, and the most wonderful substance in the Zone. I'm sharing it with you, my darling. You're frightened now, but in a moment you'll thank me. You'll thank me for everything . . . in a moment. Because you don't know what's good for you. But Grandpa does."

Jessie felt the plunger on the syringe being depressed as a pressure in her vein and a warm surging up her arm.

"Grandpa knows what's good for his little girl," the voice outside said as the needle was withdrawn. "You'll see."

Jessie's struggles were fading, and an incredible sensation of lethargy was filling her head. The pain in her arm seemed far away, and even though she didn't understand why she should be disturbed about it, the voice of her grandfather, that voice which she hadn't heard since she was thirteen years old, was making her feel better. They were going to a party, Grandpa was saying as Jessie felt herself floating through the air. When the pressure on her wrist gave way, she crumbled to the floor, her legs flopping as if they were broken.

But that was all right.

When the door swung open to reveal her grandfather, still naked and beaded over with rivulets of sweat that looked oily in the light, that was all right too.

And when her grandfather reached down and took her hand, lifting her to her feet again and saying, in a voice that sounded as if it were coming from underwater, "Come, Jessica. I'd like you to meet some of our guests," well, that was okay.

Because, after all, it was her grandpa who was taking care of her . . . just like he'd taken care of her Uncle Kevin when he was a little boy, and her Aunt Lisa, and her own mother . . .

What was her name?

What was her mother's name?

Oh, well. It didn't really matter.

Because Grandpa said they were going home.

Grandpa said.

Grandpa . . .

Said that they were both going home.

PART III

The Punishment Zone

SIX

27

All the way to the airport, Henry Parks eyed Lisa Reynolds, who started talking almost as soon as they got in the car. Parks did his best to listen, but in his mind he was running over the possible scenarios of her involvement beyond the simple story she'd given him of receiving a phone call from her killer brother in the middle of the night. He saw his options as boiling down to three separate possibilities.

One: Lisa Reynolds was telling the absolute truth, and her brother was in fact taking Jessie to the factory in Pittsburgh—which was the scene of his last, and most violent, anonymous murder.

(In his heart, Parks hoped that this first possibility was the case, because then he'd be in a position to ambush Kevin Reynolds and end this thing once and for all. Even though Lisa Reynolds was adamant about not wanting any of Henry's men checking out the factory because she said it might spook her brother, Parks had called ahead. There were guys crawling all over the place right now. If Kevin Reynolds had kidnapped his niece and started driving straight to Pittsburgh with her, there was no way he'd arrive there until at least four that afternoon, maybe closer to five. Parks, Lemon, Ellis, and Lisa Reynolds would land by four, and it was only fifteen minutes to the factory from the airport. It was going to be close.)

Two: Lisa Reynolds was the woman at the motel and was involved from the operational end of the murders.

(This was the scenario that Ellis apparently believed, and if it was true, then Reynolds could very well be leading them into a trap. Her brother could have arranged things at the factory so that he could end up killing Jessie right before Parks' very eyes—the ultimate humiliation after so many years of the chase. Or Lisa Reynolds could be rigged with a bomb that would blow the airplane out of the sky and end everything for everyone.)

Or . . .

Three: Lisa Reynolds was involved in the killings with someone other than her brother.

(This final scenario, in Parks' mind, was the most disturbing of all. What if—and this was a big "what if"—what if Kevin Reynolds really didn't have anything to do with anything? Christ! That was a rough one, and it opened up a real can of worms. What if Lisa Reynolds and some unknown accomplice had been killing people in such a way as to coincide with some of her brother's movements, making it *appear* as if he could have been in town when certain murders occurred? Parks would suspect Kevin of the crimes because of his history of emotional trouble, and Lisa Reynolds would move with virtual impunity, having thrown off her pursuers by using Parks' own prejudices against him.)

That last possibility, as farfetched as it was, chilled Parks right down to the bone.

But there was one thing that ran like a thread through these scenarios, and that was the necessity of Parks' not letting Lisa Reynolds out of his sight. Because, whether she was involved or not, she was the only hope Parks had of finding Jessie alive.

On the way to the airport, Reynolds kept her posture rigid—her knees held tightly together so that her shapely legs were cocked to her left, her hands folded on her lap, and her oversized purse tucked in between her hip and the car's armrest. But her voice betrayed a certain relief, a kind of sad acquiescence that hinted at the lifting of some weight from her shoulders as she spoke. She was, Parks thought, very much an example of the classic unwilling witness; not at all happy about her involvement, but anxious to finally tell someone else about the secrets she'd been holding in for so long.

"I think it was the shock treatments," she said, her eyes flickering from the floor, to the window, and then to Parks' face, where they settled—two pools of beautiful green. "They were what he really wanted to talk about when he called. He said that they changed his life—the treatments, and the drugs they gave him later. He said that they opened up his senses and let him see what was going on."

"He spoke like that?" Ellis asked from the front seat. Lemon was driving, and Ellis had turned around to face the back. "He just started telling you about his shock treatments on the phone?"

Reynolds sighed. "After he told me what he had been doing," she began, her eyes never leaving Parks' face. "I asked him. He said that he had been killing these people all these years, and I asked him why. I didn't quite know what else to do. I mean, I could have hung up on him, I suppose, but he sounded like he needed me."

She paused, and Parks focused on the lines of concentration straining around her eyes.

"I never let him need me before," she said softly. "So when he started talking about himself, I listened. But I didn't believe a word about the murders."

"Why?" Ellis asked.

"Because he was so gentle," Reynolds answered. "They said that he tried to hurt Natalie, our younger sister, when he was twelve. I don't know if he did that or not. I wasn't home at the time, and all I ever heard was my father's side of the story because Natalie would never talk about it. She acted like it never happened. But his guilt or innocence didn't matter, because from that time on he spent his life as more of a laboratory specimen than a human being. He couldn't have done anything wrong, even if he had wanted to."

"What makes you say that?"

It was Parks who had spoken.

Reynolds eyed him for a moment and then said, "Because

they trained him to be good. They shocked and drugged him into behaving. He used to get ill, physically ill, watching football games on TV. That's how far they pushed him. He was absolutely harmless. He was as frightened of saying or doing anything wrong as if his life hung in the balance every moment. And in a way it did. One slipup—that's all it would have taken for them to have sent him back to an institution. He'd have been trussed up and carted off before he knew what hit him. As it was, he was in and out every couple of months. But one slipup, and that would have been all. They were just looking for an excuse to lock him up for good."

"But shock treatments are supposed to make a person placid," Ellis cut in. "How could they have turned him into a killer?"

"I don't know," Reynolds said. "But that's what he said happened. He started off terrified of the doctors. But after the treatments started, he said that he wasn't afraid anymore. He wasn't afraid, because he liked them."

"Liked them?" Ellis asked.

"That's what he said." Reynolds shrugged. " 'Lee,' he said. He's been calling me Lee since he was a kid. But he said, 'Lee, I don't know how to describe it. But when they put that mask on me and strapped me down, I was so scared. I couldn't even breathe, I was panicking so bad. And when they told me to bite down on that rubber thing so that I wouldn't break my teeth when the juice hit—God. I was praying. I was really praying. But then they turned on the power and . . . I don't know. I felt the juice go right through me, and it changed everything.

" 'Lee, I fell in love. I really did. Right at that instant, I absolutely fell in love with it. I could feel the electricity rushing through my body, filling me with a peace like nothing I've ever known. That's what love is, Lee. Having something inside you that you don't understand and that you can't control. Something that might even kill you, if you let it go that far. And when you let yourself go, and start trusting whatever that thing is, and that thing starts trusting you back, and you live together, and feed off each other, taking what you need and giving all you can . . . that's love, Lee. It really is.'

"And that's what he said. Or at least as nearly as I can remember it."

"So what does the term 'Son Rise' mean?" Parks asked as soon as Reynolds' voice had fallen off.

Reynolds studied Parks' grim expression for a moment and then said, "It's a phrase Kevin said our father coined to describe why Kevin felt compelled to murder strangers."

"Your father knew about the killings?"

"Yes," Reynolds responded softly. "My father supposedly knew."

But there was more meaning beneath her words. And, leaning toward her, Parks said, "Say it, Miss Reynolds. Please. For the love of God, and the mercy of an old man. Will you please just tell me what in the hell is going on? I think you've known for a long time."

Her eyes snapped up to his.

And Parks said, "I don't think that everything you know came from a single phone call in the middle of the night. You've been in contact with him for a long time."

"He's called me now and then," she admitted.

"And he's been telling you what he's been doing?"

She nodded reluctantly. "He's been telling me things. But they've been so bizarre that, like I said, I just couldn't bring myself to believe them. I probably should have gone to the police, but . . ."

"You were afraid."

"I was afraid."

"You could have come to me."

Her silence was her answer to that.

"So, what was it that was so bizarre that it made you doubt everything he said?"

She hesitated, for just a moment, before responding, "He said that our father was still alive."

And then she broke.

"Okay?!" she shouted, the old anger welling up in her again and her hands trembling on her lap. "Okay? Is that what you wanted to hear? He said that Dad wasn't dead, but that he was alive, and telling him what to do. They were a team, and the Son Rise thing you seem to know about was a code between them. It described what happened to Kevin when he'd kill someone. He'd rise . . . he'd get an erection, a hard-on, he'd feel sexually excited. How do you want me to say it, Mr. Parks? How would you like me to tell you that my brother thinks that my dead father is alive, and that he gets off by killing strangers while wearing a shock-therapy hood?"

But Parks didn't answer. He simply stared at the woman sitting across from him, numbed and silent.

Eugene Reynolds? he was thinking.

Alive?

Eugene Reynolds was the Prisoner?

Was that possible?

Turning his head, he glanced out the window, and as he stared, Reynolds described how the explosion in the barn that had supposedly killed her father had been set up, including how an anonymous homeless person had been plucked off the street and used as a decoy for the police to find. She described how, after being liberated by his own death, her father had been free to stalk the country, killing at will, while Kevin stayed at home, using the Reynolds Genealogical Survey and Research Group's staff and computers to look up the family histories of potential victims. And she described how Kevin had continued killing when he could—but only when his father said it was safe for him to do so.

"Partners?" Parks commented vaguely. "Two men working together. But why?"

"The Gates of Paradise," Lisa Reynolds responded, and Parks looked at her in frank astonishment. "They're supposed to be satisfying my father's delusions."

Then she sighed and leaned back in her seat, running her fingers through her hair and saying, "Okay. You were right. I should have known better than to try and hold back. It'll just make things more complicated.

"The truth is that Kevin's been contacting me, off and on, for about the last five years. He's been telling me bits and pieces—details about Dad and what he and Kevin were supposed to have been doing. He wouldn't say anything specific about who they killed . . . no when, where, or how. But he was generous with the why . . . the strange stuff, the stuff that proved that he was coming in on a completely different frequency than me. Occasionally, he'd get me so worked up that I'd go home to see him. I'd be expecting this big problem when I arrived, but instead I'd always find him happy and quiet, working on building the business and sorry that he'd bothered me on the phone. When I'd see him face-to-face like that, he'd apologize and blame his medication for what he'd said, only to call me some other night after he'd been drinking again."

"So," Ellis interrupted, "this Gates of Paradise thing changed your mind about him, huh?"

"No," Reynolds said in response. "The magazine was just another goofy thing my whacked-out brother sent me. It was the police calling my mother that brought me to Cleveland."

"And it's your brother's 'sentence' described in that story?" Parks asked.

"No," Reynolds said, shaking her head. "According to him, it's my father's punishment we're talking about. Kevin's just helping him."

"Why?"

"So that he'll go away."

Reynolds leaned forward in her seat and took Parks' hand. It was the first time she had ever touched him and the sensation was abrupt, and disquieting.

"Mr. Parks," she said. "According to Kevin, our father's been torturing him since he was a kid. He's been abusing him sexually and psychologically in a systematic way that included actual medical doctors, who he paid large sums of money to fabricate Kevin's records. He's been building a monster who is totally dependent on him because the rest of the world thinks he's unstable. And he's been releasing that monster's fury and allowing Kevin to kill for him because he thinks that he has to eliminate certain people before he can go home. That's how Kevin described it. 'Dad's never going to get to go home if I don't help him,' he said. 'If I help him, then everything'll be all right.'

"He's helping Dad in order to get rid of him. Or rather, what I mean to say is that he says he's helping my father, who he says isn't dead, so that he'll go away and leave him alone. He seems to believe that if he does certain things, his torture will end."

"But what's your niece got to do with all this?" Parks asked, untangling his fingers from Reynolds' grip and taking back his hand.

Reynolds sighed. "Supposedly, Jessie's actually my sister."

And Parks narrowed his eyes.

"According to Kevin, Dad raped Natalie and made her pregnant. That's the crime that sent him here, to what he calls the Punishment Zone. When Jessie turns twenty-one, Dad is supposed to kill her, and then he can go home. So that's the story:

"My father's still alive, and my brother has been helping him kill the witnesses to a twenty-year-old crime. My niece is my sister, my father is an alien from another dimension, and my brother is actually performing us all a great service by working to get him out of our world."

Lemon sighed.

Ellis didn't move.

And Parks rubbed his eyes.

28

The limousine was waiting for them at the airport. Parks spotted it immediately, and so apparently did Ellis, who turned around and expressed silent surprise with his eyes. Lemon slid their car into a spot near the glass tunnel that connected the terminal to the enclosed parking garage, and as everyone got out, Ellis took the opportunity to whisper in Parks' ear, "How did he know where we'd be?" But instead of answering, Parks instructed Ellis and Lemon to take Lisa Reynolds to the plane, and to wait. He would catch up with them shortly, he said. And then he turned his attention to the long black car parked along the curb. It was a six-door Caddie limo with windows tinted so dark that they looked like mirrors. It had a boomerang TV antenna on its trunk, a spring telephone aerial on its roof, and, of all things, vanity plates that read, LOADED.

Loaded, he thought, clearing his throat as he stepped off the curb toward the limo.

Real fucking funny.

Jacob Krammer sat alone in the backseat, waiting. When

Parks stuck his head in, Krammer nodded and indicated for him to enter with a wave of his hand. There was a driver seated in the front seat, and he closed the glass partition that separated the front from the rear compartment as Parks sat down. This would be a private meeting.

Private, and unexpected.

"Mr. Krammer," Parks said in his most grizzled voice, shaking Krammer's hand. "It's interesting that you should be here now. We seem to be making real progress."

The inside of the limousine was done in red leather, with a seat bench in the back and another facing it over a circular table. The windows were so darkly tinted that it always looked like dusk outside. And where the television normally would have been positioned in a car used for pleasure, there was a computer screen. The machine's keyboard, Parks knew, was tucked away under Krammer's seat, where he could get at it while he rode. And there were three cellular phones lined up on the man's right-hand side. This car, despite its exterior appearance, was all business.

Krammer should have been the same age as Parks. That would have been more appropriate. He was, after all, the personal secretary to one of the richest men in the country, and his responsibilities ranged from entertaining important clients to being the corporate hatchet man who "informs employees of the dissolution of their positions." He was also the man Parks reported to about his progress in chasing the Prisoner. Having him show up here, and now, indicated that there was someone close to Parks who was reporting directly back to Sallovy—a spy, in a sense. Not that Parks' activities were a secret necessarily, but he had always resented the "money man" keeping tabs on him and telling him, by inference, what to do.

But instead of being Parks' age, Krammer was more like forty, with very dark red hair, a light complexion, and an air of authority and ease that came off him like mist off ice. He must have been born into wealth, Parks always thought. He was left-handed, wore a dark suit that was either black or that weird shade of burgundy that he went in for—the one that was so dark you could only catch a hint of red in it in very bright sunlight. And he was smiling . . .

Which wasn't a good sign.

Invariably, his smile meant that he had instructions. And Parks hated instructions.

"Congratulations, Mr. Parks," he said without preamble. "Our sources inform me that you've isolated our killer and expect to terminate him soon. That's wonderful news. It means that the time for the box has finally arrived. After nearly twenty years, it's a big day indeed."

"What box?" Parks asked, wanting also to inquire how Krammer had gotten here so fast, or if what Lisa Reynolds had said about her "dead" father could possibly be true, or if he could send some men down to Columbus to start looking back into Kevin Reynolds' telephone records to see if he had in fact been making long-distance calls in the middle of the night. But instead, he stuck with the conversation's flow because he knew that he could best save time by simply letting Krammer do his job.

From a compartment in the wall, the younger man withdrew a polished box that looked to be made of some hardwood, like mahogany, only darker. Laying it on the table in front of Parks, he said, "I assume you still carry the same .38-caliber revolver you were issued as a police officer?"

"You know I do," Parks grumbled, interested more in the box than in Krammer, and not bothering to hide it.

Opening the box, Krammer turned it to face Parks, displaying its red velvet interior, and the three rows of what Parks first took for tiny silver coins. It took him a moment to realize that the coins he was looking at were actually the butt ends of three rows of bullets—twenty in a row, sixty all together—stuck into the folds of the velvet. Without a word he took one and held it before his face, rolling it between his fingers and watching its jacket shine silver.

"High impact, military load, hollow point, .38-caliber ordnance," Krammer explained. "Specially designed to fit your type of gun."

Parks examined the end of the shell he was holding.

"There's no manufacturer's name on it," he observed.

"That's right," Krammer agreed. "There isn't."

When Parks returned the bullet to its place with the rest,

Krammer closed the case and slid it over so that it sat on the table with its handle facing Parks' way.

"Mr. Sallovy understood that he wouldn't live to actually see you find the Prisoner," he said. "So he had these bullets made for you to use when you did. They're special bullets, and I'm asking both you and Mr. Ellis to load your weapons with them."

"What's so special about 'em?" Parks wanted to know.

"They're Mr. Sallovy's way of being in at the end," Krammer replied. "They demonstrate his, shall we say, contempt for the Prisoner, because they each have, in their physical substance, a little bit of Mr. Sallovy's fecal material."

Parks glanced up.

"He defecated into the molten lead used to make them," Krammer explained.

"Sallovy did that?" Parks asked.

"When the Prisoner dies," Krammer said, "Mr. Sallovy will symbolically, and quite literally, be telling him to eat his shit."

29

It was at the end of the moving sidewalk that Lisa Reynolds started crying. She didn't want to do it, but she didn't really fight it all that hard either. She could feel the emotion surging through her, and she knew it would have been pointless to try and struggle it away. It was just too much. So, with an "Oh, my God!" and a single choked whimper, her tough façade crumbled and she clutched her oversized purse to her breast as the tears poured down her face.

Lemon was the first to notice her distress, and he grabbed her as she stumbled off the rubber treadmill that ended at a huge escalator that would take them down at least two floors. Ellis responded nearly as fast, and in less than three steps they each had a hold of one of her arms and were hustling her out of the way of the pedestrian traffic behind them. She sobbed and shook her head, trying to say, "I'm sorry," and, "No, no. I'll be all right." But her words came out garbled, and inside she knew that she wasn't going to be all right at all—not now, and maybe not ever again. It was all her brother's fault . . .

Kevin's fault.

Kevin . . .

Her little brother.

Who, despite all the trouble he'd been, she still loved as flesh of her flesh, and who she still saw as the little boy he would always be in her heart.

"They're going to kill him!" she mumbled, squeezing her eyes shut and shaking her head as Ellis and Lemon pushed her onto the escalator and held her up. "They're . . . we're going to kill him!"

They descended the two floors from the moving sidewalk level to the escalator's end, stumbled the twenty yards or so of carpeted causeway that was actually the distance under the passenger drop-off drive overhead, and then ascended another escalator that deposited them in the main lobby by the ticket counters. Reynolds' sobs steadied into a constant trembling that racked her whole body, and try as she might, she could hardly keep up with the two men holding her, even though they were carrying practically all her weight.

In front of a ladies' room near the main bank of TV monitor screens announcing arriving and departing flights, they propped her against the wall and let her cry for a few minutes before Lemon ran over to a water fountain to wet a handkerchief. Ellis asked her two or three times if she was okay, and she nodded that she was, while trying to look brave. Lemon returned and wiped her face. Her makeup was ruined. And so was her image in their eyes, she thought. She had always prided herself on her no-nonsense personality, but now, when she needed her strength the most, it had failed her, being washed away with blistering reality of what she, and these strange men who she didn't even really know, were on their way to do.

"We're going to kill him!" she mumbled, her eyes squeezed shut and her shoulders pressing cold concrete. "I just can't believe . . ."

And then she stopped, reaching into herself and producing a firm jaw and dry eyes as if they had been there all along. Gently pushing Lemon and Ellis away, she sniffed, wiped a hand across her cheek, and apologized.

"I'm sorry," she said, trying to regain her dignity. "But it just hit me . . . the reality of it. All of a sudden it was just more than I could handle."

Lemon was nodding his head.

And Ellis said, "It's all right."

"No, it's not," Reynolds said, sniffing again. "But it's too late now. It won't happen again. I promise. Now, if you'll excuse me, I'd like to clean myself up."

And both men stepped back to allow her to stand on her own.

"We'll wait over there," Ellis said, indicating a smoking area positioned across the terminal's main concourse, just before the metal detector unit. "Take your time."

Still clutching her bag to her breast, Reynolds thanked them again and went into the ladies' room, which was mercifully empty and surprisingly clean. Approaching a mirror, she felt the tears coming again, but this time, instead of fighting them, she simply let them flow . . .

Because that was normal.

She always cried.

He always cried.

Always.

She wasn't sobbing as she laid her purse on the sink and opened it. For all practical purposes her expression was one of bland concentration. It was marred only by the steady stream of tears that ran from her eyes. Working quickly, she moved with practiced fingers, unzipping compartments, undoing buttons, pulling it free . . .

It was leather and hard plastic.

Her second skin.

The mask.

The last stall in the row behind her was designed for the handicapped, wide enough to accommodate a wheelchair, and deeper than the rest. Gathering up her bag and sweeping her hand back across her skull, Lisa Reynolds pulled off her wig and locked the stall's swinging door behind herself. Her head was shaved naked like her father's. Beneath her coat and blouse, both of which she tore off, popping buttons and snaps, she wore the top half of her rubber body suit . . . her uniform . . . her real self. Beneath her skirt she wore nothing at all, so as the skirt dropped, she was left naked from the waist down, save for her thigh-high nylons and her high-heeled shoes.

She was breathing hard now, her face set in an expression of perfect indifference. She was beginning to perspire, and the tears had nearly stopped.

Son Rise! she was thinking. Now! Son Rise now!

There was nothing else in her mind . . . and there never was when the change was coming . . . nothing but the blossoming chaos of her disjointed personality.

Who was she?

She had never stopped to ask . . . well, never at a time like this, never when she was in the neutral zone, the grey area, the transitional place between male and female, man and woman.

What was she?

That question sometimes plagued her, late at night, when she was alone with all the various parts of herself that resided inside her head . . .

His head . . .

Its head.

From the bag she pulled it out, and her trembling fingers were soothed by just its touch. It was soft and hard. Firm and giving. Pink and long and masculine and so much a part of her sometimes that she could feel sensations emanating from it when it was riding around in her purse, or when she left it home in a drawer. She was attached to it with an invisible umbilical of spiritual communion that would have been impossible for her to explain . . . even if someone should take the time to ask. But that attachment was as real as the flesh covering the bones in her hand, or the tears rolling down her cheeks, or . . .

Her father's face, straining over her when she was young . . . since she could remember . . . all her life . . . except when he had temporarily lost interest in her as Natalie grew older. Then Dad stopped visiting her room. Stopped looking at her and taking her places when Mom wasn't around. Stopped . . .

When Natalie . . .

She hated Natalie!

That bitch!

She'd taken Dad away!

And *Jessie* . . .

The swirl moved in her skull, the pictures danced and bled into a single wash of aggression . . . male aggression.

Son Rise!

The penis was made of rubber and was nearly a foot long.

Son Rise!

It was supported over her shaved crotch by a strap that fit around her waist and buckled in the back.

Son Rise!

It was as much a part of . . .

Her . . . him . . . it . . . Lisa . . . Kevin . . . the Terrorist . . . as her hands . . . his hands . . . its hands.

It got harder the instant the buckle snapped behind her back, swelling until it nearly hurt. Like it always did when she/he came so close to the center, where the *other* lived. It became alive when she strapped it on, sending its invisible tentacles of pure sensation up into her from between her legs to explore her guts and move her brain and drive her so crazy that she had to pause and take a second to just stand there and feel it . . . just *feel it*!

Parks had been in the motel room!

She knew it.

There was no other way he could have known about the Son Rise if he hadn't been snooping. Like he had been for years. She/he should have killed him a long time ago, but Dad said no, said that they weren't allowed to harm Parks directly. That was one of the rules. There seemed to be an awful lot of rules.

But she was glad that all her preparations at the motel hadn't gone to waste. She'd been very careful there, making sure that the desk clerk saw her coming and going every day, sometimes dressed as a man, sometimes as a woman. She'd parked the red Corvette right out front as far as she could so no one could miss it—after borrowing it from her brother a month before. He was always willing to do anything to please her, since he associated her with much of the trouble he'd had over the years. Also, he couldn't seem to remember if he'd hurt her too—like they said he had hurt Natalie. She'd made the videotape for Parks, stuffing her rubber suit with spare blouses and jeans so that she'd look fat like Kevin, so that someone seeing the tape would automatically assume that it was Kevin or at least that it was a man;

but never a woman . . . because of the bulge in her pants . . . his pants . . . its pants . . .

Felt so hard.

And so good.

She moved the hard thing between her legs to one side so that it rested against her thigh as she withdrew the bottom half of her rubber suit from where it was rolled up in her purse. Sliding the trousers on, she rubbed the hard thing, moving it, pressing it, hurting it until she had to pause and catch her breath. The mask was hanging open mouthed from the toilet handle, looking up at her with empty eye sockets, appearing as if it wished to speak.

"We've got to hide our identities," her father had always said. "We've got to make sure we behave as if the entire world is out to get us—because it is. We're the only ones who know; we're the only people on earth who understand. It's just me and you, Lisa. If anyone else knew . . ."

"They'd nail our asses to a tree," Lisa Reynolds whispered aloud, licking sweat off her upper lip, and tasting tears.

"They all think that your brother's crazy," her father had explained. "I've spent a lot of time making sure that everyone knows that he's crazy. There's practically nothing that he could do that would surprise anyone anymore. So it's got to look as if he's the one doing it all."

"Kevin?"

"You."

"Me?"

"You're him."

"You want me to pretend that I'm Kevin?"

(The idea of playacting wasn't all that new for her. Father had been having her pretend to be different people for a long time.)

"No, you mustn't just pretend," the Prisoner said, his eyes sparkling in the dark on his side of the bed. "You must *be* Kevin. In your heart, and in your mind, whenever you go to work, you must *be* him: think like him, feel like him, see things the way he would see them, and do things the way he would do them. That way, any little mistake you make—and we all make mistakes, my dear—but any little mistake you make will look like he made it. And if it looks as if he made the mistake, then it will be him who will be held responsible should anyone find out.

"So, be Kevin.

"With all your soul."

Lisa wished, right at that second, that she had brought her wires with her. There was an electric socket over by the sink, and if she'd have brought her wires she could have used it. She could have hooked herself up and made herself feel wonderful. Like she did with men sometimes. Men who understood. Because, even though Dad had always said that there was no one else in the world who would understand, she'd found that that wasn't necessarily true. There were other men who could give her what she wanted, what she needed, what she spent all her time between killings pursuing. She just had to know where to look when she wanted to find one.

She remembered the first time Dad had showed her the place on the thing between her legs where the wires would fit. She'd been sixteen, and fascinated. She remembered the first time he had had her touch the wires to similar places on his body, and how he'd stiffened all over. Gripping the bedposts so hard that his hands went white and his face blew red with pressure. But he grimaced from the pleasure of it, not from the pain, and so did she . . . so did . . .

But she hadn't brought them because she knew she didn't have time. She was too busy to even think about such things now. By starting her spree of terror with the woman and her kids in the van, and moving all the way through Elsa McGreavy to the accident she'd caused on the freeway, she had successfully achieved the first task Dad had set for her.

"Keep them busy all day," he had said one night last week in his basement apartment, with all the pipes on the ceiling. She'd been living in the motel down the street and keeping tabs on Jessie through the microphones in her walls for nearly a week by then. Finally, cuddled up naked on the bed and listening to her stoned father speak—he'd just had a shot of his drug, and the initial, comalike stupor during which he claimed he left this world for another of ocean spray and white sand had passed, leaving him sweaty and talkative, like it always did—she began realizing why he had insisted on such outrageous risks as bugging her niece's apartment.

"When I give you the word, start a chain reaction and make the cops think that they're in the middle of a blitz," Dad said, slurring his words, eyes closed. "That way, the last thing they'll do is interrupt me when I'm in the middle of the most important thing in the world. I'll be going home. I'll be finding the tunnel out, and climbing through. I'll be free at last."

"What about me?" Lisa, Kevin, the Terrorist, asked.

And her father stopped speaking for a moment, seemed to think, and finally responded, "What about you?"

"What will happen to me after you've gone?"

This question seemed to bother Eugene Reynolds, and he got up and drank water from a thermos on his desk before answering. When he did, it seemed as if he were directing some of the deceitful brilliance that had served him so well with what he called the "cyborgs" or "cybertrons" over the years.

"You're a part of this place," he said smoothly. "My departure won't affect you at all here, but"—he smiled—"on the other side, back where you really are, where the real you is, the living creature that they used as a model for the helper you've been to me—back on the other side, you'll get your father back. And we'll be able to return to living a normal life together. We won't be trapped in this fucking nightmare anymore."

Lisa Reynolds got up off the bed and took the thermos from her father's trembling fingers, thinking about how much he looked like an insect without his clothes on, and also about how often she'd thought about killing him, like all the others he had instructed her to kill. The thoughts flashed through her mind that he had been using her since she was a child, and that he had done terrible things to her, making her crazy, making her the way she was. At first, as a little girl, she hadn't understood. But as she grew older the truth started working its way into her mind and the anger came, and the shame, loathing, and all the rest.

But at the bottom of it all, there was still the love. And also the undeniable reality of her own culpability. As much self-disgust as she harbored, and as much hatred as she directed at her father, there was still that portion of herself that accepted, and needed, the things they did. She was clearheaded enough to know that they were anything but a typical father and daughter team. And she was also proud that that was true.

So she kissed her dad and did as she was told. She'd caused the greatest upheaval in Cleveland criminal history in a few short hours. The cops from one end of the city to the other were all out looking for her/him. And there was so much attention concentrated on finding her/him that the last place anyone might think there would be trouble was at Jessie's apartment. Why, there wasn't even anyone living in that building anymore. They'd all moved out. The place was empty. Just an empty old building, without a single thing to distinguish it from anywhere else on the planet.

Except that it had the gate to hell—or to Paradise—in its basement.

And now . . .

There were athletic shoes in the bottom of her purse, and she put them on. There was a gun in a side pocket, and she pulled it out. There were gloves in there and she slid them over her fingers, eyeing the shock-therapy hood all the while and feeling the anticipation twisting through her insides as the thing between her legs ached and the mask's lips seemed to move.

Finally, she lifted it and slid it over her head. As the fine leather touched her flesh a thrill washed down her spine. Now, and for always, this was her finest moment. This instant when the transformation was complete and she became her brother, who then became the Terrorist: that creature she had first felt inside herself the night she had posed as a drug addict, would-be hooker to try and draw the Razor from a pharmacist she had eventually murdered. This was the time of rebirth. It was as if she could actually see the life force of the other creature inside her sparking its attention, lifting its eyes from some deep sleep, and blinking in the darkness inside her skull. It was as if the thing were uncurling itself from the pile it had made of its body, stretching its muscles and testing the air with its serpentine tongue. Feelers crawled through her from her crotch, touching every nerve. Tears poured from her eyes as if her body regretted what was happening to her mind but could express itself in no more significant a way than the warm flow of frustration. And she closed her eyes for a moment, took a breath, and then . . .

He was standing in the stall where she had been, holding a gun.

He was there...

The Reality Terrorist:

The man who brought death in secret wherever he went. The man who saw himself as murder made flesh, torment made human. He was clad completely in black, from the bottom of his feet to the top of his head. His face was covered with fine black leather so that only his eyes and lips were exposed—his eyes and the full lips that were even now working themselves over the well-worn stump of rubber that was positioned across the mouth hole of his mask. His teeth fit perfectly into the dents chewed into that rubber stump. His lips worked and dripped a little spit as they got comfortable. With the mask on, he could hardly speak, and sometimes, when he was exerting himself, he whistled when he breathed.

But that was okay.

It was all okay.

Because, for the Terrorist, the only reward for all the time he spent hiding, constantly in fear of being exposed, of someone running across some bit of evidence that would bring his true identity to the attention of the cyborgs and thereby ruin everything for which he had been working so long, was the chance to explode, to lash out and open up the floodgate of his own pent-up rage . . . that rage that had developed after years of being studied by his father's hired doctors . . . that rage that was engendered by a world that looked at him as mad after he had attacked his little sister with a hot iron when she was five . . . a rage that burned white-hot inside him every time he thought of what They had all done to him as the details slid into focus, one after the other, like puzzle pieces dropped randomly from a box landing as a completed picture on the floor. He sucked spit through his clenched teeth, hefted his gun and bounced it in his hand to confirm its weight, becoming whole, feeling complete. He glanced down at the remnants of his former self—at the purse and the discarded blouse and skirt—and he didn't even bother stashing them. Usually he did. Normally he was so, so careful . . .

But this time, what was the point?

If the Prisoner was right, and the Terrorist was a creature of this reality, then when the Prisoner did find his own freedom, the Terrorist could hope for only one of two things, and they were both unpleasant.

Either this reality would fold up and simply cease to be once the Prisoner was gone—which would be the merciful, and quick, end.

Or things would simply go on as before, only the Terrorist would be left without a cause.

Oblivion or solitude . . .

Neither was attractive.

So that left one alternative that not even the Prisoner had dared discuss: death. It was all the Terrorist had left. The pleasures and pains of this world—be it the Punishment Zone or an alien reality dressed in glitter—were better left behind than faced alone. So this end would be the end of it all. The task would be completed, and Henry Parks would be liquidated. The Prisoner would have all the time in the world to make whatever was going to happen actually occur, because the one man who seemed to understand, Henry Parks—that son of a bitch!—was never going to bother anyone again.

It would be glorious.

The stage was set for an epic conclusion.

It would be steeped in screams, and blood, and running feet. The Terrorist's one and true final desire was about to be fulfilled:

He was about to kill Henry Parks . . .

And he didn't care who saw him do it.

He opened the ladies' room door a crack, and, to his wonder, found that Parks was just standing there, with Lemon and Ellis, not forty feet away. It would be simple . . . so simple. It would just be a matter of drawing a bead with his gun . . .

Like this.

Squeezing the trigger . . .

Like this.

And . . .

Bang!

30

The force of it knocked Parks back so that he ended up tangled in a chair in the smoking lounge. The wooden box Krammer had given him crashed open, scattering bullets in a silver puddle as his breath rushed out of his lungs when his pelvis hit the floor. Ellis had his left shoulder buried in Parks' stomach, and the force of the young man's blow had been enough to make Parks feel as if his ribs had been broken. But almost simultaneous with the FBI man's flying tackle came the powerful blast of a gunshot, echoing through the cavernous terminal and sending the throng of suitcase-carrying travelers who, up until that instant, had been more a part of the decor than real human beings, scattering in screaming, hysterical disarray.

Parks had just arrived when the shot was fired. He had spotted Ellis and Lemon standing in the smoking lounge when the line of people in front of the metal detector reminded him that he was carrying both a gun and a box of bullets. He was just thinking how lucky it was that they were taking a private plane and would not need to pass through the metal detector, and he was also wondering where the hell Lisa Reynolds had gotten off to, when Ellis—who seemed to be studying the ladies' room— lunged at him with all his weight.

They ended up on the floor, people started running, and in a steady, deadly tattoo of ear-pounding concussions, a series of shots ripped *bang! bang! bang!* through the air, punching holes first through the backs of overturned plastic chairs and then in the cheery sky-blue of plaster walls, and then finally in the well-polished glass of the smoking lounge's big window. That window resisted the assault at first, allowing itself a shuddering, spiderwebbed spot where the first bullet hit. But when the second and third pounded their way through, the neat holes they left behind became suddenly interconnected by a road map of racing cracks, and with a heaving sound of defeat an entire section of the glass let itself fall into a glittering hail of deadly, razor-sharp chunks.

But crashing glass, screaming passengers, and terrified airline employees were all peripheral to Parks' central focus, which, even from where he lay gasping on the floor with Ellis still atop him, was the ladies' room from which the shots had been fired. As he watched through a forest of aluminum chair legs and a stampede of running bystanders, that door opened and emitted a flowing black shape, human in design, demonic in appearance. Seeing it, for real and with his own two eyes, wrapped in gleaming black rubber and studying the world with quick, dark sparkles from behind the ghoulish anonymity of a shock-therapy hood, blew terror and excitement through Parks' very being with such force that he nearly levitated off the floor. Throwing Ellis to one side and thrashing through the thornbush of chair legs and standing ashtrays into which he had been tackled, he was drawing his gun and formulating his best shot when Ellis shouted, "No! Henry! Don't move!"

And that's when things got really strange.

For, splattered through the waves of terrified passengers climbing over one another in their attempt to escape, Parks noticed a weirdly purposeful arrangement of movements that seemed to be fighting their way directly against the flow of the crowd. Like tiny insects swimming contrary to the current of ripples in a pond, there were men, all of them young, all of them wearing dark suits and grey overcoats, reaching into their breast pockets and threading their way *toward* the source of the trouble. They seemed to be moving inward from the perimeters of the terminal, as if they had been stationed at the exits . . .

And the logic of it stunned the old man numb.

"Feds!" he stammered, feeling his face flush with indignation. "You said there wouldn't be any feds!"

"I lied, Henry," Ellis was saying, holding Parks back by squeezing each of his shoulders at arm's length. "It was for your own good. I had to. I couldn't let you just kill him. They'd have put you in the chair for it, justified or not!"

"You lied!"

"It would have been premeditated murder! Henry, listen to me!"

"You *bastard*!" Parks roared, swinging blindly with his fist and striking a resounding blow on empty air. Ellis avoided his attack easily, stepping back and allowing Parks to lunge before grabbing his arm and pulling him forward, using the centrifugal energy of the old man's own muscle to send him sprawling on his stomach.

Parks looked up from where he lay, and Ellis was looming over him as tall as an office building. The younger man's hands were on his hips, and his tie was perfectly straight. His lips were serious, but there was a gleam of superiority in his eyes that was impossible to hide.

"I've been reporting back to the Bureau all along," he said, as if speaking to a child. "I couldn't let you kill him, Henry. That's the whole reason I started helping you in the first place. You've done a terrific job. You stayed on the case even when it looked hopeless, and in the end you won. But I can't let you have the trophy. As much as it pains me to say it, I'm sorry, but that's just not the way it works."

But Parks wasn't listening. Struggling to sit up, he watched from the floor as the figure in black—My dear sweet Jesus! he thought. It was Lisa Reynolds all along! A woman! A fucking female serial killer! How could I have been so stupid? How could I have missed so much?—moved quickly along the terminal, a constricting noose of FBI agents drawing guns and an increasingly thinning group of passengers hurtling past. There seemed to be no way out, nowhere for the lunatic to go. The feds had done it perfectly. Though she had taken advantage of the initial confusion her shots had caused to move farther on down the concourse and into a Pan Am passenger waiting area, they now had her bottled up in that area, where she was jerking her head around and looking for an opening. Even the bystanders seemed to be cooperating by hurrying out of the way, leaving her effectively trapped. If she gave up, she was theirs, gone forever and eternally out of Parks' reach. If she didn't—which he somehow knew she wouldn't—then she was history.

"Christ!" he thought, feeling a twang of guilt race up his gut as he realized what his body was doing . . . not so much his mind, but the very stuff of his flesh, his nerves, and the delicate system of desires that had motivated him for so many years. Run! he was thinking. Get away! You've done it for so fucking long! You've outwitted everybody, me included, for years and years and years. Don't let them take you now! Save yourself for my sake. Save yourself for *me*!

And, as if in answer to his silent plea, fate threw two separate, and yet intimately associated, obstacles into the path of the federal agents' seemingly assured victory.

The first was a stupid man.

And the second was an arriving Pan Am flight.

31

The shot that turned the head of every federal agent in the terminal was immediately preceded by the blustering shout of "Stop! Police!" that was emitted by a man whose brain was so obviously filled with visions of his own television-inspired heroics that Parks, thinking about it later, would doubt if he even noticed the presence of the other law enforcement officers. Apparently drawn by the howling fire alarm sirens screaming overhead—"When had those snapped on?" Parks wondered, realizing that he wasn't as in touch with what was happening around him as he had thought he was, and that someone had opened an alarmed, emergency exit door somewhere . . . more like everywhere—the man came puffing up the concourse, duck-shuffled to a halt directly in front of the metal detector unit, around which Lisa Reynolds had run to get to the Pan Am concourse and behind which three uniformed attendants were now hiding, drew his gun, shouted his warning, and fired . . .

Wild.

The bullet skimmed off the glass behind Lisa Reynolds, shattering it and proceeding on down to a wall, where it snapped again and ricocheted, ending up as a dent in the men's room door across the hall.

The shot startled the FBI agents, who reflexively glanced toward its source, and then hit the floor as the black-clad figure returned fire, placing a bullet in the very center of the overwrought cop's chest and blasting him off his feet so that he flew back through the arch of the metal detector itself, causing lights to flash and beepers to beep, and men and women in uniform to dive for safer cover.

It was at that instant that the door in the arrival dock opened, emitting grinning passengers who had no idea that anything was going on, and sending the Terrorist forward. The perimeter of federal agents all lifted their weapons and held their fire as their target moved to place the gawking deplaners directly in their line of fire.

From where he sat, Parks saw it all. He saw the agents champing at the bit, wanting to shoot, but unable to. He saw the startled looks on the faces of the people stumbling around in the doorway as Reynolds forced her way past, against the flow of traffic and into the tunnel that connected the terminal to the recently arrived jumbo jet. He saw the black circled nose of that jet through the window of the waiting area, and the spot where the air tunnel rested against the side of the plane. And he saw the federal agents, Ellis included now, rush forward once Reynolds was out of sight, following her into the tunnel.

What he also saw was something that every one of the federal agents missed because their minds were focused on the plane itself: on the screaming people in it, and probably on the vivid pictures they had all seen of hostage pilots being held with guns pointed to their heads. It was an awful thought, and one that could blast every other consideration out of a person's head. And it did. The agents weren't thinking about anything else . . .

So they didn't notice when Reynolds dropped from the side of the plane to the tarmac.

They didn't see it.

But Parks did.

From where he was lying he saw first the wiggling black shape of a gloved hand working its way through the tight opening where the canvas sheath of the air tunnel's mouth kissed the side of the Pan Am jet. He saw that hand become an arm as Lisa Reynolds pulled herself through. And he saw her black shape as it fell the fifteen feet or so, disappearing from his line of sight and ending up somewhere on the runway.

He was running before he knew what he was doing, pausing only long enough to snatch up a handful of the bullets Krammer had given him and stuff them in his pants pocket. He was running back down the concourse, his head nearly revolving as he reoriented himself. Almost forty years before, as a young patrolman, newly married and in need of money, he'd worked part-time as a rent-a-cop for the newly constructed airport. The place was a little different then—there had been a lot of remodeling and additions made in forty years—but its basic layout, its foundations and main buildings, were all the same. He'd walked his beat here until he knew the place by heart. And pulling up that ancient information from the depths of his mental files, he hit one of the open emergency exits and skipped heavily down the steel steps, to the waiting chill of the snowy concrete below.

"Lisa Reynolds! Listen to me! I want to help you!" he rehearsed in his head, nearly laughing aloud at the absurdity of the statement. What was he thinking: that after all this time all he had to say was, "Stop, I want to help you!" and the lunatic would simply drop her gun and say, "Oh, thank goodness. I thought you were mad at me"? She was crazy, but she obviously wasn't stupid.

So instead of shouting, Parks didn't say anything as he puffed his way along the side of the main terminal, passing parked flatbed luggage wagons, forklifts, and a lot of locked doors. He tested every one as he passed, feeling simultaneous relief and frustration at each knob that wouldn't turn. She could have gone on, or she could have gone through and locked the door behind herself, he thought, moving on to the next door, and the next after that.

To Parks' right stretched the landing strips: flat, empty, and wide. Way off in the distance, fuzzed by blowing snow and icy air, was the tree line, peppered with houses. Behind him was the Pan Am jet from which Reynolds had dropped, the source of a lot of shouting, and the soon-to-be source of a lot of running feet once the FBI agents were sure their suspect hadn't hidden on board. Ahead lay the first in a series of large bay doors used to load luggage from the terminal sorting area. Normally there should have been guys dressed in bright orange suits moving around down here, loading carts, running forklifts, smoking cigarettes and loafing. But the place was deserted.

As Parks entered the bay, he pulled up short and tried to listen for footsteps. But all he heard was his own breathing, ragged and hoarse. Where were the fire alarm sirens? When had they been turned off, and by whom? The stillness of the place was eerie, especially since he knew from past experience that it was absolutely never like this. When he'd walked this beat he'd found that anytime, day or night, there was always someone doing something in the bays. There was always something that needed moving, either in or out, twenty-four hours a day.

And then he saw the boots.

Skipping forward in an army crouch, he moved around to the north side of a parked forklift and found the sprawling body of a large, Hispanic-looking man lying facedown on the concrete. From beneath him seeped a spreading pool of blood. And one of the man's dark eyes seemed to be open.

Though his heart was still racing, Parks' breathing had slowed, and transferring his gun from his right to his left hand, he stooped, felt for a pulse in the downed man's neck, found none, and then took a step toward the "cave," which was a quarter of a mile long, narrow, and circular in structure. It looked a little like one of those ancient sewer lines you see in old movies about Rome, or the catacombs, or the Holland Tunnel, downscaled. It was done in yellow and blue tile, had a single line of fluorescent tubes running down the ceiling, and echoed like hell. It also leaked constantly, so it was always damp. Parks entered it, cocked his head, listened, and started jogging forward, holding the stitch he'd developed in his side with his free hand and breathing through his mouth. There weren't many places to hide down here, so he felt reasonably safe. But the idea of hitting the open air of the hangars unprotected made his balls try to climb back up inside him.

About halfway down he found another body, a security guard, dressed in a bright yellow, full-length raincoat and holding a big black flashlight. The kid couldn't have been more than sixteen. Look at him, Parks thought sadly. Just a kid, and a lieutenant already.

He moved on without hesitating.

Half the kid's head was gone.

At the entrance to the hangars he stopped, swallowed dryly, and tried to see inside. The interior of this area had always amazed him, especially when he was younger. It was a sight he had carried with him most of his life. Its size and depth, its simple emptiness and height, had always filled him with a sense of awe. Not that it was all that much of an architectural achievement. But just the way it looked, with its multitude of struts, beams, supports, and joists, all crisscrossed over miles of corrugated steel, dim behind an almost constant haze of airplane exhaust and poorly lit everywhere except where the planes themselves sat beneath hundreds of suspended work lights . . . it made him feel like he was underground almost, like he had stepped into a pocket of atmosphere trapped miles down . . . a deep earth cavern, a buried canyon.

And somehow that was appropriate. He remembered the same sense of size as he first stepped onto the factory supervisor's platform back at Mark O'Polo's murder scene. It was an identical sensation of reach, as if he could simply place his hand out and watch it grow, stretching out into the forbidding distance as if he had suddenly become less than solid, some elemental self that could explore great distances with his seeking fingers. The Prisoner would love such a place . . . would be compelled to seek it out . . . would be enamored by it without question . . .

The Prisoner would.

But not Lisa Reynolds.

Parks didn't know how he knew, but he understood at that instant, standing stalled in the doorway to the hangar, in a tunnel of dry tile and mildew—like a mouse in his hole looking out on the dwelling of some giant—that the creature he was chasing in her black rubber and mask was not the Prisoner he had come to identify by the unique trademarks left at the murder scenes he had studied over the years. She was not the Prisoner, but she knew who the Prisoner was. She'd told him a story involving her own dead father . . . a man. A man who was calling the shots.

A man . . .

Like her brother.

Parks could hardly believe his own thoughts. But they were there, and they could not be denied.

So it was Kevin Reynolds, or had been, all along. It was a brother and sister team—a sibling pair of lunatics who had been cooperating, covering for one another, and God knew what else.

A brother and sister.

Kevin and Lisa Reynolds.

Christ!

He could hardly believe it, even with all the evidence of the past twenty years and the past two days. No wonder he hadn't put it together. Who could have imagined it? Kevin, the sexual deviant with the record of analysis that read like a textbook for weirdos, knocking off innocent people so that he could use their bodies in his own twisted way and achieve his "rise." And his sister, shooting people and leaving their bodies alone for whatever reason motivated her to do it, for whatever bizarre thrill she was able to call her own. No wonder the feds had never made the connection between the two sets of killings. No wonder they had never believed him when he said that there was a connection. *He* wouldn't have believed him!

But now . . .

He had to get to her before Ellis and the other agents arrived. He simply had to get his hands on her and make her tell him where her brother had taken Jessie. Not a story about Pittsburgh or dead fathers really being alive. Not a story about late-night telephone calls from pitiful brothers who were confused, and not really to blame for what they did, or derelict drunks plucked off snowy streets to be used as surrogate cadavers.

God damn it! He had to get his hands on her!

And that's when the voice came down from the sky, and all the doors in the open hangar started to close.

32

"Who the fuck are you?" the voice boomed, huge, metallic, and thick. "And what's with the guy in the suit?"

Startled, Parks jerked his head up as if following the voice with his nose and involuntarily took a half-step forward. Instantly the voice announced, "What, are you nuts? He's got a gun! Don't move!"

And Parks froze with a shudder.

The sound of the huge hangar doors sliding down their tracks ahead of him was nearly deafening. There was one plane in the hangar, a Boeing 727, down a ways, looking ominous and dark in the dimming hollow of the facility's echoing bowels. Over the hard concrete floor was a veritable swamp of maintenance equipment, from hydraulic cherry pickers for hoisting men up to reach the bellies of tall planes, to rolling computer monitors for testing delicate electronics. There were tool chests as big as bathtubs, weirdly angled racks with dangling chains for hoisting heavy engine parts, golf carts full of manuals and diagrams, and wires—miles and miles of thick black wires, all running tangled over the floor as if the hangar were really a huge snake pit filled with one single serpent whose nose started nowhere in particular and whose tail ended up someplace very close to that exact same spot.

Leaning in carefully, Parks strained his eyes and finally spotted the glass cupola suspended on the wall to his left, forty or fifty feet up, where the owner of the electronic voice was hiding. It was an observation office equipped with a P.A. system and used to keep an eye on the activities in the building. The glass looked almost perfectly dark from where Parks stood, but he knew there was someone in that office, probably crouched behind a desk, clutching a microphone and straining to see the tiny spot that was Parks down near the facility's southwest corner. Whoever was up there, it was a sure bet that they were confused and scared. They had probably already alerted airport security and the Cleveland police, and that meant there would be more men in uniforms on the way to keep him from doing what he absolutely had to do.

Parks reached into his coat pocket and withdrew an ancient, brown leather wallet. Flipping it open, he glanced down at the dull sheen of the badge within: his shield, officer number 11275, Cleveland Police Department, Special Division, silver and worn, presented to him by the mayor himself as a retirement souvenir while he lay in a hospital bed, in honor of his sacrifice and dedicated service, good-bye and good luck. He studied the hangar, saw no movement, took a chance, and stuck his arm out of the cave, flashing the shield briefly before drawing his arm back. There was no shot, no bullet chipping concrete like he feared, and no sound. Just continued silence stretching far too long before being broken by the ridiculously loud voice of God again.

"To your left on the hangar wall there's a phone. Grab it."

Parks reached around, felt until he found it, and pulled the receiver back into the cave with him. Instantly a voice was speaking.

"What the fuck's going on around here?" it said—a man, scared and angry. "Who the hell was that? Why's he shooting? What's going on?"

"Terrorist," Parks said, amazed at how hard it was for him to speak. He hadn't realized how scared he was, or how old. "He's Iranian or something. I don't know what. But he's already killed some cops in the terminal, and he greased a couple of guys on the airport staff on the way down here. My name's Parks. I'm a detective."

"I think he ran through to the freight bays," the voice said, and Parks, straining up at the office box on the high wall, thought he caught a glimpse of a shadow moving inside. "I'm Lester. I supervise. I can't be positive sure that he's out of the hangar, but I think he is."

"You got a pair of binoculars up there, Lester?" Parks asked.

"Yeah," the supervisor replied.

"How about light switches?"

"I closed the doors, didn't I?"

"Can you shut the lights and give me some time to get across?"

"No sweat."

"Then do it."

One of the hardest things Parks ever did in his life was locking the door behind himself as he stepped from the cave into the hangar. As the lights went out, one row after another so that darkness spread across the concrete floor before him like the encroaching shadow of a storm cloud racing across a school yard, he crossed himself, swallowed the bitter lump in his throat, and twisted the handle on the big steel fire door so that it would snap shut behind him when he closed it. Almost simultaneous to his finally entering the hangar came the sound of approaching footsteps from somewhere deep in the cave, and he knew that Ellis or some of Ellis' men were approaching, and he wanted them kept out. But he was almost painfully aware that by keeping those approaching men out, he was making damned sure that he was kept in.

"No choice," he muttered as the last light died. "No fucking choice at all."

In the pitch-dark the slamming of the door boomed with all the authority of a land mine.

"What about the guys on the loading docks?" Parks asked the phone, which he still clutched in a sweaty hand as his last contact with the world of reason.

"Who knows?" the man in the observation cupola replied. "When the shooting started, everybody hauled ass. Far as I know, you're on your own."

"And on the other side?"

"Wait."

Pause.

"Far as I can tell, the dock's empty. Least nobody's answering my page in the office."

It was at that instant that a tiny light flashed on the other side of the hangar. It was rectangular and a washed-out grey. It started off small, stretched out over the floor ahead of it in an expanding slice, and then retreated as the sound of a slamming door echoed through the dark.

Someone had just left the hangar.

"One of yours?" Parks said into the phone.

"I don't think so," Lester the supervisor replied. "That was one of yours. Good luck, my friend. I'm afraid you're gonna need it."

"Thanks," Parks said, hanging up the phone as the lights directly over him blazed suddenly back into life and he headed for the door through which Lisa Reynolds had escaped.

Good luck, Parks thought. You're gonna need it.

Parks kicked open the door that separated the main hangar area from the freight loading dock and jumped back. What he expected was a gunshot, or the dark shape of Lisa Reynolds framed in the doorway, both arms stiffly aiming her gun at him. But what he got was even more of a shock than even a bullet might have been, if that was possible.

Just as the door banged open, a man came stumbling at him

from the loading dock area beyond, groaning, waving his arms, his face covered with blood and most of his lower jaw missing so that a terrible grimace of broken teeth and ground flesh bubbled as he tried to scream. His hair was long and wild, his clothes were the orange of the airport baggage handling staff, and his eyes were desperate.

"Help me!" they seemed to plead as the man sent yearning hands of squirming fingers Parks' way. "Look what he did to me! Look what he did!"

What "he" had done was to shoot the guy, apparently from close range, hitting him on the right side of his head just below his ear, so that the bullet passed from one side of his face to the other, taking most of his jaw with it. He must have been hiding just beyond the door when Lisa Reynolds came bursting through, and she hadn't given him a chance to run. After he was bloodied from her shot she must have grabbed him, turned him on his rubbery legs, and pushed him toward the door, knowing that Parks would be right on her heels, and using him as a decoy so that she could . . .

"Christ!" Parks exclaimed as the bloody man stumbled into him, pushing him back. "Oh, fuck!"

"There it is!" his brain said in a voice he didn't quite recognize—a calm, observational voice, kind of like a commentator on a TV football game. "That's the shape you were expecting, isn't it? The one with the grin, and the gun . . ."

"Oh, *Jesus!*"

The last voice before the shot was one Parks did recognize, because it was his own, yelling like he'd gone crazy. The wounded man, blowing a spray of blood up from his ruined throat and relinquishing his weight to Parks like a silent-movie heroine swooning into the arms of a hero, hit him with all the force of a linebacker as the black-clad body of Lisa Reynolds stepped into the backlit doorframe and lowered her gun. Parks was backpedaling, wrestling with the wounded man—who was going, *"Oggghaaa blammmaaaa!"* moistly into his ear—as the flash of Reynolds' gun bucked twice and made the struggles of Parks' burden cease. The bullets hit the wounded man squarely, one in the back of the head, the other between the shoulder blades, and their impact, even muted by the meat of the man's body, was translated into two shuddering blows that knocked Parks right on his ass. The fall was bad enough for a man of his age, but when the dead weight of the mangled man in his arms came thumping down atop him, something in his chest snapped—maybe a rib, maybe not—and he knew he was fucked . . .

That's just the way he thought of it.

"Oh, shit! I'm fucked."

And that's when the lights went out . . .

Again.

33

The situation was surreal, modified by Lester the supervisor's attempt at helping, which had been to quickly shut down the lights again, and capped off by Parks' own feeling of absolute helplessness. He was virtually trapped beneath the dead body of a man whose name he didn't even know, and as Lisa Reynolds stepped into the darkening hangar, she said, "My ass isn't gettin' nailed to no tree!" which was so incomprehensible to the desperate old cop that it was just about perfect.

Without another word, Reynolds started shooting.

Stepping forward like a robot, gun held up, body silhouetted against the light in the freight bays behind her, she fired silently, the flash from the silencer briefly illuminating the area around her arms and upper body in amazingly precise detail, so that she went from being a black shape to a monster bathed in golden light, and back, with each lick of fire.

Around him on the floor sparks flew as each bullet ricocheted off concrete, and Parks kicked furiously, sliding backward on his ass, trying to untangle himself from the dead body that seemed so determined to stay with him, and forgetting completely that he was holding a gun in his hand as his injured ribs howled beneath his shirt.

She can't see me! he thought, identifying intellectually his advantage while feeling the gorge of panic rise from his racing heart. It's pitch-dark in here! I can see her in the doorway, but she can't possibly see me in the dark!

That was true.

For an instant.

And then the door closed behind Lisa Reynolds, and they both disappeared.

The shooting stopped, silence replacing the roar of alarm in Parks' head. He quit struggling on the floor and tried to be quiet, but there was a harsh rattle in his throat that gave him away. He tried to hold his breath but his brain protested by making him feel as if he had just been pitched headlong off a high place into a bottomless chasm of perfect blackness, and he gasped, choked, spit . . .

And jumped as the darkness near him was marred by a sudden eruption of yellow sparks when a bullet went skimming off the concrete.

There had been almost no sound from the gun.

Parks was on his feet, still rattling with sticky breath, his eyes searching blindly around him, his corneas blazing with sickly green afterimages of the bullet's sparkling ricochet.

There had been almost no sound from the gun, and absolutely no indication of where Reynolds had moved to in the darkness. She must have been wearing some kind of soft-soled shoes. She must have been sneaking silently, moving like a cat, seeing in the dark . . .

No! Parks thought. She's as bad off as me. She can't see either.

And, as if to contradict his thought, a voice said, "Hello, Henry."

And Parks spun and fired.

What happened next was like fireworks on the Fourth of July, only it was brief, chaotic, and deadly. Parks' gun exploded in the dark, illuminating his hands and blasting like a rocket with force and concussion. Lisa Reynolds responded with her own silent shots—sparkling stabs of fire to Parks' left, maybe twenty feet away—and bullets slammed into concrete-block walls.

As quickly as it started, it was over. And everything went back to being dark.

"My," a voice that was weirdly not that of Lisa Reynolds said after a time. "Wasn't that exciting?"

And Parks snapped his head around so fast that he almost broke his neck. The gunshots were still vivid in his eyes, but he wasn't wheezing anymore. He was making himself not wheeze. And he wouldn't let himself talk.

Let her babble, he was thinking, standing as stiff as a chunk of granite. Let her talk. And the next time she opens her mouth . . .

"You're hit," the strangely masculine, oddly slurred voice of Lisa Reynolds said from somewhere in the dark. "You're bleeding, Henry. I can feel it. You don't mind if I call you Henry, do you? I think we've known one another long enough."

It was at that instant that the pounding started on the locked fire door Parks had left behind himself at the cave's mouth when first he entered the hangar. Voices joined that sound, but they were dull and imprecise. Even if they had been perfectly clear, though, Parks knew he wouldn't have paid them any mind, because he was too busy doing something which his brain had been telling him not to do—which was touching his face. He didn't know why, but in the back of his mind there was a tiny voice saying, "Whatever you do, don't touch your face, pal. That's all I've got to say."

But Parks did touch his face.

And when he did, he found blood.

How had Reynolds known?

It was totally dark!

Could she see like a cat?

Was she the supernatural being Parks had almost come to believe her to be after all these years?

"I'm using a Browning high-power automatic," the voice said, slurring the "s" sound in "using," so that it came out as "usching," making Parks think of the rubber stump the woman's teeth were holding. "Nine shots, fast reload. You can't get out of here alive, Henry. I could just sweep around myself, and sooner or later I'm bound to connect."

As if to demonstrate this hypothesis, a series of tiny *snaps* echoed in the dark, accompanied by yellow flashes and more breaking glass. Parks moved right, felt something brush his arm, dove left, tripped, fell, groaned, and stayed on his hands and knees until the shots were done. Then he heard the metallic *tink* of the Browning's ammunition stem falling to the floor, and the slap of another stem being loaded into the gun's handle. Reynolds was ready to go again with another nine shots, and Henry Parks was sure that he did in fact have a fractured rib. Just below his heart it felt as if someone had stabbed him with a kitchen knife. Then he panicked for a second as a new idea for the source of his pain jumped into his mind, and he felt himself over, sighing as he realized that he had not been shot in the gut.

"This whole thing goes against my principles," Reynolds said, her voice deep, and in a totally new spot, off somewhere to Parks' right. "I'm a private person by nature. Normally I tend to avoid publicity."

Then why'd you do it? Parks was dying to ask . . . but the key word there, was "dying." So he kept quiet as he chose one direction, crawled in what he hoped was a straight line, and finally found a wall. The pounding on the fire door was getting louder, and the blows fell more quickly. He had to do something. If he held out much longer, the FBI would break down that door, and that would be the end of the game. He needed to draw Reynolds to him . . . he needed to get an upper hand . . . he needed light!

As he crawled he found what felt like a hammer lying on the floor. With a quick motion of his arm he pitched it away from himself and waited. When the hammer fell, the sound it made was almost immediately emphasized by a quick *snit-snit-snit* of flashing fire, and Parks had Reynolds pegged as standing about ten yards to his left.

"Heenrrry," the Terrorist teased, drawing out the name and cooing suggestively. "Where arrre yooou?"

Parks found a wrench and threw it at the same spot he remembered as the source of the last series of shots. It hit something metallic and drew three more *snits*, which came from a place a good five yards to the right of their previous location.

God, she moved quick!

She had three more shots before she'd need to reload again.

The pounding on the fire door took on a new tone, and with a grinding squeal shoulders pushed so that the hinges gave a little and . . .

Parks caught a glimpse, just a glimpse, of light outlining the straining fire door.

He was moving in a heartbeat. Using that hint of illumination like the flash of a lighthouse in a storm, he was able to orient himself in the hangar and place himself in relation to a way out. The door to the freight docks was located directly across from the fire door, and crawling without concern for the noise he made, he headed for it, rattling tools and stumbling to his feet as the last three bullets Reynolds had in her weapon flew, two sparking against the brick wall, wide to Parks' left, and one passing right through the door to the docks, leaving a perfect pinhole of light that he used as a guiding beacon in covering the final few feet between himself and his escape.

With an exhalation of relief he found the door's hand bar, pressed, and fell through into the giddy-bright light on the docks, which blinded him for an instant and made him stagger.

What happened next confused him so badly that it left him waving his gun and mumbling incoherent curses that came out sounding like slush.

His foot hit something as he stepped from the hangar into the loading dock area. And whatever it was lifted itself once his weight was against it, pulling his leg out from under him and sending him pitching forward with terrible momentum until he was completely out of the way of the door and rolling in a ball. Then there were hands on him—big hands and strong. At first he thought that these hands were going to harm him. But then he felt himself being lifted off the floor, and the next thing he knew the hands were attached to a huge black man in orange coveralls, and another hand was over his mouth, stifling his questioning voice, and then he was pulled behind a stack of airtrays and freight boxes, with a second man leaning his face in close with a finger to his lips hissing, "Shhhh!" as the Terrorist appeared in the door.

They let her step onto the deck three feet before one man shouted, "Hey, Abdul!" drawing her black-masked attention and snapping her head around. She was just bringing her gun up with her right hand as the ammunition stem shot from its handle and her left hand slapped a fresh stem home when a man appeared from in back of a stack of orange crates behind her and brought a gleaming silver wrench that was easily as long as a baseball bat whistling forward in a deadly sweep that connected squarely with the killer's lower back. The force of the blow produced a sound like what you might get if you threw a watermelon out of a third-floor window, a *thump!* beneath which was insinuated a terrible crunch that Parks, from where he stood pinned in the arms of a man with hands like a pair of vise grips, knew was the woman's spine being snapped.

The Terrorist was launched forward—like some flopping rag doll—the Browning automatic clattering across the concrete, her arms and legs akimbo, and her head thrown back. When she landed, she jerked on the floor, squirming from the waist up with her arms working uselessly, her legs lying absolutely still. Raising her head, she tried to reach for her gun, which was five feet away and clearly out of range, but the man who had hit her—a burly redheaded brute—stepped forward, protectively bouncing the wrench in his hands like a strikebreaker preparing to wade into an unruly mob with a stick, and bringing his big-booted foot down on her reaching fingers. The sound of breaking bones tore through Henry Parks, who fought his way free from the arms of the man holding him and shouted, "Wait! Don't kill him!"

And he was then surprised by two things.

One: that there were so many baggage handlers around. After the Terrorist had been clubbed, they'd shown themselves, rising up from behind stacks of boxes and crates, ten all together.

And two: that they listened to him.

To a man, they froze when he spoke, turning their faces toward him expectantly without moving another muscle.

Just then a faint sound of breaking metal crackled in the distance, and Parks knew that Ellis' men were on the verge of breaching the fire door. Without wasting a second he shouted, "You, drag him away from the door. And you, block the hangar entrance somehow. We can't let the rest of them in yet!"

But no one moved.

"Do it!" Parks roared, and the effect his words had were like the pistol shots of a lion tamer.

Instantly, the man with the wrench pitched it away and stooped to drag the squirming body of the Terrorist across the concrete away from the door. Almost simultaneously, one man slammed the door to the hangar shut, and another jumped into the saddle of a nearby forklift, fired it up, and drove the sputtering machine right into the door. The forklift's blades slid under the door with a horribly metallic squeal, and the flat front of the machine pressed firmly to the steel, producing a thump and boom that wedged the passage shut.

Parks was moving through all this as if he were in a daze. Vaguely, he was aware that the dock workers not engaged in carrying out his orders were all staring at him, probably because of the blood even now running down his face to splatter the front of his rumpled brown suit, or the gun dangling in his limp hand. Or maybe it was because he had emerged from a perfectly black hell in which he had voluntarily trapped himself with a killer with a silenced Browning automatic. Or maybe it was because of his age, and the way he was bent when he walked, favoring the rib he was so sure was at least partially fractured, and which protested beneath his shirt with every breath he took.

But for whatever reason, there seemed to be an almost reverent air in the room as Parks moved—limped, more like—toward the nearly motionless black figure lying prone on the concrete before him. She was awake, he could see, her eyes sparkling with hatred beneath her mask, the fingers on her good hand moving, ever so slightly, the broken fingers on her mangled right hand twitching, probably involuntarily. She had to be in agony, Parks thought. From the way her legs were twisted and still, and from the sound he had heard, he was sure her spine had been snapped somewhere just over her pelvis. The pain must have been fabulous . . .

The pain.

She'll tell me everything I want to know, Parks thought grimly. She'll tell me everything I've ever wanted to know, and there's nothing that will stop me from having my questions answered.

Not the law.

Not morality.

And not that pounding on the door blocked by the still idling forklift.

"Henry?" a voice that could have been Ellis', or anybody

else's in the whole world, called from behind the door. "Henry? Let us in!"

But Parks didn't hear or see or feel anything but what was filling his eyes at that instant: the Terrorist; the helpless body of the killer of twenty years' duration. In his mind he had almost mythologized this being, and yet here he—*she*, he had to remember; it was a woman under all that black rubber—here she was, finally, lying at his feet, full of every detail he had wanted to know since his life was ruined by a madman who wanted to "get back to where I belong!"

God, he could still hear those words.

Twenty years!

"Back to where I belong!"

He stopped and put his hands on his hips.

His silver eyes were cold . . . and mercy became, at that instant, as alien a concept to the Dead Man as it might have been to his counterpart, the Prisoner—the second half of what even he had to admit was the sum total of the being that Henry Parks had become. Somewhere along the line, this had become one of the moments for which he was living. This triumph became at least partially the definition of his life. And finally arriving at it, Parks felt a strange sensation of completeness fill him, a feeling that said, very clearly in his mind, "You are nearly there. Don't flinch at the last. Do what you have to do."

Glancing around, and then down again, he noticed, as if for the first time, that Lisa Reynolds was wearing her shock-therapy hood, and in that instant his course was set.

"Jumper cables!" he called over his shoulder, pointing at the back of the forklift, idling softly nearby.

For a moment no one moved. And then the big black man who had hugged him after Parks had been tripped by the man with the wrench, stepped forward with a set of blue wires in his hands. He gave them to Parks, and then held his ground, staring at the old detective's face and then finally pointing at Parks' forehead. Jumper cables in hand, Parks slid his gun back into its holster and then reached to where the black man was pointing, up, to where his hairline had once been when he was younger, feeling flesh slick with blood, torn skin, and something hard. Working his fingers over it and grimacing with pain, he removed the . . .

Bullet.

It had been lodged beneath his skin, a black lump of lead denting his skull and sending blood streaming down his face. Why didn't it kill me? he wondered, rolling the bloody thing between his thumb and index finger. And then he understood.

This was the slug that had passed through the mangled man's head! As Parks stumbled back beneath the dying man's weight, Reynolds had fired twice, and this was the bullet that she had sent into the back of the man's skull. It had passed through his head and hit Parks. But, having been slowed by its first victim, instead of shattering bone and blasting his brains out in a spray, it had just broken the skin, barely chipping his skull enough to lodge itself there for this black man in the orange suit to gawk at.

No wonder these men were looking at him the way they were. It made Henry Parks think, You can't kill a man who's already dead. And then, with a grim half-smile, it made him place the slug in his shirt pocket.

Glancing up, he said, "Okay. Everybody out!"

But again, the guys looking at him didn't respond. They continued staring as if he had spoken some foreign language, about half of them with their eyes fixed on the shirt pocket where he had placed the bullet that should have killed him, the other half moving their attention back and forth between Parks' face and the body of the lunatic on the floor.

Parks tried, "Everybody out!" one more time, sighed, pulled his gun, and shouted, "Go!" as he fired it, once over his head.

The blast produced the effect he was looking for. Instantly, every man on the dock was heading for the exit—a single door next to a glass-enclosed office off to his right. The big steel bay doors were all closed, and as the last man disappeared through the outside door, Parks heard it snap locked, leaving him alone in the bay with a running forklift, a still thrumming series of fists pounding behind the hangar door, and the Terrorist, staring up at him silently, from where she lay crooked on the floor.

The jumper cables in Parks' hand felt a little heavy, so as much to relieve himself of their weight as anything else, he popped the lid on the forklift's engine compartment and hooked them up to the battery. Then, still without a word, he grabbed Lisa Reynolds' arm and dragged her a couple of feet closer to the forklift. And finally, he skipped over to the wall and pulled a fire ax down off its mount.

Standing over her, he bounced the ax in his hands a couple of times, firmed up his resolve, and swung the heavy blade down, smashing it into the side of the bottom crate in the stack piled up next to where Reynolds lay, making her cringe. Instantly, a clear gush of shimmering liquid erupted through the splintered hole left by the ax head, pouring into a puddle on the floor and drenching the rubber-clad figure with a beading film. The side of the crate read, "Handle with care. Live tropical fish," and, as if to confirm that warning, tiny shapes flopped on the concrete around where the Terrorist was now trying to pull herself away.

With a second and third swing of the ax, Parks opened up the side of two more crates, and soon the whole floor around where Reynolds lay was a virtual lake alive with brightly colored fish, and gleaming with an oily sheen beneath the fluorescent lights running across the building's high ceiling. Pitching the ax away, he pulled off the side of one of the broken crates and put it on the floor. Standing on this chunk of wood, he bent over and said, "Okay, Lisa, here's where we're at."

And the sound of his voice seemed to affect the Terrorist physically. Immediately, she ceased her struggles and aimed her bright, hateful eyes up at him from behind her mask, hissing breath through her teeth, and clenching her good fist.

"We don't have a lot of time," Parks said, bending down closer as if to make his words reach her more quickly. "Where's Kevin? And where did he take Jessie?"

Parks stiffened when Lisa Reynolds responded to his questions with laughter. It was the last sound he expected to hear, and when she burst out, pealing hysterically on the floor and shuddering as if she might choke on the humor of it, he found himself suddenly confused . . .

And angry.

"*I'm* Kevin, you asshole!" she suddenly shouted, trying to

raise her head and thrashing on the ground so hard that one of her feet slid on the concrete.

Her spine was definitely broken, Parks understood. If she had been capable of any movement at all, she'd have done whatever it was before now.

"I don't have time for this bullshit, Lisa," Parks said regretfully, reaching for the jumper cables and setting his jaw. "I really don't. If it weren't for those men behind that door, and for the fact that Jessie's missing, maybe this could have been some other way. But . . ."

He touched the two ends of the cables together and they produced a terrible spark that sizzled in the air and arced in chewing electric lines of static power.

"But right now, I'm afraid that you're not leaving me any choice. I was never really like this before. This is how you made me. You and your brother. You did this to me. Anything I do to you, I'm doing because of you. Just remember that. Just try to keep that in mind.

"Now . . .

"Where's Kevin? And where did he take Jessie?"

34

The first scream Ellis heard from the other side of the door between the hangar and the freight dock made him stiffen and irrationally think, "Quick! Shoot the lock off the fucking thing!" even though the lock in question was of the hand bar variety and was on his side of the door. Something was blocking their way, and no matter how hard they pushed, it wouldn't budge.

He was just stepping back from the door, options running through his head at breakneck speed, when shouting behind him grabbed his attention, and Lemon slapped him on the back, saying, "Cops!"

"Great!" Ellis cursed, turning to find dark shapes stumbling through the brightly lit hole that was the spot where the FBI had finally broken down the first door that Henry Parks had locked himself behind.

The hangar was virtually pitch-dark. There had been lights on in it when they had first arrived at the cave's end. Ellis had seen a bright slash under the door. But when they finally broke in, the lights were out—and out is how they had stayed. With the big black flashlight one of the agents had picked up off the body of the security guard in the cave, they had found their way across the hangar to this door, and been stalled. Now they were going to have to deal with the local cops.

And all the while, the screaming in the freight docks was going on and on, building in pitch, and terrible to hear.

First the gunshot and then the screaming. What the hell was going on over there?

Ellis swung the flashlight beam around and aimed it directly into the faces of the approaching police officers: four of them, in uniform, guns drawn, faces blank and sickly pale in the harsh white circle of light Ellis aimed at them.

"What the . . . ?" one of them said.

And then Ellis had the flashlight beam trained on his investigator's badge, and his voice was loud and commanding, and the next thing that happened was that the whole bunch of them was running, after one of the cops had used the telephone on the hangar wall to call up to the observation office and gotten Lester the supervisor to open the outside doors.

How long did he have alone with her? Ellis wondered as he ran. Five minutes? Maybe ten? And what was the crazy son of a bitch doing to her that would make her scream like that?

They had to shoot the lock off the freight dock door. Yeah, Ellis thought, humorlessly. Shoot the lock off! Finally, we get to shoot a lock off something! There were about ten guys standing around that door in orange coveralls, looking nervous and scared. One of them said something about how "that crazy Arab killed him. Just fucking blew his face off!" But no one seemed to hear. Everyone was locked on the sound of agony emanating from inside the building, and nothing short of an explosion would have distracted them.

They found her on the floor where Parks had left her. The forklift was still running, and there was a terrible stench in the room that smelled like burned meat and melted rubber. The jumper cables were coiled on the forklift's seat, one set of its jaws the color of copper, and clean, the other set scorched black, and thick with something ugly and burned. There was a thick haze in the air and an oppressive charge of violence—a charnel house atmosphere that made every man move a little bit slower and talk a little bit softer.

Ellis was the first one to reach the body.

"Holy shit!" he whispered, gazing down at what was left of Lisa Reynolds and feeling the tang of bile burning the back of his throat. "Ten minutes he had. No more."

The second man to the body was Lemon, who surprisingly didn't react at all. Ellis didn't quite know why he had expected the man to fall apart, but he had to admit that that was exactly what he thought Lemon was going to do: choke some epithet like, "I never would have signed up if I'd have known it was going to be like this," and vomit all over his shoes. But Lemon didn't say a word. He just appeared at Ellis' side, looked down at Reynolds' remains, and then looked at Ellis' face as if to say, "Now what?"

And in the face of such a question, Ellis wasn't really sure what to say. Henry Parks was gone. There was a second exit door down the building that was hanging open, and the only person who might have been able to tell him where the old hunter was heading was dead . . .

Horribly dead.

And then the local cops trotted up, and suddenly the freight docks were ringing with questions.

35

Seeing the airport from the runway, from actually down, on the surface, physically slapping concrete with shoes that were not inside an airplane, was a new and unique perspective for Henry Parks. And it did something for him. It settled him in a way, or, more accurately, it brought him back around a little, so that, as he ran, he could feel himself coming into himself again, shedding some of the disorientation, and yes, he had to admit it even though he had thought himself beyond all that nonsense, easing the panic that had so savagely seized him back on the loading dock. He found himself—as if opening his eyes and seeing himself for the first time in a mirror—running across the tarmac, stumbling away from the airport buildings and out toward that hazy line of houses and moving cars that bordered the field's extreme west side.

He had to move!

He had to get away!

He had to find a car!

His first impulse had been to exit the loading dock through the east door, which was the same one through which the baggage handlers who had essentially saved his life had fled. That would have put him on the parking lot side of the complex, where the brown Ford Taurus in which he, Lemon, Ellis, and . . .

Her.

Had originally arrived. He was going to take that car. But then he remembered that he didn't have the keys. Lemon had driven. Lemon had the keys.

So he'd chosen the runway side. Why? He wasn't sure. It didn't make sense. Nothing made sense. Nothing anymore! Nothing . . .

"Jesus!" he said, and stopped.

He was in the middle of a runway. The middle of a fucking runway and the wind was blowing snow over the frozen surface of the strip in shifting sheets, and his coat was open, and his face was freezing, and behind him, as he turned, was the building in which the freight docks were located, where her body was, where she'd said the things she'd said, which . . .

"Jesus," he said again, more softly.

Airplanes were moving in the distance, and people seemed to be looking at him through the long shiny windows of the terminal. There'd be cops coming soon—there had to be cops all over the place by now. But what did it matter after . . .

"Stop now," he said aloud. "Just stop."

And then he turned and finished his trot away from the airport. Painfully, he climbed the Cyclone fence that surrounded the field, cut through a couple of backyards, pounded on a few doors that were not answered, and finally headed into the street. At an intersection he yanked open the back door of a taxicab waiting at a light, and, with a garbled explanation and a flash of his policeman's badge, he hustled out the startled old lady passenger already occupying the cab. The cabdriver was harder to convince . . . Parks had to pull out his gun. Grabbing the cabbie's collar in one fist and ramming the gun barrel up under the man's chin, he wrestled him from the driver's seat, hissing, "I said get out!" with fury naked in his voice. "This is a police emergency!"

And then he got in and spun the tires, driving like a madman toward the freeway, Lisa Reynolds' voice still ringing in his head, and the image of her lying on the floor surrounded by flopping tropical fish as vivid as torture behind his eyes.

When the stolen taxicab hit the frozen freeway his chest vapor-locked on him, and he started crying . . . really crying, like a little kid, gripping the wheel and weeping hot tears that seemed as if they'd never end.

He'd killed her!

Wasn't that what he'd done?

Oh, it hadn't been with a gun or a knife, nothing so specific as an actual, physical assault. But he had caused her death as surely as if he had pulled the trigger himself. He'd stood over her like God Almighty, asking questions and sending electricity through her until she finally reached up and snatched the cable out of his hand. At first, he'd thought she was trying to stop him from using it again. But in the end he knew that it was because she wanted to possess it—to hold its power in her hand and feel its fire. Her mask was the giveaway—wasn't it? And yet he'd either missed or, more ominous indeed, ignored it all along. The psychiatric community didn't use them anymore because they were too easy for a patient to fixate on in an autoerotic way. There was something about all that leather . . .

And she'd reached up and taken the cable.

Parks resisted the urge to justify what he'd done, fought the impulse to think. He tried not to verbalize in his mind, but the words were there anyway: murder, revenge, and yes, even rape. For ultimately, wasn't that what it had done?

But what else could he have done?

She was perfectly alone in this world, an alien entity completely divorced from everyone and everything else except for her father . . .

"I just want you to love me!"

And her pain . . .

"The wires hurt so gooood!"

Both her father and her pain were intimately intertwined around her heart, like barbed wire wrapped in a bundle. They were really all she had, and they were both bad.

So he'd let her snatch the cable from him—he had let her, goddamn it! He could have stopped her but he didn't! He'd let her do it because he was sorry . . . for everything. At the instant when he saw her eyes fix on his hand, and understood what she meant to do, his sorrow was so big that it nearly swallowed him. And letting her have what she so badly wanted was all he could do. After all, he was so small. He was simply one man, standing in the shadow of something that terrified him with its simple size.

How high was madness?

Could you ever see over it?

How deep was madness?

Could you ever reach bottom?

"Just sleep," he whispered down at where she lay after the final jolt, the report of a gun echoing through the docks behind him when Ellis shot the lock off the door. But Parks stood his ground for another moment, saying aloud, "Just sleep, and dream sweet dreams this time."

And now he was crying. Before him on the freeway darkness was falling and, through the swirling loops of snow dancing across his path, the headlights of oncoming cars on the road's opposite side seemed to shatter from single beams of sliding white light to a zillion icy specks before re-forming as the passing car moved on. In the rearview he half expected the flashing red and blue of pursuing police cars, but they didn't come. And in his head he was seeing the murder scene in the factory in Pittsburgh.

It made sense, suddenly and ominously. The fucking thing all made sense.

"Don't hurt my friend—my friend who knows how to make me feel good," Lisa Reynolds had said before she died.

Before I killed her, Parks thought. Don't sugarcoat it.

"Daddy, don't hurt Mark!"

So the rack made of wood at the factory, the frame with the leather straps and dark, spooky stains, hadn't been used for torture as Parks had thought. It had been used for pleasure—Lisa Reynolds' pleasure, and for all he knew, Mark O'Polo's too. That was the secret, that was the truth. Mark O'Polo, whoever he actually was as a man, had known Lisa Reynolds, and Parks had no doubt that he had also known, or at least had some contact with, whatever other person it was that was living inside her, whatever other person it was who Parks had seen come out, near the end, calling himself Kevin Reynolds and despising the world.

"Everybody in the whole fucking world can just go to fuck!"

O'Polo had known her—them—and he'd died for it. He'd written a story called "The Gates of Paradise" for his own magazine, and that story had obviously been inspired by what Lisa had told him—maybe about herself, or maybe about someone that she said she knew. She'd probably talked about it after sex—whatever sex was to her—while she and O'Polo shared some strange, lover's hug on a wooden bed with straps made of leather and an eerie, howling wind moaning over an abandoned parking lot outside. She'd probably talked about it as a way of making contact with another person, one who apparently seemed to understand her.

He certainly understood her enough to be willing to please her in the only way it seemed he could.

So she'd wanted to reach out . . . to share something of herself with him.

But with Lisa Reynolds, the barbed wire around her heart was pronged on both sides, and anyone who knew her, or who knew anything about her, was fated to die. So it was love that had killed her. And love that had driven her . . .

Her?

No.

Parks knew that it hadn't been Lisa Reynolds who had shot and dismembered Mark O'Polo that night in the factory two weeks ago.

So it was love that had driven . . .

Kevin?

Her father?

Could it really be?

Eugene Reynolds?

... to destroy her lover.

If Parks had it right, and he was fairly certain that he did—or at least he knew that he had better have it right because he wasn't strong enough to go on much longer, and Jessie didn't have a lot of time left for him to be trying out new theories—then Lisa Reynolds was the enforcer, or partner, of someone who she loved, and who was destined, at least according to the scenario Parks understood, to reward her for her devotion, by leaving her behind. She was killing for the happiness of another person, helping that other person reach a goal that would place him forever out of her reach.

"Christ!" he said aloud, moving the car toward the exit ramp and watching his speed on the icy road.

Working it out was helping him, it seemed. Thinking it through seemed to be settling him down. Understanding...

Made him sad.

Just how real is real? he wondered, heading for Beech Street and Jessie's apartment. Who's to say what's real and what's not? If you believe it hard enough, and want it bad enough, could you get it anyway, even if it doesn't exist?

Apparently you could. Or at least Lisa Reynolds sure seemed to think so. And the one positive thing about it was that she had died with her belief still intact. Parks had made sure of that. He'd given her that much, which was about the only thing he had to offer, other than death. He'd sent her to whatever place she was destined to go, with her illusions whole to the end.

But what about the other? What about the man—for he was absolutely certain that it was a man at the heart of it all—whose delusions Lisa Reynolds had accepted as her own? What would he get?

Parks' face went grim... and there weren't any more tears in his eyes.

What would the man who had promised Lisa Reynolds solitude and desolation for her lifelong devotion get?

"One of Sallovy's bullets," Parks said, bouncing the taxi

into the Palace's parking lot and reflexively glancing up to see if there was a light on in Jessie's apartment, which there wasn't.

No surprise.

"He's going to get one of Mr. Sallovy's bullets . . . and even that's better than what he deserves."

SEVEN

36

Once the Razor was in her blood, Jessie's whole personality changed. She not only became quiet, but her body seemed suddenly malleable—as if her muscles had turned to clay. The Prisoner stood outside her cell door after he had withdrawn the syringe from her arm, listening to her voice thicken into licks of garbled noise as she slid helplessly to the floor. When he pulled the door open and stepped inside, he found her gazing up at him from where she sat, legs curled beneath her like an Indian fakir, big eyes wide, her mouth hanging open in perfect, childlike wonder.

When he put his hand out, she took it, blearily . . .

Oh, so sweet.

When he lifted her to her feet, she staggered so badly that he had to help her . . .

Just like her mother.

And when they entered the hallway and the screaming started from Kevin Reynolds' cell again, she ignored it . . .

Just like a good girl.

Which she was . . .

A good girl.

Jessie was.

Back in his subterranean apartment, the Prisoner left her swaying in a corner while he started getting ready. His hands shook and sweat poured down his face as he arranged the things he'd need on the bed. It should have taken only a few minutes to prepare, but his concentration was bad, and he couldn't keep himself from glancing over at where Jessie was trying so hard not to fall over, breaking the rhythm of his movements with her beauty, and making him pause to simply stand and drink her in.

She was magnificent! Perfect! Utterly stunning! She was the most amazing creature he had ever seen, and even the golden spirit-image of her that he had encountered so often on the Night Shore beach didn't begin to compare with the marvelous reality of her in the flesh. She was almost enough to make him glad for his confinement ... almost enough to make him bless the day he had entered the Zone. She simply took his breath away, standing there in her tight jeans and soft, brown leather jacket. Her razor-cut blond hair was a little too modern for his taste, but on her it looked right somehow, accentuating instead of detracting, giving her undeniably feminine features a slightly masculine aura that was unusual, and vaguely exciting. There was a sensuality in everything she did, an aquiline grace that could not be marred even by the intoxicated clumsiness of her present condition.

She was perfect ...

Simply perfect!

And she was his!

He wanted to hurry, but he wouldn't let himself. After all, he'd suffered for his crime, hadn't he? He'd suffered enough. Twenty-one—no! It was nearly twenty-two years that he had been struggling! He'd spent all this time alone and afraid, without so much as a moment's rest. And why was he here? Because he had loved Natalie too much, and that love had led him to transcend a taboo. It wasn't right, being treated like this. It was cruel, unusual, even inhuman, if you thought about it long enough. It wasn't the way a supposedly advanced society such as the one he had been forced to leave behind would do things. It was more like the primitive justice of antiquity, the hairy, eye-for-an-eye attitude of monkey-men ready to lop off hands and feet and gouge out offending eyes and tongues than it was any expression of civilized criminal justice. It was ridiculous. It was pitiful. It was . . .

"Almost over," he said, derailing this train of thought with a jerk and standing straight up. He'd been staring at his granddaughter—"My daughter, goddamn it! She's really my daughter!"—and his mind had wandered.

"Amosd ober," Jessie parroted numbly, her head rolling as she blinked, frowned, and licked her lips.

"That's right," the Prisoner whispered, stepping toward her. "Almost over. But only almost."

The first thing was the leash, and he slipped it around her neck, pulling it snug gently and bobbing her head. She kept looking into his eyes with that open, wondering stare without so much as a skip in her attention. And the Prisoner smiled, making her smile back.

"That's some amazing stuff, the Razor is," he said, hanging the end of the leather rope on a nail sticking out of the wall. "Amazing . . . huh, girl! Amazing?"

"Amashee," Jessie drooled.

And Grandpa wiped her mouth with his hand.

The next thing was the zipper on her brown leather coat. It slid open with a suggestive *zzzzziiIIIP!* that seemed to go on for a very long time . . . as if the zipper were twenty feet long. The jacket rustled as it fell to the floor. And then came the zipper on her jeans.

"God! Oh, God, oh God!" the Prisoner whispered.

And Jessie said, "Gob oh Gob," in return.

She was wearing pink panties beneath, and that was perfect. She was tanned, and lovely, firm and young. Her legs were smooth, and even without stockings—maybe especially without stockings—they looked like they belonged on a pinup. She was delicious . . .

So he left her jeans balled around her feet, looked at the sweater she was wearing, thought about pulling it over her head, and partly because of the leash, and partly because he had a better idea, decided against it. With a pair of scissors he took a very long time cutting the sweater open, one slow snip at a time, from the bottom, up the front to the throat, so that it parted side to side and slid down her arms. Her bra was pink like her panties . . . and her breasts were . . .

Snip!

The bra fell open, following the parted sweater and fluttering—actually fluttering—to the floor.

Her breasts were small, but perfectly formed.

He had to cut her jeans off too, because she was wearing black leather, spike-heeled boots, and he wanted her to keep those boots on—oh, did he want her to keep those boots on!

He left the panties alone for now because he had to, he simply *had* to. And then he was getting dressed.

The sounds his clothes made as he zipped zippers and snapped snaps seemed interminably amplified, cracking through the air harshly, with unmerciful plainness. The contrast between what was happening beneath his fingers and what was going on inside his head was dramatic, and, pausing at his collar, he thought, I just glimpsed the first of it! catching his breath with excitement and smiling brightly. It wasn't so much a specific thing as a sensation, but I caught it. I know I did!

What he'd caught was a snatch of feeling that demarcated one reality from another. For so very long the only evidence he had of there being two separate sides to reality was his contact with the Night Shore—his drug-induced hallucination, as someone who didn't know any better might have termed his "visits." But nobody ever had the same dream every night, and no one ever had the same hallucination every time they got high. For his entire time of sentence, that Night Shore view of the city he had left behind had been his only hope . . .

But now.

He'd felt it.

It was a sensation of separation . . . of his body doing one thing and his mind concentrating on another. As he had been buttoning his collar button, he'd been thinking about the impending trip he was about to make, and the space before his eyes had blurred, suddenly looking flat and two-dimensional. It was as if the wall had become less than solid, as if he'd suddenly found himself looking at a photograph . . .

A photograph of a girl . . .

In a sweater.
Natalie . . .

. . . was around here somewhere, he knew, walking up the stairs to the Phi Tau House and listening to the pounding of rock music thrumming inside. It was cold, and his breath made steam. It was late—nearly eleven at night—but it was Saturday, so the kids were having a party. It was a fraternity beer bash and they had hired a band, which was playing in what they called the community room, rocking the house and rumbling the street. Eugene Reynolds was drunk—again—and he had come looking for his daughter, first at the sorority house and then, on the advice of a girl with a wet towel on her head, here, at the Phi Tau House, because "It's just the best party anywhere."

So, here he was, at the "best party anywhere," looking for his daughter, and he wasn't even sure why.

The Prisoner finished buttoning his collar, and then he tied his tie, which was splashed with greed and red just like the one he had worn that night, twenty-two years before, in 1970. He'd had sideburns back then, but so did everybody. Long hair, funny suits, and high-heel shoes . . .

"Everything as it was," he murmured, feeling a thrill. "And then we'll go back to where we belong."

The trick was remembering exactly what had happened. With his memories so severely altered by the Punishers, it was difficult wading through what was real, and what had been added later. He just couldn't have been looking for his daughter while on a drunken binge. That was an addition. What had really happened was that he was trying to protect her . . .

"Yeah!"

He had heard about the wild parties the Phi Taus threw, and he had come to make sure that she didn't get involved with anything dangerous. He wasn't drunk. He was angry. Angry and concerned—just like any good father would have been.

Finishing with his tie, he turned to Jessie, seeing in her all the beauty of her mother—of Natalie—as she had been on that night.

"A girl your age," he said, low, under his breath, "in a place like that, with boys and liquor. It isn't right!"

The music didn't excite him, it sickened him as . . .

. . . he slid open the front door of the fraternity house—on which was hung a sign reading, "Check your hang-ups at the door." The dim heat and close pressing of young bodies didn't compel him as he waded his way into the darkness, it repulsed him. He wasn't interested in young girls, he didn't respond by grinning and accepting a drink when it was handed to him, he didn't try, through grand hand gestures and awkward, exaggerated dancing movements of his hips, to make the kids laugh and let him stay—an old man crashing their party, one of the enemy invading the world of the young. He didn't actually do any of that . . .

No!

"I came to save you," he said, fully dressed now and staring at Jessie. "I came, and found you half-naked, drunk, and . . ."

He grimaced with the memory.

. . . doing what you were doing!

It was coming back!

He could see it, for the first time. Up until just this moment they had blocked it from him. The Punishers had given him a hateful, guilty secret to carry, a terrible, shameful memory of what he had done to his own daughter that night to deserve the treatment he had received these past twenty-two years.

But now it was changing, behind his eyes, readjusting itself back to the way he was sure it really happened.

So, if that was the case, if he really hadn't done anything wrong, then why was he here?

If he hadn't done it, then what was his crime?

There was a blur in the air over where Jessie was standing, and before the Prisoner's eyes it began taking shape. He watched it bend and swirl for a moment before the first of Molaine's revolving head appeared, swimming up through a mark in the atmosphere, watching him with eyes that went over, and over, and over . . .

"Why?" he hissed. "If I didn't do it, then why?"

"She has to run," Molaine said, in a tone and volume of absolute authority. "It must be that way . . ."

"*Why?*" the Prisoner shouted, clenching his fists and feeling suddenly weak-kneed.

"She has to run," Molaine repeated, the revolutions of his head slowing . . . slowing . . . slowing . . . his features coming more and more into focus as the revolutions continued slowing . . . slowing . . . slowing . . .

"You *bastard!*" the Prisoner shrieked, making Jessie snap her head around to first look at him. *"I'll kill you!"*

But Molaine was gone.

And the Prisoner was moving.

He lunged across the room, waving his arms and roaring in an absolute rage. Jessie's drugged eyes sharpened, just a little, and she cowered back, more from the abruptness of her grandfather's charge than from any understanding of its motivation. Virtually exploding with rage, the Prisoner snatched the leash from its peg on the wall and yanked her away from where she had stood so obediently in the corner. He dragged her across the room, cursing and throwing spit, saying, "If you're supposed to run, then you'll *run!*" and hustling her out the door.

In the hallway she fell to her knees, and the Prisoner screamed, "*Go!* That's what they want! Run, you bitch! *Run! Runrunrun!*"

And Jessie groped and stumbled, running her fingers over doors as her elbows bumped walls. There was only one direction in which she could go, one place for her to find. And she would find it, the Prisoner knew, puffing behind her in his polyester suit and his wide, bright tie. He'd put on his wig too. So he looked good. He was a damned fine-looking man, he knew, he remembered. He could almost see himself dancing, with his collar open, all jammed together, just him and the kids . . .

"No!" he hissed. "I didn't do it!"

He watched Jessie's white skin stumble into the darkness, and faintly he heard the first of her voice, echoing back at him. What she said sent a chill through his blood and ignited even more rage inside him. It was two garbled words, but it was clear enough to him . . .

"Uncle," she was crying, even through the drug in her blood and the fuzz in her brain, "Kevin . . ."

"Bitch!" the Prisoner whispered, sweat pouring down his face from beneath his wig. "You sexy little bitch!"

"We're goin' home!"

37

There were two separate Jessies inside her head. One was doped and slow-moving, and the other knew exactly what was going on and was screaming, "Run! For God's sake get away! Grandpa's crazy! Grandpa's *alive*! *You've got to run!*"

The screaming Jessie won out over her physically. The instant Grandpa yanked on the leash he'd put around her neck, there was something about the pain biting into her that helped the frightened Jessie take control and start her body moving. But the drug-muddled Jessie still seemed to hold sway over the thinking end of things. So, as her body stumbled and ran, hands out as she bounced from wall to wall, fell, climbed back to her feet, and fell again, her eyes were wide with amazement, searching through the gloom for something familiar, something that would tell her where she was, and maybe more important, something that would give her a clue as to what the hell was happening to her. Her feet were moving as if there was some part of her that knew exactly where it was going, and there seemed to be an urgency about everything that she couldn't explain. There was a reason for her haste . . . there was . . . something happening!

There were needles in her brain that she couldn't see.

That was weird.

She knew there were needles because she remembered feeling needles that she never saw, pricking her skin in the dark . . . skin that she knew was hers but that she couldn't see . . . and mattresses . . . and light. There was Grandpa, who was dead, in a suit, with hair . . . he had been bald . . . since when? There were scissors . . . and needles . . . and . . .

"Run!"

Whose voice was that?

Who said . . .

"Run!"

?

She called for Uncle Kevin as she moved, stumbling less, hoping he'd answer. The area she was covering would have been difficult to traverse under the best of conditions, but now, half . . .

"Run!"

. . . crazy with fear, she felt as if she were on board a ship in rolling weather.

The hall was narrow, and lining either side were big, dark doors that looked as if they hadn't been opened in two hundred years. Immense sheets of dusted cobweb drifted on invisible currents of air. Shadows thickened already dim corners. There were pieces of broken furniture scattered on the floor, and the place was lit by tiny, naked bulbs hanging every twenty feet or so from frayed, dangerous-looking wires strung along the ceiling. Something about this place was familiar to her, though God only knew why it should be. But whatever familiarity there was seemed to be impelling her forward, pulling her on down the hall to the end. The paving stones were irregularly set, tripping her often. Behind her, doors slammed and a man's voice roared unintelligible words.

Uncle Kevin?

No.

Grandpa?

Chains rattled.

Blows fell.

And through everything all Jessie could do was . . .

"Run!"

At one spot she had to stop and climb down a couple of steps, using her hands on the walls for support. At another, the hall went totally dark for a stretch where a bulb had burned out, and there was a terrible, howling moment of absolute blackness where she felt disembodied, and could almost see the two sides of herself struggling for control. Finally, she arrived at a large plank door, propped open and creaking on its hinges when she pushed it. Immediately beyond that door, the hall grew wider, and more bright, the floor changing from paving stones to linoleum, and the walls becoming suddenly smooth and painted. The transformation was so abrupt that it made her stop for a moment and stand, swaying on her feet, feeling her heart laboring in her chest and hearing, faintly, the sounds of voices behind her, climbing up through the darkness of the tunnel through which she had just passed. In response to those voices, she turned and . . .

Suddenly, she knew where she was!

Around her, arranged in apparently no order at all, was a series of ancient, rolling coatracks. These racks were sagging beneath the weight of the clothes they bore, a jumbled conglomerate of time periods and styles that ranged from eighteenth-century ball gowns to Roman centurian uniforms. There were Musketeer outfits, and royal robes, chain-mail overpants, and white tuxedoes, all nearly colorless beneath a choking film of dust, and all smelling vaguely of mildew and former glory.

Dead costumes . . . in storage.

She turned, blinking. Before her the yawning tunnel that had, up to just an instant ago, been so hauntingly mysterious and new suddenly became, from this perspective, the dark, musty, completely familiar Catacomb with its big antique door. It was the tunnel beneath the theater building. The one they said ran all the way under the street. Lawrynce-Wynn University had some very old buildings—some as old as a hundred and thirty years. There were two dormitories, Oppenheimer and Lancing halls, that had been built and rebuilt twice. The story went that the Catacomb, a stretch of sewer line that had been sealed off and modified with secret rooms, had been used as a station in the underground railroad during the Civil War, hiding slaves who were on their way to freedom in Canada. The Art and Drama Center had been built on the foundation of the Mezzinger Chapel, which burned in 1952, and the Catacomb opened out onto the room used by the theater people as their costume morgue. Everybody knew about it, but no one came down here much because it was dark and spooky.

No one came down, that is, but Jessie.

More often when she was a freshman, but occasionally all during her time at Lawrynce-Wynn, she had loved the costume morgue and had visited it often. There was something about the place that whispered, "Theater," to her heart. And she loved to come and play among the costumes when there was no one else around. She'd let her imagination fly as she strolled through the rows, running her hands over dusty prints and visualizing the stages, the lights, and the mesmerized faces of all the audiences that these silent troopers had helped enthrall.

Her head jerked unsteadily as a sound caught her attention, making her mouth gape. Her thoughts were swaying dangerously, and as she moved from one idea to another, she felt a physical lurch disturb her precarious balance so that she had to grab a rack of costumes to keep from falling. When she did, stiff material brushed her belly, and looking down, she realized for the first time that she was nearly naked.

Boots and panties.

That was it.

How had that happened?

But before she could answer her own question, or realize that she had been able to ask it—which was a positive comment on the growing contact between what was happening around her and her ability to integrate it through the fog in her mind—the sound in the Catacomb grew suddenly loud and she focused on the entrance just as a figure loomed into view, stumbling up from the darkness and waving its arms.

As much from the abruptness of the attack as from any sense of danger, Jessie gasped and fell back, disappearing into the rack of costumes upon which she had been leaning. Raising a thick cloud of dust, she landed in a pile of shoes and boots as the figure from the Catacomb lumbered forward, followed by another, and then one more. The creatures made thick, guttural sounds as they moved, all lock-kneed and waving arms, and their weird, dark-eyed stares made them seem so immediately threatening that Jessie couldn't help but struggle her way back, deeper into the mess of choking cloth and leather, as they staggered and groaned their way up from the dark. Who they were, or why she was afraid of them, she didn't know. Where they had come from, or what they wanted, was even more vague, but that didn't matter. All that did matter was keeping these shambling, dead-eyed men away from her naked body, and she did just that by emerging from the costume rack right by the exit door. It took her two pushes to get the door open, and then she was through and into the sewing room, where all the new costumes were made.

Shaking the clinging remnants of tangled clothes from her arms, she weaved and ducked her way through the rows of sewing tables and machines, crunching needles and spools of thread beneath her boots and landing, hard, on a closed door. She thought for a moment that she was having the same trouble with this handle as the last—that her numbed fingers were just too stupid to work the latch—but after three tries she determined that this door was locked, and she moved on to the next, just as the first pursuing shape came crashing into the room.

The sound of its approach made her hesitate, and she turned and looked back at her pursuer for the first time. If she were not herself so disoriented, she would hardly have found him threatening. He appeared to be at least sixty years old, and was so thin that he exuded the impression that he might, at any instant, simply fold up under his own weight, his bones breaking in on themselves out of sheer weakness, his flesh deflating with a dry whiff of dust. His eyes were sunken in puffed-out wads of livid pink tissue, and his mouth hung open to reveal a lolling tongue and yellow teeth, made all the more prominent by the receding gums. His hair was filthy, and his face overgrown with what looked to be a week's worth of greying beard. His clothes were rags, his fingers were thin and limp, and every exposed section of flesh—forearms, face, legs from the knees down beneath his tattered trousers—was bruised black-and-blue, and cut with ribbons of infected welt. The man looked as if he'd been starved, beaten, and drugged. And his wavering walk appeared to be more of an escape attempt than a pursuit.

Following the leader into the sewing room came more men like him, stumbling through the door and dragging bits of costume behind on their shoes. Each was worse than the one before, and the overall impression they gave was that of an advancing, starving army, vomited up from some concentration camp and drunk with the desire to escape.

The door handle in Jessie's hand turned, and she pushed her way out of the sewing room and into the hall. Behind her, the advancing sewer army groaned and protested, and in front of her, beneath a bright, hanging light, stood something that made her scream.

The scream felt like a cleansing act, and something about it seemed to pull a certain clarity of mind up from inside her so that for a moment things burned themselves into her consciousness with all the detail and reality of a photograph. It also made her head swim, and she staggered, and caught herself on the wall, which clanged out a hollow metallic shudder, being one in a series of locker doors that ran the length of the passage beneath the main stage in the big theater. She pressed her back to the locker and eased her way around the thing that had startled her, which was standing where it could not be avoided by anyone coming out of the sewing room, grinning, and pointing to its left. She was trembling now, and that terrible, numb sensation in her mind was progressing from confusion to something very much like terror even as she stared, and stepped away from the . . .

Corpse.

And then, as she watched, the first of the starvation army stumbled out of the sewing room, right into the corpse, knocking it over from where it stood on a dressing dummy stand. Painted with the grinning whiteface of a pantomime clown, its head was cocked at a hanged-man angle, its pointing right arm was held out by a yardstick tied to the wrist and secured to one hip, and it was dressed in a bizarre, blue and yellow zoot suit kind of thing with fancy striped pants and shiny black shoes. A sign was secured to the man's chest with a pair of scissors that pierced his heart. And though it was covered with rivulets of blood, its message was still legible. It read, *Quick! Run this way!* over an arrow that was drawn beneath the words to agree with the direction of the dead man's stiff, pointing arm.

The sound of the zombie man's running into and then knocking over the corpse was absurd. And together they looked like two crazy, alcoholic bums, rolling on the floor in a struggle over a quarter. As Jessie slid along the locker doors, rattling combination locks behind her and using her hands as if she were blind, she saw two more of the stumbling men emerge from the sewing room and fall over the pair on the floor.

Then she tore her attention away, turned, and stopped.

The hall split in two directions.

And directly in front of her was a sign taped to the brick that read, *No! This way!*

Arrow pointing left.

And that's the way she went: up the echoing concrete stairs, and out, into the backstage area of the main theater.

She recognized it instantly:

The theater!

Her theater!

The realization of just where she was, mixed with the abrupt uniqueness of thinking so clearly as to identify her surroundings without having to make a conscious effort to do so, stalled her at the top of the stairs and left her hanging on a thick, bristling length of rope that was secured to a peg in the wall, and that climbed up, into the darkness overhead.

Before her stretched the backstage area of the big theater's stage. One of the things that Lawrynce-Wynn was known for was its Theater Arts Department, and the Finnegan Performing Arts Center boasted four separate stages. There were small, intimate floor-space units positioned around the main theater itself. The "big stage," as it was called by the students, was as fine a performance area as any professional theater in the city. Its seating capacity was five thousand, its stage area was over a thousand square feet, and its ceiling soared up nearly seventy-five feet from the orchestra pit, giving the room a huge, sweeping appearance that could make almost any production feel big-time. The curtain was made of plush red velvet. The lighting was expensively first-rate. And all the mechanics that operated everything from the curtain's rise to the scenery changes were packed into the narrow—though tall—stretch of backstage area that was nestled like a submarine engine room behind the stage's mobile backdrop: a wall of plasterboard sections that were rigged so that they could be pivoted, turned, and moved along a complicated series of running floor tracks, making it possible to change scenes during a production any number of times.

Lights were on, here and there in the building. And, catching her breath, Jessie realized with a start that she was not alone. In addition to the men downstairs, who were even now scraping their way up the concrete steps behind her, moving, judging by the sounds they made, so painfully slow as to be practically standing still, she saw, as she stepped from the stairs and toward the stage itself, people sitting scattered in the first twenty or so rows of seats beyond the footlights.

And that's when she thought, Drug. The word just emerged, popping into her brain as her boots echoed across the stage and she moved around a wall of bunched curtain into the gloom along the backdrop, which was painted to resemble the interior of a great ballroom. They had been getting ready for a stage production of *Gone with the Wind*, and this was Tara. Overhead hung a huge chandelier, there was a winding staircase leading nowhere stage-right, and there was a bed in the middle of the stage. That was all. No other props. Just a bed.

What was a bed doing in a ballroom?

The aisle lights were on in the theater, as were the ceiling lights, though dimly, illuminating the seating section with a thin, almost colorless grey haze that made it difficult for her to discern exactly who the people sitting out there were. There were a bunch of them, she saw, maybe twenty or thirty people, sitting absolutely silent, and not moving at all. But she could see their eyes sparkling in the semidark, and though it was strange, there seemed to be something connecting these people . . . a dark thread, moving from one to another, like a line tied around their necks and stretching over the seats.

Boom!

Jessie's boot came down on the echoing planks of the stage itself.

She was still in the wings, hiding. She had a growing awareness of her own nakedness, and she hung back, keeping herself in shadow, out of the view of her "audience," as she studied the pattern their seating arrangement made, emphasized as it was by the line that had been strung between them. It was familiar, that pattern. It was the one she had seen done in blood over the door in the factory in Pittsburgh.

Behind her the first of the starvation army stumbled up the stairs and into the backstage tunnel, making a terrible racket in the ropes and canvas without eliciting so much as a flicker from the audience by his efforts.

Boom!

Went Jessie's boot as she took another step.

The rest of her shambling pursuers emerged from the stairwell to join their bumbling leader.

And then a light came on at the back of the theater, high up over the seats, in the control booth. There was someone in the booth, she could see, silhouetted darkly by the tiny light that she knew was the one over the master control board. As she watched, whoever was in the booth raised his hands like a concert pianist and . . .

The hands came down.

And the footlights along the front of the stage blazed into life as all the other lights in the building suddenly went out.

A crash of pounding rock music blared from the immense public address system, the speakers to which were hidden on either side of the stage, in the wings, right where Jessie was standing. The explosion of bass sound took her by surprise and she jumped away, out into the open, naked on the stage as . . .

The audience didn't move.

Overhead lights flashed red, green, and blue on the bed.

And a voice from the control booth announced, "Welcome, one and all, to the best party on campus!"

38

"What the . . . ?" the security guard at the front of the Art and Drama Center building said aloud as he heard a pounding begin behind the locked lobby doors.

The guard's name was Myron, and he was starting left tackle on the college football team. It was cold; nearly seven o'clock; already dark; and Myron thought the theater was supposed to be empty. So after checking his Mace he rattled the lobby doors, found them locked, leaned his head in close, and listened to the music playing inside. It must have been as loud as hell in there for him to hear the bass so well. He thought the beat was familiar, but old, somehow. And then he remembered. It was the Bee

Gees, for God's sake. "Stayin' Alive." That old disco song from a hundred years ago. The one John Travolta walked down the street to in his disco suit at the start of that movie . . . what was it? *Saturday Night Fever.* Yeah! That was it. Myron had just seen the damned thing a couple of weeks before in the basement of the college union where it cost a buck to watch crappy VCR movies on a big-screen TV.

He was just about to raise his walkie-talkie and call the security office to say that somebody was having a gay old time in the theater building after hours, when he decided to check his clipboard first. Beneath his flashlight beam, he flipped a few pages, going over the schedule of what should and shouldn't be going on around campus on this Friday night, and finding "Special" inked in on the theater line. Squinting, he read, "Paying rental. Outside group. Friday, Saturday, and Sunday."

He shrugged, thinking, Paying group? Must be a rehearsal, just as someone screamed inside. The sound was subdued beneath the music, and muted by the locked doors. But it was definitely theatrical. Nobody would shriek like that in real life. At least Myron couldn't think of any reason someone would. It sounded like something out of a horror movie, which was the trouble with theater students: they all overacted. All ego, that was it. Center of attention all the time.

The scream came again, worse than the first time, and Myron said, "Keep practicing, honey. You'll get it yet," as he flipped his clipboard shut, checked the doors one more time—just to be sure they were locked good and tight—and headed for the next stop on his rounds, which was the all-girl dorm across the street. He had thirty-two stops to make before he would work his way back around to the theater, and he figured that, by then, either the place would be quiet or the lady inside would have perfected her scream to make it a little more convincing.

39

Parks found the door of the apartment building locked, and rattled the handle for all he was worth, shaking the door in its frame until he thought he'd rip the whole thing off its hinges.

After a moment, a light came on in the alcove, and a figure appeared behind the frosted glass. Parks let go of the handle, the door opened, and a policeman stuck his head out into the cold.

Parks pushed past him as the young man emitted a startled exclamation, and before the cop could say a word, he went running through the lobby, calling over his shoulder, "My name's Parks! Call for backup! We got a killer loose in here someplace!"

"Hey!" another cop said, materializing in a doorway and holding a coffee mug. "What the hell's going on?"

But Parks was at the steps and running down them, impervious to the confusion he had caused upstairs. Lisa Reynolds was still in his head . . . maybe more clearly than ever. Effortlessly, he drew her to the very forefront of his mind and held her there, making her recite a single sentence, over and over again, one specific statement that she had made when she was in her male identity, lying on a concrete loading dock floor, dying by inches:

"And I had to listen to her all that time, sitting alone in that fucking motel, hearing what she did while he sat in his secret room, stoned on his ass, under the basement!"

Who was the "he" sitting "stoned on his ass"? And where was his secret room? The motel where Reynolds had sat, listening in on Jessie's life through the microphones hidden in her apartment, had no basement, so wherever the "he" had been sitting had to be here . . . Parks hoped. He was taking a shot. He could be wrong, and if he was, Jessie was dead, if she wasn't dead already. He was taking a chance, but . . .

He hit the laundry room and froze in place, his broken rib screaming beneath his shirt and his vision blurred with pain. Behind him running feet caught up: the cops . . . two of them, guns drawn, looking at him as he snapped on the light, breathing hard and scared. For an instant, Parks thought that they might be ready to arrest him, that they didn't know who he was. But they didn't move. And after a second he knew that they belonged to him.

Fine.

Now get on with it.

Jessie needed him to get on with it.

When Parks moved, the silent policemen followed, and together they made their way across the echoing laundry room to another set of stairs that led even deeper beneath the building. Parks felt a chill when he snapped on the light and saw the irregularity of the stonework making up the wall beside the steep wooden steps, and the ominous darkness of bloodstains near the bottom. Then he was on his hands and knees, shooing the confused cops out of his light and studying the floor. Then he was pushing on the wall saying, "This moves. This has got to move." And then both cops were pushing too.

There were marks on the floor, scuffed through the dirt and ending right at the wall, explaining how the Prisoner had gotten the girl out of the building when there had been guards watching outside. That little puzzle had been making Parks crazy, and this foot mark solved it . . .

He hadn't gotten her out! He'd never left the premises, at least not through any exit visible to watchers on the outside.

That janitor and his laundry cart!

No amount of pushing budged the stonework, and Parks experienced a brief pang of terror that he had made a mistake. But then, with his hands on the wall, he pressed each brick individually until . . .

There!

He stopped.

One brick.

Just the one.

He reached up, and beneath his fingers the stone receded, sliding in on itself as if it were a large button and disengaging some kind of a latch so loudly that everyone in the room heard the muffled clank of old steel. A section of the wall swung in at Parks' prompting, hinged in an irregular way so that it was shaped along the staggered pattern of a mortar line.

The smell that blew in from beyond this freshly opened passage astounded the two young policemen, and Parks nearly gagged. But he recovered himself almost instantly, saying, "Come on," with a wave of his pistol, leading the way inside, and hoping beyond all reason that he and his companions were not too late.

40

As soon as Jessie disappeared down the tunnel, the Prisoner, still blowing with anger and feeling a little light-headed from the excitement of it all, produced the key to the locked cell doors closest to him . . . the ones that still contained occupants. He and the Terrorist had been busy the last month or so, collecting guests for the party and bringing them down here in laundry carts, right through the delivery door at the back of the building, until almost every cell had a resident. He'd taken out a great deal of his rage by beating these starving people these last few weeks . . . these men and women, and a couple of children too, from all over town, the suburbs, and beyond. They were drunks—one of his favorite kinds of victim since they were so easy to grab, and were almost never missed. They were also truck drivers, taxi drivers, kids walking to or from school, and prostitutes, which was another easy grab. You name it, and there was a representative here under the street. Twenty-eight in all, not including the boy who had come looking for Jessie early that morning, and the shameful son, who had come even earlier, arriving in town after a two-hour drive up from Columbus at midnight, after Jessie had left that message on his answering machine about Henry Parks and their family's unusual history.

Kevin Reynolds—*Uncle Kevin!* the Prisoner mimicked cruelly in his mind, imitating the whining, desperate intonation Jessie had used when she went stumbling down the hall just moments before—had appeared at the apartment building in the pitch-dark, running up the walk, his face full of worry and his breath hanging in lumps of steam that haloed the streetlamp light around his head.

The Prisoner had been waiting . . . not as he had been waiting for Ron Manning: in disguise, drawing the boyfriend in and then turning on him with the hammer. But just waiting as himself, so that when Kevin opened the door, there he was, standing in the alcove. The look that came over Kevin's face at the instant of realization, helped along by the light the Prisoner snapped on so dramatically, was positively delightful. It was a blossoming of absolute pain, an expression of terror and amazement so fulfilling that it nearly took the Prisoner's breath away.

"Dead!" the younger man whispered, staggering on the front step. "You're dead . . ."

And that's when the Terrorist hit him.

Father and daughter locked the unconscious Kevin in the basement cell, and while the Terrorist drove the Bronco away, parking it on a side street and walking back, the Prisoner chopped Kevin's right hand off just above the wrist with a hatchet. He then cauterized the spraying stump with a hand-held propane torch from his janitor's toolbox, and finished by wrapping the scorched flesh with almost an entire roll of black plastic electrician's tape. The dismembered hand he sealed in a couple sheets of newspaper and gave it to his daughter, instructing her to use it for leaving fingerprints for the cops to find . . . which she eventually did, pressing the hand on the windshield of the van in which she killed a mother and her son after throwing a little girl into a moving police car. She disposed of that hand by placing it directly atop the bomb she left on the floor in the kitchen of Mrs. McGreavy's house, so that when the police detonated the motion sensor with their bodies, it was the first thing to go.

There was a three-foot length of rusty chain hanging from a nail in the wall, and the Prisoner took it in his hand and let the heavy feel of it calm him a little. But just a little. He was savoring this excitement, rolling it over his soul as if it were wine on his tongue.

The time had come!

Finally . . . finally . . . *finally*!

It had come!

It was *here*!

Launching himself at cell doors, he threw them open and waded inside, driving the stupefied men blinking into the hall and screaming, "Go! Find her! *Run!*" as the chain whistled in his hand and sent them scattering at the top of their dismal speed. He had saved these three to ensure that Jessie didn't try to double back the way she had come. And he had spent the rest of his day transferring the remainder of his guests to the theater, which his daughter had rented under a phony name with a very large cash donation to the drama department's operating fund.

When the men had stumbled off, the Prisoner turned his attention to the final locked cell, the one containing his son. The hall reeked of sweat, urine, and shit. Every time he opened a cell door the stench of unsanitary confinement rushed out, gagging him with its oily strength. But at this instant, with his eyes locked on Kevin's door, he didn't even notice it. He didn't even care. All he could think of was his son . . .

His whimpering, infantile son!

This dismal, spineless puke of a boy the Punishers had given him in place of the man he remembered his son to be was disgusting, and it was time to be rid of him. But when he threw open the cell door to find Kevin still cowering in the corner where he had left him after his most recent beating, all the rage seemed to bleed out of him, and he frowned, dropping his chain to the floor with a sigh, and hissing, "Oh, fuck it! It's not even worth the time."

He left Kevin where he was, rolled in a ball in the corner of the filthy cell, holding his arms over his head and sobbing, just sobbing, a steady, pitiful sound of a mind unhinged. Everything he'd been through for his whole life, the doctors and the therapies, the brainwashing and the treatments, all seemed to have come back to him in their own way the instant he had seen his supposedly dead father's face. And now he was a wreck. He couldn't even talk. He just cried . . .

And cried.

"Fuck him," the Prisoner said, following the hall to the theater basement. "I've got shit to do!"

The Phi Tau's fraternity party was wild, loud, and dark. The pressing of young flesh, damp with sweat and heated by the flush of intimacy, mixed instantly with the alcohol Eugene Reynolds poured down his throat and produced a concoction so intoxicating that it was virtually irresistible. The pounding of live rock music thrumming in his skull sent rippling waves of nearly orgasmic pleasure through him, thrilling him right to the bone. And taken together, the whole thing seemed so ripe with potential that he could hardly contain himself. He'd been to orgies in California, and nude beach parties on the coast, he'd been the guest of doped-up film stars for whom he'd done genealogical work, and he'd been introduced to true perversion in a smorgasbord of expensive incarnations. He'd sampled every pleasure that had ever come his way, and with his experience, this little party seemed tame by comparison. But, at the same time, there was a satisfying naïveté about the proceedings, a sensation of childhood on the brink of deflowering, that gave all these adolescent boys and girls an unwholesome air that excited a nostalgic shadow in his heart, and made him feel a little like Dionysus, watching his nymphs at play.

He didn't know how so many kids all fit inside the building. And every two seconds the front door would open and another one, or two, or five would squeeze their way in, grinning and laughing, kissing and waving the bottles they'd brought. It seemed like the band played a single song all night. Occasionally, the melody changed a little, but the beat never varied, which was fine. Between gulps and guffaws, Reynolds shouted into some girl's ear—always a girl, because he liked girls—saying, "Have you seen Natalie Reynolds?" Invariably, the girl would respond with a funny look, to which Reynolds would laugh reassuringly and say, "Oh, no. It's not what you think. She's my *daughter*." Which elicited an even more suspicious response that often included a giggle. So that was okay too.

He danced and drank for what seemed like hours without seeing his daughter, or running into anyone who had. After a while, he gave her up, or, more accurately, forgot about her, abandoning himself to the booze, and the girls in the dark. As the evening grew late, kids started drifting away, staggering into the night in the direction of their dorms and holding each other up. But the kids who remained, and there were quite a few, showed no sign of fatigue, and the party continued on into the morning. But though it seemed pretty much the same on the surface, just a lot of drinking and squirming around, there came a funny kind of change in the atmosphere of the place, a growing sense of attitude. The kids who were still dancing at two, now to a deafening record player since the band had packed up their instruments and waded into the crowd in search of the girls who had been giving them the eye, were serious about what they were doing.

The Prisoner headed down the tunnel, blinking and nervous, his heels snapping on stone and his eyes stinging with the sweat pouring out from under his toupee and down his face. His brain was squirming in his head like a lizard, and, if at that instant he had felt something trying to push through his eyes, he would not have been surprised, but would have understood it to be just another step in the process of ending his sentence. He could see the party where he had danced with the children so clearly in his head that, as he entered the costume morgue under the theater building, he was brushing invisible specters out of his way. He could feel the excitement so completely that, as he moved quickly through the sewing room, he had to catch his breath. And as he stepped over where the dead student he had dressed like a clown on the costume dummy rack had been knocked over in the hall, he listened to the thumping of Jessie's boots on the backstage floor overhead as she cautiously moved away from the stairs a moment before her pursuers stumbled up behind her.

"Perfect!" he said, suppressing a laugh. And then suppressing another. And then not suppressing a third, but giving himself over to it so that it pealed hysterically through the hall and surrounded him with its joyous, triumphant sound. "Motherfucking *perfect*!"

Then he was in the control booth at the back of the theater, having taken another stairway that exited right at the booth's door. Below him was the stage, and on that stage was Jessie, hiding behind the curtain and peeking her head around. The Prisoner snapped the light on over the console and raised his hands. Jessie looked up at him, her face moon-pale in the gloom. And then he hit the switches and started the party in a single, powerful stroke.

He'd found the stage by accident . . .

So many years before.

He noticed the kids thinning out and wondered where they were going. Some couples were heading upstairs to where the bedrooms were, but others were heading downstairs, mostly boys, slapping each other on the back and leaning their faces in close to drunkenly conspire about something "really heavy" that was going on. Reynolds weaved his way around, and finally ended up in the basement, which was set up with washing machines, dryers, and a pool table. He had expected the place to be loaded with kids crashed out on the floor. But it was empty. He was so drunk by this time that he had to hold one eye shut in order not to see double, and he stumbled twice as he worked his way down the stairs to the subbasement. There he found the secret door open, and, calling, "Hey. What's happenin' guys?" he entered the tunnel, and smelled dope.

He was familiar with marijuana, and the odor didn't surprise him. The tunnel was ill lit, and there were lights on in a few of the cells, and that didn't really surprise him either. He just staggered along, glancing into dim rooms and proceeding down until he found himself in the theater across the street. There he followed the sound of music, pounding from overhead, and ended up taking the stairway that exited near the control booth, at the back of the theater's seating area.

That's where he saw his daughter for the first time that night . . .

And that's where he was now. He grinned and looked up over the console as the music he had started blasted Jessie out of her hiding place in the wings of the stage and sent her stumbling into the light. He was seeing that same view as he had seen it that night twenty years before. He was seeing Natalie, not Jessie. He was seeing his daughter, on a bed, at three in the morning, onstage, naked save for a dog collar and boots, with three fraternity brothers, while kids from the party across the street sat in the audience, applauding, calling out, laughing, and watching . . .

Natalie.

His little girl.

Natalie.

He was stunned. Eugene Reynolds, finding himself in that booth, looking down at the stage, was stunned. Then and now. Then . . . and again. The emotions were the same. He could not take his eyes off the scene as memories of the past and visions of the present mixed so seamlessly that they became but one single view for him, generated not so much by his senses, but by his mind.

He was crying as he exited the booth and stumbled into the aisle. But he was trembling with excitement as well.

The air was alive with a song—that same song, he thought, or at least one that was very much like it, with the same shuddering bass line and crazy, falsetto lyrics. The air was alive with music, flashing, colored lights, and movement:

Molaine.

He had known that Molaine would come. The Keeper's presence at the end was almost essential, for he really wasn't exactly sure what to do. He had a general idea, but the particulars were vague. He needed help. He needed direction. He needed . . .

"Natalie?" he said, pronouncing his daughter's name as if it weren't quite familiar to him, and standing stock-still at the top of the aisle. He had a gun in his hand . . . his gun, the golden one. He had a vision in his mind . . . his vision, the golden one of his soon-to-be daughter that he had seen on the Night Shore, who looked so much like the daughter he had seen on the stage . . .

Naked, beautiful, shining beneath the lights with a glaze of sweat glistening on her lovely skin as she eased herself down onto one boy and began bouncing as another moved behind her and . . .

"Natalie?" he murmured, trembling, clenching his empty fist and feeling the floor shudder.

This was the horrible, twisted memory of that night that the Punishers had been sending him all these years. This is what they wanted him to remember having seen. And worse . . . oh, so much worse . . .

This is how they wanted him to remember *feeling*!

Just this way: charged with passion, thrilled through with the sight of it, not the least bit ashamed.

He was her father, for God's sake. Her *father*! He was standing there, seeing what she was doing . . . what she was doing *right before his eyes*! And yet he felt nothing but desire for her. His reaction was total enthusiasm . . .

And that was his crime that the Punishers made him remember. Even the act, which was yet to come, which had come, which was inevitable in its coming, could not overshadow the pure essence of this so great affront. He was constructed such that he did not respond to what he had found with anger or outrage. He responded with lust. He responded by moving forward, licking his lips, mesmerized by the body of his daughter . . . so lithe, so soft, so perfect. Her face was moist, her eyes were closed, her features bore so striking a resemblance to his own that seeing her was almost like seeing himself, like watching himself transformed, like being alive in two places at once.

"And so you go!" came a voice that moved with tremendous speed, racing by and rising and falling with its own mocking purpose.

The Prisoner didn't even look up, because he knew just what he would find: the Keeper streaking through the air with his hair trailing behind him like a comet's tail, spraying his blood and spinning like a cannonball. He could not bear to see it now. He could not bear to take his eyes from the stage.

When, on that night twenty-two years before, Eugene Reynolds had emerged from the stairwell and into the theater near the control booth, the sound had been so deafening that he had only seen the people in the audience waving their arms. He had not heard their voices until he was almost all the way down the aisle, almost at the foot of the stage itself.

"She's really goin' at it this time," someone was saying happily. "She'll do ten at least; you just watch if she don't."

The voice faded as he approached, and for an instant there was an awkward absence of chatter. But there must have been something about the way he walked, or stared up at the spectacle before him, that broadcast his desire, because, almost as soon as he emerged into the glow of the stage, someone noticed him and shouted, "Go for it, Gramps!" Which made him turn and blearily look the audience over.

There were quite a few boys sitting in those plush seats, and even a few girls. They were all holding beers or drinks or each other, and they were hunkered down, with their legs up and their bottles held high. They were laughing and waving, their glazed eyes aglow. They were nearly faceless in the gloom. And they were all looking right at him.

How had he looked? the Prisoner wondered now. What was it about him that had revealed the thoughts in his mind? What was it that had told these children that he was enthralled with the woman onstage? Glazed with beads of sweat, licking her lips, moving from boy to boy, so very drunk and drugged that she could hardly speak, could hardly see, could hardly do anything but what she was doing, which she did with boys who were almost in the same shape as she. Judging by their eyes, not one of them would remember a thing about this night on the morning to follow, or any morning thereafter.

The Prisoner had followed the aisle down and was standing in the same spot he had occupied on the night of the party and seeing, out of the corner of his eye, the flowing patterns Molaine traced in the air. The Keeper was glowing in the dark, leaving shimmering lines of silver light behind himself that made all sorts of intricate conflagrations before fading from sight like the afterglow of fireworks. Blinking, the Prisoner looked up, studying the Keeper as he flew and hearing Molaine's voice speaking, as if the Keeper were not flying overhead, but were in fact stuffed inside the Prisoner's own skull. The voice was intimate, convincing, and rational . . . nothing like the robotic intonations of the past. It was understanding . . . as if it meant him nothing but success. And it was reassuring . . . as if it knew she would be able to do what he needed to do.

"Prisoner 11275," it said. "Follow me."

The Prisoner gasped as Molaine flashed past, hurtling from high over the front of the stage, and down, missing the Prisoner's face by inches and regaining altitude as he headed toward the back of the building, performed a lazy loop, seemed to hang in midair for an instant, and then dove for the stage. Trailing a bright silver streak behind himself, the Keeper flashed like a tracer bullet, straight from the rafters at the theater's rear, and right at . . .

Jessie.

Natalie.

The woman who was even now standing, center stage, swaying and squinting against the brightness of the footlights blazing into her eyes.

He shot across the darkened theater, his spinning having stopped and his features a blur of speed as his voice resounded, *"Follow me!"* through the Prisoner's brain and his long hair trailed behind him like flames. For an instant the Prisoner felt a surge of panic freeze his heart as a vision of Jessie being struck by the Keeper blew through his mind. Briefly, he saw her flying back, spraying blood and throwing her arms and legs in a crazy arrangement of uncontrolled impact, as if she had been hit by an artillery shell. But when the Keeper did hit, she didn't even seem to feel it. She simply stood there as the lightning flash of Molaine's assault drew a blazing streak through the air that started at the back of the theater and ended between her legs. The Keeper struck straight at her crotch, exploding in a decaying glitter of silver sparks and disappearing inside. Only the guiding beacon of his passing remained like an illuminated map line for the Prisoner to follow.

"Follow me," he had said.

And the glowing line faded, but remained visible for a very long time.

"Follow me."

Jessie was just standing, gazing into what must have been the total darkness of the theater as the music pounded around her.

"Follow me!"

And the Prisoner moved past the front row and headed up the stairs at the side of the stage, lifting himself into view so that Jessie turned to face him, realizing just who he was, and . . .

Screamed.

Loud.

Once.

And then again, almost at the exact end of her first panicked call, and so very much louder the second time that it seemed as if she'd do some damage to her throat. She did it because she was frightened, and confused, and because there was a second figure emerging onto the stage. Seeing that second figure, and the Prisoner, approaching her simultaneously, she screamed and screamed, stumbling backward until she had brushed the bed at the stage's center with her leg, and then scrambling around it to place the bed between her grandfather, who was to her left, walking up the stairs to the stage, and the other man, who had just emerged from behind the backdrop, shambling like the walking dead, and dragging what looked to be a length of rusted chain behind himself across the hardwood floor like a snake.

41

Jessie screamed when she saw her grandfather lift himself into view from the awful golden blaze of the footlights because of what he was . . . which was dead, and crazy, and a killer dressed in a terrible, tacky suit the likes of which she had only ever seen in the movies, with a flowered tie and a dark toupee that looked like a tarantula squatting on his head. She screamed when she saw the second figure emerge from the backstage area to her right, not just because it was her Uncle Kevin. If it had just been him, she'd have run to him for protection. She screamed when she saw him because of his hand . . .

His right hand.

Which was gone.

"They cut off my hand!" he'd moaned back when Jessie was locked in her cell . . .

Her cell?

Where the hell was that?

When the hell had that been?

He looked like death, with empty, staring eyes, and a hideous pallor to his face that bled into a bruised, shadowy line of darkness over his eyes. His mouth hung open, his body was bent and beaten, and he limped so badly when he walked that he looked as if he might fall over with the next step.

Jessie screamed because she was afraid of him . . . and she didn't know why that was true. She screamed because she was afraid of everything, and clutching her hair she tried to pull some rational thought out of the drugged muddle inside her head, succumbing to fear and frustration when all she could find were bits and pieces, snatches of memories and disembodied words.

"No!" her mouth said, and she was gratified that it did, although she wasn't sure how it had accomplished the feat. *"Nooooo!"* it shrieked again, then her knees went watery.

Grandpa followed her look and noticed Uncle Kevin for the first time. He didn't seem to know what to do, and he even raised his gun for an instant . . .

His gun?

His golden gun!

How had Jessie known that he would have a golden gun? Who had said that his gun was painted gold? Who painted a gun?

But instead of shooting, Grandpa hesitated, and then took a step back down the stairs, lowering himself into the glare of the footlights and disappearing. In Jessie's confused state of mind, seeing him reclaimed by the light was tantamount to having him vanish off the face of the earth, and instantly her full attention swayed back to Uncle Kevin, who had somehow closed the distance between himself and his niece and who was now only about twenty feet away.

Abruptly, the music overhead stopped, and with it the blazing red and green lights halted their pulsations. Absolute silence flooded in, and Uncle Kevin, whose lips had been moving without pause since Jessie first saw him emerge onstage, filled the silence with his broken, whining voice.

"Daddy's mad, Jessie," he said, stumbling another step.

And that statement made Jessie crouch and press her hands to the bed, stumbling and aiming herself so that the bed stayed directly between her and Uncle Kevin, whose eyes were rolling, whose lips were parted, whose words were vague and childish.

"Daddy's mad at me. Daddy's mad . . ."

"Uncle Kevin!" Jessie blurted, surprising even herself and making Uncle Kevin's head roll as he took yet another step, closing the distance between himself and the bed. "What . . . what's wrong, Uncle . . ."

But then a new song kicked in and the lights started revolving again. This time yellow and pink spotlights swept over everything, producing a seasick feeling in Jessie's stomach and making her stand straight up just as Uncle Kevin raised the chain he was holding and opened his mouth, tears streaming down his face and his eyes fixed firmly on where Jessie was standing as . . .

Another figure emerged onstage behind him.

Jessie's hands shot up to her mouth as she screamed again and . . .

Henry Parks aimed his gun and fired.

Uncle Kevin shuddered, spun, and nearly lost his balance. The music roared overhead, smashing down from above like thunder as hysterical stabs of yellow and pink swept the stage. Henry Parks stepped forward, both his arms straight out before him and his gun aimed steadily as his mouth moved. Uncle Kevin regained some of his composure and . . .

Jessie screamed.

And Parks fired again.

The second bullet made a spray flash up, outlining Uncle Kevin's head and upper shoulders so that, from where Jessie stood, behind and to his right, she could see a brief curtain of pink as his head snapped and his chest seemed to collapse, making a bow of his spine. Parks' muzzle flashed again, and again, and Uncle Kevin's chain dropped, his knees buckled, and he stumbled back, disappearing behind the bed as Jessie dove forward and Parks shouted again, this time something that she almost heard, and almost recognized as her name.

What she found on the floor didn't look like Uncle Kevin at all, and it broke her down. When Parks approached, gun still drawn, his voice crawling in through the terrible volume of the music roaring around her, Jessie lashed out at him, screaming and trying to launch herself from the mattress. He seemed surprised by her anger, and two steps before he reached the bed he put his gun away.

"No!" she was screaming as she reached for him, intending to grab him, punch him, scratch and hug him as "Grandpa!" she shrieked, and . . .

Parks' eyes went wide.

Then his head snapped around in response to some movement that had caught his eye, and . . .

Jessie knew that he was lost.

Before she could so much as say his name a sudden wet spot erupted over Parks' heart and he was flung back, his eyes betraying his complete befuddlement, his mouth forming an O as his hand beat the air. In that last instant before a second shot slammed into him and knocked him forever out of Jessie's reach, understanding seemed to blossom in his eyes, and with it came a terrible expression of acceptance. It was almost as if he had seen his error . . .

And then he was gone.

Just gone.

And Jessie was left alone with her grandfather, completely beyond the reach of anyone . . . because no one knew she was there.

My God! she said in her head, breaking down and relinquishing all she had left of herself to tears and trembling.

She didn't even care that she was able to think.

My God! He's going to kill me!

And the thought made her turn away from the prostrate figure of Henry Parks, lying on his back on the stage, staring up into the blazing patterns of party lights above him, his mouth open, and his chest deflated in a bloody, unnatural way. It made her turn her face to the footlights, where Grandpa was standing, hazed in golden light, lifting himself back into view and grinning with his gun in one hand, his sport coat in the other. He was taking his shirt off by the time he stepped onto the stage, having dropped the sport coat into the lights, where it disappeared as if he'd disposed of it in a fire. His face was bathed in sweat, his shirt was parting beneath his working fingers, and his gun was aimed right at her, a perfect black spot of an eye, holding her absolutely still with its deadly precision. Grandpa didn't say a word . . . and even though the pounding music would have made any statement of his inaudible, his meaning was unmistakable.

And that's when the music stopped again, and the spotlights ceased their movements, freezing dead solid and creating a series of pink and yellow puddles that covered everything on the stage.

"This is the police!" the P.A. speakers announced in tones of thunder and authority. "Drop your weapon, and raise your hands!"

Jessie probably shouldn't have done it, but she immediately looked up toward the control booth, moving her attention away from where her grandfather stood at the side of the stage and finding the figure of one policeman hunched over the announcer's microphone at the console, eerily bottom-lit by the control board's single lamp. Another policeman was moving down the aisle from the booth at a trot, his gun drawn, his young face earnest with concern.

"Thank God!" she cried, stepping away from the bed as the people in the audience—who she could now see were connected to one another by a length of red ribbon, and who had apparently been tied to their seats by means of ropes wound around their chests and hands—cheered feebly and tried to look around.

Jessie was just raising her hand, as if to wave, when the words she intended to say were cut cleanly to gabble and she gagged, clutching at her protesting throat and falling backward, first onto the bed and then off it, thumping down hard on the cold wood of the stage floor. Kicking and trying to scream, she fought at the tugging leash around her neck as her grandfather dragged her away from the bed and the P.A. exploded, "Stop what you're doing! This is your final warning!" The people in the audience changed their cheers into cries of outrage and frustration. The cop in the aisle leapt up onto the stage and aimed his gun with both hands, shouting, "Freeze!" And Jessie felt the floor suddenly disappear beneath her as a section of backdrop rushed past her and the stage transformed itself from wood to concrete as she slid painfully down the stairs.

She could smell the sourness of her grandfather's breath, even through the stars and darkness blasting her vision into mud. Her trembling fingers desperately sought to work their way under the biting leash and ease the pressure on her throat as the hot licks of moist heat exhaled on her bare shoulders puffed in time to the thumping of the stairs as she was dragged down to a landing, and then through a doorway that she tried to grab first with her hands and then with her feet. She even succeeded in hooking the jamb with one foot for an instant before a shock of pain blasted through her, doubling her up and pulling a cascade of sparkles from inside her head. Her grandfather had kicked her in the stomach as he dove over her to slam the door shut behind them and snap the lock. Stepping back over her, he dragged her another few feet through perfect darkness as the sound of pounding fists slammed the locked door.

His breathing sounded wet and painful. And there was a desperation to the way his hands reached for her through the blackness that seemed to express some silent fear, as if she might have disappeared when the closing door killed the light. Jessie opened her mouth, but when she tried to speak, her voice caught in her throat and produced nothing but a tiny click.

"Open it, or I'll shoot my way in!" the young policeman's voice suddenly ordered from beyond the locked door.

Jessie shuddered when her grandfather replied, "One move and she's dead!"

"Shit!" the cop outside said, more softly, as if to another person standing nearby. "That's just what we need."

And Jessie could suddenly see them both in her mind, the two of them, a couple of young cops standing together at the bottom of the stairs, looking like little boys, pushing their cop caps back on their heads with the barrels of their guns and scratching their chins, perplexed.

She gasped when a light snapped on. With that light came order, and she knew where she was: under the stage. Grandpa had dragged her straight back from the bed and down the stairs behind the backdrop. The room was as large as the stage overhead, but the ceiling was very low and cramped. They stored a lot of junk down here, mostly props. And everywhere there was piled furniture, papier-mâché trees, a cardboard cannon or two, and various other crap that bristled darkly at the periphery of her vision. The light came from a standing lamp, with a shade, like one that might be in any living room anywhere, and it produced so disquietingly pleasant a glow that everything suddenly became surreal.

Just as she rolled her head over to look at her grandfather, simultaneously moving to lift herself from the floor, his hands rushed at her and she tried to call out. But her words were again stymied . . . this time by something sticky and hard.

He wrapped her head six times round with duct tape, sealing her mouth and immobilizing her jaw.

"Are you all right, miss?" a cop asked through the door. "Whoever you are, mister, I wanna hear the lady talk."

"Fuck off or she's hamburger!" Eugene Reynolds shouted, leaning his face in close to Jessie's ear after he did and whispering, "You gotta talk tough like that or cops don't listen."

Jessie looked at him with wide eyes over the tape sealing her lips, and a thrill ran through her. When their eyes met, Grandpa actually winked! As if they were in this together!

Jessie was still on her back on the floor. And Grandpa was kneeling over her, looking down, almost smiling.

"I wanna talk to the mayor!" he shouted over his shoulder, addressing the cops outside. "This bussing of black kids in with us white folks has got to stop!"

He grinned and cocked his head, leaning down and adding, "That'll keep 'em busy. Huh?" as he finished removing his shirt.

He pulled off one sleeve, and before pulling off the other he placed his pistol down on the ground. As soon as he did, Jessie tried to grab for it, but her movements were muddied by the drug still in her system, and her grandfather seemed to have been waiting for just such a response. He slapped her across the face so hard that her head snapped around and her eyes crossed. The floor beneath her rippled, as if the concrete had suddenly become liquid. And then it went solid again, and there was a ringing in her right ear.

"Don't do that again, Natalie," he said, pulling the shirt

sleeve over the hand he had just used to strike her. "Daddy says no."

Natalie?

Daddy?

"It's gonna take some time to get a hold of the mayor, fella," a cop said. "Just take it easy, and don't do nothing crazy, okay?"

"Fucking plastic junk," Grandpa mumbled, undoing the zipper on his plaid trousers and pausing to look down at Jessie with an expression that seemed to soften. He ran his eyes up and down her as she tried to scoot back away from him, bumping her head on a rolling cart full of folding chairs and whimpering beneath the duct tape over her mouth.

"Oh, shush," he said comfortingly, putting his hand out as if to touch her, which made her squeal. As if disappointed, he pulled his hand back and finished with his trousers, saying, "I know this all must be very scary for you, but . . . just trust me. It'll all be over in no time. And then we'll be together. All this ugliness will end and . . .

"What?

"What did you say?"

Jessie's eyes narrowed and she froze on the floor. Her grandfather's mouth had dropped open, and his attention had focused first on her face, and then, just as quickly, down to her waist . . . no, not her waist, her crotch. He was kneeling over her, his shirt off so that his terrible pink skin gleamed with perspiration, not a hair on it anywhere, and with his trousers balled at his ankles, she could see his naked pubis. He was staring at her crotch and trembling, cocking his head, and . . .

Listening.

He was listening!

God! Jessie thought. Oh God oh God!

"I don't need you here now," he mumbled, speaking without moving his eyes from where they stared at her. "Wait, I can't hardly understand you."

Then he reached out, and before Jessie could move, he grabbed the top of her panties and tore them off. She tried to strike at him, which turned out to be a mistake, and with a protestation of anger he grabbed her right arm, forced it back, and wound a length of duct tape around the wrist, securing it to the leg of a kitchen table upon which were stacked more folding chairs. Her left hand, with which she was even now striking him, he secured to the dog leash still hanging around her neck, pulling it in tight so that her hand was tied beneath her chin.

"Now," he said, returning his attention to her crotch. "What were you saying?"

Suddenly, his head snapped back, and he looked above her, as if something invisible that only he could see had emerged from inside her and was hovering overhead. He looked at a spot in the air, his eyes firm with concentration, and his head dipping once, and then twice, as if he were agreeing with something. Then he looked down at her and said very softly, "Molaine says you need to understand."

Jessie involuntarily glanced up to the empty air, and when she did, her grandfather frowned, rubbing his hand over her shoulder and saying, "Pardon the dripping. He's always been like that. I don't think he can help it . . . and it'll go away."

He was rubbing something off her. He was rubbing something off her shoulders!

Oh, *Jesus!* she screamed in her head, glancing at the locked door and wondering, Where the fuck are those cops? Which was a thought that staggered her, and silenced all others.

The muddle in her mind seemed to have thinned, and the darkness at the recesses of her thoughts had begun to part. Suddenly, she realized, her legs were thrumming with pain, her back and neck, the side of her face, her right arm, and her throat . . .

Oh, God!

Her throat!

The pain was there, but not at the front. It wasn't at the front, it was near the back . . . if that made any sense. But it was there! It had been numbed before. It had been erased by whatever it was that Grandpa had . . .

Shot into my arm!

She had it! It was coming back. There was suddenly a chronology developing in her head. She was suddenly seeing things in order, or at least in some kind of order. That random, disjointed sensation, though persistent in its desire to hold her, was receding before a wave of mental images and physical pain . . .

Pure, physical pain.

Which Jessie actually welcomed.

With an effort she searched for it, dug through the inside of herself with inquiring mental fingers, finding the sore spots and calling out to them, embracing them, pulling from them whatever sensations they contained until, piece by piece, bits of her body started making a music of injury that blared up her spine and sparkled hot stabs of pain through the fog in her skull.

Her grandfather's fingers were still rubbing her shoulders, brushing something off her that seemed to be smearing and frustrating his attempts to remove it. She could feel the warmth of his skin on hers. And she could feel the protests of her bruised throat when he brushed the rope burn he'd seared through her old scar . . . the old scar that he'd given her in the first place . . .

Jessie gasped, her nostrils flaring over the gag of tape sealing her lips.

The Prisoner! she thought. Parks' Prisoner! The dark man of my memory . . . the memory that drove me to the police station and the dark, tall man, narrowed by perspective, who killed the happy man, and the puppet lady, and . . .

Natalie.

Natalie!

"Daddy says no."

Natalie was . . .

Jessie's *mother*!

God!

"I thought at first that Molaine looks like he does because he was supposed to scare me," Grandpa—the Prisoner—was saying as he brushed at her skin. "But now I understand. He's as much a prisoner here as I am. Everybody here's a prisoner, everybody's guilty. I'm not the only one. That's why they waved at me from the night sea after I killed them. Remember how they'd do that? They waved because, in the Zone, killing someone ends their misery . . . it ends their sentence. They might have cyborg bodies, but their souls are human. That's what threw me. But now I understand:

"I'm not the only one!

"We're all in this together!

"I'll be doing you a favor, and you'll be doing me one in return. That's the secret here! That's what Molaine's been trying to tell me all along:

"He's in as much pain as I am. That's why he bleeds like he does."

His rubbing increased in speed.

"But don't worry, the bloodstains go away. All bloodstains go away. It's just part of the punishment. And the punishment's almost over—for me and for you too! You were as much to blame as me, doing what you did. It wasn't all my fault. We both had a punishment to endure. Mine was to wait, and yours was to be my way back. You gave birth to yourself. First you were Natalie, and then you were someone else, and that must have hurt. It'll hurt when you take back my birth too . . . that'll hurt too. But it must be done. I must pass through you. Molaine says so. You must take back my birth, and be my passage home.

"And when your time comes, I'll be waiting to embrace you on the other side. Daddy will be waiting, and Kevin, and Mother, and everybody, just as we left them. It'll be a real homecoming. And it'll all be because of you . . .

"And me.

"I love you, Natalie.

"Daddy loves his little girl, so, so much."

He was speaking as if in a trance, ignoring the renewed pounding on the door, which had started with fresh vigor. He was also ignoring the new voices outside, many voices, and the pounding of feet on the stage overhead. Her attention was divided, but even Jessie could tell that there were men in the building, running around and trying to get a grip on the layout of the place. They'd find a way in, she knew, if they just had enough time. If she could just hang on long enough to give them the time they needed, she knew that they would come in and get her . . . come in and do something to her grandfather that would take him out of her life, and save her from him.

But they needed time.

And if Jessie could speak, maybe she could have given it to them. But as she was, bound and gagged, she could do nothing but watch as Grandpa nodded one last time to the air, and said, "Fini."

And beneath her plastic gag, Jessie screamed. She did it for two reasons:

One, because her grandfather's eyes had settled, and he was reaching for her in earnest.

And two, because, glancing down at herself, she saw that her shoulders and breasts were smeared over with blood . . . real blood. Real, honest-to-fuck blood. Just like Grandpa had said. Just like the madman had described. There was blood dripping down on her from the ceiling above, and her grandfather's working fingers had smeared it all over her. And still it was dripping . . .

Drip.

Drip.

Drip.

. . . down on her from above . . . from . . . what had Grandpa called it? Molaine? Down from Molaine? Invisible Molaine, who was in as much pain as the Prisoner, and who was bleeding . . .

Drip.

Drip.

Drip.

. . . real blood that splattered Jessie over and made her shriek inside and squirm on the floor because madness was changing from phantoms to blood before her very eyes and there wasn't a goddamn thing she could do about it. She could writhe and kick on the floor, pull the kitchen table with the chairs piled on it a few inches toward her, making a wood-scraping-concrete sound that didn't help her at all; she could whimper and choke, squeal and strain her head from side to side as the blood ran down her belly and her grandfather put his hands on her, whispering, "At first I thought I had to climb inside you, and I was going to bring a knife to make the way big enough for me to fit. But now

I know . . . I understand since I saw inside at the factory. I know my own soul. And it's my soul that has to go."

Jessie could feel the panic seizing her as Grandpa started rubbing himself against her, his soft flesh slick with sweat moving against the insides of her thighs. She could feel her muscles locking up, one after the other, as a horrible sensation of futility sped down her back like a shudder, and her hands started opening and closing, opening and closing, of their own accord. It was almost as if her body had suddenly become separated from her mind. She'd heard about things like that. She'd studied such intense emotions in drama classes, reading essays written by people who had survived terrible experiences in which they described in minute detail every little feeling they could remember. And what was happening right this minute made bullshit of everything she'd read. There were no words . . .

There were no words!

If she could only speak, maybe she could turn things around, like in the movies. If she could only speak, she might be able to use her acting ability to seduce him with his own fantasies—becoming everything he had ever wanted so that he would hesitate, and the cops outside would have another few moments in which to find a way to rescue her. But it was useless . . .

There were no words.

"My soul will shoot out from here," Grandpa—the Prisoner!—was saying, kneeling and pointing down at himself. "And it will pass through you to the other side. I'll be free. And if I never see another cyborg as long as I live, it'll be too soon. I won't even own one at home. I don't care what your mother says. I'll do the housework myself. No more plastic crap in my house. I've learned my lesson."

He was coming for her . . .

Here he came!

Oh, God! If this were only like in the movies . . .

But this wasn't a movie.

This was real.

Fuck the movies! Jessie thought as the Prisoner—it wasn't her grandfather, it was Parks' Prisoner, a lunatic using Grandpa's poor dead body, moving through the world in the body of a dead man . . . a corpse . . . a cadaver . . . a cadaver with eyes that saw a world that did not really exist, but that was instead the product of . . .

What?

Who cared?

Fuck it!

And Jessie gave up.

But what she gave up was not her will to live, it was her rationality. In that last instant before her grandfather could "free" himself through her, some intimate part of her humanity threw itself aside, releasing a flood of animal emotions that shot through her frozen muscles and possessed her with a desperate abandon that didn't consider consequences, but that focused instead on one, single goal: release. In that frenzy she became like an animal snared in a leg-hold trap, a creature of fear made flesh, willing to do anything to be free . . . anything, including, as was so horribly common in the wild, chewing some part of herself off in hopes of saving the rest. She was going to die anyway . . .

She was going to die!

Like hell!

It was at that instant that she saw the source of the blood dripping down on her—really saw it. And it was still another inspiration. It was not Molaine, whoever he was or wasn't. It was not Molaine, it was Henry Parks, or her Uncle Kevin, or both. From where she lay she stared straight up at the low ceiling, and through the top of the lampshade, the glowing bulb created an illuminated circle overhead. In that circle, the boards of the stage were clearly defined, and emphasizing the space between the planks, languorous swellings of red swelled, bulged, and stretched into sticky lines that ultimately dripped down as fat, glistening globules. The bodies above, lying in pools of their own blood, were leaking through the stage. There was no Molaine. There was only . . .

"Oh, Natalie, you sexy bitch."

And that was not to be.

Jessie exploded into motion, kicking out desperately at the Prisoner and eliciting a surprised response from him. She had been so still that he had apparently made the mistake of believing that she was going to just succumb, and her sudden display of nerve stalled him at first, and then angered him. He tried to strike out at her, but she had gone beyond simple self-defense, and had become a whirlwind that absorbed his punches and returned them in kind. In an instant, they were entangled together, thrashing on the floor, and the Prisoner's affections had turned to rage and he was pounding on her with both fists in the same vicious way as he must have assaulted Uncle Kevin. But Jessie didn't feel so much as a twinge of pain. The adrenaline in her system was washing the pain away, and she kicked and squirmed, trying to lock her legs around the old man's throat as he swung his fists and tried to get a grip on her legs and . . .

Something connected with the standing lamp, sending it over and popping the bulb on the concrete.

Darkness flooded the room, and the pounding on the outside door started in earnest as someone shouted, "That's all, mister!" and a gunshot rang out . . . far away . . . very far away because . . .

Jessie was still kicking, but there were hands on her throat that were pounding her head up and down on the concrete floor as she pulled with her arm and rolled with her body, sucking duct tape into her mouth in a great chewy ball, and pulling with her arm again and . . .

Something was falling down on her that was heavy and sharp, and . . .

Suddenly, there was something near her hand, by her hand, *in* her hand that was hard, and solid, and . . .

Then the crashing turned into clattering, and she was hitting, hitting, hitting, and . . .

Something went *boom!* just as loud as hell.

And she smelled smoke, even through it all.

SMOKE!

FIRE!

GOD!

And then there was light racing into the room, like . . .

FIRE!

GOD!

... was racing into the room, all a split second before dark figures appeared in the light, looking like one great mass of writhing arms and legs, as if a giant black squid were oozing through the doorway.

But Jessie wasn't watching the squid. She was hitting, hitting, hitting until ...

Someone grabbed her wrist.

And then she didn't know what.

42

Ellis shot the lock off the door at the bottom of the stairs backstage, aiming down and to his left in hopes of sending the bullet through at an angle that would minimize the chance of it ricocheting inside the room beyond. The sounds coming from inside that room were terrible. There was an old man swearing, and blows falling, and Jessie screaming in a muffled sort of way that sounded as if she were being suffocated even as she screamed. There were cops all over the theater, having arrived in response to the call for backup Henry Parks had instructed the policeman in the apartment building to put in, which was the same call that had told Ellis where Parks had gone after he ran away from the body of Lisa Reynolds at the airport. And now he was shooting off a lock, with Henry's body lying not thirty feet away, bloody and lifeless, and Jessie screaming through her terror.

For an awful moment when he first entered the room, shouting, "FBI! Don't make a move!" he couldn't see a thing. His fear was rushing in his ears, and the darkness in the room was so intense that it took a second for his eyes to adjust. When they did he almost wished that they had stayed sightless, because what he saw broke his heart.

Jessie was naked, save for her boots. She was covered with blood, and one hand was tied to her throat with what looked like a leather cord. There was a pair of bare feet aimed right at where Ellis was standing, so that the light from behind him made them look absurdly pale. The man's body was naked as well, and Jessie was kneeling next to him, hammering away with something that looked like a club. There were folding chairs heaped all around them, and what looked like an old kitchen table collapsed near an overturned living room lamp. In an instant, Ellis realized that Jessie's club was one leg of that collapsed table. And the girl's eyes, when he stepped up and took hold of her wrist, turned up to meet his with such a deep, hideous vacancy that Ellis felt his blood run cold.

There was blood all over.

There was even blood dripping from the ceiling.

They wrapped Jessie in the sheets that were on the bed on the stage and carried her to a waiting ambulance on a stretcher. She didn't say a word. After she was gone, Ellis moved around as if he were in a daze, watching police cruiser after police cruiser park in every direction around the theater building, spinning red and blue lights in crazy patterns through the cold night air, and wishing Henry were around to tell him that he'd done a good job. But Henry didn't say a word as they carried him out, wrapped in a dark green body bag. Or was that Kevin Reynolds? Well, one of them was Henry, and Ellis felt his throat go tight.

The body of the man Jessie had killed with the table leg was the last to be loaded into an ambulance. And even though the man was naked, and his face was ruined, Ellis knew who he was. He didn't say the name at any time that night, even though curious cops milling by asked him a number of times if he had any idea of "What in the living hell's been going on around here?" He didn't say a word. He just stood, trying to organize in his head all the things he'd have to do to "clean up" the mess he'd found. There were so many threads, and their untangling would almost certainly depend, at least in part, on Jessie Reynolds, and what she had to say.

But remembering that look in her eyes, and her bloodstained, deadly pale face, Ellis wondered if the girl would ever have anything to say again. He'd never seen anyone so totally terrified. And, if he was really honest with himself, in all the years he had spent on the Bureau, he had never been so scared as at that moment either. He didn't know why, but there was an air down in that awful room. A kind of atmosphere that was almost physical in its pungency. The corpse had open eyes . . . and if Ellis hadn't known better, he would have sworn they had been staring up at something hovering in the air . . . something terrible, that only those cold, dead eyes could see.

In the tradition of *THE SILENCE OF THE LAMBS* and *BODY OF EVIDENCE*

KILLER INSTINCT

Robert W. Walker

> "GRIPS WITH PSYCHOLOGICAL SUSPENSE...
> MASTERFUL."
> —bestselling author CLIVE CUSSLER

The FBI had a special code name for his unusual method of torture: Tort 9, the draining of the victim's blood. The newspapers called him the Vampire Killer. But his own twisted love letters were signed "Teach"... and were addressed to the one woman he wanted most of all:

His hunter, his prey, Dr. Jessica Coran.

__ 1-55773-743-6/$4.99

For Visa, MasterCard and American Express orders ($15 minimum) call: 1-800-631-8571

FOR MAIL ORDERS: CHECK BOOK(S). FILL OUT COUPON. SEND TO:

BERKLEY PUBLISHING GROUP
390 Murray Hill Pkwy., Dept. B
East Rutherford, NJ 07073

NAME_____
ADDRESS_____
CITY_____
STATE_____ZIP_____

PLEASE ALLOW 6 WEEKS FOR DELIVERY.
PRICES ARE SUBJECT TO CHANGE WITHOUT NOTICE.

POSTAGE AND HANDLING:
$1.75 for one book, 75¢ for each additional. Do not exceed $5.50.

BOOK TOTAL	$ _____
POSTAGE & HANDLING	$ _____
APPLICABLE SALES TAX (CA, NJ, NY, PA)	$ _____
TOTAL AMOUNT DUE	$ _____

PAYABLE IN US FUNDS.
(No cash orders accepted.)

BERKLEY INTRODUCES THE NEW MASTER OF INTERNATIONAL THRILLERS

VICTOR O'REILLY

"Heir to the work of Robert Ludlum..."
—*Boston Herald*

"O'Reilly is a literary puncher in Forsyth's weight class." —*Detroit Free Press*

"An astoundingly successful thriller...a spine-tingling showdown." —*Publishers Weekly*

"O'Reilly's tense thriller is full of surprises..."
—*San Francisco Chronicle*

"The action runs at full tilt...a complex web of murder and intrigue." —*Booklist*

"Bone chilling..." —*Chicago Tribune*

"A truly captivating, atmospheric, un-put-down-able read!" —*Cosmopolitan*

GAMES OF THE HANGMAN

__0-425-13456-3/$5.99

For Visa, MasterCard and American Express orders ($15 minimum) call: 1-800-631-8571

FOR MAIL ORDERS: CHECK BOOK(S). FILL OUT COUPON. SEND TO:

BERKLEY PUBLISHING GROUP
390 Murray Hill Pkwy., Dept. B
East Rutherford, NJ 07073

NAME_____

ADDRESS_____

CITY_____

STATE_____ZIP_____

PLEASE ALLOW 6 WEEKS FOR DELIVERY.
PRICES ARE SUBJECT TO CHANGE WITHOUT NOTICE.

POSTAGE AND HANDLING:
$1.75 for one book, 75¢ for each additional. Do not exceed $5.50.

BOOK TOTAL $ _____

POSTAGE & HANDLING $ _____

APPLICABLE SALES TAX $ _____
(CA, NJ, NY, PA)

TOTAL AMOUNT DUE $ _____

PAYABLE IN US FUNDS.
(No cash orders accepted.)

405

THE TERRIFYING MASTERWORK OF PSYCHOLOGICAL SUSPENSE!

"Insanely original." — The New York Times

"Terrifically good; page-turning terror." — Booklist

PRAYER FOR THE DEAD
David Wiltse

Two men consumed by death...

THE KILLER
spins a web of perverse obsession...
suspending his victims in a perfect moment of beauty and peace. The moment of death.

THE INVESTIGATOR
spins a web of fractured mirrors...
reflecting the killer's obsession. And making it his own.

___ 0-425-13398-2/$5.50

For Visa, MasterCard and American Express orders ($15 minimum) call: 1-800-631-8571

FOR MAIL ORDERS: CHECK BOOK(S). FILL OUT COUPON. SEND TO:

BERKLEY PUBLISHING GROUP
390 Murray Hill Pkwy., Dept. B
East Rutherford, NJ 07073

NAME_____
ADDRESS_____
CITY_____
STATE_____ZIP_____

PLEASE ALLOW 6 WEEKS FOR DELIVERY.
PRICES ARE SUBJECT TO CHANGE WITHOUT NOTICE.

POSTAGE AND HANDLING:
$1.75 for one book, 75¢ for each additional. Do not exceed $5.50.

BOOK TOTAL	$ ____
POSTAGE & HANDLING	$ ____
APPLICABLE SALES TAX (CA, NJ, NY, PA)	$ ____
TOTAL AMOUNT DUE	$ ____

PAYABLE IN US FUNDS.
(No cash orders accepted.)